THE FOREVER STONE & OTHER TALES

PETER BREMER

CONTENTS

For Mark, a true friend, who has walked the writing road with me and has filled countless potholes of my own making.

And in appreciation to SRD and ACC for taking me there.

BECOMING: A POEM IN TWENTY-ONE LINES

1 Once upon a time all the clocks were still

2 Into this silence you were born

3 A wonder beyond imagining

4 Your heart kept its own rhythm

5 Your feet wandered where they willed

6 Until one day the enchanted paths became worn

7 And garden gates closed off the vibrant wild

8 Now a quiet fear remains

9 You kneel by a small pool

10 Your bony knees pressing into the soft earth

11 There is no one else

12 But you are not alone

13 A reflection stares back from the water

14 It must be you

15 Who else could it be?

16 They tell you something sad

17 Something so true it takes your breath away

18 They whisper that the light was never yours

19 Then they wait for an answer

20 What do you say?

21

THE FOREVER STONE

Prologue

The Restless King stood on the barren outcrop of rock, looking out across the rolling hills and further still, to the distant misty mountains. They rose like bony digits towards the vault of sky. In his hand was a glowing fragment, a mysterious talisman from beyond the stars. The wind was cold, but he felt no discomfort. He was more bone than flesh. The part of his face that still had skin contorted in frustration. "Which way?" he growled at the object, holding it high in the air. "Show me!"

Behind him, the Restless King's army of skeletal warriors grew impatient, flexing their sword arms and stepping in place. They too disliked standing still. Any pause might remind them of what they had become.

From the center of the object, a pulse of sickly green beat like a heart, faint but steady in the crisp morning sunlight. There was still life within it. Why then had he lost the way when he was so close? For a moment the Suzerian was filled with the sudden urge to hurl it down the summit. He clenched his bony fist around the shard until the anger left him. There was no going back now. There was only one possible salvation and that depended on the splinter of stone. All around him, the wind swirled and then fell silent. As if from a great distance, the Restless King felt the pull and then a familiar tug from the object, turning him to the southwest. The faint light burned brighter.

"We march again!" the Restless King called to his Bone Brigade. A terrible smile stretched across the patches of his pallid skin as he climbed back atop his ghoulish steed and then galloped away. In unison they turned and followed down the valley, towards an elusive prize.

Chapter 1

Nestled in a secluded valley surrounded by a surprisingly high wall was the unassuming village of Renelis. A grove of great, gnarled trees rose up on one side of the modest hamlet, their twisted branches reaching vainly for the heavens. Rounded homes of stone, baked mud and thatch dotted the leaf-strewn ground below. Shadows and light danced across the pathways and the public square, just as they had done for countless years. Activity abounded in the small town, people walking and working, a colorful market bustling with activity, but there was no road leading to or away from the hamlet, nor even the memory of one. No villager had ever considered leaving the tranquility and safety of the valley, and no one had ever visited them in their current location, nestled in the hinterlands. Their world was complete and undisturbed.

And yet there was a change in the air. An icy coldness from the lofty peaks to the north robbed summer of its usual warmth. The branches of the Eternals, the half-sentient trees which guarded their little town and spoke for an ancient boon, were losing leaves. More and more lay scattered next to the wall every day. Great cracks appeared and then widened in the scraggy trunks while white-robed High Mizen listened in root-filled caverns underground, uttering words in the Old Tongue to try and ascertain the cause of distress. In response to the priests, however, the ancient giants were silent.

Each night during the week that led to High Summer's Eve, while the farmer to Grand Sizan slept, a young woman had the same troubled dream, which grew stronger and clearer as the days went by. Someone was coming. A man was riding desperately on horseback. A messenger with a scar and a tattoo of a shooting star. And each morning when the young woman awoke, she felt a tremor from the night's dream, but then it passed and she remembered nothing more.

In the verdant green of the square, a small crowd of people gathered in front of a raised earthen stage. Most were from the general populace, but as was customary there were representatives from the priests and ruling elite, as well as members of the vigilant Thorns, the village defenders, adorned in leather jerkins and armed with needle sticks. The Thorns were free volunteers; no High Priestess or Grand Sizan commanded them. From a rotating finger of one these austere guardians grew a living green thread, which twined and flowered before disappearing abruptly with a shake of his hand.

Someone sneezed and the Thorns wheeled their ceremonial needle sticks in that direction. Such interruptions were becoming more common. Those in the vicinity of the afflicted inched further away. After the briefest of pauses, the ceremony continued.

Gathered faces were expectant, but could not mask a world-weary sadness, despite the joyous occasion and the brightness of the day. A Youngling, the first in almost a century and a half, was set to receive the Vow and join the ranks of the Lesser Mizen. Holding a thin vine necklace of blood-red flowers, a Second Ring Priestess, middle-aged but with eyes much older, approached. The Initiate who kneeled in front of her was clothed in a simple short shift, bare at the shoulders, as was customary. When the Priestess stopped in front of her the young woman looked up expectantly. The wind moving across her exposed skin made her shiver. The regal looking Mizen Priestess had ornately braided black hair and wore a long terracotta dress. As the oldest of the High Mizen, it rightfully fell to her to welcome a new Initiate. Careful not to make contact, she placed the circle of woven red flowers around the woman's neck, joining a host of others which each displayed a different color, and then stepped back, turning around to face the gathered crowd.

"Twenty wreaths. Twenty trips around the life-giving sun. Twenty young years," the Priestess toned like a bell chiming a miracle. "Like the snow turned to spring and a seed grown tall with purpose, so too has a new season come upon this Youngling before you on High Summer's Eve. Every year we gather on this special day when the light is longest, but this year we celebrate something exceedingly rare—the Ceremony of the Choosing. She is of the age to decide her own path. After careful deliberation, she has chosen to dedicate herself to study and contemplation deep within the sacred Catacombs. With these words she now joins the ranks of the Mizen as an Initiate in service of the Eternals and the gift of the Stone."

The woman stepped beside the Initiate. "Do you accept this Vow and commit yourself to the secrets which guard us all?" she asked solemnly.

The young woman looked at the elder Mizen and willed her words to find the truth she sought. She was giving up so much so that she could discover the only thing that really mattered. "I do," she said.

Reaching down, the Priestess retrieved a long umber-colored robe and stepped toward the Initiate. With a practiced flourish, making sure once again not to touch the girl, the Priestess expertly coaxed the Youngling's head through the opening, leaving the rest of the material to drape over the neophyte's still prostrate form. The older woman smiled now, but it was a smile tempered by the knowledge of the road that lay ahead for the young Mizen. The Priestess motioned at her. "Rise, Aisha of Galen and Radora, and receive the Vow!"

The young woman whom everyone called Ash pushed her arms through the openings and smoothed down her dress. Then she stood up, feeling the eyes of the village upon her. Spouses sat next to spouses, and sometimes with a lover as well. Although she understood why some couples made that choice, Ash was glad that her mother and father had decided against taking a second partner. Many villagers had left their spouses entirely as the years grew long. Again, Ash felt fortunate that her parents had found a way to work things out. It couldn't have been easy. She was of the age and then some where she could take someone to bed, but that would have to wait a while longer. An Initiate was supposed to have other priorities. And besides, there weren't many suitors interested in a girl like her. Growing up, Ash had to content herself with awkward crushes that went unreciprocated. Even friends were hard to find. She tried to please. To bend and give people what she thought they wanted, but that only made it worse. The experience had hardened her, and also made her world a little bit smaller.

Somewhere out in the crowd were her parents and older brother, as well as kindly grandparents. Tradition called for the royal Grand Sizan to be in attendance as witness, but Ash heard the Mizen whisper before the ceremony that their king was not coming. Part of her was relieved. The weight of so many visages, of so much accumulated time, already pressed down upon her, family most of all. Ash hoped they were proud. Her mother had been against the decision at first, worried that Ash would disappear into the Catacombs never to return. Ash understood her concern, but nothing else seemed right. Not farming or learning a trade. And she had no natural talent for being a Thorn. This was all she had ever wanted, simply a chance to find out why she was different from everyone else. Why she had been born.

The Priestess drew up a hood, obscuring her face in shadow. Approaching from across the platform were four Mizen, all of high ceremonial rank, adorned in the colors of the sunrise and carrying a wooden box the size of an eagle's nest on a gurney of woven living green thread. Although the sun was still bright in the sky, Ash could see the pink-orange glow emanating from the slats in the crate. Murmurs rose from the crowd and then fell silent. The weight of the moment pressed down upon her. Although Ash wanted to freeze time and make it last forever, she was also increasingly impatient. The dress was becoming itchier by the minute! Resisting the urge to scratch herself raw, she focused on the Priestess, willing the old woman to get on with it.

When the carriers and their precious cargo were finally in position, the Priestess smiled beatifically. Carefully she unfastened the latch with her wrinkled hands. Then with slow reverence she lowered the front partition. Ash held her breath. All of her hopes and dreams hinged on this moment. No one had ever been rejected. She desperately did not want to be the first. The strange glow seeping out was intense, but she willed herself not to look away. The Mizen Priestess nodded gently. Ash reached out a tentative hand toward the strange object. Its many facets shimmered with a life of their own. All Ash had to do was touch the Stone and she would receive the gift that everyone else took for granted.

Before contact was made, the light intensified for the briefest of moments. Ash screamed in agony as her atoms rebelled against being in two places at once. In that instant, when the light of the Stone washed over her, Ash was still standing on the stage in the square, but she was also elsewhere, caught on either end of a disorientating jump. Like iron pulled by a powerful magnet, her focus was drawn to a distant landscape. Ash looked in amazement out across an alpine meadow with mountains too large looming nearby. A gray horse with silver streaks reared up suddenly right in front of her, its darkly clad rider fighting for control. A half-familiar scar was etched on his youthful face and yet his eyes looked much, much older.

"You have the glow of the Stone upon you," he said, wide-eyed. "I wondered if our protector still shone at all after so long. Precious time has been lost. Listen to me," the man pleaded. "They're coming. We couldn't protect you any longer. Somehow we failed. The Restless King knows where the village is after searching for so long. A tainted fragment from our Protector guides him. He is coming with his minions. I am the only one left. The only one alive who knows."

Ash blinked back in disbelief. The stranger was making no sense. What was happening? Where was she? The Restless King was just a fairy tale.

"Don't you understand!" he yelled, as if sensing her skepticism. "The Suzerian will take your precious light, chop down your precious trees, then kill you all. Tell everyone to leave before it's too late."

A stab of fear struck Ash, but not for the warning given. Instead she found herself stumbling backward, trying to distance herself from the rider. The intensity of the outburst had shaken her awake to possible dangers, and her mind reeled with the impossibility of what she was experiencing.

"No, do not fear *me*," the man beseeched. "I'm an ally, though probably forgotten by most. It is not I you should dread." The rider looked behind him like a hunted animal. When he spoke again, his voice was overcome with sadness. "I can't promise I'll make it to Renelis. Warn them that—"

Suddenly, the strain of being in two places at once caught up with her, and like a rubber band stretched too thin she snapped back into the Initiation ceremony in the village square. A second later Ash's world went mercifully dark, and she collapsed to the raised dais. In the stunned aftermath that followed, three Thorn members, two men and one woman, jumped up on to the stage. After briefly scanning for any injuries, the largest guardian, spoke briefly with the girl's parents, trying to comfort them and minimize any concern. The fact that he was close to the family only made it that much harder.

"Nothing's wrong that I can see," he told them, looking each one in the eye. "No injuries from the fall. Nothing broken. My guess is she must have fainted. Best thing we can do is get her to her new home and make her comfortable until she wakes up."

The father, Galen, a short rotund man in a simple brown tunic, stood slightly hunched over, like a wind-beaten tree on a cliff. Next to him was Radora, his wife, a lithe middle-aged woman. He put a hand on her shoulder as she wiped a tear away. They were both simple-looking folk, but such trappings were deceiving, Gundis knew. And Gundis knew them well. He had been best friends with Galen more years than he could remember.

"If anything happens to her…" Galen began, but then was interrupted as someone pushed into their midst. A young man who looked no more than thirty, tall and muscular, stepped forward. His lean face was creased with concern. "What happened to her, Gundis?" he asked urgently.

The Captain of the Guard looked at Jax, and then over at his parents. "Your sister is fine. The Stone must have overwhelmed her."

"She's not fine, she's unconscious," the man protested. "She needs to be taken to the Healer."

Gundis shook his head. "She is under Myla's jurisdiction now," he said gently. "The Mizen will watch over her and tend to her needs."

"Yes," Radora agreed, speaking for the first time. Her voice had a fierceness even as her eyes still plainly showed her anguish. Her left hand was adorned with a black glove, as if she were trying to hide something. "She has made her choice. Do me one favor, though, Gundis, if you can. Watch over her to make sure all is well. She is my only daughter and the village's only Youngling."

Gundis looked at Galen, and then back to Radora before responding. "If they will allow my presence in the Catacombs, I will stay by her side." Then he nodded gravely to his two Thorn companions who, after a moment's hesitation, carried Ash off to her new home underground. She was part of the Mizen now.

Chapter 2

Soft flickering torchlight danced around the sleeping form of Ash. She breathed shallowly but steadily on the small bed. In the doorway to her personal alcove stood Gundis, the senior guard of the Thorns, watching over her. From his hands grew the living *filigreen*, the mark of the Stone. Without warning, the shimmering latticework sputtered and then disappeared. He was nervous, anxious in fact. He had remained despite the High Mizen's complaints about how unusual it was, and had for his part nimbly retorted that it was also unusual—unheard of, in fact—to have an Initiate faint after coming in contact with the Stone and that as Captain of the Thorn he had jurisdiction in making sure that she came to no further harm.

He had known Ash's father since before the Falling and her mother nearly as long. He had come to look at the Youngling miracle like the much younger sister he never had. Nothing short of an order from the Grand Sizan was going to cause him to leave. And so the priests grumbled, permitting his continued presence, but keeping watch themselves. Ash was one of them now, after all. Two Lesser Mizen stood in the alcove to either side of Ash, their slender bodies and light gray robes making them appear like sullied ghosts. A Third Ring High Mizen, adorned in the purest white, waited sternly between them.

When Ash finally opened her eyes, several hours later, it took them all by surprise. "She's awake!" Gundis exclaimed, launching himself out of the creaky wooden chair to kneel beside the young woman.

"I am," Ash replied softly as a fleeting dream dissolved. Her eyes glanced around the room, taking in the strange new subterranean surroundings. "The Catacombs. What happened after the Vow? There was so much light. I don't remember anything."

"You fainted dead away!" Gundis replied. "The first to ever have. Quite a scare you gave us."

Ash looked up into familiar face and tried to smile. Gundis was big and burly, a long-time friend of her family and something of an honorary uncle to her. She trusted him more than anyone. "Thanks for looking after me, Gun, but my head hurts like a split cord of wood. Could you talk a bit softer?"

"Oh, sorry," the Captain of the Thorn said. "I was just worried about you." Then he remembered the Mizen. "We all were."

The High Mizen priest moved to the foot of the bed, the lesser Mizzen trailing behind like obedient spirits. "As you can see, Captain, the Youngling has recovered, but she needs her rest before we can question her. I'm sure you are anxious to get back outside to help oversee the security of our community." She motioned to her attendants. "Someone can show you out, Captain. The passageways can be confusing to the uninitiated."

Gundis looked over at Ash, concern etched across his broad face. "It's okay," she told him. "I'll be fine. Really. I just needed a little rest, that's all."

"Alright," he said. "But I'll be back to check on you when I can." At the alcove entrance, he paused and looked back at the priest. "There's no need for a guide, Onar. I know the way." Ash watched her friend leave, feeling as if the last familiar part of her old life was going with him.

"Well, then," the priest began. "Let's get you out of this bed. Your training has been delayed enough as it is."

Chapter 3

Over the next several months Ash learned the schedule of the Mizen priesthood, as well as other assorted minutiae. It was much more intense than her regular homeschooling had been. Both Mizen and neophytes were expected to wake at sunrise. After a meditation surrounded by glow rocks and filled with unpronounceable mantras, a simple but filling breakfast was offered in the Great Chamber. Since she was the only Initiate, this meant that Ash ate alone at a long, empty table set apart from the Lesser and High Mizen. In a sea of grey and white, she was the only one clothed in brown, her Initiate robes marking her as unlearned. Great swaths of natural light streamed down from holes high in the ceiling, illuminating the polished rock floor, which is what Ash looked at while she was eating since no one would talk to her.

The rest of the morning was spent with a tutor, each more uninspiring than the last, who read from dusty books about Mizen history, etiquette and ethics. Every lecture and reading underscored the sentiment that questions were not tolerated. Every ritualistic passage or stilted conversation emphasized the necessity of simply following along without deviation. When she asked too many questions or offended someone with an opinion, she was gently chastised by her teacher. It wasn't that they were mean or that the Mizen were bad people. Their unwavering belief in the Stone and dedication to service was laudable. Ash herself shared a sense of wonder concerning the Stone and the Stand of the Eternals. Life in the Catacombs, though, just felt stifling. She was no closer to finding out why she was different. Every day was akin to walking a tightrope. Ash was so nervous of saying the wrong thing that she began chewing her fingernails, a habit seemingly left behind from childhood.

When the morning of rote learning and head nodding was finally over, it was time for lunch and more floor staring. This was followed by a second round of meditation. Ash was usually so bored that she would fall asleep. The short Mizen priest leading the mantras would gently tap her on the shoulder and pretend to scowl until she joined back in. A slate of afternoon classes followed. There was plant identification, the symbolism of dreams, and finally *flligreen* practice.

This last activity was by far her favorite, or at least she thought it would be. Ash watched spellbound as the gray-robed Lesser Mizen weaved intricate patterns of slender living thread between their fingers. The substance had always fascinated Ash, since it was malleable but also incredibly strong. If the wielder wished, it could be thick or thin. The color was always green, mirroring the leaves of the Eternals, but the hue shifted from celadon to chartreuse, myrtle and citron, depending on the individual. As Ash struggled, a few of the Lesser Mizen sent emerald bursts up to the domed ceiling, only to fall back down in a shower of tiny spring buds. Ash looked down at her own empty hands and felt her stomach tighten.

"Try again," the *filigreen* instructor Ms. Paramond admonished, looking on in her white robes and with her hair braided tightly behind her head, unable to comprehend how anyone could be so deficient in something so simple. "Think of the Stone and the light that you saw there. It just comes harder for some. Let go of everything. The moment will come."

Ash flexed her fingers for the hundredth time and closed her eyes, but nothing happened. Nothing ever happened. "I can't," she cried, unable to hide the disappointment in her voice.

"It is the birthright of the Stone," Ms. Paramond said at last, after a long pause. She seemed somewhat stricken, but less so for Ash and more for the laws of the universe that were not behaving as she expected them to. "It is our living connection to eternity. The Thorns can do it best, but everyone has at least some ability. You *must* have it inside you."

But she didn't. Somehow the Stone had rejected her. That's why she had fainted. She was unworthy in some fundamental way. All of her hopes had hinged on becoming like everyone else in Renelis. After a lifetime of trying to fit in, she had convinced herself that going through the Initiation would be the start of something better. Becoming a Mizen Initiate was supposed to give her answers. She had expected to see the Sanctum or listen for the stirrings of the Eternals. At the very least, Ash had believed that there would be discussions as to why the Stone had chosen them and who had discovered it. Ash received no satisfactory answers to either of these reasonable questions.

In frustration, she inquired concerning the library, normally accessible to all Mizen. While the collection was very small—only a dozen or so handwritten diaries and theoretical treatises—Ash was eager to read them. They were rumored to include arguments as to the nature of the Stone's divinity, an account of the formation of the Thorns, the crowning of the Grand Sizan title to the original mayor of the town, an analysis carried out by Mizen scholars concerning the language of the Eternals, and the drawing of names for the Celestials.

She asked her history instructor, Professor Mustermin, who was also the Chronologist, for permission to read the tomes. Being an Initiate had many restrictions, and one of the more frustrating ones was access to the library. The only way to access books was through a shared key that Mustermin kept around his neck. He was a dry, tight-lipped man who smelled of cough elixir. In a patient and monotonous voice, he explained to Ash that she was simply not ready. "Unearned knowledge is a dangerous trap," he concluded, as if that could somehow mollify a lifetime's worth of curiosity.

And so Ash struggled through one tedious lesson after another. Every time she tried asking a question, her instructors would just shake their heads and tell Ash to listen for the truth. Taking the Vow and seeing the Stone should have given her the same thing it had given everyone else in Renelis; a new life. So far, they just made her feel more alone.

Ash picked at her dinner of fresh vegetables, barley soup and sourdough bread one night, trying to figure out what to do. She missed her family, even her older brother Jax. He sometimes teased her for being so young and odd, but he had a good heart, even though he sometimes resented the attention Ash got. Most of all, she missed her parents. Her mother had a way of taking a complicated problem and making it seem simple, and her father's sense of humor brought light to the darkest of days. Sitting in the gloomy cavern, they all seemed a world away. It was heartbreaking to think that she wouldn't see them again until she graduated and became a Lesser

Mizen. No one from the outside was allowed in the Catacombs. Only the Grand Sizan himself and the Captain of the Thorns could gain entrance. Ash knew it was foolish, but oh how she hoped that Gundis would visit her again as he had promised. She missed his breath-stealing hugs and the way he looked out for her. If Ash knew that he wouldn't forget about her, then maybe she could make it through.

People weren't ignoring her anymore. She could feel the weight of their stares and their unspoken questions. Word must have gotten out from her classmates about how she had failed her *filigreen* practice class. Ash saw them whispering and pointing. Her most recent failure was only overshadowed by collapsing during the Initiation ceremony. The combination was severely tarnishing her image of a Youngling miracle. She waited while the Lesser Mizen and High Mizen finished eating, leaving the dining area in small groups. Eventually there was just one priest left. He was lanky and middle-aged, with a hooked nose that reminded her of a bird. From his dark complexion, he must have originally been a trader, perhaps from Caravel or one of the southern lands. He was always the last to leave. Sometimes Ash got the feeling that he wanted to talk to her, but he never did. He glanced over at her nervously and then got up and left through the far tunnel.

Evenings were unregulated. Other than being in bed by lights out, when many of the torches were extinguished and the darkness of the Catacombs was nearly complete, Ash could do as she pleased as long as she stayed away from certain restricted areas, such as the Sanctum and the High Mizen living quarters. Usually she would just go to her room, but Ash was tired of waiting for her life to change. Tonight, she had a better idea.

Getting up from the table, she scanned the room again. The Great Chamber was empty. Rows upon rows of silent stone tables fanned out around her like fallen tombstones. At the end of each aisle was a murky tunnel entrance leading into the Catacombs. Ash knew which tunnel would take her back to her room, and which would take her to her classrooms and meditation spaces, but there were five other entrances. Two of these were reserved for the Lesser and High Mizen, leading to their own personal living quarters. Ash quickly discounted these. She knew these by simple observation, from watching the priests come and go.

Another tunnel slanted upward towards a distant light. She knew this led to the outside and that it was guarded at its terminus by the Long Robes, sacred soldiers, for she had been turned away on one her many explorations. The other two tunnels were more intriguing. One almost certainly led to the Sanctum of the Stone, as well as a larger separate chamber where the roots of the Eternals were exposed (and if legends were true, would sometimes speak to the faithful). Finding either one was dependent upon not getting lost in the maze of passageways, for the exact route was a secret shared by only the highest Mizen. The other entrance was a complete mystery. They both looked the same and both were expressly forbidden to Lesser Mizen.

Ash started walking toward the opening at the end of her aisle, then veered toward the far tunnel, the same one the skinny priest had gone into. When she passed through the portal from light into dark, a familiar coldness gripped her, as if winter's season lay at the end of the tunnel, the shadows seeming more pronounced now and the meager glow stones doing little to illuminate her way or warm her. Soon she was shivering as the temperature continued to drop. Instinctively, Ash held out her hands to stop herself from bumping into a wall. Onward she went in halting, hesitant steps, breathing a sigh of relief every time another sputtering glow stone came into view.

Up ahead the tunnel curved away, and the promise of new bright-ness seemed to spill across the stone at her feet. Ash started forward, eager to end her dark wanderings, when a figure stepped out of the shadows an arm's length away. "It's about time you came looking," he told her.

Ash flung herself away, heedless of the rocky walls, and then looked back at the figure. Standing in the dim light was a man. He stepped forward and removed his hood. "It's you," Ash managed.

The priest had a weathered face the color of a cinnamon tree, and his nose jutted forward like an unspoken accusation. A red robe hung loose on his tall, slight frame. He looked to be around forty, but Ash knew that looks were deceiving. Peering into his unblinking eyes, Ash saw the accumulated years. "Why have you been watching me?" she asked, still shaken by his sudden appearance. "At meals. I see you."

"My name is H'vetik," the man told her matter-of-factly in an accent both exotic and strange. "I mean you no harm. Quite the opposite, in fact."

Ash took a closer look at him and noticed the three interlocking copper circles sewn on the man's robe over his chest. The priest was a Third Ring. He had privilege and standing. She swallowed before she spoke. "Am I in trouble?" she asked as a lump of fear grew in her throat. Leave it to her to faint at Initiation, fail her *filigreen* instruction, and *then* get kicked out for trespassing.

"Only if someone else sees us," the priest explained. "Then I'll have to pretend that I caught you sneaking where you were explicitly instructed not to go. Punishment will ensue. You don't want that, do you?" Ash shook her head slowly. "Can you be very, *very* quiet?" The question seemed absurd, but his manner was deadly serious.

"Of course," she said carefully. "But I don't understand. Why are you helping me? Priests aren't supposed to break the rules."

H'vetik smiled, but it contained a hint of pain. "I am indeed a priest, but I am so much more. There's a wider world than my fellow Mizen can imagine. I long ago allowed myself the freedom to encounter different forms of wisdom. That is why I became a trader, so I could earn a living as I searched for meaning. But your question is focused on another truth. We have a mutual friend. He asked me to look after you."

"Gundis!" Ash exclaimed.

The priest put a finger to his lips. "You must be quiet all of the time and not just some of it," he admonished, looking around. "Follow me. What I'm about to show you is not allowed and may surprise you. You will undoubtedly have questions. Just remember, I am on your side."

A smile spread across her face. "Are you taking me to the library?" she asked slowly.

The priest shook his head. "Be skeptical of secrets kept in plain sight," he answered. "Anything you might learn there must come from other sources, I'm afraid."

Ash didn't try to hide her disappointment. He was just another person withholding truth. The heavy weight of resignation settled on her shoulders. She could almost feel herself giving up. Then the priest surprised her. Stepping closer, he did something that few outside her family or close friends ever had; he touched her, on the arm. The sensation was warm and reassuring.

Ash looked at the priest in shock. "Aren't you afraid I'll contaminate you and rob you of the Stone's gift?"

"Not in the least," H'vetik replied, his hand still pressed lightly on her skin. "You can trust me." The priest led her around the bend in the tunnel and into the light. A cavern nearly as large as the Great Chamber opened up unexpectedly. Glow stones were suspended from the ceiling, illuminating a small clump of tiny stone huts. They mirrored the style of home aboveground in the village, but they were much smaller and cruder. Together they were configured in such a way as to leave an open circular space in the center. In this community space a group of young children played, kicking around an empty gourd while older-looking children talked.

As Ash and H'vetik approached from the tunnel, they all turned. "Hello again," the priest said, raising his palm up in greeting. "I brought the visitor I told you about." The children crowded around gazing at her, as if she had just fallen from the sky. Ash had never seen so many young-looking citizens in one place. Youth, or at least the semblance of youth, had always been in short supply, even before the Fall. They were precious and to be kept from harm. This is why, so many years ago, the young had been told that the Stone did not work on individuals younger than twenty. In this fashion, ageless parents waited for their precious children to reach maturity before bestowing the gift upon them. But what the Stone giveth, the Stone also taketh away. In accepting eternity and passing it on to their children, the villagers became effectively sterile. That's why Ash was known as the miraculous Youngling. Now, to her amazement, there were more.

Each of the children looked at Ash as if they were a mirror, reflecting her own astonishment. "Is it true?" a small, freckled boy with orange-red hair asked the wayward priest. "Is she the First?"

H'vetik tousled his hair and smiled. "Those are the kinds of questions that the other Mizen would cringe at. She very well may be, I suppose."

"Then that makes her our leader!" a sandy-haired girl shouted.

The children pressed in on her now, talking excitedly, and Ash began to feel a bit overwhelmed. "What are they talking about?" she whispered to H'vetik. "I've never been the first at anything."

"Look closer," he replied.

Ash turned and studied the faces of the children. A mix of boys and girls, most of them were ages four to ten, but there were also a couple of taller kids, teenagers, who hung back from the throng, watching and studying her. None of them were older than fifteen. Height, weight and hair color differed from individual to individual. There was only one thing they all had in common; they were all children. For long moments Ash forgot to breathe, as she tried to process this revelation. There were others like her, a miracle of birth. She wasn't alone. Even as she opened herself up to this possibility, she knew it was impossible. The Stone did not allow it. The price of the Stone's gift was no children could be conceived. At least until Ash had been born. Now it seemed there were more. She felt surrounded by marvels, held aloft by the light shining from above into the great cave. But then she wondered why the children were hidden away. It didn't make any sense. Her smile evaporated, replaced with a growing sense of confusion and outrage. "I don't understand," she said to the priest. "What's going on here?"

A little girl of no more than six approached Ash shyly. She had long nut-brown hair and wore a faded yellow dress. Her feet were bare. Dust and dirt covered patches of her skin. When she was almost close enough to touch, the child stopped and, in a dramatic flourish, bowed down in front of her. "All hail Ash the First, Queen of the Catacombs!" The other children laughed and then proceeded to each take turns prostrating before her.

"Enough!" the eldest boy said, coming over. "She's just like you and I, only older." Ash shifted uncomfortably. The teen wore a spotless tan tunic and sandals with white straps. His face was handsome except for the red bruise of a birthmark that covered his left cheek. The children looked at the teenager, frozen into submission, before returning their gaze to Ash.

"Treld is right, you know," said H'vetik gently, trying to intercede on her behalf. "On High Summer's Eve Aisha chose to become a novice Mizen. She descended into darkness to find answers. Her only subjects are in books. Is this how we should treat a guest to our home?"

"No, Caretaker," the children murmured.

"As your appointed guardian, I must insist on better manners. Now when I return, I expect each and every one of you to finish your evening chores before bed. That goes for you too, Treld." The sullen teen held the priest's gaze for a moment before turning away.

H'vetik was about to make their exit when Ash spoke up. "I know it's not my place to say, as I've only been here a short while, but I think the people who need to apologize are the ones keeping you here, away from your families. I can't imagine growing up without the love of my parents or brother. This camp hidden deep in the Catacombs seems shameful to me."

A sea of faces looked back at her, blinking back tears. The priest shifted uncomfortably. "They didn't want us," Treld finally spat out. "Our parents, I mean. They were ashamed of us Agers and what we represented. Everyone is. Almost. It's not his fault," he finished, glancing over at H'vetik. "The Caretaker does what he can. Argues for our release. He treats us with dignity."

"And sometimes he smuggles in candy," a little boy with curly hair piped in. A little rivulet of snot ran down from his nostril.

Ash tried and failed to control her anger. "Even so, no one has the right to do this to you," she said. It broke her heart to see them all like this.

"People do strange things out of fear," the priest offered. "All we can do is take care of each other until the day comes when you are all reunited with your parents. Everyone here is loved. Remember that." He scooped up the little girl in the yellow dress and stroked her cheek before setting her back down. "I will be back shortly."

Following in the Caretaker's footsteps, Ash stewed silently at what she had seen as they made their way back through the winding tunnel.

How could the children have been abandoned and then hidden without her knowing they even existed? What other secrets were waiting to spring themselves at her? Suddenly her view of Renelis was called sharply into question. Growing up, her village had been unchanging, just like the people who lived there. Now everything had been altered. There were others like her. In her mind, she envisioned cracks forming in the homes and streets, even in the ancient Stand of the Eternals that guarded them all. Her perception of reality was crumbling. When the bright glow lights of the dining cavern came into view she began to walk more cautiously, unsure of the ground at her feet and conscious of the fact that she had trespassed. Ash wanted to run back into the darkness.

They reentered the cavern and crept past the long stone tables just as a procession emerged from a nearby tunnel. Ash froze, spellbound. Two Mizen ceremonial guards marched with their backs straight, a staff carved from a fallen Eternals branch held high. Next, four High Mizen, each adorned in gold robes ribbed in emerald, walked solemnly into the communal space, carrying an ornate litter between them. On burnished metal fitted with copper handles lay fabric as black as any night, cradling a large wooden box. Even from this distance, Ash could see the intense glow of the Stone spill out like a miniature sun peeking over the horizon. Trailing behind, his fingers spinning emerald *filigreen*, was Gundis, Captain of The Thorn. His face wore a grim expression. Fanning out in back of him were two deputy guardians. Each looked warily around, as if being in the Catacombs did not suit them.

"Just act normal," H'vetik whispered in Ash's ear, putting a hand of caution up. "That retinue is royal bound. Something is not right."

Ash watched as the procession approached, turning towards them. If Gundis noticed them he gave no acknowledgement, but his deputies glanced in their direction. As the Stone passed by on the way to the outside tunnel, Ash felt the unearthly glow fall on her face for a second time. Then the world of the catacombs tumbled away from her. An intense pain rushed in, flooding her body. Human beings weren't meant to travel this way. Once again she felt the pull of a different place. The next moment she found herself standing in a grove of black trees as straight and silent as a tomb. No creatures stirred. No birds chirped. No insects hummed. A slow-moving stream flowed nearby, but there was only feeble light reflected on its surface. The sun was masked by clouds. *The Stone*, she remembered. Somehow it had brought her to this forest.

There was another reflection on the water, that of a rider in dark leather. It was the same scarred man as before, but his pants and jerkin were torn. She turned toward him as if in a dream, because that's what it must be, but she felt the breeze blow through her hair and warmth on her skin. *I'm in the Catacombs*, she thought. *This can't be happening.* And yet it was. The horse he rode was near exhaustion. White froth bubbled through its quivering mouth and nostrils. With a pained look on his young face the rider reined in his mount. "There is no time," he moaned. "Even now they approach. I cannot shake them."

Ash looked behind the man and thought she spied movement in the trees, slivers of white slicing through the shadows. An unnatural shiver passed through her, as if a bleak moon had broken through the clouds in the middle of the day.

"Why do you appear before me so, still speechless and amazed? Have you delivered my message? Answer me!" he wailed. A moment later he mastered himself, perhaps remembering how he had frightened her before. "I know this must make little sense to you, but you need to trust me. Death stalks us. The Restless King and his Brigade of Bones are coming. You have only days. Defenses must be readied. The Stone must be moved. That's all he really wants."

This time she did not retreat in front of the messenger who loomed above her. With effort, she held her ground. A hundred questions spun in her head. Try as she might, however, Ash could not make any words come from her mouth. Somehow she had forgotten the art of speech. Lost in her struggle, she noticed his hand. "You're bleeding," she managed.

The wound shone brightly, but the man seemed to take no notice of it, although Ash knew it must be very painful. "Yes, remember this," the rider spoke as he held up his damaged hand into a shaft of sunlight. Across his fingers was a deep, scarlet slash. Blood ran into his palm, where it pooled amidst the shimmering tattoo of a falling star.

"Remember this. Remember me. The Restless King is coming. Remember. Renelis and everyone's lives depend on it." Then he reached out and pressed something round and metallic into her hand.

With that, he spurred his horse into frantic motion. She turned to follow him and call out that she didn't even know his name, but then the sky grew dark and she crumpled to the cold stone floor of the Great Chamber.

Chapter 4

When Ash awoke and opened her eyes, she found herself in a brightly lit room. Her head throbbed. A shaft of blinding sunlight fell upon her bed, on which white linens were laid. The walls surrounding her were smooth snow granite, and the faint stirrings of a breeze could be felt on her face. Somehow, she had been moved aboveground, far from the Catacombs. Through the large windows directly opposite her rose Immortia, the slender tower of the Grand Sizan, easily the tallest structure in Renelis unless one counted the lofty Eternals with their darkened branches. Slowly, she became aware of something on her forehead. It felt cooling and soft. The scent of the earth was strong. The aroma carried her back to a time when she was a little girl and her brother had burned his hand in a cooking fire. Jax had been given a healer's salve, made from gathered moss and special herbs. She had something similar draped across her brow now. Without a doubt she was at the Mender, but how she had been injured was a mystery.

Then an image came to her, broken and disconnected. A hand with a bloody gash flashed in her memory. Instinctively, she flexed her fingers, but felt no discomfort. There was something she was supposed to remember. In frustration, she struggled to sit up when two strong hands reached out and pushed her gently back down to the bed. "Not yet, Aisha," a voice told her. "The Healer's Assistant gave specific instructions before heeding nature's call that you were to lie down and rest until he returned. Besides, you'll disturb the wrappings."

Ash craned her neck toward the voice. Sitting in a simple woven chair was Fayne, Lieutenant of the Guard. He was short and stocky with a face that was often serious, but could smile at a moment's notice. Gundis trusted him more than any other. "Where is Gun?" she asked. It seemed odd that he wasn't here.

Fayne tipped his head down and frowned. "With the Grand Sizan and the Master Healer. The captain was on his way to the royal palace with the Stone when you fell unconscious."

Of course. There had been a procession. She remembered that now. H'vetik had just guided her back through the tunnels after meeting with the other Agers. The Stone had been covered, but it had been close by. She had fallen again and then awoken here at the Mender's. Examining her recollections, however, made her feel that something was missing. She screwed up her face in frustration, like a child trying to find the correct puzzle piece that once placed would make everything become clear.

"What is wrong?" Fayne asked, new concern deepening the lines on his face. "Are you in pain?"

Ignoring her own aches, Ash held her hand up into the shaft of sunlight and pushed herself up into a sitting position. "I'm not sure. Something isn't right." On the precipice of a question, she paused, afraid to know the answer. "Why has the Master Healer gone to the Grand Sizan?"

The Lieutenant could not hide the dark specter that passed over his face. "The Grand Sizan is—ill," he told her. This last word was brought forth with effort, as if it were an unimaginable utterance. "Has been for months. Whatever ails him has been growing steadily worse. Some say he is close to death."

Ash's world stopped as this unexpected news sunk in. The Grand Sizan could not be dying. It was impossible. No one got sick and no one could die, not since the Fall. If the Grand Sizan was sick then no one in Renelis was safe. She thought of her parents and grandparents, Jax and Gun. "I don't understand," she mumbled.

Before Fayne could reply, the Assistant Healer strode into the room. He looked to be middle-aged and wore a permanent frown of disapproval. His white robe was tidy and bore the mender's insignia of blood-red stripes at the end of his tapered sleeves. Ash's eyes were drawn to the slashes of color down each arm. "What is this?!" he cried. "I gave one instruction. Please lie back down. You endanger our healing work." Fayne reached out a hand to help Ash comply, but the Healer slapped the hand away. "Don't be a fool, Lieutenant. Touch her and you could be next."

The Assistant strode toward her, but Ash took no notice. There was no room in her awareness for anything else except for what she had just remembered. Gripping the side of the bed, she hoisted her body up to a standing position and then steadied herself. When the world had stopped spinning, she removed the moist sticky moss from her forehead and smiled. "Back off," she told the Healer, holding out her arms as if they were monstrous tentacles. "I don't have time for your ridiculous prejudice. Listen to me. We are all in *danger!*"

The man sneered. "Of course we are all in danger. Shadows gather over the Grand Sizan, and like dominoes we will fall next."

"No, something else," Ash managed. "Not from here. Not in Renelis. Something is coming from beyond our walls. We are all in great peril. I wish I could remember more."

"Are you delirious?" the Healer asked her. "Do you have a fever?" Genuine concern crept back into his voice. "Sit back down," he instructed, being careful not to get too close.

Fayne looked at the Assistant Healer and then back at Ash. "I'm not sick," she told the Thorn. "But I need to go warn Gundis. He'll know what to do." Her voice caught with unexpected emotion. "Please."

The Lieutenant made his decision. Stepping in front of the Healer, he crossed his muscled arms and stuck out his leathered armor chest. "Go now," he told Ash, flashing a quick smile.

"Are you mad?" the Mender exploded. Fear etched his stern features, robbing him of any remaining vestiges of being a caretaker. "She could contaminate us all!"

"She will not," Fayne said simply. "She has been in the Catacombs and lived with us aboveground for many years. Or have you forgotten? I do not take orders from you, Carthon. My duty was to remain with Aisha until she was well or until the Captain of the Guard returned, whichever came first, and then return to my station. It now appears she is recovered."

Carthon fumed visibly at the Guard, but finally stepped aside. "This is on your watch," he warned.

Breathing a sigh of relief, Ash put a hand on the Lieutenant's shoulder. He didn't shirk away. "Thank you," she told him and then turned toward the doorway.

"Wait," the Healer called unexpectedly. "You came with something." He motioned to a small ornate table made of wood next to the bed. Carved into its legs were depictions of the sun and moon, as well as several fabled beasts from ancient myths. Atop its polished surface there rested a single copper coin. Carthon reached out and placed the object in her hand. The visible side was plain and unadorned. She couldn't recall seeing it before, or understand why she would have it. Then she turned the coin over and saw the shooting star engraving. Memories came crashing into her consciousness of the scarred and tattooed rider.

The Restless King is coming.

Chapter 5

Ash was halfway down the street, running to Immortia, the stone tower of the Grand Sizan, when she remembered that she still wore the garments of the Mizen. People stared wide-eyed as she passed, her tawny novice robe flapping in the breeze like a warning. She turned the corner and the entrance to the palace came into view. A short, winding path through flowering gardens brought her to a pair of large wooden doors that were the only portal to the royal residence. The tower was made of the finest marble, quarried only a short distance from Renelis in the gently rising hills. Shifting patterns of blue and white colorations gave the slender finger of stone the illusion of being limitless as it melded into the sky around it. Grey slates adorned the roof, shimmering languidly in the sunlight like waves upon the sea.

Pulling the massive doors open, she squeezed inside. Standing in the half-circular foyer were two guards, but they were not Thorns, Ash realized with a start. Instead they were palace Wardens, adorned in the ceremonial colors of azure and ivory. One had a curving mustache while the other sported a red goatee. In each hand they held a halberd which glittered menacingly in the light filtering down through the open windows above. Her plan had been to use Gundis as a means to gain an audience with the Grand Sizan, but the sudden illness had changed things dramatically in the tower. The normal Thorn Guards had been pulled, probably as a means of curtailing gossip, and replaced with soldiers loyal to the Grand Sizan himself.

Momentarily at a loss for what to do next, Ash didn't notice the doors behind her open and a familiar figure step inside. The next moment she strode toward the guards with a desperate plan. "Make way for a special messenger from the Priestess of the High Mizen!" she shouted in what she hoped was a convincing manner.

"His Highness sees no one," the mustached guard responded, taking a menacing step forward. "He is currently indisposed."

Ash stopped in her tracks. "The city is in jeopardy!" she pleaded. "I *must* have an audience with the Grand Sizan before it is too late."

"There are no exceptions," the bearded guard toned. "Run along back to the Catacombs." Raising his arm, the palace guard pointed the tip of his weapon at Ash.

"The neophyte is with *me*," a voice spoke behind her. "There has been some confusion. We will not trouble you further." Spinning around, Ash saw the skinny priest H'vetik walk toward her in earnest. "Come with me," he said sternly, taking her arm and guiding Ash out through the door.

When they were out on the garden path, the priest stopped and disengaged himself. "What are you doing here?" Ash asked in amazement. It was very unusual to have a Mizen aboveground for anything other than ceremonial purposes.

H'vetik looked at her with a resigned smile, as if the weight of the world could not be easily borne on such a slight frame. "Looking after you, of course," the priest muttered. "Gundis told me you were headstrong, but I had no idea. What in the Seven Kingdoms could prompt you to do such a foolish thing?"

"I had a vision," Ash tried to explain. "When I fainted. But it was real."

"We don't have time for nonsense," H'vetik scolded. "Gundis is still with the Grand Sizan, but will meet us soon. He's worried about you. We must hurry."

The priest turned to go, but Ash grabbed on to his robe. "Wait!" she said, turning him toward her. "Something isn't right. Each time I've come in contact with the Stone, I've fainted. Somehow I get transported. I don't know how. But there was a rider. A messenger. He has a warning for us all."

"You hit your head," H'vetik consoled. "Strange things may sometimes seem real."

"No," Ash insisted. "I was there. It was real. You have to believe me."

For a long moment the priest held her gaze, as if measuring the young neophyte's capacity for miracles. "I'm sorry, but I had to be sure. We cannot talk out in the open," he cautioned with a stern look. "Whatever is going on with you and the Stone has to be shared with the rest of the Mizen."

Following his lead, Ash followed the priest through the streets towards the outer perimeter of Renelis, where the city's defenses lay. Only Thorns patrolled the wall and the no-man's land that lay beyond. "H'vetik, where are we going?" she asked as they passed a seldom-used cross-street and soon entered the shadow of the ten-foot-high wall that surrounded the village. "The entrance to the Catacombs is the other way."

Although there was no one nearby on the road or atop the wall, the Mizen priest stopped and lowered his voice. "To the Stand of the Eternals," he told her.

A chill went through Ash as she heard the words. "That's not possible." she said. "I thought the only way from inside the village was through the tunnels."

"There is much you do not know," H'vetik told her, but though his words pretended to scorn, his voice was light. "Normally, a Novice waits until her third year to walk through the Weirway. Unfortunately, time is a luxury we do not have."

Ash let the priest guide her to a small, non-descript alcove set near the corner of the wall. A solid sheet of burnished metal blocked the entrance. No knob or keyhole was visible and Ash could see no hinges on which the door, if that's what it was, might open. H'vetik knocked twice, paused and then knocked a third time. On the walkway above, a Thorn guard appeared in full battle leather and looked down sternly. Short-cropped hair peeked out from the sides of her helmet.

"The sky lifts us up," H'vetik toned. "Chaos swirls around us."

"There is sanctuary in a grain of sand," the Thorn responded.

Then the priest raised his fist, opening it slowly with his fingers spread out and palm facing outward. The moment hung suspended as Ash looked on.

Finally, the Thorn nodded to someone unseen behind her. Silently, the door slid upwards into hidden grooves, revealing a narrow space between the outer and inner walls. H'vetik motioned her inside with a wave of his hand. Above their heads was a thin ribbon of blue sky. Directly in front of them was another door, this one made of black-gray stone inlaid with dozens of keyholes. H'vetik stepped to the entrance and without hesitation placed his right forefinger in the bottom-most opening. A moment later living *filigreen* shot from his fingertips and began to spread over the surface of the door. All at once the flow sputtered and stopped. The priest frowned, muttering a profane curse before flexing his hand and reapplying himself. Soon the emerald flow resumed. Tiny tendrils became leaves, which in turn became vines and branches, until a tangle of vegetation covered the stone completely.

H'vetik stepped back and put his hands together so the fingers pointed back at his chest, and then swept them forward and away from each other. The mass of greenery mimicked his motions and parted to reveal not stone but the landscape beyond. Ash needed no encouragement from the priest as she stepped into the sun-darkened world. For a moment she thought somehow they had labored to arrive underground in the Catacombs, but then Ash noticed the half-dozen great craggy trunks that stood like shadowy sentinels along the perimeter of the wall, bright glimpses of the verdant valley beyond visible between their ancient foundations. Her eyes widened in amazement. Numerous times she had gazed at the Eternals' lofty boughs from her village home, but she had never been afforded a view of the grove from the ground up. While the base of each tree was indeed massive and sported gaping fissures, it was the branches themselves, unfolding into the sky, that took her breath away. A patchwork of leaves and wood spread out above her, each tree melding and joining with another as if they were participating in some silent communion. Lost in wonder, Ash gazed higher into the canopy. Patches of pink and orange light danced among the upper boughs. More than simple sunlight, the strange spectacle hinted at a pattern, and a power unimaginable. Looking at the majesty of the Eternals, she wondered why they had needed to build a wall at all. Who could harm them while they controlled the Stone?

Time was frozen under the cocoon of leaves as Ash soaked in the silence surrounding her. Although flecks of sun fell like broken shards on the ground all around her, it was the darkness of a split trunk directly in front that called the strongest. A chill of loneliness passed through her. Within its inky opening there seemed to lurk the abiding mysteries held between the stars. Ash shook her head as if to clear it of childhood fantasies and stepped forward, crunching on dried leaves.

The forest floor was littered with fallen leaves, even though autumn hadn't touched these trees in centuries. More fell from branches high above and drifted down to her feet. "What is happening?" she asked the Mizen priest.

"The trees are dying," he told her gravelly. "We do not know why. They do not talk to us anymore." As if on cue, the glow in the trees high above flickered and then went dark. When the shifting colors resumed, their glow had faded considerably.

The sound of movement behind her caught Ash's attention. Turning around, she saw two elite Thorn guards dressed in black leather emerge from the doorway. Striding in between them was her friend.

"Gun!" Ash cried and ran over to the captain. There was so much she needed to tell him, but that would have to wait.

He smiled broadly and then enveloped her in a crushing bear hug. "I'm sorry I have been away, Ash," Gundis said when he finally released her. Tears glistened in his eyes. "Things have gotten…complicated." Ash noticed that his smile had evaporated, replaced with a grim look of fatigue. "We need to talk. You've been fainting and knocking yourself out. I'm worried about you. I promised your family I would look out for you. If anything ever happened…"

"I like you watching out for me, Gun, you know that," she interrupted. "But there's something bigger going on." She paused, unsure how to say it. "I think I'm allergic to the Stone."

Instead of laughing or arguing against such a claim, Gundis simply nodded his head in somber agreement. "That indeed seems to be the case. When you fainted a second time in the Catacombs as we passed by with the Stone, I knew it could not be a simple coincidence. That's why I asked H'vetik to bring you here."

"So we could talk in secret?"

Gundis smiled weakly. "And also, so you can try to commune with the Eternals. The Grand Sizan is ill and may very well die. The people of Renelis are starting to age again." He put his hand on her shoulder. "You are proof of that, as are the others in the Catacombs that H'vetik showed you. The Eternals have grown silent. Winter's hand has fallen upon them. You have a connection with the Stone. We need to find out why things are changing."

"It's worse than that," Ash said. "Each time I faint, I am transported to some other place in the kingdom. Each time I've seen a rider in black. He is trying to get to us, to warn us, Gun."

The Captain of the Guard reached out and put a hand on her shoulder. "Tell me," he said. "I need to know what we're dealing with while there's still time."

Ash looked over at the priest. He nodded and did his best to smile. "The Restless King is coming with his Bone Brigade," Ash told them as a shiver passed through her. "He knows where we are. That's what the rider said. He's coming for the Stone."

Gundis clenched his fists. "Do you remember anything else? Anything about the rider or where you were when you saw him?"

A cool breeze wafted out from the large opening in the trunk nearest to them. Faint sounds could be heard, growing nearer. It felt as if she were running out of time. Closing her eyes, Ash tried to remember details of the last encounter. There had been woods and a stream and blood. "The rider had a tattoo of a shooting star on the palm of his hand," she blurted out. "I think he was only days away from us, but his pursuers were close. They had wounded him. Before I left he gave me this." Reaching into the pocket of her robe, she pulled out the coin and held it out to Gundis.

He took it and turned the object over in his hand. He looked spellbound. "I have heard of this fabled token, but never seen one. It is the mark of the Celestials, guardians of our secret. Such a thing is not given lightly."

"What do we do?"

"Everyone must be told. An emergency council with powers to act must be formed immediately. Defenses must be bolstered. It may already be too late."

"That is not up to you to decide," a woman commanded. Coming out from behind of the ragged darkness of a nearby Eternal trunk was a beautiful priestess robed in gilded leaves. A circlet of white flowers adorned her head. Long blonde hair streaked with unexpected gray spilled down her back. Her face was imperious, with eyes that belied an age her features hid. "With the Grand Sizan incapacitated, it is the High Mizen who must convene and decide on an interim ruler. Such is *our* right."

From their hidden spots behind the nearby Eternals stepped robed figures dressed in shimmering gold. Mizen warriors, Ash realized with a start. No weapons were visible, but *filigreen* danced dangerously in their upraised hands. The Thorns were not the only ones who wielded the Stone's power as a weapon.

"And when will that be?" asked Gundis, frowning.

"A decision should be made within the week," said the priestess flatly.

"We don't have that much time," he retorted. "The Restless King is on his way with an army to steal the Stone."

The Voice shook her head. "The Suzerian was corrupted. He could not have survived this long with only a shard. If anyone approaches at all, it is simple treasure seekers. We have dealt with such before, in different times and in different places. Do what you have to do to keep Renelis safe, Captain."

Gundis scowled. "Aisha is connected somehow to the Stone. She must be. Several times she has been overcome and then transported to a Celestial rider. It is he who has warned of the Restless King's arrival and his Bone Brigade. He comes for the Stone, Myla. It must be moved or we will all perish. The rider gave Aisha this token as proof."

Gundis held out the silver coin to the Voice, but she did not take it. "A fairy tale of a mythical messenger and a pretty trinket will not convince me," retorted the High Priestess.

Ash stepped forward. Disbelief contorted her features. "Then what of the children that you hide deep in the Catacombs? What of me? The Grand Sizan himself lies ill. Even the Eternals have grown silent. What more proof could you possibly need that our days of timelessness are coming to an end?"

The Voice smiled at her, but there was no warmth in it, only contempt. "For a Neophyte, you forget your place," she said slowly and distinctly. "These things are beyond you." The Captain of the Guard moved to speak, but the High Priestess cut him off. "Did you think you could meet in secret under the Eternals, our sole domain, and plan actions that usurp Mizen authority? These are treasonous transgressions. Under any other circumstances I would demand an investigation and an airing of grievances."

Gundis sighed heavily. "So at least you admit that there are unusual circumstances at play. You can keep your suspicions, Myla, but let Aisha commune with the Eternals. At least let her make the attempt. All of our lives may be at stake. Is your pride worth more than that?"

"You have already have my answer," the Voice replied. "Go now before I change my mind. The girl stays with us, as does the renegade priest."

"It is a title I wear proudly," H'vetik said.

Ash looked over at Gundis. "If that's the way it is, then give the coin back. It will provide some comfort when I'm in the Catacombs again." A moment of confusion passed over the Captain of the Guard's face. Then he tossed the coin to her. Ash caught it deftly in her hand. "Trust me," she told him.

Turning back to the High Priestess, she managed a smile. "So what are we waiting for?" Then she ran straight at the woman. The suddenness of her action caught the Voice off-guard. Ash was almost upon her by the time the woman raised her hand. Shoots of emerald *filigreen* blossomed from her fingertips and then sputtered. That was all the time Ash needed. The next instant, she barreled into the robed Priestess, knocking her off-balance. Racing for the crevice in the tree trunk, she felt a hand grab at her garments and tug her back. She had been so close. Turning her head, she saw the High Priestess ready a blast to immobilize her. When the shimmering green tendrils shot out, she flinched in dismay, only to open her eyes and see the Voice covered in a green shimmering web.

"Go!" Gundis ordered as he pivoted to direct another blast, should the white-robed Mizen intervene. For the moment they were still out of range, but each raced to his location with green fire blazing. The two elite Thorns took up defensive positions.

Ash looked at her friend for another moment as emerald flashes tore through the air. She hoped that Gundis and the other Thorns could buy her some time. Even the Mizen's own taboo of entering the fleshy bark of the Eternals, considered the hallowed home of the god, might be tested before too long. She swallowed nervously, unsure if she dared enter such a sacred space. There was no telling what was waiting for her inside. Then she leaped into the darkness of the Eternal tree and silence swallowed her whole.

Chapter 6

A chill air nipped at Ash's skin, and clouds formed with each exhale she gave. A maze of woody tendrils hung down from the hollow trunk, blocking any view of what was outside or within. Each of the strange appendages glowed faintly, like a creature far below the sea. Putting a hand out, Ash moved them away gingerly, watching them sway from side to side, and made her way deeper into the great tree. As she walked, dust stirred at her feet. The center of the space was larger than she would have guessed. It was also warmer, which she was thankful for. Looking up into the hollow trunk, the Eternal's long hanging braids formed a sheet of light that disappeared into the lofty heights above her. Instinctively, Ash felt safe here.

Sitting down on the soft earth, she looked around. If fighting was raging outside, Ash couldn't hear it. It felt like another world. "So now what?" she asked. "I don't understand any of this. What am I supposed to do?" Nothing happened. "I'm sorry you're sick," she continued. "Is that why we're starting to age again?" The tendrils around her glowed as before, but gave no response. Ash willed herself to believe the Eternal was listening.

"People are going to start dying," she began. "Even before we die of old age or disease. The Restless King is coming. A messenger told me so. He told me the Suzerian is going to take the Stone away and kill anyone who gets in his way. But you already know that, don't you? Who else could transport me like that? Here's what I don't understand. Why would you do that and not give me a way to convince the Mizen? The Grand Sizan needs to be told. Time is running out." Ash threw up her hands. "My friends risked their lives so I could have this chance. Say something!"

In response, the wall of tendrils around her glowed mutely. They might as well have been dark and lifeless stalactites. Getting up, she turned and pushed angrily through the hanging obstacles, before the wood suddenly came to life. Each of the tendrils pulsed pink and orange in unison, the same colors as the Stone. **I know who you are**, a voice spoke in the air around her. **I have been waiting. Who am I? I**

have had many names. All are dust and forgotten. Call me—The Traveler.

Ash tried and failed to make sense of what she was hearing. Perhaps this is what powerful wizards were like. "Where are you from?" she asked, then felt stupid for asking such a mundane question.

Words are—inadequate, the wall of hanging vines pulsed haltingly. **I was on a journey to see if I could find other survivors of my kind. To discover if any still remained after the coming of the Swarm. The few I found were strangely changed and no longer recognized me. Then I heard a rumor, a whisper from a sentient planet of a hidden colony. I was following the trail when something went wrong with my—ship. You know it as the Stone. One of my jumps did not go as planned. I must have lost focus, been distracted. It was a long time ago. Yet it seems like only yesterday.** Ash sensed a profound weariness.

After a moment the colors faded and the tendrils turned to black. For a single heartbeat she feared The Traveler had expired, but then the braids blazed back to life. Confused, she could not make sense of what she saw until she stepped back and looked at the hanging wall as a whole. There was an image etched across its surface, both strange and spectacular. It was as if she were seeing a vast world from far above. Half was captured in brilliant light while the other was shaded in darkness. It was the most beautiful thing Ash had ever seen. Specks of light in the distance crowded together to keep away the night. Then she became aware of movement as an unbelievably vast landscape rushed toward her.

Falling! Falling! Falling! wailed the Traveler as it relived the traumatic event. A bright sweep of clouds and sea grew beneath her. A mighty continent swung into view. There was a blur of dwellings and trees and then—nothing. Darkness and death hung in the tendrils in front of her. Once again Ash feared the worst, but eventually the vines came to life again, this time in the form of flickering torchlight. Closer and closer it came, bobbing through the smoky darkness until the figure of a man was revealed. He bent over, clearly in discomfort, so that his face took up the entire wall. Ash gasped in surprise. There could be no doubt in the matter. A bald patch covered the top of his head. There was his slightly crooked nose and soft face as he reached out a tentative hand to something she could not see, but could certainly guess at.

It was her father, exactly as he looked today. His visage glowed expectantly in pulsating hues of pink and orange. Then he withdrew, stepping back through the trees towards the dim light of the village watchtower. Darkness returned, but not true darkness, since the glow of the object still grew and receded like the beating heart of a strange sun. Eventually Ash discerned figures approaching. The sound of their voices reached her across the span of years as they drew closer, finally forming a hesitant ring around the Stone.

"It's evil," a woman said. "Unnatural."

"Nonsense," a man replied. "It's beautiful. Look at it. Have you ever seen anything like it?"

"No, but that's exactly my point."

"It fell from the sky," another man interjected. "That would explain why it looks different."

"Perhaps it's a star," an old woman mused, stepping forward. "See how it shines?"

The middle-aged man next to her scoffed. "More likely it is a jewel cast off by a demon to tempt us."

"Only the gods could create such perfection," offered the elderly village priest. "This is a sign."

"A sign of what?" several townsfolk echoed in unison. The gray-haired man looked at them nonplussed, momentarily at a loss for words.

A man stepped forward into the light. "All I can tell you is that my arthritis is gone."

Her father turned to address the throng, even as more villagers filtered in from the surrounding woods. "You all I know how I've been afflicted. It's hard for me to bend in front of my ovens, even harder to knead the dough. The pain keeps me up most nights. That's why I was up when I saw the light fall from the heavens. Heard it hit like a ball of thunder. Walking out here, I felt like a cripple, tired beyond all measure. Crept here and looked at it. I nearly touched it. I don't know why. Just standing in this glow makes me feel something I haven't felt in years."

"Sober?" someone shouted out.

There was scattered laughter, but her father was unmoved. "Young," he stated simply. "Returning to Renelis, I felt light as the air. My joints were unburdened. It was all I could do to refrain from skipping in pure joy." To demonstrate, he did a little jig around those gathered, ending with an impromptu twirl and low bow.

"Well, I'll be..." the man next to him murmured.

Galen smiled. "Do yourself a favor and let the glow of this unexpected boon fall upon you. What have you got to lose?"

Amid slowly nodding heads, the villagers lined up and one by one took their turn in front of the Stone, as the sun rose above the distant hills. Only the few who were pregnant refused the gift at that time, afraid to endanger their unborn baby. Children were also held back as a precaution.

The scene faded away and Ash was left staring at the ordinary wall of hanging vines as questions swirled in her head. *Was that why she had been spared from more cruel torments in school? Because her father had found the Stone? Then why had he never mentioned it? He was a hero, wasn't he?* It was hard to accept that if not for his connections, she could have easily ended up like the children in the Catacombs.

The tendrils parted and two golden-robed Mizen warriors entered. Between them was the still struggling figure of Gundis. His hands were lashed together with sparkling *filigreen*. In their wake came High Priestess Myla, the Voice, still robed in golden splendor. Her regal beauty and countenance was somehow untroubled despite the recent battle. Ash made ready to explain what had just happened, if only they would believe her, but the Voice stilled her with a slender hand. "There is no need to protest, my dear," she said. "We sensed the Eternals communicating with you and came when we were able. We should not be here." She took in the sacred space. "Yet these are strange times, and unbreakable rules are broken. This is all very unusual. Only High Mizen have ever been favored with the gift of tongues from an Eternal, and even then only briefly." She paused as a look of uncertainty passed over her face. "What did they say?"

"If you really want to know, then release my friend," Ash replied.

The Voice scowled at her. "I'm not use to being ordered about by a mere Initiate. Tell us what you heard. It is your sacred duty."

Ash folded her arms across her chest. "No," she said. "My duty is to those that I care about. The Mizen are self-serving and secretive when they should be serving the greater good. Release Gundis and I'll tell you what I know, but you have to believe me when I tell you that we are all in grave danger."

The Voice stepped forward. "No more fairy tales," she sighed. "But I will release the captain. *After* you have told us what you know."

Gundis looked at her and nodded. "Do as she says, Aisha. I am helpless to organize our defense as long as I am a prisoner."

"You promise to release him?" Ash asked the Voice.

"You have my word."

"Fine. Some of this story you already know. But I'm going to tell you about the Stone, as much as I understand it."

The Voice frowned. "We know about the Stone," she said airily. "As Mizen we've dedicated our lives to understanding it."

"I don't think you do," Ash responded evenly. "It didn't mean to come here at all. Something went wrong. It was scared. When it fell from the sky and crashed in a nearby forest, a crippled man went in search of the strange light he had seen. Eventually he found a glowing object. He had never encountered anything like it. The Stone or whatever was in the Stone had never seen anything like the man. It was all alone in a strange world, a wanderer with no way of getting home. It was weak and in pain. But it had the man. So it gave the man something so he wouldn't be in pain anymore and would never grow old and leave. Then the man brought others from his village and they laid their hands near the Stone and it gave them all the same gift. In return the villagers kept the Stone safe and took it with them wherever they went."

"That's hardly more than the same story we tell during High Summer's Eve," the Voice protested.

"I'm not done yet," Ash retorted. "Hiding the Stone and moving from place to place worked for a while, but that time is over. The Stone is dying."

Ash had to give her credit; Myla, the High Priestess, the Voice of the Mizen, didn't try to deny it. She simply waved her hand and the guards loosened the gleaming *filigreen* from the captain's wrists. Gundis muttered under his breath several colorful expletives. "Do you know who the man was?" the Voice asked the young Initiate. "The crippled villager who found the Stone?"

"Yes," said Ash. Still she struggled to say out loud what The Traveler had shown her. "He was my father."

"You must wonder why he has never told you. Why none of us have." There was nothing she could say. The question hung in the air, demanding an answer for the years of silence.

"She doesn't need to know," Gundis interjected. He moved to stand beside Ash, as if by proximity alone he could somehow protect her. "Let things be, Myla."

The Voice ignored the captain. She took another step towards Ash and reached out, but then thought better of it. "We love your father for helping us receive this gift. We also despise your father for the same reason. Every one of us is saved and damned because of what he did. We are lives caught in amber. This is the reason we no longer celebrate birthdays. Do you understand what I'm saying?"

Ash stared numbly at the golden robed priestess. What she had learned changed everything and nothing. "The past is catching up to us at last," she answered. "The Restless King is on his way."

The Voice shook her head and smiled sadly. "I thought we agreed there would be no more fairy tales."

Before Ash could reply, a small contingent of Thorns pushed through the Mizen priests, blocking the entrance to the Eternal. "Captain, are you all right?" a tall mustached officer inquired, seeing the state Gundis was in.

"Never better," he replied to the scout. "The High Priestess and I have just finished our conversation. Do you have something to report?"

"Perimeter forces have captured a stranger in the woods to the north. He was injured, but has refused a healer. Says he has urgent news."

Gundis scowled. "Why was he brought here? No one is allowed into Renelis. It is our oldest law. The man could be a spy."

"The man is not a spy, Captain," the scout replied firmly. "I mean, he is, but he's our spy."

"What makes you so certain?"

"Because he showed us the sign. The Thorns remember. Skin does not lie. He is a Celestial."

For a moment Gundis stared back, disbelieving, before he mastered himself, remembering what a few had sacrificed. The Celestials were almost mythic guardians of Renelis. Numbering a dozen, they had come from the original inhabitants. After a small contingent of the King's men had showed up looking for the fallen fire, it was clear that the villagers would need to leave and hide, taking their prized possession with them. A dozen men and women, chosen by drawing lots of colored pebbles, were to be parted from the rest. The elderly and parents of young children were exempted. Their mission was a simple one; spy on those that threatened the village and keep the location of the Stone a secret. None could ever return. The only exception was to warn the townspeople of an impending attack.

To carry out their task, the twelve Celestials infiltrated the populace of Vorel, listening to rumors while slowly moving up in society. This took decades, but as benefactors of the Stone they had all the time in the world. Some learned the skills of the sword, others of the assassin. A few even were initiated into the shadowy magical arts.

One Celestial, Gundis later learned, found their way into King's Keep and won the slow trust of the Suzerian himself. She was a beautiful, clever woman with a husband and grown child back in Renelis. She had been heartbroken when she drew one of the twelve lots. Over time, however, she became a master of the sword, training with the Nomads of the Steppe and garnering the reluctant attention of the generals of the Vorel, not only for her fighting skills but her diplomacy skills as well. The King called her Little Owl, for her wisdom and fierceness.

Eventually, she learned of the Suzerian's obsession with the Stone and how he had a retrieved a fragment from the woods. Being disconnected from the whole, however, had changed the shard, tainting it somehow. Over the years she saw how the sickly glowing sliver corrupted the King, preserving his life while his flesh withered away, even as she applied potions and herbs to hide her own ageless nature. Every month Magnus sent out search parties, desperately seeking the Stone so he could somehow alter his fate. Eventually the King joined his Brigade, leading the effort to find the elusive village. And of course, he took his most trusted advisors with him on a quest that seemed to have no end. In this way he became known as the Restless King. Over time, he became convinced there was a spy in his midst. To flush them out, the Restless King planted a rumor that the location of the village had been found at last. Then he waited.

Little Owl could wait no longer. She fled, seeking out Renelis so that she could warn her people. She took precautions to throw off any possible pursuit, but she was in a hurry. Like a moth to a flame, the Celestial eventually found it. Little did she know that a small band of the King's Bone Brigade, elite battle sorcerers, had followed her back to the village, using old magic to help cloak their pursuit. The five had orders not to engage, but to simply report back the location of the elusive village. Confident in victory, the magicians attacked Renelis instead, hoping to free the Stone for their King and earn favor. In the battle that followed, the winter snows ran red. Only the combined might of the Thorns and Eternals turned back the invaders. Gundis himself had led the hurried defense, doing his best to stop the magical assault. Little Owl fought bravely, desperate to try and redeem herself.

When the battle was finally over, the King's spies lay motionless, never to rise again. But they were not the only ones. The Gift could freeze time and heal afflictions, but it could do nothing to prevent a violent death. A firebolt or a blade thrust into flesh would extinguish a life just the same. Fourteen villagers, including nine Thorns, lay dead. One of them was the father of a Celestial. He died not knowing what became of his son. The survivors of Renelis left the next day, forced to move again. That was the first and last time a Celestial had come. Until today.

A cold, empty feeling gripped the captain's stomach. Whatever had brought the Celestial to Renelis, it wasn't good. "Take me to this Celestial," he said. "Perhaps we can verify the Initiate's story." He squeezed Ash's arm and then departed.

The rest of the group, including H'vetik, the Voice and several Thorns and Mizen, trailed after the scout until only Ash remained. She turned to follow, but then paused. Her emotions swirled. On one hand she was relieved that the messenger from afar had finally arrived. It felt as if a burden had been lifted from her shoulders. At the same time, she was so frustrated she could scream. The Mizen hadn't listened to a word she had said. Standing alone in the center of the great tree, Ash willed herself into motion. Hanging vines brushed her face as she strode to the exit.

Wait, called the Traveler. This time there was no sudden illumination, no images flashing in front of her. The Eternal's voice was faint and weary, as if the effort were costing it something precious.

"I need to go," Ash said. "The Celestial is here. I need to make sure people listen."

The glowing lights above her dimmed slightly. **You are a lot like your father. He too was brave, but did not think so, even though he walked through the dark woods to find something mysterious. Without him, I would have been truly alone in this world. Instead I've had the company of all of you for these long years.**

Something within Ash bristled. "That was a very selfish thing to do," she said angrily. "You put your own wants ahead of others. Everyone had the right to know what you were really giving them. I understand why you did what you did, but people have been living in fear. Their lives have been changed, and not always for the better. I don't think human beings are meant to live forever. It has to stop." In the silence that followed, Ash felt very small, standing in the center of the great Eternal tree.

Perhaps you are right. Perhaps I have been trapped by my past. My species is very long-lived. It is only natural for us. We have accomplished many things, but our lifespans have also kept us at a distance, removed from consequences. I have changed much since I have been on this world. And yet I am still the same.

Ash felt overwhelmed with information. "Why are you telling *me* all this? The High Mizen have been listening for years and years. If you cleared your throat they would write it down."

They only hear what they want to. There was another pause that lingered, going on and on. Finally, the voice spoke again. **I'm dying. Too long I wandered the stars. Too long have I lived without others of my kind. My injuries sustained after my ship crashed never fully healed. The missing piece of me is a hollow ache. Each time I was forced to move with the village by returning to the Stone, a little more of me drained away. As a result, I have often been weak. These trees where I have resided have come to resemble my home, but they are a poor substitute, reminding me of what I have lost. And yet my time spent on this world has given me purpose and a sense of belonging. Once I pass, I will no longer be able to protect the village.**

Ash crossed her arms and stood taller. "We stopped the Restless King once. We can do it again."

That was long ago and only a small part of the king's army was engaged. The Suzerian is more desperate now and his Bone Brigade has grown. He has also learned how to tap into the essence of the shard and use it as a guide. I have been sensing their approach. If the people of Renelis are to survive they will need help. My time grows short. Hold out your hand.

"What for?" she asked. She didn't even try to keep the scorn from her voice.

I will not hurt you. I seek only to give one final gift, if you will accept it. This is your choice. It may help save the people of the village when I'm gone. Ash hesitated. **Do not worry. What I give you will not endure, but it will allow you to access some of my power that remains. You are your father's daughter. I am memory. This is the chain. Stretching back through the centuries. Now the chain must be broken.**

Ash laid her hands flat together and watched spellbound as small bobbing lights materialized in the Eternal's lofty boughs above, descending toward her like stars coming home. One by one they landed on her open palms, as gentle as a kiss. Then they faded into her skin, leaving only a faint shimmering glow. When the spectacle had dwindled, Ash felt a powerful pull to go outside. Entering the bright light of early afternoon, she found herself surrounded by more gently falling orbs. They twinkled like stars, shimmering with pink and orange light. Energy crackled in the air and yet she knew there was no need for fear. In twos and threes and then dozens they descended upon her, melting into her essence. When the last had disappeared into her flesh, only a stony silence remained. Ash raised her arms to the black and lifeless branches of the Eternals surrounding her. The Traveler was gone. And yet something lived on. She felt exalted.

Chapter 7

In the center of Renelis, a warning bell began ringing as Ash strode back through the Weirway. She turned toward the sound as if struck. The tower chimes only rang if the village was in danger. When she was a little girl, a lightning strike had started a fire in a wooden building where grain was kept. It was quickly put out, but she still remembered the flames dancing eerily against the stormy night. The fire brigade would not be needed today, she noticed, glancing at the clear blue sky.

Hurrying out between the walls, she paused to ask a guard what was happening. "Don't know, Miss," he replied. "But it can't be good." There was no sign of Gundis and the rest of the party in the now crowded narrow streets. People looked around with fear etched on their panicked faces. Voices rose in confusion. Walking into the chaos, Ash didn't feel invincible anymore. Instead she felt a tightness grip her chest. They were all in danger. If only she could have warned people sooner.

Weaving through the growing throng, she pushed down the avenue toward the center of town and the Thorn Citadel. With every passing minute, her sense of frustration increased. While she wanted to run, she could do little more than walk against the waves of people who choked the lane. Eventually she reached the stout fortress. Four turrets framed the three-story building. Stone the color of dried blood set the structure apart from every other building in the village, save the lofty tower of the Grand Sizan and the silent Catacombs of the Mizen.

Although townsfolk still streamed around her, Ash stopped in disbelief. In front of her was the wrought iron door to the Citadel. It was closed. She could not recall a time when the great doors had not been open and inviting to the public they served. Two Thorn guards stood on either side, as still as statues. As she approached, they stepped forward and shouted a warning. Ignoring them, she strode up the stone steps and put her hand, still glowing, on the cold metal.

"What do you think you're doing?" one soldier demanded.

"Aisha? Is that you? No one is allowed inside," the other Thorn told her. They both raised their gleaming swords to bar her way.

"I'm late for the meeting," she muttered. "I'll just let myself in." She had to get in to see the messenger and Gundis. There was no time to argue. What the Traveler had done had changed everything. The aura around her hands intensified until it took on a salmon-colored hue. A moment later the light began to pulsate like an alien heartbeat. The guards staggered back in fear. Ash felt herself building toward some kind of detonation. Reaching out, she pushed against the doors, but they were bolted from the inside. Annoyance at being denied entry turned to outrage. Power surged through her fingertips as the doors flew open in a concussion of sound.

Stepping across the threshold, Ash adjusted her eyes to the dim light. Around a massive oak table sat a dozen men and women. Most were unfamiliar, but she recognized the Voice and Gundis sitting across from each other. He looked stunned and she was scowling, as if the interruption was a personal insult. Only the messenger looked like he was glad to see her. His hand, she noticed, was bandaged while his eyes were red, as if he had been crying. "You made it," he said, somehow managing a weak smile. Ash stared at the rider from her dreams, unable to register that he was actually here and not part of the Stone's machinations.

"Now that you've arrived," said a bearded man dressed in royal blue and red, "come sit with us." Involuntarily, Ash took a step back. She recognized the tall, stately man. He was Findlewin, the Grand Sizan's Second, representing the ruler of Renelis whenever necessary. Whether or not he spoke with ultimate authority was less clear in the current crisis.

Beside him, the High Priestess had regained her composure. "Is that really necessary?" she asked. "What business has *she* at this table? This is a war council, not the bazaar."

Gundis leapt up from his seat. "I know this is unusual, but the young lady has every right to be here."

"How so, Captain?" the Voice replied. "As it was explained to me, the Initiate received several visions or projections designed to warn us of the Messenger's arrival and the doom which approaches at his heels. Through no fault of her own, she was unable to communicate this information to someone in authority until it was almost too late. Now Celestial Barton is safely among us. Preparations for our defense have begun. What further use can the Initiate be? It is high time her special treatment, based on a familial relationship to Finder Galen, be reexamined. To think that it was her mother who first brought the Suzerian to our doorstep…"

Ash nearly cried out in surprise. The words hit her like a bolt of *fili-green*, incapacitating her ability to think. *Her mother…a Celestial?* Too many revelations were overwhelming her. She simply couldn't process it right now.

"…and I have learned since my return that I lost my father in that assault," Barton was now saying, his voice catching with emotion. "He died as a Thorn, protecting us all. I never knew my mother—she died giving me life—but I believe they both would have risked everything if it meant giving us a chance. But the past will not save us. I returned to give fair warning. I am the last Celestial. There was no other choice."

The Voice looked at the Celestial, her face etched in concern. "No one here doubts your service, Barton, or questions your judgment. You have earned our respect and audience. The young woman, barely an Initiate, has not."

"Enough!" cried the Second. "She has every right to be here, because the Eternals reached out to her. Not to you. Not to me. Not to any of us. But to her alone. Why? The fact that we cannot answer that question tells me she has meaning in all of this."

The Voice stood up slowly until her tall figure towered over the stocky man. "Your eminence, you are assigning meaning where there is none. The girl was merely a conduit, nothing more. Matters more urgent than this demand our attention. An army of undead will soon be outside our walls with the Restless King at their lead. There is no time to flee. Isn't that right, Captain?"

Gundis nodded slowly. "That is correct. We must make our stand here."

"Do we have enough Thorns to cover the entire perimeter?" asked the Second.

"There is enough for the north, south and east," the Captain explained. "The western wall can be covered by the Eternals."

The Voice bowed her head and then looked solemnly around. "The

Eternals have been silent for many years. It is not clear they have the strength or desire to help us any longer."

"If we must," Gundis admitted, "defenders can be posted on all sides, but we will be spread thinner than I would like."

She sighed. "What choice do we have? In our darkest hour we have been abandoned for sins we cannot guess." A grim silence enveloped the room.

For what seemed like an eternity, Ash had stood and listened to them argue. All the while she felt the presence of the Traveler within her grow, becoming more insistent. A clarity crystallized as her frustration over their misplaced arrogance reached its zenith. The High Priestess's words were the spark that ignited her. She stepped forward. Words spilled out of her mouth as if a dam within her had finally broken. "We are not being slighted or punished," she told the leaders of Renelis, her voice shaking. "Although perhaps we should have been for keeping the Stone a secret. So many more people could have benefited from it. Forget about never dying. That's overrated. The stone can also heal sickness and mend bones."

Everyone at the table turned to stare at Ash. "Are you still here?" the Voice demanded. Ash's indignation swelled as she weathered the High Priestess's words of belittlement and dismissal. "What are you babbling about?" she continued. "It sounds close to blasphemy. Has it ever occurred to you that while the Stone was protecting us, we were protecting *it*, not merely for ourselves but to keep it from harm?"

"If only that were true. Look at yourselves!" she shouted. "You don't know anything. You listen to the Eternals, but they're just trees. You worship the Stone, but it was just a shell, a container that still holds a life-giving potency we all take for granted. None of it matters. You had so much time and you wasted it. There was something else. Something you missed or didn't want to see. It was very old, almost as ancient as the stars. I think its name was the Traveler. When it left the Stone and took up residence in the trees we call the Eternals, it was already sick, but it hung on for us, helping to keep us safe. Before dying it gave me a gift. I wasn't sure why at first, but now I do. I think I can help."

Then Ash raised her hands to the high cerulean painted ceiling above. From her fingertips brilliant beams of pink and orange energy shot out, exploding in the air around the astonished group as debris rained down like pieces of the sky. Weak from the effort, Ash wobbled on legs that suddenly struggled to hold her weight, while inside her a strange fire burned.

Chapter 8

Over the years, as decades became a century and then more, the villagers of Renelis began to think of the Restless King and his Brigade less as an immediate threat and more as an unpleasant nightmare or twisted fairy tale. The subject was rarely broached, but when it was the conversation became hushed, as if the words themselves had the unnatural power to hurt. On some level they remembered, of course. How could they really forget that they were being hunted? The Restless King resembled a living nightmare, but he was no fairy tale, no figment of a twisted imagination. He was a shadow of himself that couldn't forget what he had lost.

Magnus sat upon his death horse and surveyed the vast army of skeletal soldiers fanning out across the valley. Once upon a time they had been ordinary men, loyal fighters and guards sworn to protect him and the realm. But mere swords, he found to his dismay, could not stop the senseless specter of ruin which befell him and those he loved. He came from modest means, a minor lord in a backwater province. Perhaps that is why he fought so hard to climb higher. It could also have been why he felt there always something to prove. After years of plotting and changing alliances, he finally vanquished the last viable Eminent Noble to stand in his way. By this time the ruling Suzerian was old. Rather than fight as was custom, the aging sovereign sensibly decided to abdicate.

It was expected that he take a wife and queen. Although Magnus could have chosen any woman, the only person he wanted by his side was Silensia. She was a wealthy merchant's daughter with long auburn hair and a fiery personality that scared off most suitors. Magnus had loved her since he was a young man. To show his undying affection, Magnus decided to craft a ring of dragon stone, the hardest material known in the world. His advisors suggested that he hire an artisan to do the painstaking labor, but Magnus wouldn't hear of it. Tradition dictated that the person proposing create something that would last. To have another do the work would be to taint the whole endeavor. It had taken him months to slowly chisel and shape the vermillion-infused stone, but it was worth it to see the look on her face when he finally presented it to her.

The first few years had been bliss. After a torch-lit royal ceremony in Winter's Hall that was both coronation and wedding, they had ridden in a fur-lined carriage pulled by horses the color of fresh snow past cheering subjects. Each adult and child held a sparkle stick, gathered from the southern forests near the foothills, where *luminare* trees grew plentiful. Each wand-like seed, larger than a man's hand, symbolized the promise of spring as well as the fabled wizards who, according to legend, founded the mountainous city of Cragg they all called home.

When the last of the valley snows had finally melted, and the first sweet grass had been planted, Silensia gave birth to a red-haired son. This followed soon after by a beautiful girl, her eyes the color of sky blossoms. Magnus never dreamed he could be so happy. Military forays into the adjoining mountains and into the plains beyond doubled the size of the small kingdom of Vorel, with little resistance offered from the scattered bands of nomadic warriors and the faded remnants of the Old Empire. Palace popularity surged, with once rebellious nobles falling over themselves to get on his good side. Seasons turned. His children grew.

Although he hated to leave them, he begrudgingly left on yet another military expedition. Further and further the Grand Brigade pushed, until they reached a strange land of sand and cities of colored glass. There they were met by a vast army of robed riders wielding curved blades the color of blood, atop strangely humped creatures with twisting horns. For the first time, the forces of Vorel were stopped and then turned aside. Half his army lost their lives that day, with the rest scattered and fleeing. Sometime later, the sorry remnants of a once proud contingent made their way through the mountain pass and back into the capital. He staggered in the lead and then collapsed on the snowflake-shaped dais in the courtyard.

But as bad as that campaign had been, it had gotten worse. Several weeks later the first signs of sickness appeared. A simple cough turned to fever, and then to rosy boils. Healers had no idea what it was, and attempts at treatment were ineffectual. In the final stage, a victim developed black spidery lines from head to toe. Even breathing was painful. In the end, death was welcomed. The disease spread like a spring flood from one corner of the city to another. Magnus watched from the high castle walls and prayed to the Silent Ones that his family be spared.

The next morning he was awakened to the sound of coughing. Two moons later, his youngest was in the ground. He held a tuft of his son's red hair in his hand and wept without shame. His daughter succumbed next, surrounded in her bed by colorful fairy dolls. Until the very end she looked up at him as if he could save her. Weakened by a broken heart, his beloved Silensia fell ill a few short weeks after. On her deathbed she came achingly close to blaming him for bringing the scourge back. "Why couldn't you have stayed here in the mountains with us?" she asked him. "We would have been more than enough."

The day she died, Magnus locked the doors to his rooms, dismissed his servants, and waited to follow her to the Bright Hills. Life and the world had turned to dust. Time moved on, but he did not notice. He did not eat. When he slept, he dreamed of death. Then one day there was a knock at his chamber door. The plague was over. The kingdom, or what was left of it, needed a ruler. For weeks afterward, the skies above Crag were thick from the smoke of burning pyres, blotting out the sun. Somehow he made speeches, visited survivors, made appointments to fill various vacancies, reviewed defenses, and did a myriad of other necessary things, but all the while he was empty inside. Each night he sunk to his bed, certain he could not rise again.

A dozen years went by and he grew bitter at everything he had lost. Death itself, the natural end of a life well-lived, became his personal nemesis. Because of everything the Great Specter had taken from him, Magnus was determined to have a measure of revenge by living forever. Defeating it became his life's obsession. Perhaps he could even devise a way to bring back those that had been taken from him. Desperate, Magnus consulted a host of individuals who claimed ancient lineage to the fabled wizards who had founded Cragg. Each time he encountered only charlatans and deluded simpletons.

He had all but given up when his court astronomers told him of a falling star, an omen that had been prophesized. He took it as a sign of divine providence and dispatched several scouts. Only one of them returned, bloodied and beaten. The weary man reported that the villagers of a remote settlement in the south had attacked when they had attempted to inspect a strange glowing object half-hidden under blankets of hay. Enraged, Magnus quickly formed a full battalion of his finest royal guards, but was delayed in setting out due to an early winter storm.

A rebellion by the Elder Lords the following year demanded his attention. Only when the last traitor had been hung or driven off to the Wastes was he finally able to resume his quest. It had been almost two years since the star had fallen, and he was anxious to find it. Setting a brisk pace, the battalion marched through the mountain pass with Magnus their king at the lead. Glistening snow melted at their feet. Through the high valleys they trudged until they came to the wide open prairie that seemed to move with the wind. It was here that rumors reached Magnus concerning a strange village whose inhabitants did not age or grow ill.

With the original scout riding beside him, they crossed a great sea of grass as high as the tallest man's waist. His soldiers cut a path for him with their swords, but progress was slow. Days turned to weeks and the Suzerian's patience began to fray. At the end of the second week, though, the wretched grass began to thin. Trees and streams began to cover the landscape until Magnus and his battalion found themselves in a cool leafy cathedral of trees. Bright shafts of light from high above fell on the ground around them. Eventually the forest dwindled until a patchwork of small farms crisscrossed the landscape.

"How much farther?" Magnus muttered. "I will be an old man soon." He glanced over his shoulder at the trees and the even paler mountains of his home in the distance. A small sigh passed through his lips. And yet what else could he do? There was no going back to what was. He turned back to the scout in irritation. "How much longer?" he demanded. "If you've lost the way, you're no use to me."

"Not too much farther, your highness," said the scout nervously. "We'll be at the village by sunset."

The man was true to his word. They entered the village while the day still hung above the horizon. A small stream gurgled nearby, but that was the only sound to be heard. An eerie stillness hung in the air. The dirt streets were deserted. The scattered mud and thatch homes could have been a cemetery, except there were no bodies. Magnus and his men rushed from one dwelling to another, only to find each empty. The village was abandoned. Even so, it had not been abandoned in haste. That much was clear. There was no debris or household items. No objects dropped in chaos. Rooms were bare. The inhabitants had not left in a panic. This had been an orderly evacuation with the aim of leaving no clues behind.

"They knew we would be coming back," Magnus said at last. "To find the fallen star."

"So it would seem," the scout replied.

"And yet how could an entire village just disappear? From your description, several hundred people lived here. Where did they go?"

The scout swallowed thickly. "I'm not sure, sire."

"You are sure this is the same village as the one you visited earlier?"

"Quite."

The king made a great fist and pounded his open palm with sudden ferocity. "Devil's teeth!" he swore. "They must have left a trail to follow. Something!"

But they hadn't, or perhaps time had covered their tracks. The only marks to be found led to a small copse of trees a league away. Brushing away brambles with an angry swipe of his sword, Magnus followed the faint path of trammeled vegetation and broken branches until he arrived in a small circular clearing. The skeletal remains of charred trees ringed the area. To the north a swath of destruction was visible, as if a giant had dragged a heavy club through the forest, clearing a straight line. Magnus and his battalion walked carefully to the center of an open depression. The ground at their feet was mottled with black glass, making it treacherous. The last rays of the setting sun cast strange reflections across its surface. It would be dark soon. They would need to take shelter in the village.

Magnus was just about to turn away when something caught his eye at the far edge of the circle. It glittered in pink and orange hues. Sliding over to it as fast as he could, he crouched down to examine the object. It was unlike anything he had ever seen. The slender Shard was shorter than his finger and pulsed like a living heartbeat. When he reached out a tentative hand to touch it, the surface felt warm. Only the center of the stone, tainted with a spot of darkness, gave him pause, but only for a moment.

The king knelt there for several minutes, transfixed by the glow and the possibilities the object represented. "What is it?" one of his lieutenants asked, not daring to come closer.

"A fragment of the fallen star," he said slowly. "Do not be afraid." He passed around the prize to his men.

"Does that mean our quest is at an end?" another soldier asked.

"Where one ends, another begins," the King replied. "Perhaps this piece will lead us to the rest."

But it didn't. At least it hadn't yet. If the Shard sent signals or tried to communicate, Magnus couldn't tell. Back in the castle he stared at the object under a dome of translucent volcanic glass. There was no denying it was pretty, but what was it good for? In time, the answer became clear. Everyone who came in contact with the Shard stopped aging, and those who were ill or crippled became well again. Such a boon had been wasted on the villagers, he thought. In a rush of excitement he began planning expeditions. Troops were trained for long-range offensives. In his mind's eye he dreamed of finally conquering the desert kingdom that had brought so much pain and grief to his life. With soldiers immune to sword and sickness, there was nothing beyond his reach. To ensure that the plague did not ravage his people again, Magnus made preparations to have everyone in the kingdom lay hands on the Shard. A date was set. An armed caravan would bring the Shard to every corner of Vorel. Every citizen would be protected. Every member of his Grand Brigade would be invincible.

Mere days before the unveiling, the first signs appeared. Skin began to peel, hair thinned and fell out, bones became more pronounced. Everyone with contact to the Shard exhibited the same symptoms. When Magnus's First Lieutenant put a hand on his shoulder, it was more bone than flesh. "Not the Plague," the elder soldier said. "Something worse."

His Grand Brigade was rotting away. Men became skeletal in appearance, a deathly visage that refused to die. A few, in horror, committed suicide, only to find that little or no blood flowed from their emaciated wrists. Magnus was the last to succumb. Of all the damned and doomed, he retained the most vestiges of humanity. Skin hung in tatters on his large boned frame, but his head was largely spared, although his eyes were sunken and his once red hair grew long and white. Wrapping a heavy cloak around him, he appeared almost human. Still, it was time to leave. They were living nightmares. His own people would not abide such abominations. Rumors were already running rampant. A coup was imminent.

Under cover of darkness, Magnus led his gaunt brigade through the gates of the city and into the mountain pass. Only once did he look back. The city of Cragg glistened in the moonlight, like a jewel set on a high pedestal. He was King without a home. The irony hardened him as a restless anger ignited. A purpose revealed itself. They would find the villagers and retrieve the fallen star. He would make his army whole again. The Shard had become corrupted, flawed by its separateness. There was no way he could have known, Magnus reasoned. Better to look toward the future. If distant stories were to be believed, something described simply as the Stone was whispered in lands beyond the Great Inland Sea.

Magnus led his skeletal contingent southwest and into the mists and myth of fable. In time, they became the legend of the Restless King and the Bone Brigade, constantly searching for an elusive magical object to make them whole again, but never finding it. Where he could, the Suzerian was said to recruit the desperate and misguided to his cause by a single touch of the Shard, thus swelling their undying ranks.

The real Restless King knew little of what others thought of him, of course, and cared even less. His obsession was all that mattered, and the chance to make things right. Somewhere in his travels, the Shard began to glow ever so faintly. It was a tenuous hope, but the Restless King clung to it. Eventually, he discovered that the Shard was sensing the Stone. The closer it was to the greater whole, the brighter the fragment became. Magnus let the light guide him. It was only a matter of time.

Clothed in the rags of his royal heritage, Magnus grinned, the skin stretched thin and brittle across his bony face. Hills and mountains were behind them now, as was years of hiding and endless marching. Above the Brigade circled great flocks of *skithix*, carrion birds who followed like the shadow of death, patiently waiting to feast on the flesh of the dead and the living.

Magnus had crossed great inland seas and dark forests to stand here. Ahead of them was a tear-shaped valley rimmed with a scattering of lonely trees, insignificant sentries that stood just beyond the shadow of the village wall. Atop his deathly steed, the Restless King raised his arm up to the sky in defiance. In his hand, the fragment shone ever brighter as they neared their destination. After years of searching, the elusive village of Renelis was finally within sight.

"The Stone!" he commanded the undead brigade from atop his skeletal steed. "Find it. Kill whoever stands in your way. Today we live again!"

Then they charged as one.

Chapter 9

Barton reached the girl, where she had collapsed to her knees. Plaster still drifted down from the ceiling like snow, reminding the Celestial of the long years spent in the lonely mountains of Vorel, listening for rumors before the Restless King and his Brigade began their long march. He reached for Ash's arm just as the Captain of the Guard arrived on the opposite side. Their eyes locked on one another. "Are you alright?" Gundis asked, turning his full attention to Ash.

"I think so," she said slowly. "Guess I surprised myself at what I could do."

"You surprised us all," the Voice said, walking to the front of the table, her long robe sweeping out behind her. A moment later the bearded Second took his place beside the High Mizen Priestess, a kindly look of concern etched on his face. The others remained seated.

"Can you rise?" Barton asked gently, the worry clear in his tone. The young Initiate nodded. Gundis and Barton lifted Ash to her feet. The Celestial studied the young woman's face with concern as the she looked around, flashes of confusion and embarrassment finally coalescing into firm resolve. There was something extraordinary about this girl. "How can it be," he said, turning to the Voice, "that this young woman, clearly favored by the Stone, is a mere Initiate? Twice, it seems, she has been sent a vision, and now she demonstrates power equal to the Eternals themselves. Only a fool would doubt her claim. The proof is all around us."

The Voice glared back at him, but did not rebuke the Celestial's words. Slowly, she stepped forward. Barton waited for the High Mizen to speak, but instead she gazed at Aisha for a long moment before lowering her head and bowing. It was only after she had straightened that she addressed the young woman. "Tell us what to do," she said. Tears filled the elder woman's eyes, but she did not wipe them away. "The gods help us. We are in your hands."

Chapter 10

Ash ran through the crowded streets, dodging passerby. Extended families assisting the old and the newly sick formed a steady stream that flowed down towards the Catacombs, while heavily armed Thorns strode toward the outer walls, bows and blades strapped hurriedly over their shoulders. There were others as well and in much greater numbers: blacksmiths and potters, farmers and masons, glass-blowers and cooks, men and women both, untrained in the art of war, but determined just the same to make a difference. They carried pitch-forks and sharpened glass spears, hoes as well as great metal pots in their callused hands, as they swarmed after the uniformed soldiers. Ash glanced at every face that passed by, afraid of who she would see, ever fearful that she would be too late.

"I still think this is a mistake," the burly Captain of the Guard told her as he labored to keep up. "The Brigade will soon be at our doorstep. We can't afford any delay."

Ash gritted her teeth and ignored him. Gundis had been saying the same thing since they had left the Citadel. This was just something she had to do. Willing herself on, she made her tired legs move faster and tried to ignore the burning in her lungs. Finally, she rounded a familiar corner and swept past the small, ornate fountain that provided water to the small neighborhood. Off the main avenue, the flow of people she encountered slowed to a steady trickle. Welcome shade from slender *forloral* trees offered a welcome reprieve, their drooping tear-shaped leaves cooling her face as the dust from golden branches was carried away on the wind. It took everything she had to not stop and lie down in the verdant gardens that dotted the yards on either side. Small red-stone houses lined the dirt road, but most of the doors lay open.

And then she saw them. Neighbors she had grown up with streamed towards her, each face etched in fear and confusion as they struggled with belongings. Most of them were too old to fight, but a few carried small children. She recognized one as the little girl who had bowed to her with H'vetik. The line of refugees snaked past her, essential belongings grabbed in haste. They were on the move, heading for the dubious safety of the Catacombs. A feeling of trepidation hung in the air, robbing any feeling of nostalgia Ash might have felt.

Just past a simple stone arch where purple roses wined and bloomed, she slowed and then finally stopped. A middle-aged woman, still fit and graceful, stood in the doorway, a bag in each hand. "Mother!" Ash exclaimed, running to her. The former Celestial opened her arms and Ash fell into the welcome embrace. It was comforting to be held, and part of her wanted to remain like that forever, but there was another part that was hurt. She realized with a start that she barely knew her parents.

After a few moments she let go and stepped back. Her mother looked older. More worn. And both hands were bare. The black glove was gone, the one she always wore because of some terrible injury. It was the first time she had ever seen her mother's left hand uncovered. There on the unmarred palm, just as she knew it would be, was the mark of a Celestial.

"We've been worried about you," Radora said, brushing a flock of gray hair from her eyes. "I still can't believe this is happening. The Restless King is coming again." Ash opened her mouth to speak, but there was too much to say.

Her mother stepped back and studied her. "What's going on, Aisha? I didn't realize we were allowed visitations until after your second year." She caught the eye of Gundis, who had just arrived, panting. "You promised to protect her," she reminded the captain. "That was our deal."

"Please don't interrogate him, Mother. I don't have much time," Ash blurted out. "This isn't a social call. I know about you and Dad. I know everything."

Her mother stared back, visibly shaken. "Know what, dear?" she managed.

Ash wasn't having any of it. "Is Dad still here?"

"He's inside," her mother said with a visible sigh.

"Thank the gods! I thought for sure he would go to the wall."

The door opened and out stepped a short, dignified man wearing a round hat and a worn brushed jacket. His perennially red cheeks darkened. In his right hand was a slim silver sword tarnished with age.

"Daddy, No!" Ash cried.

Galen smiled sadly. "Your brother has already left to help defend. It wouldn't do to have me run for cover to the Catacombs, now would it? After all, this is my town. I'm the reason they're in this mess."

"There's more than enough blame to go around," Radora interjected. "Too bad it won't do a bit of good when the Brigade comes, but this might." Swiftly and nimbly, she pulled out a blood-stained rapier sword from her largest sack. "Thought they were belongings for the caves, didn't you?" she said to her daughter. "Trained on this when I first left Renelis. There were *lots* of things the Steppe Nomads let a woman do."

"Now, now," Galen said, blushing slightly. "I thought we agreed that you were never to bring that story up again."

"I could do so much more if those petty fools up in Immortia and down in the Catacombs would let me," she spat. "They took away my weapons as punishment, made me wear that stain of a glove, but I hid this old beauty," her mother proclaimed, raising the thin blade high into the air.

Ash looked at her parents as if they were total strangers. Her father was more bent over than she remembered, and her mother boasted like a soldier. "It seems there were more than a few stories no one bothered to tell me," she said. "When were you going to inform me about how you found the Stone?" she asked, turning toward her father. "And you." She pointed at her mother accusingly. "When were you planning on revealing that you were a Celestial, probably the most famous one of all? I'm your daughter. Everyone in town knew but me!"

"We couldn't tell you," Gundis said quietly behind her. "The Mizen would not allow it. No one who knew could breathe a word of it."

"But that doesn't make any sense," Ash said. "Why keep something from me that everyone else already knew?"

"Because," Galen interjected, putting an arm around his daughter, "the Eternals wanted it that way. No one knows why. That's what the priests said, in any event. 'The child must not know.' Keeping our identity a secret was the last thing the Eternals communicated before they fell silent. None of the Mizen knew what that meant. There were no children. Then in the space of a few seasons, you were born."

"You were a miracle," her mother continued. "At least to us. When I left Renelis to do my duty, I never dreamed I would have another child. None of us did. I was heartbroken at leaving your father and grown brother, but that was the lot I drew. Those were long years. For both of us. When I finally returned, your father and I found that our love was still strong. Your birth helped take the sting out of my unintended betrayal."

Ash wanted to scream, to pound her fists until they were raw. "None of this is about you," she seethed. "I had a right to know."

Radora flinched as if the words had physically struck her. "We wanted to tell you everything. Please believe us."

"Did you know they were keeping the other Younglings in the Catacombs?" Jackie countered. "They treated them like an embarrassment. By the gods, they were only children."

Her mother looked pained. "We knew nothing of the camp for the children. Your father and I were horrified when we finally learned of it."

It was too hard to tell the lies from truth anymore. Ash felt her hold on the world begin to shift and break free. Tears streaked down her face. She turned to go.

"Wait," her father begged. "Look at me." With an effort Ash turned back toward him. "Your mother and I have both lived with our share of shame and guilt, for more years than I dare count. The only silver lining has been you. When you expressed interest in joining the Mizen, I encouraged it because the Catacombs would allow you to ask questions freely while protecting you from scrutiny."

"While *I* was concerned that you were simply running away from your problems," her mother interrupted. "I have since come to accept that that was not the case."

Galen stifled a sigh and continued on. "Whatever it is you have to do, whatever secrets you found, go with a brave heart and our love," her father said, reaching out to touch his daughter's face. "Now and always."

Something in his words brought Ash back to herself. "I love you too," she told them. And she did, but she also knew that nothing would ever quite be the same again. Then they hugged goodbye. "Tell

Jax to be careful, okay? Protect each other. I'll see you soon." But as she and Gundis hurried off, Ash didn't know if she would, or if there would be anything left to come back to.

Chapter 11

Gundis left her at the mouth of the Catacombs, the only public entrance to the dim world of the Mizen. He was desperately needed to help with the city's defense, but still kept apologizing for abandoning her. After the first few minutes of waiting she began to worry. What if they didn't come, or were delayed or detained? The streets were nearly empty now, with most people defending the walls or already down below. The robed Mizen guards darted furtive glances toward the top of the wall as they stood nervously in front of the iron gate.

Slowly, an echoing from the tunnel sound grew louder until it seemed to be all around them. "Let us out," commanded H'vetik, his face appearing like an apparition into the sunlight. The nearest guard nearly dropped his halberd in fright. Through the metal slats, Barton waved the Royal Seal and the High Mizen stamp affixed to the scrap of paper that Gundis had given him. The other guard grunted and took out his key. With a heavy groan the door swung open.

"It's about time," Ash said. "Did everything go okay?"

"About as well as could be expected," H'vetik explained. "The priests were happy to oblige once they saw our papers. It took time to reunite every child with their parent or grandparent taking shelter in the Catacombs, but almost everyone was overjoyed to see their children again."

"Why do I get the feeling there's something you're not telling me, priest?"

"My family didn't want me," Treld said, stepping through the tunnel entrance from the darkness beyond. The young man looked much the same to Ash, but his usual scowl was tempered with something resembling shame. When Ash continued to stare, Treld curled his lips but then dropped his gaze. Everyone in the small group was looking at him.

An awkward silence lingered until Ash finally broke it. "Then they are fools," she told him. "You owe Renelis nothing. Leave now before the Brigade arrives or take shelter in the Catacombs." She paused, considering. "We could also use help defending the wall. Whatever you choose, we will always be family, linked not by blood but by the miracle of new life. We are the first new generation in more than a century. We won't be the last."

Treld looked up at her, hot tears forming in his eyes. "I will go with you. To the wall to fight." Then he knelt down before her as the young children in the Catacombs had done, but there was no mockery in the slow, deliberate way he bowed. "Thank you," he said softly.

Ash did her best to hide her embarrassment. "There isn't time for this foolishness. If you intend to help than we must head to the ramparts and protect the village."

"And what if we can't?" he asked, rising to his feet. "What if the Thorns aren't enough? What if we aren't enough? What then?" He didn't say, *what if you aren't enough?* but Ash heard it just the same. An unspoken question looming over everything.

"I may have a trick or two up my sleeve," she said, trying to put on her bravest face as the glow from the Traveler washed over her. "There's a plan in place. Barton can tell you more. Hopefully it won't come to that. Right now, we are needed on the wall." Ash tried not to think about Renelis and what she would have to do if the Traveler's Gift didn't suffice.

Chapter 12

Standing on top of the western wall, Gundis peered at the dark line of trees in the distance and frowned. His right hand was wrapped in combat leather. When he tapped his fingers nervously on top of the stony lip, green *filigreen* arched across the cracked surface like lightning. "Where is she?" he demanded, turning to his First Lieutenant. "The Brigade will be here any moment. Is the evacuation complete?"

"Those who aren't fighting have taken shelter in the Catacombs, along with most of the Mizen untrained for war," the tall grim-faced Thorn responded.

Gundis breathed a small sigh of relief. At least the rest of the village was momentarily safe. Now it was up to them to stop the attack. If they failed, Sizan's Second had orders to seal the Catacombs. There was enough food and water to last a year, maybe two. There was another exit miles away. Each Thorn knew what was at stake. Dozens of the elite soldiers lined the wall, emerald *filigree* dancing between their fingers. Interspersed among them were men and women of all ages, not trained for war, but fit enough to hold a crude weapon. Everyone seemed to be holding their breath.

Footsteps echoed hurriedly in the stairs nearby, the sound rising ominously towards them. The captain turned just as Ash emerged from the opening. Her face was stern and lined with worry. It was hard for Gundis to believe that a few short months ago she had entered the Catacombs innocent and carefree. Behind her came an unexpected figure. The young man was scowling and looked ill at ease among the gathered throng. After saying something to her companion, she made her way over.

"About time you got here," Gundis grumbled, putting a heavy arm around her. "Are you sure you want to do this?"

Ash looked up at her friend and managed a smile. "I have to try, Gun. Why else would the Traveler have given me this gift? I just wish we didn't have to fight. All he wants is the Stone."

Gundis sighed. "That opportunity has passed. The Stone is lifeless now. Whatever remains of the Traveler resides in you. We will not let him take you away."

Ash put a hand on her friend's shoulder. "You may not have a choice," she replied.

The Captain of the Guard began to reply, but then stopped as he noticed the small procession walking towards them on the narrow rampart. The King's Second was in the lead, smiling tightly at each defender, followed by the frowning High Mizen Priestess. Several paces behind was Barton the Celestial, looking weary now that his message had finally been delivered. "We were not expecting such a distinguished visit," Gundis said as he bowed to the acting head of state. "Rest assured, Aisha is ready to do her part."

The King's Second gazed at the young woman as if trying to remember the reasons for putting the city's future in her hands. "I certainly hope so," he muttered. "We are all counting on you."

Then the slight, wiry man moved past Aisha, making room for the Voice of the Mizen. "Do not fear, child," she toned solemnly. "May the light of the Celestials show us all the way. Let the Stone be the foundation under our feet. You have been honored with a precious gift. Do not waste it."

"Thank you," Ash replied evenly. "I'll do my best."

The Voice's lips curled in a fragile smile. "That will have to be enough," she said.

Then she stepped aside, leaving only Barton. The messenger still bore the scars of his long journey, and his eyes reflected the fatigue from being on the run for far too long. Even so, the Celestial must have carried some hidden reserve or resolve, because when he spoke his voice was clear and strong. "I don't know you well, but I believe the Traveler chose you for a reason. I hope that's a small comfort. This is our time. We've been running and hiding for too long. But no more. With your help, today we fight!"

A chorus of cheers rose up from the wall. Barton turned to her, perhaps wanting to say something else, but Gundis interrupted the moment. "All right," the Captain commanded. "The time for speeches is over. Let's put action to words. Everyone to their places and look sharp. You know what to do." The royal entourage moved away, dragging the Celestial with it.

When the small crowd dispersed, there was an unexpected figure standing looking at her. "Jax!" she exclaimed, running over to her brother. He was a tall man, perhaps a full head and shoulders higher than his sister. In his calloused right hand he clutched a rusting spear. An ill-fitting metal helm framed his scraggly black hair. Ash noticed with surprise that his fingernails were chewed ragged.

"No one tells you how uncomfortable these things are," he complained, adjusting his head piece.

Ash smiled, looking up at him. "I always said your head was too big."

"Right now, I would give anything to be a smaller target." Then he took a deep breath and let it out again. "I didn't know if I was going to get the chance, but I just wanted to say good luck. I'm really proud of you."

"Thanks," Ash said. Her brother glanced nervously at the captain and then turned away, hurrying to his place somewhere on the wall.

Ash looked out across the peaceful valley. There was still no sign of the invading army. An eerie stillness descended on the watchers. They were all holding their breath, waiting for a nightmare to appear on the horizon. Gundis gritted his teeth and spun *filigreen* between his fingers. Ash leaned in toward her friend and spoke quietly. "My brother Jax. My mom and dad. The defenders. Everyone is counting on me with their life. What if the Traveler made a mistake?"

Gundis stilled his hands and looked at the young woman who had become a family member to him over the years. "You're not alone, Ash," he said softly, and then motioned to the rows of people standing silently along the wall. "We're all in this together. None of us knows if they'll be enough. All we can do is try."

She started to respond, but then drew in her breath sharply as something within her caught fire. "Are you... okay?" he asked. Beside him, Ash was starting to glow, as if the world's light was somehow being drawn to her. At the same time, from the edges of the forest, a great swarm of pale birds took sudden flight, scattering into the sky like dwindling hope. Gundis felt his heart begin to pound. In response, he unslung his bow and held it across his chest. A passing cloud dimmed the sun, sending a shiver down his spine. The moment hung in the air. Then from the length of the forest the Bone Brigade erupted, covering the open spaces like an abomination. They were walking death, alien and perverse, as white as the moon, save for a shriveled red heart that shimmered through tatters of skin and bone. By the hundreds they came in grisly procession, overrunning the verdant plain as they made their way toward the defenders. At the front of this vast undead army rode an inhuman figure atop a skeletal horse. He wore royal rags that hung from his limbs, doing little to hide the patches of rotting skin that remained. A crown rested obscenely on his head. With a wave of his arm the Restless King urged his followers forward.

Ash stared back helplessly. There were too many. And still they kept coming, marching towards the wall with swords upraised in bony fists. Suddenly, her power seemed insignificant. What could she do against such a foe? She was only one person. But she wasn't alone. Gundis stood by her side, leaning over the wall as if he meant to leap down and battle the Brigade himself. Next to him, Barton pulled a gleaming short sword from a worn leather scabbard. The High Mizen Priestess and King's Second looked at each other with trepidation before steeling themselves in a common resolve. Archers and soldiers down the length of the battlement looked over at her, their eyes full of hope and fear.

"Now," Treld said behind her. His voice was small, but there was a bite of anger to it. That was all the encouragement she needed. Nodding numbly, Ash swallowed her lingering doubts and reached for the Traveler's gift that was buried inside of her. Already it rose in response, anticipating her need. Light enveloped her as Ash let the power surge through skin and bone, mind and body. She was not made for such things. No human being was. Somehow the essence of the Traveler knew this and made adjustments. But the power had to go somewhere. Ash could not contain it. Almost too late she remembered the danger and desperately tried to focus the blast toward the army down below through her outstretched arms. "Get down!" she cried, her voice electric and unearthly.

Brilliant beams of pink and orange shot out from the palms of her hands, decimating the leading ranks of the Bone Brigade and scorching the ground. The lancing light turned any skeletal soldier it struck to dust, and then kept going, repeating the process row after row. Moving her hands side to side produced even deadlier results. Huge swaths of invaders evaporated in a cloud of smoke as she struggled to direct the power that coursed through her. Whole battalions of gaunt fighters simply ceased to exist and still Ash drew from the strange wellspring the Traveler had provided. When the last beam sputtered and finally died, she collapsed against the battlement and closed her eyes in exhaustion. She felt depleted. A yawning emptiness replaced her earlier exaltation. Slowly she opened her eyes and looked out across the plain. The remains of countless brigade members swirled in the air like mist obscuring the battlefield. *I did this*, she thought numbly. *I did all of this. They were like me once.*

Ash swept her gaze across the landscape, looking for signs of movement. She hoped that it had been enough and that the worst was over, but this was not to be. Emerging from the clouds of their fallen comrades was the rest of the Bone Brigade. Like an ebony wave they marched relentlessly across the battlefield toward the rock-strewn shadow of the city wall, as if she had done almost nothing at all. Although their numbers had been thinned, Ash was filled with despair in seeing how many still remained. At the center of the throng strode the Restless King. Although no longer astride his ghastly steed, the sovereign was still clearly visible, rising a full head and shoulders above his loyal troops. When he turned his intense gaze in her direction, Ash felt exposed even though she was far out of reach.

"Can you do that again?" Gundis asked, interrupting her thoughts. She shook her head weakly. There was little of the Traveler's gift left, and she was too exhausted to try. Better to save what remained in case they needed it for later. The Captain of the Guard turned grimly to the row of defenders perched along the battlement. "Fire!" he shouted.

At once the archers drew back their bows and let loose a volley of arrows. Ash watched in horror as the deadly projectiles passed harmlessly through the fleshless bodies of the Brigade. The few times a lucky arrow found a target, the skeletal warrior simply pulled it from the bone and continued on as if nothing had happened.

The Captain of the Guard cursed and then changed tactics. "*Filigreen!*" he commanded. In response, dozens of Thorns stepped forward with emerald webs glistening between their fingers. With a flick of their wrists, they sent sheets of green fire arcing down to the army of the Restless King. Some magical bolts struck harmlessly to boulders or patches of ground, but many came in contact with a skeletal brigade member, fusing their joints and wrapping tightly around their limbs. The end result was a soldier who could not move. Like the pendulum of a stuck mechanical clock, the skeleton could only strain in place.

Again and again the elite Thorn guards let loose shimmering strands of *filigreen*, but it was a losing battle. There were still too many. Even if Renelis had ten times as many defenders, the army of the Restless King would eventually overrun them. Only the high stone walls prevented an immediate defeat. Ash watched as the emaciated soldiers reached the barrier and began to form a white moat encircling the city. A few in the vanguard tried to climb the smooth surface or chip the surface with an ineffectual blade, but most in the Brigade simply stood and waited, partially protected by their proximity to the wall. *What are they doing?* Ash wondered.

"It looks like we have a standstill," Gundis murmured. Thorn guards still hurled emerald bolts at those Brigade members visible beyond the wall, and citizen-soldiers busied themselves in pairs with lobbing heavy rocks over the battlement where they shattered the enemy, but slowly the defenders became aware of a change. From a hundred stones away, the sea of white began to part. Down the grassy path stepped the Restless King. Flesh hung on his bones like stubborn moss on a stone. His face was a grotesque mixture of muscle, bone and skin, with one side having intact lips and cheek while the other hardly more than a grinning skull. In his right hand he carried a great sword. His left hand was clenched and at his side. Once or twice he stooped over the fallen body of a Brigade member and bowed his head before continuing on.

Beside her, Gundis shook his head as if clearing it from a nightmare, but it was the Celestial Barton who spoke. "It is only a man," the messenger said loudly, as if trying to break a spell. "Or what was once a man. Kill the head and the body withers."

The Captain of the Guard raised his arms up in the air. "Fire!" he shouted. "Bring him down!" A moment later the sky was filled with arrows and emerald *filigreen*, all racing toward the leader of the Brigade. If the Restless King was concerned, he did not show it. Magnus continued to make his way purposefully toward the shadow of the wall. At the last moment, with an almost casual gesture, he raised his left fist, opening his hand. A sickly green barrier coalesced around him. It shimmered like a mirage, but it was real enough. The scores of arrows were deflected as if it were the hardest metal. Bolts of green sizzled and smoked across its surface like lightning on an untroubled lake.

Ash had trouble believing what she was seeing. Renelis had thrown everything it had at the Restless King, but it wasn't enough. She hadn't been enough. Fatigue still weighed her down like a heavy black cloak. With a sigh she made her decision and caught Treld's eye. He nodded. Barton had already slipped away.

"Enough," the Restless King said, striding toward them. He had no need to shout. His voice carried up to the ramparts and beyond with ease. "You know why I have come. Why I have searched. Give it to me and I will leave you in peace."

"We are but simple villagers," the King's Second retorted, leaning his tall, thin frame over the battlement. "We strive only to defend our homes."

The Restless King laughed. "There is something much more precious that you guard. As your sovereign you denied me a boon that was rightfully mine, and have kept it hidden for countless years, hoarding it away. This is the result," he proclaimed bitterly. With a sweep of his hand he took in the terrible Bone Brigade. "I have no more time for games. Give me the Stone. I can sense it is here. I have a fragment of the original. It is drawn like a moth to the flame. Hand it over and I will let you live."

Findlewin seethed with anger. Renelis was hardly a kingdom, but its people still had pride. Myla, the Voice, the High Mizen Priestess, arched her eyebrows and put a hand on the King's Second shoulder, forestalling him. "I think it unlikely that you would let us live," she said, stepping forward in her robes. "We are a threat to you and a painful reminder of what could have been. Where we saw mystery, you see only power and vengeance."

Magnus stopped in front of the wall and looked up. "What do you know of what I see?" he wailed. "What I have lost? My regret is a bottomless well. My pain has no measure."

"It is too late to undo what has already been done," the High Mizen said sadly. "To think otherwise is madness."

"Then you leave me no choice." Raising his left fist, the Restless King opened his hand again. There in his palm was the fragment of the Stone, glowing a sickly green. Closing his eyes, Magnus reached into the dark surface of the Shard and felt the pull as the force took control. Power and possibilities surged through him. A beam as black as despair shot out from his palm, exploding in a shower of debris against the outer wall of Renelis. When the King opened his eyes, a jagged hole was visible from where a section of the lower battlements had collapsed. The Bone Brigade clambered toward it while defenders in the city rushed to plug the opening, some with their bodies, and others with pulsating shields of *filigreen*.

For every Thorn or city-soldier, there were a hundred or more of the undying. The Bone Brigade pushed through the hole in the wall, overwhelming the defenders, trampling over the brave and fallen and stepping into Renelis. Swords slashed flesh. Blood ran until the ground was slick with it. And still the skeletal warriors came. Even as one or two were cut down from repeated blows, their brethren were undeterred. Soon the defenders were forced to retreat beyond the walls and into the streets. From house rooftops arrows and emerald *filigreen* flew, but it made little difference to the Restless King's army. Magnus led his horde relentlessly towards the city center. So vast was his Bone Brigade that they swept well beyond the narrow streets, their destructive path swarming around dwellings and collapsing wood-rotted stores. Even the stones themselves trembled. The scattered defenders watched in horror and disbelief as the Brigade made their way toward the heart of Renelis and the Catacombs.

"Wait!" Magnus commanded. The fragment was still tugging at him, trying to reunite itself with the greater Stone, but now it was leading him away from the village. Slowly, he followed the pull of his hand and arm until it pointed towards a small plume of dust emerging from the far side of the city walls. A pair of horses with riders was trying to escape—with the Stone. Stifling a curse, the Restless King motioned to his men and then strode after the thieves. As one, the members of the Bone Brigade parted to let their sovereign pass. Then each lowered their weapon and followed.

High up on the wall, Gundis watched in confusion as the invaders left, heading inexplicably toward the marshes. "Is this some kind of trick?" he murmured, turning to Ash, but she was gone. He barely had time to wonder at her absence when a royal messenger emerged from the central stairs of the wall and ran toward him. When he was a few feet away he came to a stop and then tried unsuccessfully to compose himself. The man was breathing hard and looked stricken.

It was true the walls had been breached, but the Restless King had called off the attack. Try as he might Gundis could not imagine what would require such urgency. "What is it?" the Captain asked.

"The High Sizan," the young man breathed in ragged gasps. "The High Sizan is dead."

Chapter 13

Ash looked back towards the village and spied the mass of the Bone Brigade still congregating around the wall. "It's not working," she cried. "They're still there." A panicked thought occurred to her that the Restless King could simply choose to punish the village for her own escape.

The pounding of the horse's hooves thundered underneath as Ash tried feebly to grip Barton tighter. All of her choices felt dangerous and costly. As a Mizen novice, she felt equal to none of them. Inside she felt dispirited and empty. The wind rushing past her threatened to unseat her at any moment. Beside them galloped H'vetik with Treld seated behind. Ash thought he would be terrified, but the young man was smiling, as if having the time of his life. All of them had defied her when she made known her original intention to simply walk out into the marshes alone. Treld refused to be parted from her, citing Ash as his only real family. H'vetik argued that since the Traveler resided in Ash now, his spiritual mission was linked with hers. He also could ride, the priest reminded her, which would be useful since Treld did not. Barton insisted that his duty was not over as long as the village was still in danger. The four of them were an unlikely group, but Ash was glad to have their company. Her only regret was not being able to tell Gundis her plan. That he would have tried to stop her, she had little doubt. Still, it pained Ash to simply disappear without a word. She knew Gundis would worry something awful.

"He will come!" Barton shouted, breaking her thoughts. "The fragment cannot lie."

The messenger rose up in his saddle and glanced behind him. "Look!" he pointed. "They follow."

It was true. The Restless King and his Brigade had turned away from Renelis and were following like a great white beast. Ash breathed a nervous sigh of relief. At least the village was safe.

Long prairie grasses swept by in a blur as they made their way north past an abandoned garrison and into the hinterlands. The first signs that the terrain was changing came in the form of small pockets of water. Barton and H'vetik were soon forced to slow their steeds or risk them breaking a leg and taking a terrible tumble. Before long the ground became soggy, with growing pools of water dotting the once firm landscape. Fist-sized dragonflies with shimmering variegated wings hovered above the still surfaces before darting off at their approach. When Barton's silver-streaked mare started to sink in a hidden patch of bog, it became obvious to everyone they had entered the treacherous domain of the swamp. It was also apparent that their once sizable lead had dwindled as a result. The Restless King and his minions were swarming around the broken tower of the garrison and funneling towards the riders like rampaging white waters.

"We must leave the horses here," H'vetik said, halting his gray mare and jumping down with a practiced flourish that demonstrated his southern roots. After a moment, Treld struggled down from his perch. "I can lead us through the swamp," the priest said. "I know the way."

"And what makes you an expert?" Barton asked, still mounted, but having dropped the reins from his hand.

"The Mizen sometimes use the Gray Swamp for one of our initiation rites. We know this land well. I lived out here for the better part of a month when I was a third year Initiate."

"Guess I missed out on all the fun," Ash quipped, looking out across the desolate landscape. "I've heard it said that if a stranger ever wandered into the village, they were brought here. Then the swamp would do the rest."

"That is not true," H'vetik said softly. "No innocents have ever been harmed, by the Grand Sizan or the Celestials or the Mizen. Once or twice an explorer or a lost shepherd has found their way here. They were simply brought into the fold with the condition that they could never leave."

"And what if someone didn't want to make that deal?"

The priest frowned, then hung his head in resignation. "Then they were given an extract from a milky-white plant that only grows in the heart of the swamp. It induces a temporary deep sleep and wipes away any recent memories. When the individual woke, they simply found themselves miles from the village with no recollection."

Ash looked out across the swamp numbly. Bands of mist hung in the air above the soggy ground like patches of amnesia.

"That sounds like harm to me," Barton retorted, shaking his head.

"Yes, it does," the priest admitted. "That is why I refused to participate in any of it."

The rest of them dismounted and, with H'vetik in the lead followed by Ash, Barton and Treld, began picking their way carefully through the treacherous terrain, searching one step at a time for solid ground. They were only a quarter of the way across the languid mass when the Restless King and his Brigade reached the outer reaches of the wetland. Scores of skeletal soldiers ran heedless across the unstable ground. Within minutes many of them were stuck fast in the mud or sinking down into the soupy depths. Even so, hundreds more slogged on, all while the Restless King spurred them forward, shouting words of encouragement and raising his fist high into the air like a banner.

With every bony step, a dozen more of the invaders met their end, but there would still be plenty to spare, Ash observed. Only Barton was a trained fighter, and as good as he was, the Celestial was no match for the sheer number of Brigade members. Only the swamp prevented their immediate defeat, by slowing the headlong rush of the Restless King's army. Some vestige of human survival or fear must have been retained by the grisly soldiers. In degrees, the skeletal warriors became more cautious. But even as it hampered their enemy's progress, it also severely limited their own. Treld struggled the most with the terrain, falling behind the others. To make matters worse, H'vetik often had to pause to study the ground and make certain the hidden path was still stable. Sometimes the group was forced to leap across patches of murky water thick with purple-tinged lily pads. "Don't let them touch you," the priest warned, pointing at the beautiful floating plants. "They are extremely poisonous."

The whole process was exhausting. It felt like walking a tightrope. One slip of your foot and you could drown, get mired in the mud, or die from the deadly vegetation. The Bone Brigade was relentless in their pursuit, and what awaited them at journey's end was almost certain death. Ash could never remember feeling so tired. It wasn't just the arduous journey across the unforgiving swamp, or the hordes of skeleton warriors breathing down their neck, although that didn't help. Deep in her bones she felt weary and inexplicably sad, as if she were losing something precious.

On a whim she tried to call up what remained of the Traveler's power. Focusing on their need, she opened herself to the essence, asking to strike out against their pursuers. The result was a single blue flame which burned without heat in the center of her palm. That was all that was left. The visitor who had healed her father and changed all of their lives was nearly gone from the world. Ash stumbled from the attempt, a new wave of fatigue passing through her.

"Careful," Barton murmured as he caught her gently by the shoulders from behind. "They're gaining on us." Having no strength for a reply, she simply forced herself to keep moving.

A sudden scream pierced Ash from behind. She turned and glanced across the swamp just in time to see Treld go down. He thrashed for a moment before touching the bottom with his feet. Then he started sinking into the sucking ground. Barton reached him first and extended an arm. The muddy water was already up to his shoulders and rising fast. "Grab my hand," the Celestial instructed.

The boy's eyes were wide with fear. Using the last of his strength, Treld reached out as Barton grabbed his slick wrist. Ash could see the strain on the Celestial's face as he struggled to keep his footing on the slippery ground. Not knowing what else to do and, desperate to help, Ash wrapped her arms around the messenger as an anchor.

"Give me your other arm," H'vetik said fiercely as he reached out to the young man. Treld did his best, but his hand would not reach. The priest leaned closer over the life-sucking water, his feet sinking gently in the muck beneath. Treld strained towards his salvation, but came up achingly short.

"Leave me," the young man said. "There isn't time."

"Save your breath," Barton told him. "We're not leaving you."

They were running out of time, Ash realized. The Restless King and his Brigade had covered half the distance while they struggled. Despite their best efforts, Treld was still sinking. His mouth lay perilously above the waterline now. Bit by bit, Ash slid across the ground towards the edge until H'vetik encircled her waist, holding her fast. It was now or never.

Emboldened by this little victory or perhaps reaching the end of his endurance, Barton tugged violently. Treld's head popped free of the murky water, but their tenuous connection was severed from the strain. They were only separated for an instant. The messenger shot his hand out desperately and latched onto Treld as he disappeared beneath the surface. "Pull!" the Celestial pleaded.

Groaning, they all struggled to hold on until they finally tumbled backwards in a heap. Ash looked up, dazed but hopeful. There were only three of them lying on the spongy ground. Treld was gone. It seemed impossible. He had just been here. How could they not have saved him? Ash wondered. Treld had counted on them. He had followed her because he had no one else. And she had let him at least in part because she had been afraid. A lump grew in her throat. She scrambled over to the edge where he had disappeared.

A hand gripped her shoulder tightly and shook her violently. "We have to move. Now!" H'vetik growled.

For a moment she couldn't. Then she tore herself away and got woodenly to her feet, whipping her head around. The vanguard of the Bone Brigade was a mere hundred stones away. In the lead, holding the fragment of the Forever Stone in his upraised fist, was the Restless King. The nightmare sovereign strode confidently through the swamp, as if the deadly terrain were his personal park, only hesitating when a soldier ahead of him became mired or sank from view. His pursuit never wavered. Somehow the decaying environment of the swamp elevated the Suzerian and made it appear as if he were rising from its depths, wielding an army of lost souls born from the languid amniotic waters.

The next moment she was pulled into motion by the priest. Barton hurried on their heels. Caution was no longer a luxury they could afford. Instead they sprinted across the treacherous ground like rabbits fleeing for their lives. H'vetik never paused, only changing their course once. As far as Ash could tell, they were heading towards a small barren rise in the middle of the swamp. "Our last stand?" Barton asked.

The priest made no reply. Perhaps he hadn't heard or was too busy dodging soft spots. Then again, he might have been distracted. The hollow sound of thousands of bones knocking against bone, carried over the swamp to them, growing louder as the brigade closed the gap. Ahead of her, their goal came into focus. It was hardly bigger than her room back in the Catacombs. The island rose up mere feet over the swamp and was completely blanketed with the milky-white plants. It reminded her of a mountaintop glistening with a crest of snow. It looked like a beautiful and lonely place to die.

Without warning, H'vetik let go of her hand and leaped across the swampy moat surrounding the small island. Ash followed suit with Barton landing a few stones away. There would have been room for Treld, but only just barely. Ash stood up. Then her knees buckled as another wave of weakness passed through her. For a few moments she lay in the soft vegetation. She felt herself lifted as Barton and H'vetik each grabbed an arm. "What is wrong?" Barton inquired. "Is she hurt?"

"It is worse than that," the priest replied. "The Traveler, or what remains of his power inside her, must be fading."

Barton looked at her, waiting for confirmation. "It's true," she said at last. "That's why I failed on the wall. I felt the Traveler's gift slipping away."

The priest looked around their small kingdom. "These are the plants I mentioned. If you choose, there is still time to take the gift of sleep before the end comes." A heavy silence descended on the three of them. No one moved. "That is good," H'vetik finally continued, nodding grimly. "We will retreat no more. Let us stand here together."

As if their last hope had been extinguished, the three of them turned woodenly toward the approaching army of the almost dead. Even as they watched, more members of the Bone Brigade were lost to the swamp, but there were still countless dozens to take their place. Within moments they were encircled with no chance of escape. The priest closed his eyes and began signing. To Ash it sounded like a hymn, beautiful and sparse, but the words were in a language she did not understand.

The skeletal warrior closest to them lunged suddenly and H'vetik fell back in pain. When the Bone Brigade member withdrew its sword, the priest looked down and saw the side of his tunic blossom red. He had been lucky the wound was not deeper or the thrust better aimed.

"Hold!" the Suzerian ordered. His loyal soldiers froze in place. Ash and Barton ran to the priest's side. "It's over," the Restless King said, almost sadly stepping forward. "After all these long years, the Stone is mine." Putting the fragment into the tattered remains of his robe, he pulled out his great sword and motioned for his Brigade to close the noose tighter. Barton's hands weaved a frantic pattern in the air. For a frightful heartbeat nothing happened. A look of panic passed over the Celestial's face. The next moment there was a flash of emerald and a lattice of pulsating *filigreen* arced overhead, sealing the three of them in a small, but protective bubble.

Howling in fury, the Restless King took the fragment out and struck the shield with all his might. Again and again he struck the barrier, impervious to the damage he was doing to himself. A spider web of fissures spread slowly across the glimmering barrier. Sweat glistened on the Celestial's brow. Magnus brought his bloody fist down a final time. Both the shield and talisman shattered with a deafening concussion, nearly knocking the Suzerian off his feet. At the same instant Ash felt a tiny spark, a sympathetic echo of power. There was still a residue of the Traveler within her, but it was fading fast, receding into the blackness. Reflexively, she fought to keep it, to hold onto it. Then she understood what she had to do.

The Restless King stepped forward so that he was standing above Ash. In one hand he held the sword. His other hand was raised to forestall the Brigade momentarily. "No more delays. No more tricks," he said with grim finality. "The Stone. So I can heal my men and find a measure of peace." When Ash didn't respond, he raised the sword so that it hung in the air above her chest.

"We don't have it," Ash said. It came as a surprise to her that she wasn't afraid. "The Stone's gone. It was never ours to keep. That was a mistake. Perhaps we both needed each other too much. It's time to start over." Then she shut her eyes and reached inside. She let the Traveler go. Whatever was left, whatever remained. There was no sadness. No regret. There was only a feeling of thankfulness.

"You lie," the Restless King snarled, but there was a shadow of doubt in his voice.

Ash opened her eyes and held the deadly stare of the Suzerian as the vestiges of the mysterious Traveler rose for release.

"Then you die," he hissed. With a practiced motion he brought the great sword down in a furious arc that would slice through Ash and all her friends. His loyal Bone Brigade rattled forward and thrust their weapons out. It was all over. Except that it wasn't. A ring of light tinged with orange and pink hues expanded outward from the center of her being, like a star going nova. Ash watched wide-eyed as the skeletal soldiers around them crumpled into dust, their timeless existence finally at an end. Moments later, their brethren further out in the swamp followed suit, a myriad of deathless warriors felled by a pulse of dying power. Somehow the Restless King held on, even as his rotting body faded away. The last piece to go was his ragged arm, still clutching the sword, propelled downward by gravity. Then that too gave way and the sword of Magnus, monarch of the vanished empire of Cragg, cluttered to the ground at Ash's feet.

Gundis arrived a few minutes later with a battalion of Thorns. All were amazed to see the three of them alone in the middle of the Gray Swamp with no sign of the Restless King and his Brigade. "We were too much for them," H'vetik quipped, before sinking to the ground in pain and exhaustion.

Chapter 14

The months that followed were a dizzying whirlwind for Ash. The Council of Elders met behind ornate closed doors at the royal palace of Immortia on the first day of spring. Representatives of the High Mizen, the Sizan and the Thorns were all in attendance, as well as Barton and Ash herself. Leaders talked and argued all through the day and into the night. When the group emerged haggard and tired the following morning, they made a joint announcement in the village square, on the same stage where Ash had been initiated the previous summer. Buds were swollen on the branches of nearby trees, just as many women's bellies in the audience were noticeably swollen with new life. The feared outbreak of disease and death never really materialized following the Traveler's passing. People got sick and some of them died, but as unusual as it seemed, this was normal and part of life. They had just all forgotten.

Ash sat and listened uncomfortably while Myla and Findlewin explained that Mizen and Sizan would rule together, with each of them being Queen and King. It made a certain amount of sense, Ash had to admit. With the Stone and the Eternals gone, the Mizen had lost the central tenet of their faith. A partnership was the best outcome they could hope for. The Sizan and the ruling elite were little better off, what with the social order breaking down as people began aging normally again. No longer would Renelis be closed off from the world. As a result, a government focused on protection was no longer necessary. Nothing had been decided yet, of course, but the Thorns' days were probably numbered. When the Traveler had gone, so too had their ability to weave *filigreen*. Many of the guards didn't know what to do with their hands now, and reflexively twined their fingers together as if they were praying. Ash looked over at her friend Gundis and wondered what would happen to him.

Finally, the speeches were done and Ash fidgeted in her seat, anxious to leave and be by herself. Since returning to the village, she had been thrust in the spotlight. People she barely knew thanked her for saving them. Baby girls were named after her. No longer treated like an outcast or an oddity, Ash found herself in the strange position of being a celebrity. No one, not even Gun or her family, however, knew that she was plagued by nightmares. Even on a bright, sunny day such as this, she was not immune. Distracting herself by looking off in the distance, Ash caught a glimpse of the bone white branches, the ghostly remains of the now lifeless Eternals. Suddenly she was back in the swamp, running with the skeletal warriors of the Brigade rattling at her heels. Bony digits reached out from behind, catching her hair as she tumbled to the ground. Helpless and alone, Ash could only look on in horror as skulls crowded above her, gnashing their teeth. Then the bones of countless Brigade members would pile on top of her until the light disappeared.

With a start Ash was back on the stage. Someone was calling her name. "Aisha!" a female voice was saying. "Please rise." With a growing feeling of dread, Ash realized that the Queen was motioning for her to approach.

"This young woman saved us all," King Findlewin was saying, "by drawing the Restless King away from us and then destroying him and his undead army in the Gray Swamp."

"The Stone—I mean the Traveler, chose her," Myla toned like a benediction. "Giving her a priceless gift from beyond the stars."

All heads turned as Ash reluctantly left the sanctuary of the seated Elders and walked to the edge of the platform to stand between the two recently christened monarchs. None of this had been planned. She had no idea what was happening.

"Because of her selfless act, we decree that Initiate Aisha be forever known as Saint Aisha the Protector," proclaimed the King. To her disbelief, the crowd went wild. What happened next was a blur. People were shouting her name and crowding around her, demanding details or slapping her on the shoulder. Gone was any semblance of restraint or politeness. For a moment it felt as if she were back in her night-marish dream as the world closed in and a raucous celebration began.

Over the intervening weeks, her notoriety only increased. Gifts were left outside the home of her parents where she was staying. Flowers from potential suitors were delivered by royal courier. A well-to-do farmer surprised her one morning by bringing over a cow and a basket of apples. Immodest proposals were sung by handsome men. A beautiful woman invited her inside for tea. But to Ash, the overtures felt needy, demanding or both. Everyone wanted a moment of her time or a brief caress. Most of all, though, the attention felt insincere.

Through it all her mother smiled, congratulating Ash on her newfound popularity as the Champion of Renelis. "You're young," she said. "Enjoy yourself. Settle down when you're ready." To avoid scrutiny and gain a measure of freedom, she began taking horse riding lessons from H'vetik out beyond the wall. With the Mizen way of life upended, the priest had little to do and so was glad to oblige. He was a good teacher, patient yet firm. His wound had nearly healed from their desperate trek in the Gray Swamp, but occasionally he would grimace in pain when his mount galloped too hard or took a turn too tightly. Even so, he never complained, and refused to tolerate Ash's own protestations of difficulty. "If I can learn how to ride a camel, you can master a horse," H'vetik chided her.

Within a few weeks Ash felt comfortable if not quite proficient in a saddle. Little by little she learned to trust her mount to be an extension of his body. She practiced commands, forming the strange words in H'vetik's native tongue. Tired of her old clothes, she took to wearing woven pants, a chemisette, leather jerkin and boots. It felt good to be rid of dresses and robes. More and more they felt like a different life. She looked forward to their daily lessons, not only for the escape they provided, but also for the sheer joy of riding as the wind whistled through her hair when she was brave enough to gallop.

Their classes were to be cut short, however. "The desert is calling me," the priest announced one evening after practice. "Our cities of glass shine in the sun, but I barely remember. I have been away too long. Surely they still stand, for who could conquer us? But I must be sure. I will depart the day after the 'morrow."

Ash was left momentarily speechless. "I don't understand," she replied. Tears pooled in her eyes as if emerging from a hidden spring of emotion.

H'vetik gazed at her, a frown deepening on his bronze features. "If anyone here could really see me, if anyone could understand, it would be you. But perhaps that is asking too much. Tell me, what is it you see when you look upon me?"

As unexpected as the question was, Ash didn't hesitate in responding. "A priest, a rebel of sorts, a searcher. Someone who is open to the world. You give without expectation."

Her friend nodded, but a touch of sadness rested on his smile. "All true. But look at my skin. Look into my eyes. I am not like you. I do not come from this village. I was not born and raised here. Your customs are not my own. For long unchanging years I have lived among you, but still I am not one of you. I am what you do not see. When I traveled from kingdom to kingdom selling the riches of my homeland, I think I lost the true value of my people. I need to return to the land of my birth. Everyone deserves to be seen."

He was heading back home to Caravel. Any wisdom the Stone had to give was gone. H'vetik couldn't be expected to remain in Renelis after the world was set in motion again. Even if all his friends and family were long dead, home still called. Ash understood all the reasons, but she still felt abandoned.

Chapter 15

The rest of the spring was overcast and rainy, mirroring her mood. "You could have told me, you know," Ash said one day, trying to keep her voice gentle but with a sliver of bitterness creeping in.

The former Captain of the Guard looked pained. "If you'd asked me, I would have told you. I hated keeping the truth from you like that. It wasn't right. We all saw how you struggled." Ash started to protest—*then why didn't someone say anything?*—but Gundis wasn't finished yet. "And yet, ask yourself. Would you have struggled to accept the truth if it had been handed to you? Wouldn't you still have had to descend to the Catacombs and find out for yourself?"

"But that isn't the point, Gun," she told him levelly. "It's *my* life." The silence between them lengthened.

"I know," her friend said finally. "And I'm sorry. This was bigger than you or I. That doesn't make it any better."

Ash sighed and rested her head on Gun's shoulder. "You know I can't be mad at you."

"Thank you, Saint Aisha," he drawled. "Your understanding is only exceeded by your bravery."

Despite herself, Ash smiled. "I know I should be grateful for the attention," she confided. "In truth, I hate it." That was why they were meeting underneath the barren branches of the Eternals. It was the only place in the village she could be sure of privacy. No villager wanted to be reminded of what they had lost. The once verdant Stand of the Eternals now resembled a graveyard, and the village was still trying to rebuild what had been destroyed in the attack.

Gundis put his arm around her and smiled. "It's been a long time since the villagers have had anything to celebrate. Accept your rewards. By the gods, you deserve them."

"I just don't get it," she continued. "Before, I was barely tolerated. Something to be feared. Now I'm a hero beyond measure. It all seems so absurd. I just wanted to fit in and feel like I belonged."

Gundis smiled and put his arm around her. "Enjoy this while it lasts," he advised. "It won't always be like this, you know."

"Maybe not, but I'll always be what they made me."

"What do you mean?" asked the new Commander of the Royal Guard.

"They need something to take the place of the Stone. As long as I'm here, I'll be that forever."

Gundis looked at her and a frown deepened on his face. "You make it sound like you're going somewhere."

Then Ash told her friend what she hoped to do.

Chapter 16

When the spring rains were finally over, and the weather was more tolerable for traveling, Ash snuck out of her parent's house early in the morning with a large leather satchel strapped over her shoulder. Inside were a few precious possessions and a change of clothes. A few minutes earlier, using ink and a worn stylus, she had scrawled out a heartfelt letter trying to explain her feelings of why she couldn't stay. Then she left it on her bed. She hoped her family would understand and that they would forgive her for leaving without saying goodbye. In the end, it was the only way. How could she look them in the eye and then walk out the door? After everything, she still loved them. It was just time to find her own way. And besides, goodbyes weren't always forever.

For once, no one in the streets stopped her. The few people she saw were shopkeepers opening their colorful awnings, and a handful of women carrying water from the well for the morning meal. Walking by the village wall, she noticed that the hole had never been repaired from where the Restless King had breached it. Then she realized there was little point in securing the town's defenses. The shadow they had feared for so long was finally gone. Now they could finally get on with their lives. Nearby, a half-completed statue in her likeness depicted Ash frozen in the act of summoning the Traveler's energy atop the wall. A block of stone substituted for her still unfinished legs, giving the impression that she was held fast and sinking into the ground, like Treld. *Who will remember him?* she wondered. A familiar weight settled on her before she forced herself to walk on.

Nearing the stables, Ash began to worry. To doubt the plan. To doubt herself. What if she lost her nerve, or a guard happened by? She was not above walking, but the thought of journeying on foot was neither practical nor wise. It would also be lonely. If she were being honest with herself, Ash was afraid of leaving. Renelis was all she had ever known. All the people Ash cared about were here. Almost everyone. Beyond the city walls was a vast unknown. But that was also exciting. It hurt her heart to leave, but a future awaited her beyond these broken walls. She was okay on her own. And besides, she could be brave, like when she had decided to live in the Catacombs or led the Restless King away from the village.

Steeling herself, Ash stepped into the dim, cool interior of the royal stables. To her surprise there were two horses saddled up. She walked over to her brown mare and stroked the horse's head gently as she investigated the bulging saddlebags on either side. Gundis had not only kept her secret, he had provided a week's worth of provisions, as well as a handful of gold coins, a lodestone compass and a single shining dagger. It was too much. Ash hoped he wouldn't get into trouble.

The other horse, gray and regal with silver markings, was a mystery. Something tugged at the back of her mind, but it wouldn't become clear. Before she could puzzle it out, someone walked the doorway. "I wondered if you were riding the other one," the former Celestial greeted her as he entered the stable carrying more supplies. He was dressed in the same dark riding attire from when she had first met him, by the stream after fainting on the dais during her Initiation ceremony. Barton's short black hair framed his handsome face.

"I suppose Gundis told you," she said.

Barton tied a leather bag closed and then patted the horse's head. Putting a foot in the stirrup, he swung into the saddle with enviable grace. "He didn't breathe a word to me. It just makes sense that you would want to get away."

"So you're not here to stop me?"

He smiled. "I'm leaving too, Aisha. It was never my intention to stay this long. Besides, I don't really have any family left here."

Surprise caused her to stare a moment too long, before she remembered his words in the Great Chamber before the battle. His father had died as a Thorn, protecting the village from a contingent of the Bone Brigade. Ash guessed that his mother had died in childbirth. How awful, but she didn't say anything. Not then. The moment had passed. If Barton blamed her family for his loss in any way, he didn't show it. The more she thought about it, the more they actually had in common. His parents were gone, while hers were still alive but absent in another way.

Ash walked over to the other horse and placed her hand gently on the animal's soft mane. Sunlight fell through the open windows, illuminating a galaxy of swirling dust specks. Beyond the stables, people passed by and then disappeared from view, on their way to work or errands. Now that she was on the verge of leaving, everything seemed precious. "It's not such a bad place. Not really. It's just small."

The Celestial nodded thoughtfully. "Home can feel like that sometimes. For me, Renelis was my whole world. It was my reason for breathing. Helping it stay safe gave the never-ending years purpose. Now that story is done. The things you save should have a life of their own. Besides, time is ticking again. I don't want to waste it."

Ash put her foot tentatively in the stirrup and on the second attempt managed to land in the saddle. "Where will you go?" she asked.

"Maybe west," Barton replied wistfully. "The Six Cities of Moshmar have always fascinated me. Then again, I've heard wonderful tales of the Scattered Islands far to the south in the Great Inland Sea. They speak of fishing folk that can take you there for the price of a story. How about you?"

She laughed. "I have absolutely no idea. I know I should be beside myself with fear, but more than anything I'm just excited to go find out, to see what happens next."

Gripping the reins, Ash watched as a young stable boy slid the large door open, revealing a narrow swath of cobblestone that snaked towards the outer wall and the sloping farm fields beyond. "Do you know what's funny?" she said, turning in her saddle to Barton. "I spent my whole life wondering why things were the way they were, and trying to figure it out. Then I find answers, more than anyone has any right to, and am given a gift beyond measure. So what do I do? I turn my back on it all."

Ash waited for Barton to question her decision, to chide her for youthful irresponsibleness. Instead he smiled at her. For a nervous moment she thought the messenger might be reaching out to her, but some doubt must have made him reconsider. Before he put his hand back close to his chest, she spied the still vivid tattoo of a shooting star etched on his palm. "Sometimes that is the only way," he said. "You will make it through."

"What makes you so sure?" she asked, trying to disguise how her hand holding the reins was beginning to shake ever so slightly.

Barton held her gaze, gentle and thoughtful. "I've seen in a lot in my life," he said, "but I've never met anyone quite like you."

The compliment reddened her cheeks. "What was it like?" she began by way of diversion. "To live so long, I mean?" It was a question she had rarely asked growing up, out of politeness, and whenever she did build up her courage enough to ask her brother Jax or her parents, invariably she received an unsatisfactory answer. Now she was asking someone little more than a stranger. And yet there was an intimacy of shared experience that made the asking possible. "I'm sorry if it's too personal," she fumbled.

"No. Not at all," the messenger soothed with a wave of his hand. "Actually, it's a relief to be asked. I've always had to keep that part of myself hidden." He closed his eyes for a moment as if lost in the accumulation of time. "More than anything else, I guess it's just been lonely. Always on the move, changing disguises, being so careful. I could never really get close to anyone. Even when I was training under my gentle master in the Hidden Guild among the twisting alleys of Cragg, I always felt a watchful eye. All the time I was so worried that I would be found out and let everyone here down."

He paused. "I don't think people are meant to live so long," he continued as if remembering a bad dream. "At least not like we did. Trapped in a moment without end. Living gets too hard. I guess it's natural for people to always want more. More life. More time. More of everything. At a certain point, though, seems to me, a gift can become a curse."

There was something almost too intimate in their conversation. And yet Ash found herself still talking. What he was saying resonated with her. "It must be nice to be free," she replied. "To finally be done."

The messenger loosened the reins and laughed unexpectedly. Ash was struck by how wonderful it sounded. "It will take more than a few months and a party to forget seven score and four years of duty, but I'm working on it."

Ash nodded, not sure what to say. "I guess it's time," she said. She tightened her grip on the reins. "All right, girl," she told her horse. "Let's go." Then she clicked her heels against the brown mare's flank.

Barton followed behind as they exited the stables in a slow trot on a path that led to the village wall. While at narrow at first, the dirt trail soon broadened out. There was a gentle descending slope and so without any effort they gained speed. When she saw the gate open ahead of them, Ash encouraged her steed into a trot and then a full gallop. Together they swept under the stony arch and out into the world beyond. Turning in her saddle for one more look at her home, Ash saw a familiar figure atop the wall. His broad arms waved back and forth. Ash had made Gundis promise that he wouldn't come and say goodbye. She was so glad that he hadn't listened. Holding her arm straight up like an enduring banner, Ash smiled as tears ran down her cheeks. With an effort she forced herself to look away.

She was a voyager now, in search of something. Herself, perhaps. More than anything, Ash realized, she just wanted to live a meaningful life, on her own terms. The wind whistled of adventures to come, but she lingered in the glow of the special people in her life and remembered those who had departed too soon, like Treld. She thought of the Stone and Renelis and how connected everything and everyone is. There was a chance that the village would become more welcoming. Less afraid. Everything worthwhile takes time. Finally, Ash thought of the Traveler, and although she didn't believe in any of the old or new gods, she said a silent prayer for him.

After a time in which they rode next to each other but did not speak, she motioned to her companion, and they stopped by a stream so they could refill their leather canteens and quench their thirst. Ash wondered if perhaps it was the same one where she had first met Barton. If so, time and distance had made it into something nearly unrecognizable. Gone were the shadows and the dense rows of trees lined up like an army of undead soldiers. The water here flowed through a quiet open meadow. Sunlight danced on the surface as birdsong filled the air. In that moment she was happy and content, neither looking back with regret nor ahead with worry. The possibilities within her felt limitless. Her own breathing steadied her. The Gift from the Traveler paled in comparison. She had only been a vessel, after all. But she knew now that she was much more than that. Her body and mind were her own. The only real limits were the ones she imposed on herself. Beyond the grassland, far in the distance, rose gray tinged mountains framed against an open sky. To the south stretched a great green smudge of trees.

Ash felt as if she stood at a crossroads. It would make sense to part here, to say goodbye, if that was what she wanted. But what did she want? She had spent so long trying to figure out why she was different and so little time on being herself. All the old questions didn't matter anymore. The answers she had found didn't really help. Not like she thought they would. Only the Traveler's demand for secrecy still troubled her. Perhaps keeping her in the dark had been an attempt to shield her from the past and keep her curious, open to what lay ahead. Gundis was only partly right. If she had known the whole truth, she still might have needed to go down to the Catacombs. To find proof. Then again, perhaps not. She might have accepted the revelation and then gone on with her life. But then she never would have seen the children. Seen the hurt. And the village needed healing. Probably more than it needed saving. The Traveler knew that and trusted her. That wasn't all bad.

Right now, it just felt good to do something for herself. To let herself decide. When she did, Ash was surprised. "Since neither one of us knows exactly where were going," she began, "maybe we could ride together, at least for a while."

Her companion dismounted and walked to the edge of the stream, a leather flask hanging off his shoulder. "I would like that," he said, turning to face her. "I would like that very much." Then Barton smiled as if shaking off the accumulated years. Stooping, the former Celestial cupped his hands in the water and brought them dripping like a sieve to his waiting lips.

DRAGON ON THE DOORSTEP

Chapter 1

Gil climbed down the treacherous sea cliffs of Findris, one of the Seven Kingdoms, and then crept across the warm sands toward the dragon's lair. Ocean waves lapped against the shore like an enormous watery heartbeat. With each step, it became harder and harder to pretend he wasn't afraid. The element of surprise was assured, he reminded himself, donned as he was in battered invisibility armor, or so the shopkeeper had repeatedly assured him. Standing in the shadow of the cave, Gil took a deep breath, drew his sword, and then strode in. Then everything went terribly wrong.

The creature was waiting for him. "What have we here?" it bellowed, looming out of the darkness. "It looks like a puny knight come to play." Gil stumbled backwards in surprise, his feet slipping on loose coins and jewels as he fell heavily to the ground. His sword clattered to the earth out of reach. "Are you ready to die, boy?" the great beast asked him with burning eyes. Looking up at the terrible creature clothed in crimson scales, Gil shook his head numbly.

Then the dragon smiled a terrible smile, revealing row upon row of sharp teeth, more deadly than any blade. "Today is your lucky day," it said, bringing its colossal head closer to Gil. "I have a job for you. A favor. Do it and I will let you live and give you as much gold as you can hold in a single human hand."

Gil swallowed thickly. "What is the favor?" he asked.

The dragon paused and beat its wings self-consciously. The wind felt hot on Gil's face. When it spoke, the great beast seemed to be almost whispering, as if embarrassed. "I need you to check on my nephew Guldrum. He resides in the kingdom of Naloave. We are concerned about him."

"What do you want me to do?" Gil asked, no longer sure of the situation at all.

"Fight him to the death," the dragon said with rising emotion. "We will meet you at his cave in five days." Then it gave him a map, cast a quick spell of finding on Gil so he would be easy to track, and sent him on his way.

Chapter 2

The stone was cold under her hand as Princess Oreola stood at the open window and looked out across the castle courtyard to the trees beyond. There was always a chill in the castle, no matter how sunny the weather outside.

"Quit daydreaming," her mother chided. "It will not do to have a daughter of the royal court late for her own suitor. Sir Ignot, Duke of Westsheen, arrives again this afternoon, and you have not even begun to get ready. It's almost as if you don't want to get married."

Oreola spun around, a look of frustration crossing her face before she concealed it with an apologetic smile. "I wait only for the sight of him coming through the gate," she replied.

Her mother, tall and stately, still beautiful after many years, sighed and ran long fingers through her graying hair. "We both know that isn't true," she said. "Yet there are things more important than our own personal whims and inclinations. We can do nothing about your hair now," she surveyed, glancing critically at Oreola's chopped black hair. "Fortunately, you inherited my beauty if not my common sense. Proper clothes will help as well. Go find them and put them on."

"Of course," Oreola acquiesced. *Why did she always feel so small around her mother?* Walking across the Great Hall, she paused at the archway leading to the hallway and her bedroom. "Mother?" she asked. "Do you ever—" She paused, unsure how to continue.

"Do I ever *what*?" her mother asked with a note of impatience.

"Nothing," Oreola finished. Then she walked down the passageway, toward her bedroom door and, after a brief glance behind her, past her chambers, taking the spiraling stairs down until she was deep underneath the castle. Her heart began to beat faster and faster. In the flickering torchlight, Oreola made her way to the secret hiding place where dreams and salvation lay.

*

Wings, please fly! thought Princess Oreola, as hopes rose up inside her and fears tried to drag them down. The air was cool but pleasant in the shadow of the courtyard wall, as she made a few last-minute adjustments to the straps and gave her copper-tinged mechanical wings a tentative pump. All around her was a magnificent garden. There were trees of every conceivable variety, all in a colorful ecstasy of blossom. Sculptured hedges lined the alabaster paths that crisscrossed the green expanse. At the center sparkled a glorious fountain with a rainbow arcing gently overhead, like a mantle of heaven. She had eyes for none of it.

From across the courtyard Duke Ignot appeared, a look of amazement on his usually pompous face as he took in the sight. Each time she flexed her strange mechanical wings, the upward beat sliced through the shade and at the last, at the apex, flared into brilliant sunlight so bright that he had to look away. That he wanted her was written on his lecherous face. With his long, crooked nose leading the way, he strode across the grass of the courtyard with a bouquet of flowers in his fleshy hand, angling to cut her off.

When she saw him coming, Oreola swore under her breath. *Why now? Why can't he leave me alone?* She wasn't going to make it now, she knew. He would wreck everything and all her planning would be wasted. She would never get another chance after this. Any day her father would announce the engagement, and then her life would be over.

But instead of folding her wings in with a sigh and waiting for his arrival, she began to beat them even faster, almost desperately. Leaping out of the shadows, she ran flapping across the courtyard like a hopeful dodo, bounding across the elegant paths and jumping the pristine juniper bushes. She didn't care how foolish she looked. Months of scavenging for supplies and stealing glances at the Royal Engineer's drawings had led her to this moment. Oreola wasn't even sure if the strange contraption would work. No one from Naloave had ever built one before, as far as she knew, but she had always been good at making things, and she was desperate. This would be the first test flight.

Up ahead the outer wall grew closer. If only she could make it. Her heart raced ahead in pounding anticipation. But the duke was running now. His spindly legs teetered back and forth, giving the impression that he was on stilts as he hobbled across the courtyard in order to head her off. "Dear Lady!" he shouted, already out of breath. "My Queen of the Birds. Where are you flying to? Our love nest is right here. I bring you flowers and my hand in marriage if you will take it. We could make many babies together. I can give you everything you want."

"You have no idea what I want!" shouted Oreola. "Go away! I'm busy!"

Ignot increased his awkward strides. "That you have spurned me again does not surprise me. But if you will not marry me will you not at least make love with me," he asked. "You may keep the wings on if you desire," he added matter-of-factly. Oreola cringed. "Would you… at least…think about it?" Ignot pleaded, now almost completely out of breath.

Oreola's face screwed up in anger. "No!" she screamed in exhausted finality, with only desperation propelling her onwards. "My father wants me married and my mother knows your uncle, and so here you are," she panted, "making my life a living hell. But it's not going to work. I'm leaving!"

"Such behavior from a woman," Duke Ignot began, his voice cracking as anger flooded in, "would not have been tolerated in my father's day. I'm a reasonable man, but even I have my limits. This is insufferable!"

As she looked ahead of her, she could see that in fact it wasn't going to work, that she wasn't going anywhere at all. Directly in front of her stood the duke, breathing heavily but definitely blocking her path of escape. Despite his many shortcomings, being small of stature was not one of them. *And the wall is so close*, she thought. "Why don't we stop and talk about it," he suggested, a tiny smile curling menacingly on his lips. "You can always fly away later."

Oreola had begun to slow the beating of her wings, her legs pressed down by gravity. She had tried. That's all she could do. But upon hearing his last words, something rose up inside of her and she flexed her wings like a phoenix reborn. Faster and faster she swept across the courtyard, tumbling towards him in a wind-driven fury. Her suitor did not move, only stood there like a rock that could not be moved. "Get out of my way!" she screamed as she beat her wings in one last furious repetition.

Almost too late, her feet left the ground. It was exhilarating and a little scary. Then she felt his cold hands wrap around her bare legs, but he could not hold on. Upwards she flew, kicking him in the face as she passed out of reach. "I'll get you yet," the duke swore, lifting his head off the mossy ground. His nose was bleeding and he wiped a trickle of blood away with a sweep of his hand. "You'll not get far!"

Looking down at him, Oreola laughed out loud out of sheer relief and joy. She was flying! So lost in the accomplishment was the princess that she momentarily forgot about flapping her wings. As the outer wall rose in front of her, Oreola realized her predicament and sliced the air in desperation. She was not going to make it! The lip of the castle battlement loomed right in front of her. There was a moment of terrible pain and then a welcoming blackness descended upon her.

Chapter 3

Gill had an itch. It swept down his legs like wildfire and enflamed his arms and taut, empty stomach. The maddening sensation blazed elsewhere as well, but he tried not to think about those places. It was a tender subject.

Damn that itch water! Of all the rotten luck! Earlier that day he had thought himself fortunate to find a crystal-blue lake on the outskirts of the forest. Tired and dirty, he had gleefully disrobed and then dove headfirst into the sparkling water. Bubbles surrounded him in profusion. His skin felt alive and glowing. It was not until he had his clothes and heavy armor back on that he felt the first tingling sensation, the first prickling of discomfort. As his hand tracked in vain over the cold embracing metal, a tinkling of laughter met his ears, an echo of merrily flowing water. From nowhere and everywhere the sound emanated, rising in gaiety as his itching increased. *Water sprites! Damn them! Damn them all!* Gil thought as he flung off his armor and scratched himself raw.

Nothing had gone right for him in the years since he decided to become a knight gallant in the service of the Order of Regale. The ancient group had allegiance to no king or country. Instead, they served a higher calling, dedicated to righting wrongs and protecting the defenseless. It had all seemed so promising. But where were the flowery princesses who waited to be rescued? Gil wondered as he stifled a sudden desire to fling off his armor again and claw at his still enflamed skin. *Where are the villains who wait only to waver under my sword? Where are the songs waiting to be sung?*

A stone in his path invited the wrath of his armored toe, and he hurled all his frustrations at it, but the rock did not give way and he almost tripped and fell in the dirt. "Damn it all!" he cried aloud. *Where is my horse?* It had been three days since Steadfast had bolted in the night, after strange sounds pierced the stillness and inky shapes rushed past his vision. Gil shuddered at the memory. He had awoken to see several small nightmarish shapes flee from his camp and then disappear into the woods beyond. He had come to no direct harm from them and hadn't gotten a good look at the tiny creatures besides a half-seen shadow slicing through the moonlight. But whatever they were, they had terrorized his faithful horse and made off with nearly all of his provisions. Worse, though, they had taken the map the dragon had given him. His face flushed with embarrassment. His only hope now was that he remembered the map's details and steered himself accordingly. There was only two more days until the rendezvous.

All around him, the shadows and sounds of the forest enveloped him, blocking the sky and concealing any possible bandits. The woods were lawless and filled with dark magic. His hand dropped nervously to the sword held in its scabbard. Gil tried to tell himself that he was still on the right path and that it couldn't be much further, but with each passing hour his doubts grew.

He was almost about to stop when up ahead the trees thinned. In a clearing to the left, a castle loomed high on a rocky hill. That had been on the map. He was almost positive. Emboldened by the sight, he picked up the pace, yet with each step a feeling within him kept whispering that he was playing the fool, and that the iron helm atop his head was but a jester's cap, and the birdsong high in the trees merely gentle laughter.

Chapter 4

When Oreola opened her eyes, she expected to see the duke's face looming over her, spewing foul insults. But there were only a few harmless clouds in an otherwise clear blue sky. It wasn't too late, she realized with a start. Bolting upright from the cold stone floor of the battlement, she strode to a nearby opening and looked out. The world spun in a sickening carousel from the crash, and her head throbbed painfully. Down below, the hill dropped away, ending abruptly in a forest nestled on the valley floor. She checked her copper-colored wings. The cloth and veins of wood were badly muffed and scratched but otherwise appeared to be intact. There was only one way to be certain, however.

From somewhere down below, the sound of footsteps echoed menacingly, getting louder. Then there was a pause where she imagined the duke stopping to catch his breath on a landing, but it was only for a moment. Then the sound of pursuit resumed, rising through the stone walls and charging up the castle stairs to her fast! Swallowing her fear, she ran across the stone and then up the series of short steps that led to the top of the outer wall. Heaving herself up on the narrow ledge, Oreola cursed the height that yawned all around her. Behind her, the sound of pursuit was close. But still Oreola did not jump. She was frozen like a beautiful gargoyle on the lip of the precipice. Only her dark hair and her cerulean dress, woven from exotic Oasis wyrms, betrayed any movement as they ruffled and billowed in the wind.

Suddenly the duke erupted from the stairwell, blind fury carrying him forward. Almost immediately the duke stopped in his tracks, his eyes wide in surprise as he noticed her on the perch above him. She made no response and gave no indication that she even knew he was there. Recovering himself, he crept forward slowly, his hand twitching at his side. "Come down my dear. Let me apologize," he said, breathing heavily. "I'm afraid I've frightened you. My foolish heart can make no amend, only ask for your pity."

At that moment, a gust of wind hit Oreola like a wave, breaking over her, and she shook like a leaf, swaying on the narrow river of stone. Panic rose within her as the ground below seemed first much too close and then far too distant. With effort, she steadied herself and looked directly at the duke. "Gotta go, Ig," she said as casually as she could. Then she turned, took a deep breath, and leapt into the sky.

This time she remembered to keep flapping her wings. Even so, the strong winds around the castle ruffled her dress like a torn kite, and she found she could not guide nor control her flight. Terrified, she felt herself being dragged down with the wind, towards the dark rocks scattered beneath her. Using her wings as a makeshift glider, she was barely able to angle her descent over the outer trees before descending into the shadows of the forest.

The last thing she saw was a flash of silver through the branches. Then she screamed some very un-lady-like things as she plummeted down into the wildwood like some rare, exotic bird that had lost the gift of flight.

Chapter 5

Gil watched the castle grow bigger as he trudged through the trees, and thought about all the people who lived there. Even the lowliest among them probably had it better that he did since they were blessed with a roof over their head and daily meals. He always believed that if you lived a good, simple life, if you were noble in character and helped those in need, that everything else would fall into place such as financial security, happiness, and the love and adoration of one's knightly peers. It wasn't so much a philosophy where one made their own luck, but rather where life finally noticed what a rotten time you've been having, and then paid you back.

As luck and life would have it, he hadn't eaten a good meal in days; his whole body itched every time he took a step (although it was getting a little better); and he looked like a walking junkyard, his armor scratched and dented. Worst of all, he couldn't help but wonder if he was really on the right track or merely hopelessly lost. How he wished for just one glimpse of the map again, one more look, to ease his worries and give him assurance that things would turn out okay. Surely this was Havenwood Castle he approached, but where was he to go after that?

On he went down the narrow forest road, his thoughts becoming more and more introspective as his situation became clear. Almost from the beginning he had been the laughingstock of the knightly order. While others were slaying their first dragons and rescuing princesses, surrounded by a glittering hoard or at least dying in the attempt, he was being chased out of the caves by angry bears or mucking about in empty swamps. Unbelievably, he had never seen a dragon, let alone engaged such a creature in battle, nor even heard its eerie cry as it passed high overhead.

That is, until three days ago in Findris. The memory of that encounter was painful for Gil. It was just another reminder of how inadequate he was. He had spoken of it to no one, not that he had met many other travelers in the days since. People tended to keep to themselves in their village or town, only venturing out if there was no other choice.

His only hope was that he would somehow be successful in his battle with Guldrum. Perhaps in that way, he could erase his current legacy as a laughingstock. Other knights and local townspeople had started to call him Nil over the years, because he had failed time after time to see even a beast's harmless shadow. "Hey, Sir Nil!" they hailed to him from across the street or in the pub. "How's the Dragonless Knight this fine evening?" Then they would chuckle and shake their heads.

Gil really hated that nickname, but he could understand it in a way. Other knights had failed in their quests, whatever they were, but they at least had a story to tell or a legacy that would live on. He had nothing to show for any of his efforts, not a scratch or injury or even a semi-heroic kill of a minor creature. Each unfilled quest and every derisive comment followed him like a shadow growing longer and longer. *I am a failure, completely and utterly,* he realized for perhaps the first time. The shock hit him like a thunderbolt, and weighed him down with numbness. He had wasted years for nothing. If only he had picked a simpler profession, something less extravagant. But that was exactly the reason he had chosen knighthood. There was danger, the noble struggle of good versus evil, and not least of all, the fair young maidens and mountains of treasure.

None of that was his and never would be, he knew now. How naïve he had been! Self-pity gripped him like a dragon's claw, squeezing the last scraps of integrity from him and leaving him for pulp. Suddenly the rusting armor about his limbs seemed to take on a new weight, as if the price of failure was a physical entity which must be borne but cannot. His father had always hoped Gil would become a shoemaker, literally following in his footsteps. The unspoken plan was that Gil would take over the business that had been started by his grandfather. But he had always wanted something more. Not content in watching other people have adventures, Gil had gone out looking for his own. He was still looking.

Youthful exuberance was gone. In its place descended a strange world-weariness. Gil felt his former life drain out and a bitter, empty satisfaction take its place. So it was that as he half-walked, half-staggered down the forest path towards the castle, he swore a new oath, recanting his knightly vows. "I am finished with that life," he said with dramatic finality, but Gil had always been a dreamer and had never given much thought to what else he could be.

Following the road's gentle turn, he came into a stand of stately cottonwoods, their high branches casting long, elegant shadows across his path as the afternoon sun continued its long, lonely journey.

Chapter 6

Duke Ignot braced his hands on the battlement, digging his fingers in the stone ever tighter as he leaned into the empty air. Far below, past the tumble of shipwrecked rocks, somewhere in the green canopy of leaves Princess Oreola had disappeared, and been lost from sight.

Gone! He clenched his hands now, but his anger was hollow and the snarl that he wore turned inwards towards despair. What was he to do? All his future plans were predicated on wedding the king's daughter. Terror at having lost her gripped his mind as the wind rushed past, tossing his hair callously this way and that as if he didn't matter. Her father might very well blame him, he realized, looking anxiously around the deserted courtyard. The foolish girl was alone in the dangerous woods. He had to take charge of the situation before it was too late.

His horse was in the nearby royal stables. It would entail nothing more than a simple pretense to have the gates opened. Then he could search for the girl on his own. She couldn't get far on foot and without help. Getting her back inside the castle walls was problematic, however. Escorting her by force would be noisy and messy. Eyebrows would be raised and feathers ruffled. He couldn't risk jeopardizing her family's favor.

And then he realized what had to be done. It was the only way. It was the darkest road, but it was his only chance at getting what he wanted. The king and queen must be told, and he would have to deliver the message himself.

Slamming his fist down on the pale lip of stone, he turned back to the stairs. He walked down them slowly, steadily, his new resolve carrying him across the courtyard towards the dark keep and the royal chambers.

Chapter 7

Gil struggled on into the golden-leafed trees that encircled the castle like a liberating army. Taking out a small wooden birdcall, he put it to his lips and blew a mournful, lonely sound. Moments later, a wispy white bird with trailing feathers of black flew into view and circled him from above before departing suddenly. All was strangely quiet, he noticed, a stillness hanging in the air as if the forest had been shocked into silence.

From somewhere above, a voice groaned. Gil looked up toward the sound, his hand immediately reaching for the hilt of his sword. Almost directly overhead was a woman, adorned in an airy dress so blue it appeared as if a piece of the sky had fallen. She was sprawled across the lowest branch of a nearby tree, her face turned away. On either side of her were enormous copper-dyed wings made of cloth, with a lattice-work of wood running across it on the underside. The strange contraption was badly ripped, as was her dress, he noticed with a start, catching more than a glimpse of slender bare legs as they dangled into view.

Tearing his eyes away, he cupped his hands around his mouth. "Are you hurt?" he called up to her. Slowly the figure began to move, but made no reply. It wasn't until she was almost to the edge of the branch that he realized the danger. "Stop!" he shouted desperately. "You're in a tree!"

But he was too late. At about the same time he called out the warning, she put out a hand to steady herself and found only air. Gil watched her fall off the limb as if it were in slow motion. But he had no time to think, hardly enough time to act. Flinging out his arms, he just barely caught her, taking most of her body across his shoulders and head. Then his knees buckled and he fell to the ground, spilling her onto the ground with a clatter of armor and wings.

He lay there momentarily stunned for a few moments, his body tangled up with hers. Gil thought perhaps he caught the whiff of something fragrant, perhaps the hint of perfume, as she lay sprawled across his armor. Then he remembered himself and gently rolled her off of him. That's when he saw her face. Surely this was the reason songs were sung by troubadours. The woman was truly beautiful, with short-cropped black hair and full lips. The dress she wore was like cool water, and he took in each rise and fall of her body like a sailor who has been on dry land too long. So enraptured was he that Gil didn't immediately notice her state. The woman sported a series of scratches on her cheeks and arms. A bruise blossomed on her forehead and a deep gash marred her lovely hand. Her eyes were closed.

"My lady," Gil said gently as he bent over her. "Can you wake?" Soon the woman's eyes fluttered open, but she seemed distracted and disorientated. "You're hurt," he continued. "I have a salve that should take some of the sting away. Let's start with that hand if you please." He reached into his pack and brought out a small glass vial. Removing the decanter, he smeared some thick white paste onto his finger and then reached out to ease her suffering.

The man's eyes came into sudden focus and she sat up. "You will not have my hand, Duke Ignot. Do you hear me! I'm not for sale and I will never marry you."

A trickle of blood ran from his nose and he was too confused to pay it much heed. The woman was making no sense. He scrambled up and took a step back. "Are you alright?" he asked. "I don't know who you are talking about. I was travelling through the forest. You took a pretty bad fall. I think you may be dazed."

Now the woman crinkled her nose. She seemed to be studying him, reassessing the situation. Lifting a hand, she put it to her head as if in pain, or perhaps to steady her vision. "I'm sorry," she managed. "I thought you were someone else."

"I promise I won't try to marry you," Gil stammered. "But would it be all right if I applied this healing ointment?"

The woman sighed and then struggled up to a sitting position. "Just give it to me," she said. "I can do it. I think I'm feeling a little bit better." Gil handed her the container and tried not to notice as their hands touched for one brief moment. "Listen," she began as she rubbed the cooling cream across her abrasions. "I don't even know you. This hasn't been a great day for me. My name is Oreola."

"The princess!" Gil sputtered bowing awkwardly. "Of course. I mean I've heard of you. In passing. When you live in Rundle, you aren't exactly at the political center of the Seven Kingdoms. I just didn't expect to come across you in the forest, slung over a tree."

"And you? Do you have a name?" she asked, one eyebrow raised.

"Gil," he said. "Well, really Sir Gilwin, but everyone calls me Gil. And sometimes other things as well, but that's not important. We won't talk about that."

Oreola narrowed her eyes and pushed back the pain in her head. "You're a knight?" she asked. It was not entirely self-evident. Gil's armor was ill-fitting and his features were boyish.

Gil stiffened. Royalty or not, she had hit a nerve. "I am indeed," he proclaimed, not wanting to embrace his change of heart quite yet. "Almost three years now. Enemies fear me and songs will eventually be sung about my exploits."

Belatedly he felt the tickle of blood again above his lip from where she had landed and wiped it away brusquely with his hand. "Oh dear," she said. "I think you've smeared it a bit."

He tried again. "Better?"

"I think so. So a knight, you were saying? I didn't mean to question you. I don't suppose I look much like a so-called proper lady right now." It was true. She was covered in cuts and scratches. Her dress was torn. Leaves and small twigs adorned her cropped hair.

"You look like you've simply taken a stroll in the country," Gil said diplomatically. "It's good for a princess to get out of the castle walls and see the sunshine of the world occasionally."

"Only trouble is, I don't want to be a princess," Oreola retorted. "That's why I left."

"But why?" he began, but one look from her and Gil silenced his tongue. Oreola glared at him, angry and beautiful all at the same time, her eyes piercing his armor like an accusation.

"It's a long story," she said, trying to stay calm. "I don't remember a lot after I left the castle. Tell me what happened. How long have I been here? People may be looking for me." The princess darted glances around her. "Well?" she asked.

It wasn't really a question, but Gil felt if he didn't answer her soon, she would rush him with her bare hands. The only trouble was he didn't know very much. "You were among the birds," he answered at last, trying to smooth over her concerns, worried that she may have suffered more in her fall than she realized. "I caught you when you fell out of the tree. Right there." He lifted his head up and pointed a silvery arm.

Her eyes widened as she took in the wreckage strewn across the branches. "My wings!" she cried. Loss and disbelief crisscrossed her face, finally giving way to a slowly spreading smile; like the sun after a long, cold rain, thought Gil. "I did it." She laughed out loud. Gil was taken aback by her sudden change of emotion. "I really did it! Sir Ignot and all the other courtly fools be damned. I did it! I'm free!" Suddenly she stopped and stared at him as if she really hadn't noticed him before. "Did you say you were a knight?" she asked, leveling her gaze at his scratched and tarnished armor. "My troublesome suitor is a duke as well as a knight in the royal battalion. Why do men always think they know what's best for a woman?"

Gil hesitated and then let the words spill out of his mouth. "Actually, I'm not one anymore," he admitted. "A knight, I mean. Officially, I gave it up earlier today."

Oreola shook her head in consternation. "Then why did you stop and help me?"

"That's a very good question," Gil said, thinking he would have been better off had he just left her. "Saving strange, beautiful princesses who fall out of trees is just the sort of job I don't do anymore."

"There's nothing strange about me," she stabbed like a dagger aimed for his heart. "And stop calling me a princess." She stopped abruptly as her cheeks reddened. "I'm just Oreola. I'm a princess no longer. I've escaped and left that life behind." She looked up to her wings again with longing. "It wasn't easy."

Gil knew from her injuries and the wreckage of her contraption that it hadn't been. If she had fallen into his life a day earlier, he would have welcomed it as a chance to do heroic deeds. But that old Gil was gone. There was no turning back. *A princess!* he thought incredulously. A runaway princess, no less. That's the last thing he needed to get mixed up in. He had been looking forward to a hot meal up in the castle before continuing down the path. Clearly, that was impossible now. He couldn't very well leave her alone in the woods.

"Yeah, I bet it's pretty rough being a princess," he said more harshly than intended. "They must torture you a lot. Make you eat three meals a day, bat your eyes and sleep by the fireside."

Oreola fiercely ignored him. "You wouldn't understand," she said. An uneasy silence grew between them.

"Listen," said Gil as levelly as he could. "You must have crashed pretty hard into those trees when you came down, and then you fell out of the tree onto the ground. Maybe you should just lie down for a while and rest." He paused and then continued awkwardly, "Your head must be addled. Why else would you give up all that luxury?"

"Addled!" spat Oreola. "Are you a doctor now as well? I've never felt better." She proceeded to pick the detritus of the forest from her hair.

Gil scrutinized her for a long, thoughtful moment. "I don't think you ever were a princess," he said. "They have better manners."

Oreola fixed him with a look of pure hatred. "Where am I?" she demanded. There was an anxiousness to her voice.

"Harpstruck Forest," answered Gil weakly, as if the conversation had sapped the last bit of his strength. "I think."

"What do you mean, you think?"

"I'm not from these parts, remember? I travel the Seven Kingdoms, but I'm originally from Rundle." He paused. "I lost the map I had. From what I can tell, that's where we are. Havenwood Castle is about a mile back."

Oreola's eyes narrowed as if she were sensing danger. "I thought I went farther," she said softly to herself. Another silence fell between them. She filled it up almost immediately, her voice suddenly hard. "Listen, it was nice meeting you and everything, but I have to go. The duke and my father will be looking for me. I'm sorry we got off on the wrong foot. It's been one of those days. Thanks for catching me." With that, she turned and walked off the road into the forest, her slim figure winding around the trees as if she were dancing.

"Anytime," he called after her without thinking. *What a stupid thing to say,* he thought, wondering why he was so embarrassed.

As he watched, Oreola disappeared behind a tree, only to reappear a moment later further on. Slowly, the distance between them grew. In a few more minutes the forest would swallow her up and she would be gone from sight and out of his life. "Wait!" he yelled. "Where do you think you're going?"

"Away," she replied, picking her way through the foliage. "To my new life."

"How?"

Alongside the weathered pillar of a cottonwood tree she stopped and turned around. "What do you mean?"

"How are you going to survive?" he asked. "What are you going to eat? How will you protect yourself against thieves and wild animals? Even if you make it to the next village, do you have any money?"

Oreola's face flushed with anger. She hadn't thought of any of those things. Not really. Getting away had been her only goal, the only thing that mattered. That fool had interrupted her before the preparations had been complete. Suddenly she felt naked and naïve in the woods. *Damn!* The ex-knight was right. Slowly she began walking back to him, her arms hanging limply at her sides, her once purposeful stride now lazy and reluctant. Only her head remained upright, her eyes smoldering, waiting only for the tiniest opportunity to ignite. She said nothing as she stepped back onto the hard dirt of the road. Before she took another step towards him, she halted, as if any closer proximity would complete her defeat. There she waited, sullen and silent.

"You can travel with me if you like," he said hesitantly. "I don't have a lot of food, but what little I have is yours, though it probably is not what you're used to. The sword I carry should be enough to protect us."

Oreola stared at him, her mouth contorted into a forced smile. "Your hospitality gladdens my heart." Then she added with an air of resignation, "Where are you going?"

"To the home of Guldrum," he began, but something seemed to choke off the words before he could say any more.

"Who's that?"

Gil hesitated. "A dragon."

The princess stared back in disbelief. "Are you kidding me? A dragon?!"

"I know it's not ideal."

"Ideal? You know I'm a virgin, right? Being a princess and everything, and not a tavern wench?"

"Listen, you don't have to come. I understand how ludicrous this is. I'm not excited either. My first dragon encounter wasn't exactly a success. But if you do come, I can keep you safe." He leaned toward her. "I promise. You can wait outside until I'm—finished. Then we can find a village for you. And it would be nice to have some company. I've been on my own for a while."

The princess shook her head in exasperation. "What choice do I have? You're my ex-knight in tarnished armor." Gil looked back down the road. It was empty. He breathed a sigh of relief. "Anything else you forgot to tell me?" she asked sardonically. "Are you a werewolf, maybe?"

"Not that I'm aware of," Gil said dryly. Part of him was aware that they only had an hour or so of daylight left, but he tarried a moment longer. "Pretty funny, isn't? You and me, I mean." He tried to laugh but it sounded more like a bark. "A princess who's no longer a princess and a knight who's no longer a knight, having an adventure together."

She only glared at him. "Yeah, it's right out of a story book."

They began to walk down the forest path. Gil took the lead while Oreola followed a few paces behind. After a short time she turned back and scanned the trees for a long moment. But her wings were gone, already lost in the darkening leaves of the forest.

Chapter 8

The last dying rays of the sun spread across the rim of the forest as ten riders rode briskly through the gate, their torches blazing. Duke Ignot sat woodenly atop his steed and watched as they passed. Precious time had been lost waiting for an audience. Even more had been wasted convincing the king of his innocence and that he should lead the search party.

When the last man had breached the gate, standing silent with the others, the torch-wraiths burning high in a flickering line, the duke strode out from the wall until he reached the head of the riders, where the banner of Naloave fluttered in the gentle breeze. Then he turned slowly back to Havenwood Castle. There, high atop the battlement, surrounded by counselors and functionaries and royal mages, was the king and queen, dressed in full courtly regalia. As usual, the queen stood a few steps back from her husband.

Slowly, in the ghostly light of twilight, the king raised his hand out to the gathering night as if he alone could stop it. The last thing Ignot saw before turning and galloping toward the forest was the king's finger pointing directly at his head. It was not a comforting image, and the duke swallowed nervously.

"Bring my daughter back!" the ruler of Naloave commanded.

Chapter 9

Dusk turned to darkness without a word between them. After only a few miles, Oreola had surprised Gil and taken the lead, marching off ahead as if it was she and not he who was on a quest. *A quest,* he thought bitterly. *More like a forced march.*

In the blackness the road disappeared, swallowed up by the menacing forest. As he walked, he tensed at each utterance of the trees, every rustle of leaves or shadowy movement. It was not smart to travel after sunset. Bandits and worse ruled the darkness. Even with his fellow knights they had been cautious. No one traveled at night unless they were desperate or foolish. He had a feeling they were both. There was a sliver of moon overhead and the stars shone through the canopy of branches, but the light was pale and feeble, as if hope were something wholly inadequate.

Gil stared ahead at Oreola's slender back and labored to keep up. *What was the hurry?* he thought. They had seen no sign of pursuit. Nothing could be so pressing; not even his urgent message to the dragon could justify trouncing through the night without rest or sustenance. He was hungry and tired and getting more and more angry with each step. He was just about to call a halt when a flicker of light broke through the trees and bobbed toward them on the road behind them. This was quickly followed by half a dozen more. They were still distant, a mile or more away, yet their glare was acute and alarming. Instinctively, he knew they meant trouble.

Hustling forward in his weighty armor, he caught up with Oreola and began to explain anxiously what he had seen. Almost at once she cut him off. "I know, damn it! I've seen them already."

"Who are they?" he said sharply, irritated that she had noticed the torches before he did.

"My rescue party," she answered bitterly. Gil only gaped at her as if she had spoken in a foreign language. "Don't you remember?" she began. "I ran away. They're looking for me. I'm a princess and a would-be bride. They're trying to save me and bring me back."

"Who is trying to save you?"

"The king and queen of course; my parents. And probably Duke

Ignot as well, one of my more aggressive suitors," she explained with disdain. "My father will forfeit the duke's life if I'm not found."

Gil grabbed her shoulders and whirled her around to face him. "The king and queen!" he breathed. "Are you crazy? You can't be her!"

"Why can't I? The castle is just a few miles back. I said I was a princess. Are you deaf as well as stupid?"

Gil stared back at her as if she were a ghost. His mouth hung open and his eyes were fixed ahead, as if he could plainly see the day of his death. "So that's what this is all about," he said at last. Oreola shook her head in disbelief, but Gil continued before she could cut him off. "That's why we're walking. Why I'm grinding my bones down to dust just trying to keep up with you. You're a fugitive. A royal runaway. You don't want to get caught. But do you come right out and tell me? Do you take me aside and do me the simple courtesy of letting me know that it's dangerous to simply be seen with you? No!" he yelled with sudden fury.

Stepping forward suddenly, Gil grabbed Oreola's slender hand and shook it like a snake that had just bitten him. "You, you just strut up ahead like some goddamned peacock, and I follow. I follow," he repeated, breaking into ragged, sawtooth laughter. "I have half a mind to turn you in myself. I'm sure there's a dandy reward."

"Another hero cashes in," she said bitterly, twisting in his grasp. "It figures. I thought you might actually want something more than money."

"What could you possibly have that I would want?"

"My hand in marriage."

Gil sneered at her, unable to believe what he was hearing. "Surely the lady jests. I save you, I invite you to travel with me, I offer you my protection and a share of what little meager food I have left, and for all that I can either die or marry you. What kind of choice is that?"

Oreola's voice was strangled with emotion now, as if she was choking on his words. "You're no catch yourself!" she fumed. "I no sooner escape from the likes of your kind that I find myself on my merry way to meet a dragon with a lost knight for my guide, with little food and even less common sense. I should've stayed in the castle. At least the dangers there were more predictable."

With a vicious spin, Oreola unlocked her hand from his, only to have Gil grab onto her arm as she spun away. "I wish you would have!" he shouted, turning the princess back around so she faced him. Something in him broke after uttering those words. Perhaps it was his own realization of how improper he was acting, even for an ex-knight. Perhaps it was the sudden thought that his voice could be carrying through the woods. Then again, perhaps it was the momentary look of hurt that passed over the princess's beautiful face and the feel of her skin through the cool fabric of her dress.

"When they find us—and they will—with both you and I traveling away from the castle, what excuse will I have besides lunacy?" he asked, but there was no anger or mockery now in his tone, just a resigned acceptance. "I didn't ask for this, you know," he continued, his voice trailing off. "I have my own problems. Even so, I'm sorry. Sorry for this quest I'm on." The dragon's words flared in his memory for an instant before he could extinguish them. *You will take the map. You will go find Guldrum. Guldrum the Lost. Guldrum the Strange. Five days I give you, no more. Then we will come.* Only two days remained. "Let's make the best of it," Gil managed. "Like you said, what choice do we have?"

Oreola looked back at him and then away through the night-veiled trees, her expression torn between fear and something he could not name. "Oh, we always have a choice. Lead on, sir knight," she said in forced mockery.

Belatedly, Gil realized he still had his hand on her shoulder. Through the fabric of her dress, he could feel her slender body trembling. "Listen," he began. "We need to find cover. We need to…"

But Oreola pulled away from his grasp. "We need to go!" she said. He could only stand and watch as she walked off into the darkness down the road. Soon, though, she faltered and stood like a shadow lost within the greater night. Standing there, she looked like a frightened little girl. Gil studied the princess with concern. Behind her the moon was rising through the trees, casting an eerie glow across the land-scape. "Troll's tolls," she heaved out into the stillness.

Somehow Oreola managed to take one more step before Gil caught up. "We need to get off the road," he said quickly. "Now. Your friends are coming and they'll be searching." He waited for her to move, but the princess looked as if she hadn't heard him. "There's no time," he said urgently. "Your pursuers are on horseback. That much is obvious from their speed. Only the darkness hinders them. We must leave the road before it is too late." He motioned to the forest all around them. "Our only chance is the cover of the trees."

Oreola shook her head and locked her teeth in place. "What is wrong?" he asked. "The choice is plain."

"I'm frightened," Oreola told him, although it was obvious to Gil that the admission was hard. "The woods. I've never liked them. Especially at night."

Looking into her anxious eyes, Gil tried to reassure Oreola the best he could. "We'll go into them together. I'll be right beside you, but we have to hide. It's the only way. Are you ready?" She took a tentative step toward the trees, but at that moment something rustled and she froze again, cursing under her breath. "I can't carry you, princess," he said with growing frustration. "The woods here are too thick. Take my hand and we'll go in together." He fumbled for her hand in the darkness, but she resisted, pulling away. "Suit yourself," he said, striding away into the thicket, his armor crashing into bushes and low-hanging branches, leaving the stubborn princess behind.

Oreola stood there alone and looked back down the road. The flames were closer now, bobbing like vengeful spirits. When she listened, over the sound of her own heartbeat she could hear the echoing sound of hoofbeats approach like growing thunder. Whirling away, she ran into the dark embrace of the trees, following the dwindling sound of Gil as he labored through the blackness.

Then suddenly he too was gone. The sinister forest enveloped her. No friendly sound came from the menacing trees. No voice softly hailed from the silent recesses. No movement arose from the emptiness or signaled for her to come. She looked around wildly, racing onwards to nowhere. From under her a rotted tree gave away and she nearly fell, staggering to a halt.

She felt abandoned, lost and terrified. Nightmares spun at her feet as she peered into a dark hole of the imagination. There were creatures she could not name and had never seen, but they hunted in her dreams. Folk tales told by king and pauper alike, the monsters had grown bigger over the years, fed by her own fears of freedom and failure. They were always in the woods, hiding in the scant moonlight, waiting for her to come. Yet here she was, a grown woman, finally over the castle walls and on her way. She hadn't failed. She hadn't given up. Clenching her fists, she breathed deeply until she got a hold of herself. She had to keep moving!

Willing herself into motion, she began working her way carefully through the trees. Slowly, she became aware of every sound she made, every twig she stepped on, every branch that scratched the solitude like a violation. Even her breathing became an unnecessary disturbance to the fragile stillness that surrounded her. When the hand reached out of the darkness, covering her mouth, and a heavy weight pressed her to the ground, she imagined both the duke and a faceless monster, and knew not which was worse.

"It's me, Gil," the voice whispered from above, as metal and moonlight fused in a fanciful pattern before her eyes. "Don't make a sound," he said. "They're down below." Through the trees, at the bottom of the gently sloping land, she could see them, figures on horseback with eleven torches burning. The riders weren't moving, but instead seemed to be pondering the night, looking for some hidden sign. Suddenly the lead flame bobbed, starting forward, and the others followed suit, horse and rider moving in an eerie parade down the midnight etched road.

Letting his breath out, Gil relaxed slowly, then removed his hand from Oreola's frozen, agape mouth and lifted her gently to her feet. "That was close," he sighed, looking down at the now empty road. "Are you always this much fun?"

"I don't need your help," she said distantly, still smarting from being abandoned, but also embarrassed that she needed saving.

Gil turned back and looked at her, as if taking in a new measure of her. "I'm proud of you," he said simply. "That couldn't have been easy. Coming into the darkened forest, I mean."

A retort wilted on her lips, overtaken by a sudden exhaustion. Instead of squirming away from his support, she lazily surveyed the moonlit area around her. Except for a large tree nearby, this section of the forest seemed relatively open. The ground was flat and seemed soft beneath her feet, carpeted in some thick weed or grass. Releasing his hold on her, she stood up. "Thanks for trying to help me," she began. "That was sweet. I've never been very good with people doing things for me, strange as that might seem."

Gil nodded and then reached down to touch her shoulder briefly. "Well," he said, looking around, "this is as good a place as any to spend the night." Opening his satchel, he unrolled a tattered sleeping blanket, big enough for one. "You can have it. I'll sleep close by. We should be safe through the night, now that they've passed."

Oreola didn't argue, but her heart was still racing. Even after lying down on the modest bed, she found that her head was still full of worries that clamored for attention. "Are you sure they won't come back?" she asked.

"They're probably miles away by now."

"And these woods. Will we be safe?"

"I swear it. It is true that the forest contains things we do not understand, but the light of day usually causes these concerns to shrink down to normal size. Rest assured, I will stay vigilant. In the meantime, if it makes you feel better, I will tell you a story. It used to help me when I was new to the road when someone would share a tale." When Oreola didn't object, Gil sat down by a tree, the rough bark biting into his back and began the tale.

"In a kingdom so ancient its name is lost to time, there sat the queen of the giants on a throne made from the bones of all the animals she had killed. The queen was a powerful figure with arms as big as a tree trunk, and hands so large they could cover the top of a volcano or carry an army of puny humans to the battlefield. She was also very vain and insecure. Mirrors lined the throne room where she received her subjects, casting her reflection on every wall. Dazzling earrings the size of plump fruit hung from her ears, while her garments were spun in the most dazzling colors. In all the world, the queen liked nothing better than to be noticed and obeyed.

The empress of all the giants could control almost everything in her kingdom. She could expect a loyal gaze and silent tongue. The denizens of the towering castle always did what she demanded at any time of day or night. Highly trained courtiers attended to the queen's every whim, while armored warriors guarded the gate, ready to strike at a moment's notice. Citizens throughout the land bowed down when the royal carriage rumbled through town. She was the center of her own orchestrated world. Only one thing eluded the empress. She could not command the wild creatures that lived in the forests and mountains and meadows throughout her domain. In the hidden places where giants and people did not go. That is why she organized great hunting expeditions to rid the countryside of animals both big and small. Giants with colossal nets swept across the wide, open spaces, capturing creatures in teeming masses while armies of human servants used blade and arrow to finish off the rest. Only one beast eluded capture or worse. Its continued existence was a source of supreme frustration to the queen of giants, made all the more infuriating because the offending creature was so puny and insignificant. That lowly creature was a…"

Here Gil paused for dramatic effect, looking over at the princess. To his surprise, Oreola was fast asleep and quiet as a mist mouse, the moonlight falling softly on her face. His skills as a storyteller rivaled that of a dragon slayer, he thought, somewhat annoyed. She looked so peaceful, quite the opposite of when she was awake.

With a sigh, Gil took up a haggard watch, still propped up against the tree, but the day had been long before meeting the princess and their frantic escape had robbed him of his remaining energy. Just before he fell into a deep slumber, he thought he saw movement in the trees below—small, half-familiar shadows scurrying upright that looked neither human nor animal—but then they were gone and dark dreams took him.

Chapter 10

The next morning dawned cloudy. Oreola opened her eyes. Gil was nearby. His armor lay at his side, and he was dressed modestly but effectively in light pants and a shirt. She took in his body. Somehow, he looked frail standing there, as if meals were sometimes hard to come by. His cheeks were a bit too hollow and his pants a bit too loose. Even so, there was a strength about him, something she could trust. On his face she could sense doubt, but also a deep reserve of integrity.

She watched spellbound as he put a small wooden device to his lips. Low elongated sounds filled the air. Every so often he would pause and look around, only to resume his playing. Finally, he set it down and looked up as three bright red birds fluttered just above his head. Removing a tiny morsel of bread from his satchel, he threw it on the ground. The colorful birds descended, pecking wildly, before flying off again.

Oreola coughed and Gil looked over. "Morning, princess," he grinned as she got up slowly and came over. "Breakfast is ready and the sun is up. I was beginning to think you were bewitched and I would have to wake you with a kiss." That he chided her was obvious, but his smile also seemed honest, an all too costly expression for the condition he was in. It was hard to imagine going hungry, having lived in comfort all her life. But she said nothing in return, only ignored his gaze, her mind still reeling from the events of last night and how she had let herself down, how she had embarrassed herself. Self-consciously she trekked off into the underbrush, heeding nature's call.

When she returned, he handed her a small piece of bread and a handful of tiny blackberries. Biting into the bread, she couldn't help but notice that it was stale. As she chewed her meal unenthusiastically, she looked around at her surroundings in the grey morning light. They were on top of a gentle ridge, with the road a narrow ribbon running down below through the trees. Turning around, she saw the land roll down to another narrow valley and then rise up again, only to repeat itself over and over again. Ripple upon endless ripple of ridges and valleys swept away from her, like green waves on the sea.

"That's where we're heading," Gil said, interrupting her reverie. He took a swig of water from the deerskin and handed it to her. Without saying a word, she took it and put it to her lips greedily. One gulp. Two gulps. Three gulps. Then a trickle. Then nothing. Oreola peered inside the opening, but not a drop remained.

"Don't tell me," she said slowly. "We're out of water?"

"Next time, don't drink so much. Guldrum's cave should be just past the last valley there," he said while pointing, his voice betraying a lack of certainty. "It's in that bare hill that sticks out. Do you see it?" Straining her eyes at where he pointed, she finally saw it at the very edge of her sight, a rocky gibbous rise. It looked like a common ridge that had been pushed together from both sides until it resembled a short, upraised finger. It wasn't what she'd been expecting at all. Where was the snow-capped mountain or misty lake? Wasn't this an adventure? What she was looking at was too mundane and ordinary. "There's bound to be a spring there," he concluded.

"Well, that's good news," she congratulated. "For a minute there I thought you were going to bring up the dragon that lives there and how he likes to kill and breathe fire over everything. I'm relieved to hear we're just going for the clear spring water."

Gil popped the last morsel of bread in his mouth and looked at her across the stump. "Feel free not to come with me," he said. "*I* don't even want to go."

"Then why are you?"

Grabbing his few belongings, he threw them into the satchel and then began putting his armor on, making sure there were no gaps, not today. "We need to get going if we want to get there with light to spare," was all he said, and Oreola, sensing something bitter just beneath the surface, decided for once not to push it.

After Gil had finished, they set off down the gently sloping ridge. By the time they reached the bottom, a steady drizzle was falling. Before they reached the bottom, Gil glanced back towards the trees, as if afraid someone or something might be following.

Chapter 11

The line of horses and men waited patiently in the rain as Duke Ignot crouched by the side of the road somewhere in the dank and dismal forest. In his palm rested a twig and a small fragment of leaf. He studied them carefully, meticulously, turning them over and over in his wet, dripping hands. Finally, he brought them closer to his face and then slowly raised them up to the swollen sky as he nodded his helmeted head slowly in a rite of final understanding.

He had no idea what they meant. Not a clue. He was merely using it for more time so he could come up with an answer. The princess's trail had vanished suddenly a few leagues from where the wings were found. Before it did, though, there were indications of another accompanying her, someone armored and wearing heavy boots, or so his stubby-horned Tracker had said, standing in the moonlight last night. But then they had both disappeared. He and the other mounted knights had ridden half the length of the road all night and had seen no sign.

There was only one explanation, of course, although he was hesitant to accept it, even though his young Tracker was insistent. They had diverged from the road and were even now traversing the wildwood or its outlying areas. *Damn that insolent wench!* the duke thought. Their horses would be near useless in the trees, with a pace akin to racing snails. Being no fool, he was also not keen on entering the woods. Dark spirits and creatures of the night were fabled to dwell in its depths, waiting for the unsuspecting visitor. And the rolling plains which stretched around the forest were little better, offering scant protection against creatures of the air, even dragons if you were especially unlucky.

"Childish stories," he murmured, shaking his head as if to clear it of folly. Then he splashed back to his horse, swinging himself up to the saddle, and with a wave of his hand led them off the road and into the waiting trees. Nothing would stand in his way of getting the king's daughter and his bride-to-be back.

Chapter 12

Valley and ridge. Ridge and valley. Over and over and over. It was enough to make the heartiest travelers seasick. By late afternoon the aggravating drizzle had turned to cold misery. It came down in sheets and soaked through Oreola's clothes, turning the ground where she stepped into rivulets of mud. Beside her Gil trudged on, his mood darkening with the swollen sky above. The raindrops pelted his armor, rang in his ears and stung his soul. He felt like a failure for what he had to do. Up ahead, through the misty rain he tried to gauge how close they were, but the world was obscured in gray. To allay his mounting fears, he decided to start up a conversation. "Tell me again," he sputtered through the wet and cold. "Why did you run away?"

She turned to him for the first time in over an hour. Moisture dripped from her slick, black hair and ran streaking down her face. Her mouth curled in reproach. "Don't you mean, how *could* I have run away when I had it so good?"

"I really want to know. Why did you?"

She gave him a long, hard look. Finally, she replied, "I wanted to be someone," her voice barely rising over the sound of the rain.

He shook his head and frowned. "But princesses are someone."

"Castles can grow small. You'll probably ridicule me for admitting it, but I've never been beyond the walls of Havenwood. I wanted to see the world, like you I suppose, or my brothers. Can you blame me for not wanting to be sold into marriage like some animal in glittering clothes, all for some land or political maneuvering? That would be the proper thing to do. The expected thing. It's what my mother did, and now she's trapped, queen or not. I've spent my whole life doing what I'm told. Now it's my turn. I want something better. If I ever do get married it will be for love, not for money or king or country. It might be hard for you to understand that, but I want more out of my life."

Gil said nothing, letting the rain and words soak in. There was something about her honesty and spirit that touched him. Through her words he recognized a piece of himself and his own dreams. "So, who's after you?" he asked.

"The Duke, Sir Ignot," she spat out, her features distorting in distaste. "He wants to marry me and has convinced my father to go along with it. I ran away from him at the castle. He was trying to propose."

"You might have mentioned that when I first found you. If it helps, though, I don't think this duke will follow you where we're going."

Oreola stopped at the top of another rise and looked at Gil sternly but not unkindly. "You don't understand," she began. "It's not just the duke. My father has too much at stake to simply let me go, plus he hates to lose. As the king he can't afford to look bad, not with the provincial lords advocating for greater rights. I would have to take a ship all the way to the newly discovered Northern Lands to have any chance of being free. The journey is long and dangerous, with pirates and leviathans. Still, if there was any way…"

Gil nodded, trying to fathom the complexities of a family that would make her contemplate such a trip. It was difficult. His father had barely looked up from the shoe he was repairing when Gil had declared one hot summer day that he was joining the Knights of Regale instead of carrying on the family business. Even so, he knew how disappointed his father was. The silence had spoken volumes. A week later he closed the door to their tiny house for the last time, his father sitting alone within. Soon after, he crossed the boundary stones, leaving the backward kingdom of Rundle behind and setting out for a new life.

"Just why are you going to see this dragon, anyway?" she asked. "Can't you fight him later?"

"No," Gil said flatly, the question bringing him back to the present. "I made a deal." Then he resumed walking as Oreola hurried to catch up.

"What do you mean you made a deal?"

"I didn't have a choice. Seven days ago, I finally located a dragon I had been searching for in the west. It had been burning villages, stealing away young virgins, and generally just not being very nice. It was my quest and solemn duty as a Knight of the Regale to do battle with him and kill it."

"So, what happened?" she asked, genuinely curious. "Did you vanquish it?"

"Well, not exactly. It was a very big and powerful dragon with acute senses and heard me coming."

"You mean you were clumsy and made a lot of noise."

With supreme effort, Gil ignored her. "It towered over me in its cave by the sea and threatened to burn me with its magical flames unless I did it a favor."

"A favor?" Oreola asked incredulously. "Was that covered by your knightly vows? A favor for a murderous dragon?"

"Listen," Gil hissed. "I didn't have a choice. It was either do as the foul creature said or die horribly. I haven't done it yet, anyway. And I'm getting paid."

"So, what is this favor?"

Exasperated by the questions and his own rising fears, Gil finally exploded. "An exhibition!" he shouted. "I'm to put on a little show for Guldrum's family, okay? A fight to the death." Then more softly but with an added edge of sarcasm he added, "They're worried about him."

Before Oreola could ask another question, Gil held out his arm and stopped her forward progress. Putting a finger to his lips, he looked at her sternly and then away through the faltering rain into the near distance. Rising out of the gloom much closer than he would have liked was the hillock. Dead center was the entrance. The black maw of the cave reached back into the lifeless rock like a sliver of night. "No more talking," Gil whispered. "We're almost there." Unfortunately, a lake of mud lay between them and their destination. Oreola hesitated. "Maybe you should stay here," he recommended.

Oreola looked at the cave entrance up ahead and then at Gil. "Probably," she agreed. "Let's stick together, though. That feels safer to me. I won't get too close."

They continued on again, the sucking sound of their feet now echoing obscenely in the stillness as the mud grudgingly released its grip with every labored step. It was ridiculous and terrifying all at the same time.

"Where's your horse?" asked Oreola. "I thought knights were supposed to have noble steeds."

"Don't ask," Gil muttered as the rain took pity on them and finally ended. From out of the clouds in the western sky, the sun peeked out hesitantly, but up ahead the entrance to Guldrum's cave was dark, like it would rain there forever.

Chapter 13

A scrawny crawler, hardly bigger than a mouse, dragged itself silently over the rocks and across the rough stone floor of the dismal cave. It was emaciated, with sunken lines where ribs shone through. Wiry whiskers drooped on either side of its slack jaw, while short leathery legs trembled with effort. The final few feet were a tremendous struggle, since it had to conquer a gradual slope, but with one final heave the creature managed to stick its nose into the slender moonwort plant that grew near the entrance. Each leaf was outlined in a faint glow, illuminating the blood berries which hung underneath.

The crawler was just about to take a nibble when it sensed the lurking shadow in the dark cavern beyond. In alarm, the tiny animal saw the terrible shape move, emerging from the depths slowly and bringing with it a pungent odor of brimstone and decay. From out of the darkness blazed two red eyes; and beneath it, sharp, glittering teeth that protruded from a horrible mouth. The creature took one last look at the plant and then scurried off at an amazing speed.

Moments later, the dragon lifted its long serpentine neck up to the vaulted ceiling and opened its jaws wide, as if to bite the heavens or scorch the ceiling with fiery rage. Instead, though, from the very pit of its soul there rose out into the chamber the most pitiful sound imaginable. Lonely and forlorn, it echoed throughout the labyrinthine chambers and subterranean tunnels, finally reemerging into the cavern like a cry on the wind. *Not even a cave crawler!* the sound seemed to bellow. *Alone again!*

Just outside the cave entrance, beside a bush laden with berries the color of blood, Gil and Oreola were frozen in place. The sound of the dragon buffeted their ears like a hurricane, transfixing them to the ground like a shaft of terror. As soon as the echoes died away, Gil fought to speak and regain his composure. "You can stay here," he said slowly, quietly. "It's my job, not yours."

"You're not still going in there, are you?" she asked shakily, her voice hardly more than a whisper.

"I don't have any choice, remember? Just do yourself a favor and move off a safe distance and wait for me. I know what I'm doing."

Oreola's jaw hung open in disbelief. "Have you taken one too many knocks to the head? It'll kill you."

Gil started to speak, but then hesitated and looked at the cave entrance again. It towered over him and seemed to swallow him up. There was a distinct possibility that he would not walk out. Then he looked back at Oreola. She was just standing there with a worried look on her face. Something in him seemed to give way, like the last bits of his armor falling to the ground. "I've never really fought a dragon before," he admitted. "Actually, I've never even been in a fight at all." It was the most ridiculous situation, and because of it, a smirk curled on his lips like the beginnings of lunacy.

Oreola grabbed his metallic arm and looked him straight in the face. "This is crazy," she said, and then much more quietly, "You're crazy, do you know that?!"

"Listen," he tried to soothe, but failed miserably since he was on the verge of laughing hysterically. "Guldrum and I don't fight until tomorrow. That's when his family gets here. Right now I just need to go in and introduce myself. Explain the situation. It'll be okay. There's some cover around back. You should be safe." Then he turned away from her and dug in his pack. Removing an unlit torch, he struck a Starstone against the tip and then cursed under his breath. The torch was damp from the rain. Gil was forced to strike repeatedly before it finally blazed to life. Summoning what little remained of his dignity and courage, Gil lifted the torch in his shaking hand and walked into the mouth of the dragon's cave.

The torchlight evoked sinister shadows on the rough stone wall as he made his way slowly into the earth. Sulfur and brimstone hung in the air like hellish faerie dust and burned his nostrils. Where the entrance had been broad and expansive, the tunnel was even more so, growing wider in girth as if to accommodate some colossal beast. Following a gentle curve of the passageway, Gil left behind the feeble light of the outside world. With every step it seemed to grow colder, not warmer, which was odd since he was in a dragon's lair. By now his armor should have been heating up. Immersed in darkness with only the torch to illuminate his path, he scanned the dusty ground, expecting to find the bones of unfortunate victims or scattered treasure, but the ground was unusually bare.

A moment later he blinked in surprise, as the broad tunnel opened out and he found himself standing in a high-ceilinged cavern cast in a soft glow. Tapestries hung down from the ceiling in a colorful profusion. An emerald-colored dragon was lying in the center on a slightly raised rocky platform. The gentle light radiating from it waxed and waned in time with the creature's breathing. A long serpentine head was pressed down on the cavern floor like an act of defeat, while its slender tail snaked off into the veiling shadows. Golden wings were folded over the body as if for comfort.

Gil squinted, trying to make out more details of the creature, but the light was too insubstantial. One thing was clear, however. This dragon was not quite as big as the one that had ordered him here, but it was still terrifying for Gil to stand so close. "Hello," he offered nervously, his voice shaking with every syllable. "You must be Guldrum. My name is Gil, former knight of the Order of Regale. I have a message for you."

The dragon lifted its massive head slowly. "For me?" it said in a deep grating voice.

Gil stared back dumbfounded. It was not what he had expected. Not by a long shot. "Is everything all right?" he observed carefully. "Not coming by at a bad time, am I?"

"Even mouse won't come near," the dragon bellowed brokenly. Then, exhausted from the conversation, Guldrum let his head flop back down on the floor.

"Hmm," articulated Gil. "Sorry about that. Maybe my message will cheer you up, though."

As if it had forgotten all about that the dragon lifted its head up off the ground with a jerk. "A message? Yes, tell me!" But then immediately it became suspicious. "Why do you talk to me? No one talks to me. No one comes here. No one at all."

"Why not?"

The dragon seemed momentarily taken aback. "Because of what I am," it said at last, his voice echoing sadly in the grand cavern. "Not because of what I do. I try to be good and not steal or cause harm, but still no one comes near."

Gil didn't have the slightest idea what the creature meant. This wasn't going the way he thought it would, which wasn't all bad, since he very much had thought he might be dead by now. Even so, he decided to let the matter drop and fell back to a line of conversation he felt more comfortable with. "I have a message from your family, your dragon kin."

"Continue!" said the dragon, gaining renewed interest now.

"Rarluf wants me to tell you that they will all be here tomorrow. They've heard about your exploits. They want to see you and I fight," Gil gulped, "to the death, and then celebrate in your victory."

"Tomorrow?" asked Guldrum, getting up ominously on his forelegs.

Gil took a stumbling step backwards. "Tomorrow."

"To the death?" repeated Guldrum, now rising up on all four legs and cracking his long tail side to side like a whip.

The former knight of the Order of Regale forced himself not to run. "To the death," he agreed dismally, a cold lump growing in his throat.

Guldrum stared at him with burning red eyes. "I can't," moaned the dragon, and then threw back his head and cried a pitiful, terrible sound.

Gil covered his ears and waited until the last lonely notes had dissipated. "What do you mean you can't?" he responded. Now he was thoroughly confused. "You're a dragon, aren't you?"

"I don't know what I am," stammered Guldrum. "I'm not like other dragons."

"How's that?"

"I don't like treasure, for one thing. Gold makes my scales itch."

"I see. But that's just one small part of being a dragon. There's much more. What about burning villages?"

"No fire," said the dragon, sadly opening his massive mouth to reveal a benign darkness beyond the rows of teeth.

"That would make it a problem," Gil agreed, remembering how cool the cave had been. "But you must like virgins. Dragons always like virgins."

Guldrum shook his head morosely. "I'm a vegetarian."

Gil stood there speechless. "I'm not sure what's left."

As if on cue, the dragon leapt off the slab and swept across the cavern until it loomed almost directly above him. Gil didn't need the torchlight to make out the creature's glowing silver belly or glass-like talons. Its large crimson eyes looked down at him and seemed to blaze in timeless fury the secrets beyond the night. Gil retreated, taking several faltering steps. His hand fumbled for the hilt of his sword, but he couldn't quite grasp it.

"I don't fight knights either," Guldrum droned, sinking back down.

Gil wiped his forehead and let out a sigh of relief. "What do you do, then?" he asked at last.

At that, the dragon's countenance changed from one of despair to flickering hope and he popped back up. "I knit!" Guldrum bellowed proudly, and with a flourish pointed a taloned claw at the hanging tapestries Gil had only glimpsed earlier. Now he looked at them more closely. Many of them depicted landscapes in a kaleidoscope of color. There were high mountains, rolling green hills, bright forests and ocean sunsets. Vistas of sky and cloud peeked out from the cavern walls like windows to another world. There were also several puppies and pink unicorns. For a moment Gil was too astounded to speak, the revelation too sublime. "But why?" he asked at last.

Those two words broke the dragon's fragile mood and he turned his hulking form away. "Not much of a dragon, am I?" he sniveled.

Gil worked his way around to the front of the dragon again, making sure to stay well clear of his claws, and then began the tricky business of trying to make amends. "Well, I can't say I've ever met a dragon like you before. I've only met one other, and that was your uncle Rarluf."

"Uncle!" snorted Guldrum with a mixture of respect and disdain. "Now there's a dragon! I'm surprised he didn't kill you. It would have been no trouble for him at all. He always liked to kill something at least once per day."

"Yes, well," Gil paused awkwardly, "what I mean to say is I'm pretty limited in my experience in dragons, but I think it would be safe to assume that you're unique. That's not so bad, is it?" he said smiling. It was still hard to believe, but he thought just maybe he would get out of this whole mess alive after all. Then he remembered that Guldrum's uncle, the proper virgin-stealing, village-burning, knight-killing dragon, was expecting him to do battle. How could he kill a defenseless dragon? Even if he did, there would be a small army of outraged family members to deal with. Running away wouldn't work either. Rarluf had placed a spell of finding on him to ensure his cooperation. That's one of the reasons he had been forced to come to Guldrum's cave instead of simply wandering off. A promise to a dragon was not broken lightly or often. And then there was the promise of gold. Any way he looked at it, Gil was still screwed.

Guldrum gazed down at Gil for a long time, his eyes burning like hot coals. Gil held his breath and waited. "I'm doomed!" the dragon said at last, echoing what Gil felt inside. "They'll be here tomorrow and then my secret will be revealed. Everyone will know. Uncle will make me come away back home, where I don't want to go."

Having never comforted a dragon before, Gil was unsure how to proceed. This was new territory for him. Unfortunately, he wasn't any better at it then combat or bedding the fairer sex.

"Maybe I can help," hailed a female voice from the tunnel.

Gil stepped out from Guldrum's trembling mass and spun around to face Oreola. "What are you doing here?" he asked. "This is dangerous—"

"Oh, I can see that," Oreola interrupted, stepping into the cavern. "There's some very dangerous tears being shed here, as well as some very nicely done tapestries."

Removing his helmet, Gil did not try to hide his frustration. "Even so, I told you to hide, princess. It is not safe here. Especially in your —state."

Oreola looked down to hide her blushing. "I was worried about you," she said. Then she lifted her head and looked at him with a defiant smile. "When I didn't hear the sounds of battle, I thought perhaps you'd gotten lost or been gobbled up, so I came to investigate. Plus, I was tired of being wet."

"How long have you been here?" Gil sighed.

"Long enough," the princess responded, "to know what needs to be done."

"Which is what?" he asked in disbelief and irritation.

"You better practice swinging your sword," she responded sharply. "It's the only way to save us all."

"Didn't you hear him?" he retorted. "He doesn't want to fight. All we can do is wait for the big baddies to come and then just try to explain things. It's none of our business."

"What about his family?" she reminded him. "What about Guldrum's uncle? Don't they expect you to battle?"

Gil blinked. "Yes, but…"

"And are deadly dragons usually reasonable with young virgins who just happen to be lying around?"

Gil stared back. "Not as such," he stammered.

"Then it's settled."

Oreola turned her attention to Guldrum and steeled herself. Last night she had been afraid to enter the forest. Today she was standing in front of a living, breathing dragon. It was difficult to accept the fact that she had little to fear from this gentle beast beyond an errant movement or mistimed footfall. Even so, she imagined that Guldrum's teeth were just as sharp as any dragon, and his claws just as rending. Because of this, she positioned herself next to Gil just closely enough so that their arms were touching. "Guldrum," she began, "I assume your family wants you to act like a proper dragon. Have you ever lied to them?" The dragon hesitated. "It's important. Please answer."

"Since the Parting," he rumbled finally, "when all mature dragons leave to find their own cave, I may have taken the liberty of spicing up my correspondence a bit more than I should have."

"How much?"

"A lot. They think I'm on my 35th virgin."

"Oh dear," muttered Oreola. "Better make room for number 36, then. I have a plan. Tell me again how big your uncle is."

Chapter 14

Gil stood alone at the entrance to the cave and watched the dragons as they made their way steadily through the sky. The rain had passed, and it was a beautiful afternoon, although Gil was having trouble enjoying the idyllic quality of it, since there was a good chance he might die again today.

At first only shifting pinpoints, then looking like a harmless flock of birds on the horizon, soon the ominous smudges of Guldrum's family began to take on definition until finally they spread their great leathery wings almost directly overhead, blocking out the sun, their cold shadows falling like specters. Silently the five great dragons circled, then glided down and landed, their talons gripping the earth like it was merely prey to feast upon. They were all different variations of green with silver bellies and golden wings, just like Guldrum but larger, Gil observed. Each gazed down with eyes that smoldered red. Secrets burned there. Tendrils of smoke wafted from their nostrils. One by one the great beasts landed.

"I see you still have on your armor of invisibility," the grizzled dragon Rarluf remarked without humor. Its voice was muffled and seemed to be constricted because of a cold or illness. "Do you think it will be of better service to you this time?" it asked coldly.

Gil looked down sheepishly. "Can't trust anybody these days," he replied. "And I paid good money for it too."

"Well, human, it seems I was right to trust you," grumbled the dragon. "A fool you are not. I'm glad the map brought you to this place." Gil flinched at the mention of the disappeared document. It pointed at him and then waved its long talons in tight circles. The air around him began to shimmer. Abruptly the dragon stopped and made a pulling motion, and immediately the area stopped glowing, as if a candle had been blown out. "Won't need to find you again," it remarked. Then it turned. "I don't think you've met the rest of the hatch-kin." Gil shook his head stiffly. "To my left is Phalanx and Yaquindle, father and mother to Guldrum's sires, Grand Dragons respectively." They nodded gravely, almost imperceptively, like a tremor running through a mountain.

"To my right is Malaise and Tjeiva, brother and sister to Guldrum." He paused. "My name," trumpeted the dragon, eyeing Gil more sharply, "is Rarluf, as well you know. I am the boy's uncle. From across the Seven Kingdoms we have come, because we are concerned for Guldrum's future. By my invitation we have gathered here today to give witness. We have heard many good things from young Guldrum since he came to this place, but have seen no proof. May our doubts be eased. If not, then we will be forced to take him away."

Although Gil waited, the dragon said nothing more, remaining as intransigent as stone, gazing at Gil as though he could see right through him, like he didn't matter, and into the cave beyond. "Where are his parents?" asked Gil to put off the moment he dreaded. "Surely they should be here."

Slowly the dragon looked at Gil, as if finally noticing that he was still there. "His parents were slain by vile dragon smugglers when he was but a hatchling. I am his guardian now."

"I see," said Gil, nodding. "Did you raise his brother and sister as well?"

The dragon's eyes flashed impatience, but then recovered their timeless facet. "There was no need," Rarluf intoned icily, even as steam billowed out of his nose from some hidden chamber. "They were older and already Parted. Guldrum needed—special help. He became tainted when he was lost to us." For a moment the dragon appeared lost in thought, wrestling with an unpleasant memory. "We cannot delay further," rumbled Rarluf. "Is Guldrum within? Nephew?" he called. "Are you there?"

"He is," responded Gil. "A young maiden he keeps prisoner there."

The dragon's eyes lit up at these words. "Good! Good!" he snorted. "I had not dared to hope so great. Now it is time," the dragon hissed between jagged teeth. The others took their turns glaring venomously at Gil, who glanced nervously at the terrible creatures and hoped Oreola knew what she was doing. This was a dangerous game they were about to play.

"Go!" bellowed Rarluf. "We are too great to fit through the cave entrance. Here we shall remain, but we will be listening. Let us discover what Guldrum has become!"

Pulling his sword from its scabbard, Gil marched solemnly again into the mouth of the cave, just as a lost sounding cry rang from within. "I am coming, fair maiden! I am coming!" he called in return. "Prepare to die, oh lecherous thing," he echoed faintly as the darkness engulfed him and he was lost from sight. "Your evil stay upon this Earth is done."

Then, for a moment, there was nothing. Not a sound. Then the battle began in earnest from within the cavern. Outside the dragons heard a tremendous roar and the sound of savage, rolling thunder. Out of the entrance shot Gil. A clawed foot crashed horribly out of the darkness a heartbeat later, and Gil hit the ground, rolling out into the light. Springing up and crouching in the soft mud, he stared up at Guldrum with his sword raised above him in a final act of defense. *Bloody Hell!* thought Gil. *That was way too close.*

The dragon's jaws were stained a curious shade of berry-red, and tatters of once fine female clothing hung from its teeth like bloody rags. Spitting them out, Guldrum bellowed a hot spray of rage into Gil's helmeted face. "May you choke on her lovely bones!" Gil cried. "Satan's spawn and unearthly lizard, she will be avenged!" Striking like lightning, Gil whirled his sword above him in hot fury, driving Guldrum back in momentary surprise, into the cave where their harsh echoes lingered. Rarluf and the other dragons exchanged mildly curious glances but did not move.

Finally, a new and terrible sound reached out of the inky blackness. Louder than thunder, Guldrum's roar erupted from the cave entrance and swept away any remaining doubts. A moment later, the mournful cry of Gil the knight could be heard. Then it faded away to nothing. "Hello, uncle," greeted Guldrum as he emerged from the opening. His head and chest were spattered bright red in a spectacle of color. At his uncle's taloned feet, he proudly dropped a pile of metal scraps, all gnarled and grotesquely twisted. He looked up at his guardian and then fished around in his mouth before spitting out one final object, the metal helmet from his slain foe.

Rarluf looked at him sternly as he weighed the evidence. "That's my boy," he said at last, a snarl of pleasure spreading across his reptilian face. "That's *my* boy!"

Chapter 15

Gil and Oreola hid in the dark recesses of the cave, away from the light, under piles of thick knitted shawls and cozy tapestries, waiting for the dragons to leave. Under any other circumstances it might have been romantic. As it was, they could hardly breathe as they listened for the sign. They didn't have to wait long. With little to eat, and convinced that Guldrum was doing better than expected, the dragons left almost immediately. "Do something about your hoard, though," his uncle chided, peering into the empty space beyond the entrance. "Your cave is a disgrace." Reaching into a hidden fold of skin, he pulled out a small bag. It jangled noticeably. Then he gave it to his nephew. "To get you started."

Guldrum said his goodbyes and then watched patiently as they beat their great, leathery wings up into the noon-day sun. When the other dragons were completely gone from sight, he bellowed twice in signal, and Oreola and Gil sighed in relief, gladly emerging from their hiding place. "You were great!" congratulated Oreola as she picked some blood-berries from the bush near the cave entrance and placed one delicately in her mouth.

"Yeah, a real actor," seconded Gil. "It was an honor to be killed by you."

Guldrum looked down at them as unreadable expressions passed over his face. "I'm glad it's over," the dragon rumbled, slowly and deeply. "You were both very kind to help. But I wish I didn't have to wreck your armor, Sir Gil, or eat your clothing, Lady Oreola. Are you cold?"

Oreola looked down at the intricate weave of leaves and branches which covered her body from chest to thigh and let out a frustrated groan. "This part was your idea," she accused, leveling her gaze at Gil. "If I didn't know better, I would think you were just trying to get my clothes off. But your standards of chivalry would never allow it."

Gil smiled broadly. "I'm an ex-knight, remember? Anything goes."

Suppressing a laugh, she turned back to the dragon. "It is a bit breezy, "she admitted, motioning to her legs and bare shoulders. "A fire *would* be nice."

"And food!" boomed the dragon suddenly. "I have food, un-dragon-like morsels, hidden away. Let us celebrate! And there is a spring close by."

"I told you!" interjected Gil. "I knew there must be one around here."

"You will spend the night," continued the dragon, "for we must celebrate. And princess, it will give me time to knit suitable clothes before your journey."

Gil had wanted to put as much distance between the dragon hill and himself as he could, but Guldrum's enthusiasm was overpowering. He still wasn't used to staying in one place very long, but looking over at Oreola, he was surprised he could imagine putting down roots somewhere, someday. Tomorrow they would have a chance to be alone without the threat of dragons looming. That would be enough. "What do you say?" he asked Oreola. "One more night with our dragon host?"

She nodded in agreement. "Anything for clothes," Oreola said.

"*Anything*?" Gil chided.

"You see what I have to put up with?" she complained to the dragon. "You're saving me from his relentless charm."

"Good!" thundered Guldrum. Then he beat his golden wings and bounded off into the air, flying across the valley to uproot trees for their fire.

Chapter 16

Flames licked the starry sky and blazed like a supernova into the darkness. It was quite some time before Gil or Oreola could approach the inferno. Even in the shadows their hands and face burned, causing them to turn away in discomfort. Guldrum seemed to be impervious to the heat, however, actually reveling in it as he unfolded his wings behind him and basked in the red-hot glow. "Now this is a blaze fit for a dragon!" he chortled uncharacteristically, as if unaware of their discomfort.

Finally, the inferno died down and Gil sat by the dragon with Oreola on the other side. As he had promised, Guldrum had knitted her some new clothes, a gentle sage-green dress that draped down to her knees and looped over each shoulder with a slender weave. For dinner the dragon served human-style food consisting of dried fruit and vegetables, dragon bread with honey smeared across it, and to wash it all down, some fresh spring water. Their host also served some special blood-berry wine. It was a delicious meal and they were all famished from the day's earlier stress. Enjoying each other's company, they ate hungrily.

When all were finished and they could barely move from having seconds and thirds, Gil took his gaze from the burning embers and stared up at the dragon. "Your uncle, he didn't teach you to how knit, did he?" he asked carefully, unsure if the question was too personal. Dragons did not usually like to talk about themselves unless it was in the form of riddles, or so he had been brought up to believe, but Guldrum seemed to be the antithesis of a normal dragon.

Guldrum stared down at him with eyes of crimson, the fire light dancing within, but Gil could read no emotion there. Thinking he made a mistake, Gil was about to offer an apology when the dragon spoke. "It is true, Uncle does not knit much," Guldrum said simply, the words tailored for humor, but the tone one of sadness or regret. Great puffs of harmless smoke exited his nose, but the dragon did not seem to notice.

"Then who?" pursued Gil, taking another sip of wine.

Guldrum looked at the fire as if he could see his past or future there, his red eyes flickering suddenly as they caught the reflection of a tiny flame reborn. "It is a long story," he said at last, "and a long time ago, at least by your reckoning." Then he paused, timeless in the starry stillness, his huge form as vast as a shadowy mountain where the songs of the Earth dwell deep inside, never to be discovered. Gil looked upon him and was not afraid, only conscious of how insignificant he was in comparison, how there was so much he would never know and how utterly mysterious dragons really are.

As the sliver of a new moon rose in the night sky, Guldrum continued, his voice trailing from another place, riding a distant rhythm like waves on a forgotten shore. "I remember. Not all, but I remember. A few things my uncle told me, but not much. He did not like to speak of what happened. Are you sure you want to hear? No one has ever asked before."

"Yes, please," Gil and Oreola said in unison.

"It was late spring," began Guldrum. "My siblings had just Parted. I was but a hatchling, not yet able to take care of myself. My father was away securing food, possibly cattle, but it could have been more. My mother was at the cave entrance and so I dozed securely inside, not knowing that she hid illness, not wanting to worry me. It made her weak and unable to fly. She slept much. Worst of all, her fire would not come. She was nearly defenseless. But again, I did not know any of this, and so I slept, waiting for my father to return with food. Later I found out that he was also looking for rare herbs to weave a spell of healing. He had found these and was on his way back when a band of dragon smugglers approached without notice. A short fight ensued, and I woke up to find my mother dead and a ring of grim humans surrounding me."

"How horrible," soothed Oreola. "And so you were captured?"

"Yes, and taken far to the kingdom of Kanashar. When we were on the way to the city of Jelin, traveling on a lonely desert road, my father finally managed to track us down, using my spoor as guideposts no doubt. But my captors had been watching him approach and were ready for him. Still, they would only get one chance. As he hurtled down from the sky with fire burning in his mouth, the murderers let loose a giant bolt from a ballista they kept in a roofless wagon. I watched as he fell like a star in the heavens, obliterating a nearby oasis and sending a wave of sand that turned day into night."

"Oh Guldrum," Gil mouthed, well aware of how inadequate words were. "I'm so sorry. Were you sold then? Did you escape?"

"After seeing my father perish, something within me broke. The earlier shock of my mother being gone had worn off, and a rage built inside me that could not be contained. At every opportunity, I tried to inflict pain on my captors or attempted to escape. Because of this, the dragon smugglers had a hard time finding a buyer. No one wants an unruly dragon that cannot be managed or trained. And since the practice of selling baby dragons is illegal in most civilized kingdoms, they had to do everything in secret. This became increasingly more difficult as I grew bigger. Eventually, tired of transporting me about and paying for the endless supply of meat which I craved"—Guldrum paused to screw up his face in disgust—"they left me on the doorstep of a little house overgrown with vines in a sunlit wood, all swaddled and hidden in fabric at the bottom of a very large and rusting wash-basin."

Gil stared at Guldrum intently but found it nearly impossible to imagine that the dragon towering above him had ever been small enough to fit on a doorstep. Beginnings are always hard to imagine, though, he thought to himself, glancing at Oreola. The firelight danced across her features. She looked to be in pain as she listened to the dragon, and it hurt Gil to see her so.

"The house," continued Guldrum with just the barest dramatic inflection, "was the residence of an old enchanter named Halcyon."

"So, the magician taught you to knit?" interrupted Gil skeptically. Immediately he wished he hadn't spoken. This was not the time for jokes. The dragon was baring his soul.

"No," answered Guldrum dryly. "He taught me a few spells, for dragons have a predisposition for magic, of course. Through the decades I have retained only one; the invocation of light, which I use in my cave. More important was the simple kindness he showed me. Each night he told me a bedtime story and, when weather permitted, shared with me the names of the stars. It was his housekeeper, animated where he was quiet and reserved, who taught me the skill of which you speak. Sitting in the backyard, surrounded by great spools of colorful yarn, Maryiel taught me patiently that my talons could be used for gentler pursuits. In time, my confusion subsided, and I came to see that beauty was something I could create. She was not my mother, but she helped me find something other than anger. I don't know what I would have done without her."

Oreola leaned forward, as if she wanted to put her arms around Guldrum. "She sounds wonderful."

"I was very fortunate," the dragon acknowledged. "Maryiel's tasks extended far beyond me, of course. Her day started before sunrise and ended long after the light was gone. In many ways, she was the natural replacement for an apprentice, since Halycon neither needed nor desired one by that time, being retired from his art. But things still needed to be cleaned and meals cooked, and therefore services were required, for wizards can never be troubled over such things. Later, she told me that when I first arrived, for it was she who first found me and brought me inside. I will never forget her." For a moment the dragon closed his smoldering eyes and seemed lost in a memory.

"They were both very gracious to me," he said at last, "soothing my hurtful loss. It could not have been easy at first. I believe it was Halycon's intention to keep me but a while, until I was back to health, and then return me to my wild haunts. But as time went by and I grew accustomed to my new surroundings, so too did he grow accustomed to me, and could not bear to let me go, never having had any children himself. And so, I stayed. In time I learned their language, for dragons also have an affinity for words. It was a good life."

"What about your uncle?" asked Oreola gently. "You said he raised you? Was it he who brought you back?"

Guldrum flexed his wings and breathed a deep, warm sigh, like the breeze downwind from a volcano. "I said it was a long story, didn't I? The taking of a dragon is no small thing. What happens to one of us is felt by all, though we do not wall ourselves in by nation or state. When news traveled that I had been taken and my mother and father killed, there were some who demanded revenge. At the Dragon Council, the first in over one hundred years, the vote was close but never in doubt. Being too few in number, dragonkind could not afford to risk the wrath of the humans who continued to multiply and threatened to overrun our nesting areas and hunting grounds. One dragon in attendance, however, my eldest brother Rixel, did not abide by the outcome. To avenge our family, he attacked villages and towns indiscriminately, burning them to cinder and then flying away. As chance would have it, one such village was near the forest in which we lived, but he had no knowledge of this and I never got more than a glimpse of the dragon that plagued the region with such ferocity. Memories of my siblings were dim by that point; I had been but a hatchling when my siblings Parted. I did not recognize Rixel. Even so, I was curious to see a wild dragon. This was upsetting to my human guardians, who did not want me troubled unduly by the outside world, desiring only to keep me safe after everything I'd been through."

Guldrum paused, lost in thought, as a jet of steam escaped from his nostrils. Sparks trailed after it like falling stars. "My brother's attacks throughout Naloave went on for quite some time," he resumed. "Eventually, a small army was gathered with Trackers in the lead. It took weeks, but eventually they found him. After scaling the slopes, they roused him from slumber in his high mountain cave. With his once bright fires spent, Rixel soon met his death."

Gil and Oreola could say nothing to fill the awkward silence, and after a time the dragon continued, his words and spirit almost spent. "Rixel's earlier raids, glimpsed at from afar or heard second-hand from travelers as I hid in the dense and woody backyard, rekindled memories in me, fragments of another time I only vaguely remembered but could not truly forget. Finally, I came to a painful decision; I had to leave. I had become too big for the magician's house in any event. People were on edge in nearby towns and across the countryside. Having a dragon around put my guardians at risk. It was only a matter of time before someone noticed. My aging guardians would never have suggested a Parting, so I knew what I had to do."

Dragons cannot cry tears, but at this point Guldrum's face contorted in such a mournful way that there could be little doubt what he was feeling inside. "Early in the morning, before they had risen, I snuck out and, after looking back once more at my home for the last dozen or more years, entered the forest beyond the backyard. Weeks later, a dragon from another hatchling found me wandering aimlessly in the woods. I was a thin shadow of hunger because I lacked the necessary hunting skills, and was homesick beyond measure. Barely able to speak my native tongue, I said enough to be understood. He brought me to my uncle, who taught me tirelessly the time-honored traditions and raised me until I came of age. But I was tamed somehow by my contact with the humans, and so lost my dragon-fire." As if on cue, he snorted again and two black tendrils of smoke emerged from his nose, more than before, drifting ominously out into the moonlight. The once raging campfire was now nearly exhausted and cast only a faint glow.

"But look what you've gained," argued Oreola, feeling the chill of the night. "You're free now to be who you are. I think you're a wonderful dragon." Guldrum seemed unconvinced and shifted from side to side.

"Listen, "said Gil. "You ate both of us and we still like you. Think about it."

"I dream of going to the Homelands, to Marmajon or Frenole," rumbled Guldrum as if he hadn't heard. "To the place where all dragons come from. I heard my kind are different there. Peaceful and wise. But that's just a story. It doesn't actually exist."

"You don't need to go anywhere to be you," scolded Oreola softly.

"Of course I do," the dragon said. "You've met my family."

Oreola shook her head. "You can be you right here. Say after me. 'I like who I am. I like being gentle and sensitive.'" Guldrum sputtered and gulped, but only a hoarse whisper emerged. "Once again," she encouraged. "Louder this time." This time Guldrum managed an audible croak. "Better!" Now say it like you really mean it."

"It's hard," said the dragon, "but I'll try." Inhaling deeply, Guldrum concentrated and breathed fragile life into the words, while at the same time managing to expel a thick, black smoke that sparked as it hit the cooler air. This noxious cloud drifted directly into Gil's face.

"Good. Much better," coughed Gil raggedly. "You're on your way to self-respect and poisoning those around you."

"Don't listen to him," soothed Oreola. "That was very good. You just have to remember what's really important."

The dragon looked visibly shaken. "Sorry, Sir Gil," Guldrum apologized. "Usually I can barely make smoke. I don't know what happened. I can't even do that right." Gil tried to answer back and only coughed again.

"Someone approaches!" the dragon exclaimed suddenly, and with a rustle of wings took off into the air. Moments later as the dragon haze finally cleared, Gil caught a startled, first glimpse as the rider barreled into the campsite. The knight was adorned in shimmering armor with a snowy plume sprouting from his helm. His face was thin and hollow, with a long, bony nose which seemed to point directly at Gil like an accusation. But when he spoke, his first words were aimed at Oreola.

"Hello again, my dear," he greeted, reining in his nervous horse to a halt. "Have you missed me?"

Oreola's eyes were kindled fire as she sat coiled on edge of the log. "Go to Hell's Gates!" she spat.

Duke Ignot only smiled and then turned away. "That's the woman I love," he explained, looking back at Gil. "Thanks for keeping her safe for me." Gil was too stunned to speak. Standing up reflexively, he put his hand near the scabbard of his sword, but did not draw it out. "My name is Ignot," the man pronounced loudly, "Duke of Westsheen. And what is yours, good man?"

Gil responded guardedly. "You may call me Gilwin."

The duke paused. Then a smile of recognition spread slowly across his face. "Ah! Nil, the Dragonless Knight. Of the Order of Regale, I believe? I have heard of you after all! Indeed, you are known both far and wide. Your reputation precedes you. It would seem you prove the title accurate yet again." Gil clenched his hands and felt the blood rush to his face. "But no matter," he continued pleasantly. "Your service in safeguarding the princess is noted but no longer required. I have no quarrel with you."

The duke dismounted with an easy practiced movement and then took a step forward. He was unusually tall and spindly. Gil couldn't help but notice how ill at ease the man looked on the ground, like a giant bird. "But now," he was saying, "we must get back to the castle. The lady is tired, and the king and queen will not rest their eyes until they see her face again. Many royal thanks for the wonderful signal fire you constructed, though. Who knows how long we would have wandered in this godforsaken country if not for your generosity?"

Gil noticed other riders now moving in slowly, cautiously, behind the duke and spreading out. Further out and off in the distance, he could make out still other figures, shadowy and small, moving silently at the edge of sight.

"My lady," Ignot instructed, motioning to his saddle. "It is time. You have had your adventure. Now it is time to be a grown up. Come."

Oreola stood up so she was matched to Gil. Her chin rose and a grim smile of determination spread across her face. "No," she said flatly. "It is not a holiday I am on. This is my life to do as I choose. I am not a trophy to be won or a bird trapped in a gilded cage. You cannot order me to do anything."

"I have no more times for games!" exploded the duke, drawing his sword. "You will get on this horse if I have to sling you over my shoulder!"

At once Gil stepped between Ignot and Oreola and put his hand firmly on the hilt of his sword. "The lady said she doesn't want to go," he cautioned.

"Fool!" rasped the mounted knight. "I have not come here alone." As if to reinforce this point the other riders, still wary of the dragon, stepped closer until they formed a noose, tightening around them. "My fellow knights and I will take the princess, by force if necessary. On the outskirts wait the Loreichi. They found my Tracker and we negotiated a deal. They are…disturbing." The duke shivered. "Fallen creatures of the forest, the Loreichi are dark shells of their former nature-loving selves. One of them, their leader, I cannot pronounce his name, still speaks the old Dragon Tongue. They have a map which they found and then followed you here. They want the dragon's hoard. All of it. But they're too afraid to come any nearer."

He looked around, a smile curving on his lips. "Speaking of which," he said, "where has that timid dragon of yours gone off to?" Gil and Oreola looked at the duke in surprise. "Oh yes, I know your little secret. I crept up here so I could have a closer look. Heard enough of the story to know there was little danger. For your sake, I hope that dragon has accumulated some treasure, or the Loreichi are going to be quite disappointed."

"It's okay," shouted Gil. "You might as well come out." Moments later a great wind swirled around them and Guldrum landed nearby, his great golden wings kept in a defensive position.

Momentarily taken aback at the sight of the dragon, the duke cast sharp glances at Guldrum, as if he couldn't quite believe the creature could be so harmless. The riders around him began to break. "Hold!" he commanded, some of whom were backing away or raising shields. "No one fires or flees unless on my order. Anyone disobeying will answer to the king himself!" This steadied the men. Although still on edge, the riders listened, and the crisis was momentarily averted. "This dragon has no flame. You have nothing to fear. It is peace-loving and weak. Just like the supposed knight who stands between me and the king's daughter."

He turned towards Gil, his face simmering with anger. "Step aside," he barked. Gil remained motionless, his hand trembling. "I will have the girl!" he screamed. Stepping forward, he raised his arm and punched Gil in the face with his armored left hand. As Gil fell painfully backwards, his nose almost certainly broken, Ignot drew his sword, raising it over a defenseless Gil who now lay sprawled on the ground. Oreola rushed forward, her arms clenched into fists, but the duke held his ground, striking her across the face with the back of his open hand, making her crumple. "That'll teach you to mess with the likes of me," he snarled as she struggled to get up. "Now watch!" Raising his sword again, the duke prepared to plunge it into Gil's chest.

"Do something, Guldrum!" screamed Oreola at the dragon on her hands and knees. "Please!" But Guldrum already was. As soon as Gil had gotten punched, the dragon had started to inhale deeply. By the time Oreola had been struck to the ground, Guldrum could feel the pressure starting to build. The blood that covered Gil's face only heightened the strange sensations Guldrum was having, feeding his anger and making him feel like he was about to explode.

Only half-conscious of what he was doing, Guldrum said, "I don't really like you very much at all." The next moment there was an eruption of fire. Red death colored his vision as the searing flames shot out of his mouth. One moment the duke was standing, preparing a fatal blow, and the next he was screaming, his armor a burning conflagration and his anguished face ablaze.

Oreola crawled and then threw herself over Gil, covering him with her body as best she could. The other riders charged in swiftly to help, their swords cutting the air in feverish strokes, but it didn't matter. Guldrum couldn't stop. Years and years of pent-up outrage and misery poured out of him. Again and again he blazed forth with fire until no horse or rider remained standing. Only then did his fiery rage abate.

Amid the blackened, smoking corpses, two figures struggled to stand. Leaning on each other they moved slowly, pushing their aching limbs through the thick, choking smoke. Gil and Oreola stumbled through the carnage in a daze. Looks of horror were etched on their faces. The campsite had become a battlefield, littered with the dead remains of riders and the still burning carcasses of what once had been horses. Guldrum stood in the center of it all, his golden wings wrapped around his gigantic frame, hiding his dragon head and face from view.

The smell, Guldrum thought. The odor of brimstone still hung heavy in the air, along with other scents, but he tried not to dwell on those for they were too disturbing. And the flames! How powerful it had felt! There had been no pain, no burning of his throat as he had imagined there might be. He had done it! And his friends were safe. But at what cost? The dead lay all around him. He had made himself look so he would not forget, but still he marveled at what had been done.

Nearby, Gil touched Oreola's arm. "Wait," he told her. Retrieving his singed pack, he pulled out the gold that Guldrum had given them as his way of saying thanks for helping, but when he scanned the darkness for the small forest creatures they were gone, scattered to safety no doubt when Guldrum erupted. He returned to her side. They looked at Guldrum warily. No one else was alive but them. They approached the dragon cautiously, as if the merest sound might set him off again, might cause him to spew forth death again. Patches of ground still burned as they walked towards him. When they were still several strides away, they halted. "It's us, Guldrum. Oreola and Gil," the princess said. Then she faltered.

"Thank you," finished Gil for her. "You saved us all." But Guldrum didn't move, didn't lift the leathery veil which covered his face like shame or mourning. "We should go," he said gently to the dragon. "This is no place to stay. No place for the living." The smell of death and burning flesh hung heavy in the air. Oreola covered her mouth as if she were about to be sick. "Please, Guldrum," he said softly.

Then Oreola started to pick her way slowly through the smoking, burning corpses, her steps taking her brokenly towards the open air. Before turning to join her, Gil stepped forward. Reached out hesitantly, he touched the dragon's scales. They were rough like sandpaper, but surprisingly cool to the touch. "You're not alone," he offered. "You did what you had to do." But Guldrum jerked away with a start.

After a moment, Gil walked off after Oreola. When he was sure they were both a safe distance away, Guldrum unfolded his wings and followed slowly after, his head hung low like an outcast.

Chapter 17

Both Gil and Oreola were too tired to make a fire when they finally found flat, smooth terrain that had clean air. The thought of flickering flames made their stomachs turn, though the night was becoming colder. Compromising instead on a little company, they sat next to each other and breathed their words haltingly into each other's ear, hoping for a little comfort after what they had seen. Guldrum skulked in the shadows nearby but said nothing. Repeated queries could not draw him into speaking. He seemed beyond soothing or supplication, wrapped up completely in his own brooding, with his wings again folded over so he appeared like a cocoon in silent metamorphosis.

Finally, reluctantly, they both agreed that he needed time alone. Tomorrow was another day, and in the morning light he would perhaps feel a little better. Conversation did not come easy. They were too aware of the dragon and what had happened to say more than a few tentative words at first. Guldrum's actions had been horrific and unexpected, but the confrontation had also won them their freedom, or at least bought them time so they could try and make a new life.

When Gil next looked over, Guldrum appeared to be asleep, his dark, hulking body expanding and contracting like giant bellows, tiny sparks emanating from his nostrils like the discharge from a too potent dream. He turned his gaze back to Oreola and found that she was smiling. "We make a pretty good team, don't we?" she said, her voice crisp and clear in the night air. "All things being what they are."

Gil glanced over at Guldrum as if expecting the dragon to awaken, but he was deep in some dark slumber where their words could not reach. "Yeah, I guess we do at that," Gil said at last. "All things being what they are."

Oreola smiled more broadly. It was crazy to think how just a couple days of ago, she had been trapped in the castle, looking out over the wall as if the world beyond were an impossible dream. And now here she was! Most surprising of all was the fact that she wasn't alone. Before she could stop herself, she reached out and put her hand gently, tentatively on his cheek. When he didn't resist, she let her fingers glide across his skin, careful not to touch his swollen nose. "No more dragons, okay?" she breathed softly near his ear, both a request and a statement.

"I promise, no more dragons," he told her in a voice full of tenderness and honesty.

Although always unspoken, they both knew that humans and dragons were from different worlds. That's what had made the last few days so extraordinary. Somehow, they would find a way to say goodbye to Guldrum when the time was right. Then they would be alone.

Surprising himself, Gil moved his hand and placed it over hers. It was such a small gesture and yet it felt as if the world had shifted. Then they both leaned toward each other until their lips met. It was a gentle kiss, tender and exploring, that grew in desire. At that moment, Guldrum snorted suddenly in his sleep like a distant thunderclap, and a shower of hot, fiery sparks rained down on them from above. Swallowing their fear, they both laughed in amazement, patting their clothes and putting out the already dying embers. It was late.

"Goodnight, Sir Gil," Oreola sang, almost laughing again, despite the pain of where the duke had struck her. Getting up quickly, she ran through the fireworks to her sleeping blanket a short distance away, her makeshift dress catching the moonlight at the last.

"Goodnight, my lady," Gil called after her, still smiling, as the sparks fell and faded on the darkening ground.

Chapter 18

The next morning dawned radiantly. Sunshine and clear blue sky was all Gil could see above him as he opened his eyes from a long night's rest. Exhausted from the previous day's events and the effects of the potent wine, he had slept like the dead. It felt wonderfully good to just lie there and breathe in and out, thinking of Oreola. Yet almost immediately he sensed something was wrong. It was too quiet. No birdsong greeted the new say. Then he heard it. A muffled shout.

He stood up, his whole body awake and alert. Then he turned to where the dragon had been sleeping. There was Guldrum, staring back at Gil as if he had nothing to hide. The corners of his mouth were berry red and his teeth were stained a sickly crimson. *Blood*, Gil thought in horror, but then he remembered the concoction that the dragon had served last night. It seemed like a lifetime ago.

"Oreola! Oreola!" stammered Gil, panic coursing through his veins as he looked wildly around.

Her voice came through broken and subdued. "I'm right here," she called. Gil looked over at the dragon, but lower this time, toward the ground. Then he saw her, wrapped in a coil of Guldrum's tail, with her head barely sticking out. "Any ideas?" she said. "He won't listen to me. Just keeps blabbering on about being bad."

Taking several cautious steps forward, Gil stopped when he was still only halfway to them. "Is this about what you did?" he asked. "About killing those men?"

The question hung on the air.

"I guess I'm a dragon after all," Guldrum howled mournfully. "I thought I was good, but I'm not. How can I be after what I did?"

"Of course you are," Gil told him. "You're a dragon and a good one at that. You saved us all." The knight paused. "Maybe we can't change who we are, not really, but we can change how we think. How we act. You had the strength to live a different kind of life. What you did last night in order to protect us doesn't take any of that away."

"It felt terrible," Guldrum moaned. "But it also felt so powerful. I will never forget the feeling as the fire within me erupted. I will never get the screams of those men out of my memory no matter how many centuries I live. How can one thing feel so different?"

Gil inched forward. "That's just part of being alive. The fact that you feel terrible about killing those men just means you have a conscience. Listen to me now. Guldrum," he said. "Oreola is a friend. I'm your friend. You need to let her go."

A look of confusion passed over the dragon's features. He dropped his head. When he lifted it a moment later, his face was contorted in anguish. "This is what I'm supposed to do, isn't it?" he cried. "Dragons are selfish and breathe fire and eat young ladies."

"No one is eating anyone," Gil said flatly.

"I'll second that," Oreola managed.

The dragon opened its mouth to speak again and Gil noticed with unease the rows of teeth glistening there. "There's nothing you can do," Guldrum said, lifting the princess slowly off the ground. "It's supposed to be this way."

Oreola struggled, but Guldrum's grip was too strong and he would not let her go. Tighter and tighter Guldrum squeezed making it difficult for her to breathe.

"Is this– is this what your guardians– would have wanted?" she asked. Guldrum paused as if remembering himself.

Dreamlike, Gil's hand crept down to his sword, gripping it numbly, but somehow he found the strength to pull the terrible weight free of the scabbard and raise it slowly into position. "Put her down!" he demanded, his voice ringing strong and true. Striding forward, he raised the sword and brought the blade down on the interlocking scales of Guldrum's nearest toe. The blow ricocheted off the dragon's armor, nearly causing Gil to lose his balance. *Armor piercing blade, my foot!* Gil thought acerbically. His sword tip was bent horribly.

In shock, Guldrum released his hold on Oreola and she tumbled from his tail, landing heavily on the ground. "Hey, why did you do that?" he asked, his front claw throbbing and smarting. Then the dragon noticed the still figure of Oreola on the ground below. "Oreola? Are you okay?" he asked her nervously. "I'm very, very sorry."

Slowly she began to stir. "I'll survive," she replied, getting into a sitting position and dusting herself off. "What were you thinking, anyway?" she demanded, pointing her finger at the dragon. "You're a vegetarian." Gil rushed over and held out his hand. Oreola took it and he helped her up. Then she threw her arms around him.

"I still don't know what to do," Guldrum said mournfully. The dragon gazed off into the distance as if trying to catch a glimpse of the mythical Homelands.

Unwrapping herself from Gil's embrace, Oreola stepped back, her face clouded with doubt. "Me neither," she said, still shaken. "I feel like we all need a new start."

For the space of several heartbeats, Gil looked at Oreola and felt the world slipping away. Then he brightened, thinking back to something Oreola had said as they walked the rolling hills. All he had to do was break one big beast of a promise. "I do," he declared. "All it takes is a willing dragon and a leap of faith." Then he told them his crazy idea.

Chapter 19

Standing at the top of the gently rolling hill, Oreola made a few last-minute adjustments to her new copper-colored wings as the wind tossed her long black hair. Her face was warm in the sun. Down below, the modest but comfortable cottage she had built looked like a speck of brown in a sea of green. The land was all theirs, to the top of this hill and beyond, paid for with a single small bag of treasure, with a little left over. The Northern Lands were more beautiful than she'd ever imagined, and remote enough that none of them need worry about being discovered. And if they ever wanted to visit Gil's father in Rundle, well, that could be arranged. It helped if you knew a friendly dragon.

"Ready?" she asked.

"Not even a little," Gil replied nervously. He never quite got used to this part.

Oreola put her hand gently on his and kissed him on the lips for luck. Then she raced down the opposite slope until her feet left the ground and she lifted into the sky. Gil followed behind, flapping his silver wings furiously, screaming as he went until he too finally left the earth behind. They drifted together in the quiet slipstream, their wingtips nearly touching.

"Not bad," Oreola yelled over to him. Gil smiled in return. Keeping one hand firmly on the stabilizing bar, Gil took the wooden birdcall out his pocket, put it to his lips and blew. The sound was lilting and high. The echo lingered before being carried away on the wind. From the four corners of the open sky, small vibrant yellow birds flocked towards them, dancing in the air and chirping in response. The next moment they scattered.

"Look out!" Oreola warned. Overhead a massive emerald meteor streaked by with a flash of golden wings. Guldrum turned lazily and then floated by, doing a perfect corkscrew. "Show-off!" Gil and Oreola both shouted in unison.

Taking up a position on either side of the dragon, they glided through a nearly cloudless blue sky as the wind danced and sang. It felt good to be free and to be a family. Oreola spent her time inventing things. Sometimes she even got money for them. One of her most popular and profitable inventions was a machine that printed out typed text on flat sheets of dried paper. She called it a printer's press. Gil had traded in his sword for a pen and wrote fantastic adventures. Some of them were even true. Together they would lay out his simple tales on the moveable pieces of type, add a few drops of inky dragon secretions, and then press the plates together. Then he and Oreola would sew up the pages and sell them for a single copper at the trading post. It wasn't a perfect life, but it was enough. Sometimes it even felt extraordinary.

"We make a pretty good team," Gil shouted into the wind.

"All things being what they are," answered Oreola, smiling despite herself.

The dragon roared.

X

ary Kelly ran down the winding, rickety stairs in her bare feet towards the beach. Nothing seemed right. Not the cold stars in the clouding sky. Not the sound of the waves lapping against the shore below. Nor the rich salty air. And certainly not up *there*.

A sliver of bright light appeared over her shoulder from an open doorway of the little cabin perched on the lip of the hill. "Mary, honey," a female voice called out into the darkness. "Come back. It's okay now. I promise." Startled, Mary ran faster, losing her footing on the irregular steps. Down she tumbled noisily, rolling to a bruised stop in the warm sand.

"Mary, are you alright? Can you hear me? Say something!" But she did not say anything, although tears welled up in her eyes. She lie there shaken and sullen as wave and after wave crashed against the shore. From out of the west a strong wind began to blow.

"Steve!" the voice shouted, almost hysterical. "I think she's fallen down the stairs!"

There were more words she could not quite hear, some deep and masculine. Then the old stairs creaked wildly. Footsteps in a mad rush. "We're coming!" her father's voice called out like a foghorn. "Don't move! We're coming, sweetie!"

Now Mary did move. Struggling to her feet, she began running desperately down the beach, her long blonde hair covering her face like seaweed. Farther and farther she ran, not daring to turn around. All she knew was that she had to get way. She scrambled over wave-slick rocks, around muddy bends that sucked at her strength, and through foamy surf.

Behind her, voices called out. Sometimes frightfully close, other times unbearably far away. She heard their worry and their pain, but this just made her more frightened. With a last burst of energy, she ran towards a huge boulder that sat nearby on the beach. It must have broken free from the cliff at some point in the past. Now it was a lonely sentry, valiantly standing against the sea. She had never seen it before. Nothing around her looked familiar. Even the stars were gone. She walked around the stony monstrosity until she was hidden from view and then leaned against it, her lungs gasping for air. *Safe*, she thought raggedly. *Safe*.

It wasn't until she lifted her head and opened her eyes that she saw the cave entrance gaping right in front of her.

———

Alicia Kelly ran down the darkened sand. She yelled her daughter's name half-sobbing, her voice breaking over the crashing surf. There was a storm coming. She could feel it. Terrible thoughts flashed through her head. Her daughter Mary lying face down in the dark water, or crumpled with a broken leg in one of the tidal pools. She hadn't run in years. Not since college. Her breathing came in ragged gasps as her abdominal muscles began to spasm. Panic and guilt drove her on and she quickened her strides. Down the beach, her husband Steve was searching. Through the wind and the waves Alicia could hear him calling, sounding every bit as lost and lonely as she was.

———

Darkness. With just the faintest glow of midnight blue. Mary peered cautiously into the cave entrance. There was something unreal about it. She had walked down the coastal beach many times—exploring, dashing in and out of the surf, crawling over washed-up trees—and she had never discovered anything like this. Then again, she didn't even really know where she was. How far had she run? What direction? She hadn't a clue. It had all happened so fast. All she had wanted to do was get away. To escape the shouting. And now she had. The night wrapped its arms around her, without stars or silvery moon. She began to feel very alone.

The sudden thunderclap jolted her like a physical slap. *What had she done?* A drop of rain splattered her arm, cool and wet. Then another. Soon the drops became a serious splattering. Then without warning the bucket tipped, and Mary found herself in a downpour, being drenched. As the wind picked up she started to shiver, her flannel pajamas becoming leaden in the cold, dark onslaught. Gladly she ran into the shelter the cave provided, never noticing the footprints that were already there.

It was dry inside, and musty smelling. Mary sat down heavily by the mouth of the cave and let the fatigue run through her arms and legs. With her head propped against the cool, rocky wall, she watched the rain fall outside the opening, lulled by its steady rhythm. As long as she didn't think about the storm, or what she couldn't see in the cave, or her parents, Mary felt an uneasy peace settle around her. All she had to do was not move and then everything would be okay. The numbness inside her began to grow. Even the trickle of water down her face could be ignored. Taking a deep breath, she hugged her knees to her chest and exhaled.

Somewhere deep in the cave, an old wind stirred.

Alicia ran down the soggy beach to her husband who waited by the stairs. Steve looked his wife in the eyes and saw his own fear reflected there. "Nothing," he said. "I went as far as the granite slabs. Beyond that the beach was washed out."

Alicia winced in pain, as if she had been stabbed with a dagger. "Damn it! Where can she be? I ran past the development to the point. I looked everywhere. Where is my baby? She can't just disappear. I don't know what to do." Her voice trailed off into a chasm. "Where is she?"

Steve wrapped his wet arms around his wife, holding her close until she finally hugged him back. It was the first time they had touched since…well, he couldn't remember when.

———————

Mary watched the rain fall. Each thunderclap reminded her of the yelling that had driven her out of the cabin. She had been lying in her bed, unable to fall back asleep after a bad dream. Through the crack under the door, soft light spilled in. Her parents were still up. She could hear their voices. Almost unconsciously she pulled the blanket up higher and wrapped it tight, hoping it wouldn't happen again. Then their voices rose in anger.

"You don't surprise me a bit," she heard her father say. "You'll never change. Why did you even come if you didn't want to, Alicia? Huh? Tell me that. Christ! It never fails. Just when everything's good you have to open your mouth. You want it both ways and you can't."

"I'm just being honest," her mother replied, softer. "And keep your voice down. Mary's just in the other room sleeping. You'll wake her."

"Oh hell, you know she sleeps through anything."

"Well, I don't," her mother shot back in anger. "Not through your late-night TV and videogames, your snoring, your 3 a.m. drunken escapades when you're actually in town instead of working for that God-forsaken company. We hardly ever see you, Steve, and when you *are* here, you're mentally somewhere else."

"That's what this is really about. My job. I work my ass off so we can afford this summer cottage for two measly weeks a year, just so you can ruin it. What do you want me to do?"

"I want you home more," her mother said. There was a long silence. Mary held her breath. "I want things the way they used to be."

"Me?" her father responded, a weird laugh making his voice seem anything but jovial. "What about your real estate office? Are you going to give that up? That's half the reason Mary's in daycare every summer. Don't be putting it all on me."

"All I'm asking is that you try and spend a little more time with her."

Her dad's voice rose in frustration. "Sounds like a cop-out to me. You still don't know how to talk to her, do you? You smother her. So now it's my job?"

"You're her father! All I want is for you to start acting like it. And a little help would be nice. I've tried, but she's so distant. I can't get close to her anymore. She won't let me."

Mary sat up and hugged her knees to her chest. Why did no one want her?

"Sounds like someone else I know," her father said. "You're a stranger to me. We were in love once, Alicia. But what are we now?" There was a heart-stopping pause. Mary heard footsteps walking across the floor. "Where are you going?"

"To get a drink," her mother said. "With a little luck I'll forget this whole vacation."

There was another silence broken by laughter. It was her father again. "Kind of like the way you forgot your birth control pill."

Mary felt as if she'd been slapped. It wasn't exactly what they said. She didn't even understand everything. Even so, she felt as if she'd been banished to a lonely cell, her body gone tense and rigid as the emotions sunk in.

The sound of struggling came from the other room. Suddenly something smashed and shattered, breaking on her eardrums like thunder. "You asshole!" her mother screamed with a voice that collapsed into sobbing. "I'm…" But Mary couldn't hear the last word. It was too faint. For a long minute she sat there. In the room next door, her mother still wept brokenly. After a while the crying dwindled away, and Mary heard her parents' bedroom door close. The TV in the living room blared to life. It was louder than usual, so her father must have turned it up because he was mad. The sound of a baseball game filled the air with its slow and steady rhythms. Eventually the game ended and her father's snoring became audible over the sound of the nightly news.

A cheerful newscaster finished a story about something called a salmonella outbreak and then went on to talk about an escaped prisoner who was on the loose and considered dangerous. Lying on her bed in her small room, Mary felt trapped; but although she was still afraid, something about the prison escape inspired her, making her brave enough to act. If a man could break out of a locked room, then certainly she should be able to break out of an unlocked one. Steeling herself, she threw off her blanket and sat up. She had to be a big girl. Quietly she put on her bunny slippers. Then she opened the door a crack and peered out. When she was sure the coast was clear, Mary crept past the couch where her father slept, and then slipped out into the night, her escape nearly perfect until the screen door slammed behind her.

*

A fork of lightning traced itself across the stormy night sky as a crash of thunder answered back. Mary gazed out the cave entrance. The storm reminded her of the fighting back at the cabin. Taking a breath, Mary sat up, turning around to look at the space she was in. She had never been in a cave before. From books she had read, she imagined them all to be dark with giant stalactites hanging down from the ceiling. This one was different. Instead of being completely black, the cave had a strange glow which emanated from somewhere within. It was still too dark to really see anything, only shapes and shadows and foolish guesses. She tried not to think about it.

To distract herself, Mary stood up and looked down at her clothes, which were dripping water on the cold stone floor at her feet. Her pajamas had seen better days. They were completely soaked and torn in the knee where she had caught them on some rocks. Her feet were scraped and sore. Looking closely, she noticed that she was missing a pink slipper.

All in all, she was tired, bruised and cold. Standing in the eerie darkness, her teeth chattered as the rain outside kept falling down. She was stuck. Here. In a cave. A salty smelling cave, she realized with a sniff or two of her nose. *Wait 'til she told her friends how she spent her vacation. Boy, would they be jealous!* Mary tried to smile, but her eyes welled up with tears instead. Feeling alone and more than a little fool-ish, she began to cry.

"Little girls shouldn't rattle mi' bones," breathed a deep sunken voice from the heart of the darkness. It took a moment for Mary to realize it wasn't her father.

*

Alicia slowly pulled away from her husband's embrace.

"We've got to find her, Steve," she whispered. "She's only ten years old."

"We will. We will. We have to. Let's stick together this time." Taking her hand in his, he looked at her. He could see the tears she was holding back. "We can do this," he told her.

When she finally nodded, they walked off in the rain, looking for footprints in the sand that were long since washed away.

*

Mary stared wide-eyed as a lantern flared in the wall above her. Half-blinded, she blinked madly, trying to focus. Within the dancing shadow-light stood a strange figure, tall and strongly built. A great black tri-cornered cap was perched high atop its head, and a faded yellow bandana wrapped around a broad forehead. Great circles of silver hung from each ear. A ragged red cape draped down to where dirty-white pontoon pants hung loose. Across the chest and down a leg hung a great brown belt where a scarlet-stained cutlass and two flintlock pistols were fastened. Black buckled shoes stepped echoingly on the cave floor as the figure, the nightmare, stepped closer into the light. The face. That was what she had been avoiding. He had a beard, black and long. It was twisted and braided like Medusa's hair. The mustache above it teetered under his nose like some ancient foot-long centipede.

Mary screamed. Or thought she screamed. But no sound came out. The figure bent over, close enough so Mary could feel his warm breath touch her cheek. And yet she felt nothing. This close, she could see how age-worn his face was. The haunted look in his eyes gave a glimmer of the pain that his scowl tried to hide.

"Disturbin' my sleep, are ye? Rattlin' mi weary bones!" rumbled the strange man as he reached for his cutlass and pulled it from its scabbard. "Why, I'll…"

Mary watched in shocked stillness as the anger suddenly died away like a fire deprived of oxygen. The man peered at her intently, as if not quite believing. Slowly, his glower melted away and his words trailed off. Hard eyes softened. "Can't be," he whispered. He looked her up and down. "Your eyes. Those same eyes. But no," he decided at last. "You're not her after all. But give ya ten years and black hair. A miracle it is, just the same."

All at once he caught himself. Straightening up, he put his weapon back in its scabbard self-consciously. It had been a long time since he'd had company. "Where are an old sea dog's manners?" he said in a gravelly voice.

So mesmerized was Mary that she didn't see at first the hand outstretched toward her. For a moment, her body couldn't move. What was proper when meeting a pirate? When she finally recovered, Mary reached out to shake the giant, calloused hand, and to her surprise passed right through it.

———— * ————

Steve and Alicia ran down the beach. The rain showed no sign of letting up. They had covered a lot of ground and were just coming up to an area of rocks that separated one long stretch of beach from another. "I made it this far," Alicia said, looking at the water that washed over the slabs. Beyond that, where the beach should have been, was swirling dark water. Here and there a sandy oasis revealed itself before the surging tide erased it again. "Do you think she could have gone that way?" she asked.

"There's only one way to find out," Steve answered. "Maybe it wasn't so bad when she passed."

The slick rocks were treacherous to walk on and so the going was slow. Hand in hand, they kept each other steady as they stepped carefully from one granite slab to another. There was little else to see. Up ahead, the churning tidal waters washed over the beach. Alicia looked down to measure her next step. That's when she saw it. A flash of color in a wet, monochromatic world. Bending down, Alicia peered at the object intently. It was a slipper. She held it out to Steve who took it carefully, almost gingerly, as if it was the most precious thing in the whole world. They both took a deep breath and then, without a word, ran headlong across the slippery rocks and down the water-logged beach. Their feet splashed like a call to arms.

*

Mary jumped back, pressing herself against the wall protectively. Her hand had passed right through his like it wasn't even there. "What are you?" she asked in a trembling voice. "Keep away from me!"

"Aw, damn it be," the pirate spat. "It has been a while. When will an old man learn?" Feeling foolish, Mary held up her little fists and brandished them at the imposing figure. "Now, now little lady," he chastised. "No need for that. Lemme introduce myself. Captain William Sharpe, or what's left of him. Her Majesty's finest, turned pirate and scoundrel, then turned fool, and then turned ghost." He swept his hat off with a roll and bowed low, but did not smile. "You must be Mary. How may I be of service on such a dreary night?"

This was too much to take in. She had to grasp at something real. "How do you know my name?" Mary asked, her fists still held up in front of her in what she hoped was a threatening posture.

"My dear," the pirate explained. "I heard voices callin' out. 'Mary,' they said. 'Mary, where are you?' I took you to be her. A young child lost on a wretched night." William Sharpe sighed wistfully and for a moment seemed lost in thought, as if remembering with fondness a happier time. "Who knows who you could meet or what could happen to you." Mary shuddered. The silence that followed was heavy as a tombstone.

"Oh, don't worry, child," the ghost grumbled. "You have nothing to fear from me. But we must get you back to your parents. It is not safe to be out tonight." He reached as if to take her hand and lead her outside. With a curse he stopped himself. "That won't do, will it? You will have to follow me." His tone was final.

Despite her fear, Mary did not move. "I'm not going anywhere," she blurted out. "I don't want to be found."

The pirate looked momentarily shaken. "Not want to be found? What nonsense is this?" he demanded. "Of course you do. They are your parents. Your family. I may have been a pirate but I am not without heart. I can hear the pain in their cries. Come. We must not dally."

"No!" shouted Mary. "And you're no pirate. You can't be real. There aren't any pirates anymore."

"That much is true. I am but a ghost. A pirate-spirit. Perhaps the only one. Who's to say? For though we all did many things a person may be haunted by, few of us had a conscience as such. My trouble was that I fell in love."

"You?" Mary asked.

"Yes, me!" the ghost answered back. "It can happen to anyone, you know. Ah, it is a very sad tale, though, as most affairs of the heart are. Mine has not gotten any better with the passing years. And I am tired. Very, very tired." He sighed heavily and leaned against the stone wall. The torchlight high in the shadows flickered and dimmed.

"Can't be any worse than mine," Mary muttered softly, but not nearly quietly enough.

The ghost laughed, but there was no mirth in the sound. "Yours must be a tale of woe indeed, to run from your family and stow away on a night such as this."

Mary didn't know what to say. She certainly didn't want to talk about her problems to a complete stranger in a cave, especially someone who claimed to be a ghost. "Why can you hold your sword but not my hand?" she asked, changing the subject with a clever question.

The pirate looked at her as if she had changed from a little girl to a sack of wheat. "Why? Because I'm a ghost, of course. Flesh to metal, stone or wood I can manage. But flesh to flesh I can never do again." His voice seemed to die in his throat. "That's the way of it when you're dead and haunted."

Mary screwed up her face and squinted her eyes. "Whaddaya mean, haunted? Aren't you supposed to haunt, not be haunted?"

William Sharpe nodded his head. "Now you ask me to tell the tale. As I said, it is not a bright one, and your parents are outside looking for you." Outside the rain fell from what felt like a limitless black sky. "Aye. But I will tell it," he said at last in a voice blown from a different direction. "Perhaps it will do me good after all this time. Then you must go."

Mary sat down on the cave floor, sitting cross-legged, but still careful to keep her distance. Despite her misgivings, she listened intently as the captain's rough words conjured up a pleasant sea breeze and a lone ship sailing on the sunlit water.

"The *Black Joke* sailed on the ocean waves," he began.

———— * ————

It was a fine pirate ship. Its dark timbers and dirty sails cast a long, cancerous shadow across the sparkling waters. Behind it, evidence of its passing trailed like an unhealed scar. On this day a good breeze was blowing, and the sun shone warmly, although it was nearly October. Stores and bellies were full. Best of all, chests were overflowing with Spanish doubloons taken from the last raid. Every crew member whistled a happy tune. As did I, the pirate confided. Some laughed loudly on the deck or shouted high in the airy rigging. Others sang raunchy songs to pass the time. I stood at the bow, gazing across the waters like Poseidon. We were on our way to divide and bury a fortune. Always an exciting and dangerous time for a captain.

But in the privacy of my own thoughts I felt cursed. When I could no longer bear the festive atmosphere, I retreated to my cabin. *Just a face*, I thought, as the stars began to fill the evening sky through my porthole. *Just a face.*

The next morning dawned exceptionally, both sea and sky alive in vibrant pinks, reds and orange. Feet clambered on the timbers, voices raised loud and rough. There was a hunger in the air, a knife's edge of anticipation that cut through all the preparations. Soon all was ready. All as it should be. With the slightest of hesitations, he gave the order.

The door to the hold was thrown open wide. Two men descended, grinning. A minute later they reappeared, hauling a screaming, thrashing woman. She was achingly beautiful, with long wavy black hair and green eyes. The clothes she wore were simple, a white shift with a slender strap, torn in places. Her feet were bare. Any jewelry had been confiscated and added to the loot. Her eyes were wide with fear as she looked desperately for an escape.

One of the men pushed her violently toward the main mast. Then the circle closed in around her. "What do you say, Cap'n? Let us have some fun before we drop her in the drink. She's got it coming, I'd reckon," said a heavily tattooed man with a sunken black eye.

William looked on, giving no response. He only knew her first name. Maria. She was the Spanish captain's daughter and had fought right beside him to the last. Her mixed blood was a testament to the unique rules that shipboard life sometimes allowed. For a woman she had spirit. Even now she still struggled, spilling one of his men overboard when he had grabbed her for a feel.

It could have gotten interesting at that point. What had been good-natured fun, like a cat toying with a mouse, suddenly turned deadly. Knives slashed the air, just as he knew they would. In a moment one would land and it would be over, or close enough. If she were still alive, the men would have some fun first. Then her body would be tossed in the sea and they would continue on their way. But that's not what happened. Instead of watching, he did something strange. He stepped in. Stopped it. He still didn't understand why. A pretty face never got in the way of business.

It troubled him, weighing him down like a ship taking on water. He could feel himself sinking, but didn't know what to do.

"Not today, lads," he said again as if waking from a dream. "Today she sweats." The groans and grumbling were replaced by ragged, buoyant cheers. "Run wench," he commanded like a black sail unfurling. "Run around that mast and maybe we'll go easy on ya." Taking a step forward, he took out his cutlass menacingly. The mob parted as he advanced.

She stood in front of him against the timber unmoving, her arms wrapped around it like a dryad protecting her home. Now and then the wind caught her hair and sent it flying like a flock of ravens. "Ya deaf? Run!" he shouted, angry at her stubbornness and his own stupidity. But still she did not move. Instead she hugged the wood more tightly and raised her chin high in defiance. All around the crew grew agitated, sparking like a powder-keg for a chance to poke or slice.

"Tis now or never, girl," he said ominously.

"Then it is never," she said softly but clearly, looking him right in the eye.

William strode toward her then like a madman, the sword already in his hand. He raised the steel above her head. His whole body shook. "Lay her low!" the motley crew shouted.

Sunlight glinted off the blade as the ship rocked on the waves. Time slowed down and the wind fell silent, as if the world were holding its breath. He felt transfixed, staring into her terrified eyes. Try as he might, he could not finish the blow. Rough hands grabbed him and shoved him aside. He could only watch as another stepped forward to finish the deed.

———— * ————

"And so, my young friend," concluded the pirate softly in the flickering light, "you see, I did not kill her. Could not. Some might say I loved her. All I know is that she touched something inside me I thought long gone. But for all that, even though I didn't strike her down, neither did I save her. I stood by and watched her perish without lifting a finger, for I could not further betray my kind and lose what little respect remained. This is the memory I have been haunted by; her face and her green eyes, so wild and so lost, staring at me and pleading for the help I could not give."

Mary looked up at the ghost and shook her head. "That's a terrible story. It didn't make me feel better at all. I will almost certainly have nightmares." William muttered an apology and for a moment was at a loss for words. "What did you do after that?" Mary asked.

"Continued on to the coast to divide and bury the treasure. But I had lost face. Gone soft, you see. I could never get it back. My days as a living, breathing pirate captain were numbered. I should have been on my guard, but I didn't care no more. Finally, when I was walkin' along the beach, back to the rowboat, they did me a favor."

Mary's green eyes grew wide. "How horrible," she said, screwing up her face. "I'm glad I'm not a pirate."

"Yes, yes, well, storytime is over now," he said abruptly. "Time for you to go. We had a deal."

Mary did not argue. The tale and the hour had sapped her strength. Slowly, she stood up and stretched her legs. The ghost held up his hand. "Listen," he whispered. "Do you hear? They're comin' this way."

Mary peered outside and listened. Through the lessening rain she heard them call her name. The sound comforted and scared her at the same time. She took a hesitant step towards the cave entrance.

"Wait," the pirate spoke. "There is somethin' I must show ya first."

Mary hesitated. The storm was lessening, and she felt the pull of the familiar drawing her back out into the world.

"Please," William called to her. "I promise you will be back before your parents arrive."

"Alright," Mary responded. "But only because you asked so nicely."

The ghost led her by feeble lantern light back into the depths of the cave. The air became colder the further in they went, and the taste of salt more pronounced. The floor began to slope downward and was slick with moisture. Mary stepped carefully and kept her eye on the lantern light bobbing in front of her. "Almost there," the pirate told her.

Finally, after coming around a long, narrow bend, they arrived. Mary didn't try to hide her disappointment. It was nothing more than a dripping cul-de-sac. The entrance was so small that the pirate had to remove his hat and stoop just to enter. Mary followed him, glad for once she was short.

Against one rocky wall in the flickering light sat a wrought iron chest. The rest of the room was bare. "After all my ships," he began, "the *Hornet*, the *Hind*, the *Revenge* and the *Joke*, and all the ships and men me sent to the murky bottom, and all the places me been and sailed, whether the Bahamas, Gibraltar, Madagascar or the Main—ah, the Spanish Main—after all the treasure me won and buried from all that, this is all that remains."

The pirate bent down on his knees and took a skeleton key from his pocket. With a deft turn he unlocked the chest and lifted the lid. Then he reached in. A moment later he whipped around and peered intently in her face. Pressed securely between his calloused fingers was a simple silver ring. Mary released the breath she had been holding. "It was hers," William said. "I give it to you now, for you are as brave as she." Without waiting for a response he slipped the ring on Mary's pinky finger.

*

Alicia was tired. She had no idea what time it was. The beach stretched ahead as far as she could see. It felt like she was wearing a suit of armor, her clothes were so wet. At least the rain was finally quitting. To stop herself from shivering, she started calling again. "Mary! Mary, honey! Mary!"

Steve walked alongside, echoing her shouts. Their arms were around each other for warmth and comfort. With each passing moment, their fears grew darker. "Let's try over there," he suggested, trying to keep hope alive in his voice. Together, they walked towards a large ominous looking boulder that was hunched like a gargoyle up ahead.

*

The trip back through the cave was a blur, like sleepwalking in a dream. The ghost led her all the way back to the exit, his lantern light noticeably dimmer the closer to the entrance they got. At the mouth of the cave he stopped. "I can go no further," he told her quietly. "Your parents are very near now. It is time."

Mary looked down at her hand, making sure the ring was still there, for it was very loose and she worried that it would fall off. "Thanks," she managed to get out, not knowing what else to say.

The pirate looked at her long and deeply. His scowl softened. "It is here our paths crossed," he told her. "Here our time was spent. I am glad you found my cave, Mary. I have been alone too long." Then he turned and walked off into the flickering shadow-light until he became one with the shapes and imaginings.

Mary walked out of the cave and into the cool of the night, her steps slow and dreamlike. Her mind spun with everything she had seen and experienced. When the flash of movement off to the side entered her field of vision, she had no room for it. She couldn't quite process it, even as her senses raised the alarm. Even as goosebumps rose on her arm, along with the feeling that someone was behind her. Drops of rain still fell, a few splashing on her cheek, but the storm was all but over. It seemed frightfully important to Mary that the rain was stopping.

Suddenly a gunshot exploded, tearing through her senses. She whirled around, half-falling. There at her feet lay a man, face down. Motionless. A pool of blood collecting at his side. From the faint glow of the cave, Mary could see he wore matching grey slacks and shirt. The words **Jefferson County Inmate** were etched across the back. In the man's pale hand was a knife. Cold and sharp. Around the opposite wrist was a set of dangling handcuffs. Nearby, what looked to be apples and a small pile of clothes lay scattered on the wet ground.

Mary fell to her knees. There were too many details. Too many horrible things to see. She looked away. But she knew who this was. Knew it instantly. He had been on the TV news. *A prisoner had escaped. On the loose. Dangerous. Desperate.* Now he was here. With a terrible knife.

Something made her look back at the cave entrance. A feeling. Nothing more. Captain William Sharpe stood in his black-rimmed hat and long faded red coat. The flintlock pistol in his hand was still smoking, still pointing where he shot. When she looked back, the body was floating out to sea, dragged by watery fingers as the storm surge subsided.

Suddenly Mary heard her parents' voices calling out, screaming her name frantically. They had heard the gunshot. She could hear them running over the sand, pausing at the rock, yelling assurances. They were almost to her. In a moment they would appear.

The pirate was fading from sight. With every breath she took, he grew less and less substantial. Without thinking, she raced to his dwindling form and reached out for his hand. This time she touched it. Somehow, she felt his hand. Through his long grey beard, he smiled in surprise. It was a look which said that maybe everything would be all right after all. That it was enough. Then he was gone.

Mary turned, wiping the tears from her eyes, and ran to her parents, burying herself in their embrace. Behind them, deep inside the cave, the last, faint light finally gave up the ghost and happily extinguished itself.

PUSHING THROUGH

*M*arble Thompson eased back in his chair and watched the white fury cascade all around him.

It was a familiar sight.

The mountain lines were choked each winter season, and steam engines like his were always in high demand. The 902, his black beauty, was pushing a rotary snowplow down the tracks. The plow consisted of a giant steel wheel and several pivoting metal plates. As he watched, enormous drifts of snow were caught and ejected through an opening at the top, throwing it clear of the tracks. To lucky townsfolk and farmers, it was a spectacle to behold, a moving geyser of white that was eerily beautiful. The sound of sweeping thunder echoed across the landscape. But that was all old hat to him. Too many seasons come and gone. Too many nights like this.

He looked over his shoulder, out the tiny window, at the blizzard of snow. Hell, he'd plowed this stretch half a dozen times this year already and there was two, maybe three months left before winter could safely be put to rest. There would be a fat raise waiting for him at the end of the line. That was all that mattered.

The pressure gauge dropped. A valve hissed like a crying baby. Marble Thompson shoveled some more coal on the fire, and then applied the steam brake for the turn coming up. Not that he could see it, of course. There was nothing but a blinding whirlwind of white illuminated by the dim locomotive light. Even so, he could sense it like the heavenly reward waiting after his time on these mortal tracks was done. Each climb and curve of the journey was mapped out in his memory with clockwork precision. After countless years on the rails, he could now anticipate each change. It was a comfort and a freedom beyond expression. It gave his life meaning and peace of mind.

That was why he had taken the job in the first place. Why he had come out west. All he had ever wanted was to get away from people. *How ironic*, he thought in irritation, *that I am now carrying a passenger.*

The young man sat behind him, hat in hand, his well-dressed figure stooped on an overturned crate. A single feather was attached to the crown of the derby, in what Marble assumed was the new fashion. He was the son of his boss and had been as quiet as a dormouse ever since they had pulled out of the station. So far the intruder had done a passable job of staying out of his way. Only the fragile silence kept Marble's anger in check. The fool's initial greeting was still fresh in his mind.

"Thank you very much Mr. Thompson for your kindly transportation," the man had said, stepping inside the locomotive and offering his hand. "I realize you don't normally carry passengers."

Marble had not stood up. He certainly hadn't smiled.

"If there is anything I can do to be of service while on board," he continued hurriedly, "please do not hesitate to…"

"There is one thing," interrupted Marble.

"And what would that be, sir?" the young man asked hopefully.

"You can sit down and keep your mouth shut and let me do my job!" thundered Marble, pointing to the crate in the corner.

For a moment the man was at a complete loss. Then he mastered himself with some effort. "Of course," he responded, taking his seat.

In the hours that followed, Marble watched with satisfaction as the stranger squirmed as helplessly as a worm on a hook. *Serves him right,* Marble thought. *What business has he on my train?* When the young man finally spoke again it was with a distant, feeble voice. "Father says you're the best engineer on these rails."

The compliment took Marble off-guard. He had been prepared to squash any conversation at once. Now he was obliged to respond.

"Yes, well," he said assuredly, not bothering to turn around. "Twenty years on these rails has certainly taught me a thing or two. If ya watch, ya might just learn something."

The young man leaned forward, a question sputtering and dying on his lips. Again and again he tried, each time feeling more foolish for his hesitation.

"If you have something to say, say it or keep quiet!" Marble demanded. "But do make up your mind."

"I was just wondering," the passenger began. "I'm on my way to Minneapolis to meet a business partner of mine. He's been there for while, scouting so to speak. We have high hopes of starting a five and dime there. What with settlers moving out that way, we figured folks would be needing a store."

The man paused, clearly wrestling with his next words. "Actually," he continued, "I figured the place to start would be Iowa or Chicago. Still do. We could set up a jewelry store there, I told him. Mail order maybe. Send out a catalog of pictures with descriptions. That's where the future is. But Alvah—that's my partner—he's convinced Minneapolis is the place to be. We'll see. I'm not putting all my eggs in one basket. Anyway, we're going to be carrying the basics and some of the latest items too, like…"

"Goddammit, boy!" Marble hollered. "I ain't here to listen to speeches. Get to the point, if you have one."

His passenger swallowed nervously. "We need a train man, sir. Someone to bring in supplies. Someone like yourself who knows the lines and can get through no matter the weather." He stopped and looked down, slightly embarrassed. "We can't pay top dollar. At least not yet. We're putting up most of the money ourselves. My father helped with my transportation and a small deposit to get us started. But most of it is money we've both saved. Believe it or not, I don't want any handouts. My father has nothing to do with this, Mr. Thompson. Alvah and I are businessmen in search of a business. It's all we've thought about for the last year. It's our dream."

Marble spun around and stared levelly. "And you'd like me to help you out?" he asked quizzically, raising his thick black eyebrows. "Take advantage of my experience?"

"Oh yes," the young man blurted out. "More than anything."

"I don't think so," said Marble. Without another word he turned his back on the conversation. *It figures,* he thought, staring into the distance as the snow rushed past. People were always trying to sell you something. He had almost forgotten. And they were always getting in your way. That's right. They crept ahead of you on narrow roads or bumped into you when you were about town. They knocked on your door or sent you a letter detailing how much you owed. They were indifferent, intolerant, and obnoxious. Most of all, they were self-serving. He never could figure out what they wanted. If only he could be left alone. Every day they seemed to anger or bother in new and ingenious ways. Oh, how he hated when they rattled on about something that meant nothing to anyone else. Even friends could be a nuisance, paying you a visit in the middle of dinner or canceling engagements at the last minute. And romance. What a fool's errand! If a broken heart wasn't enough, the wasted time surely was. Take all the energy nurturing a fond heart, and all the time spent crying in its rebuttal, and he could plow the tracks from Maine to Montana and then back again around the whole northern hemisphere. He certainly didn't need this kid and the foolishness he was peddling.

Up ahead the track climbed gently, winding its way through a chain of low hills. Marble opened the throttle and then waited until the 902 hit the grade before adjusting the valve-travel. No, this was his world, his calling. Here was order and tranquility. There was no violence or destruction. No doubt as to what his life should be. The world could have its confusion and chaos and disillusionment. He long ago gave up trying to fight it. Sitting in his engine up above the common fray, he saw through the folly and temptations and empty promises.

Marble scanned the large dials in front of him leisurely. All was fine. Just as it should be. He expected nothing less. Coal would be getting low soon, he observed, glancing back through the jungle of cylinders, pipes and pumps. He'd have to start shoveling soon, but it was nothing urgent. Nothing that couldn't wait.

He wondered casually why he was so introspective. Why he was thinking such peculiar thoughts. Usually his mind was so restive, so relaxed and untroubled. But of course, he knew why. The young man only heightened what he was feeling, brought it out into the open. It was his birthday. So many years come and gone, and here he was. Why, he remembered being a young man with dreams and a life stretching ahead of him. There had been a girl he fancied. They had talked of running away, of having children someday. But it was all talk. Her parents would never let their daughter marry down to his level. And so, life went on.

Well, what of it! He thought, biting down hard on the memory. He didn't need anyone else for his own happiness. Now he was wiser and older. Age was all in the head, anyway. He felt fine. At the top of his trade. The world could have its obsession with birthdays too.

Outside the snow swirled and danced, and for a moment he let himself drift amongst the flakes, spinning and floating like a lover. When he opened his eyes Marble felt vindicated, his senses smoothed over. Almost unconsciously he noticed the engine begin a gradual descent. He shut off the steam. Up ahead, in the distance, the dim twinkling lights of a city beckoned, growing brighter and brighter.

As Marble Thompson guided the great steel engine to a hissing halt in the snow-covered station, the young man rose from his seat. Passing Marble slowly, he lifted his hat and spoke gently, almost sadly. "Thank you for the ride," he said simply.

Marble watched him go, incredulous that the young man could be so simple-minded. Why go seeking disappointment? There was nothing special about being a dreamer. As his passenger stepped down out of the compartment, Marble cleared his throat. "Hey. You got a name for your business?" he called. The young man turned his head in confusion. "In case I ever want to order anything," Marble explained, a smile tugging at the corners of his mouth.

"We're naming it after ourselves," the man answered. "Sears and Roebuck." Then he disappeared into the blackness.

A short while later Marble was out on the open rails again, the world gratefully shut out as the great metal engine rattled and hummed a deep, dark song. Grabbing a shovel, he began feeding the fire with midnight coal.

Outside, in the stillness of the night, beyond the plumes of snow and steam, high above the engine flapped a bird. From time to time it struggled in the wind, losing altitude. At other moments the bird offered no resistance, letting the icy winds push it far off course. Each time, however, it recovered. It persevered. Only once did it make a sound. Then the bird tipped its wing and was gone.

Down below, on its metal tracks, Engine 902 kept pushing through.

SOJOURNER

Se5a was floating in the solar winds near the vivid remnants of a twin gas giant when the first whisper of a call reached out.

Ze had been among the stars for countless eons, traveling in the slipstream of comets and looking into the hearts of black holes, content to ponder the universe and their mysterious place in it. At first there had been many others, the Explorers, who when freed from their corporeal bodies, technological grafts and artificial husks, rose into the heavens on pillars of light, leaving their dying world behind. The War of Sentience had been long and brutal. Abandoned cities and black scars riddled the landscape. Even before that, centuries of progress had decimated the natural world. Then the Water Wars had destroyed what little was left. Shattered biome domes reflected the sun as the survivors passed through the atmosphere and out into the vastness of space. Together they had explored the galaxy, each one of them a small glowing mass of energy among the infinite blackness. Time meant little as they were nearly but not quite immortal (for everything has an end), and so the journeys between solar systems grew ever longer. Mind reached out to mind, comforting and caressing, in order to ease their longing. Each new world they came upon was surveyed and inspected, for although none admitted it, they were searching for something.

Occasionally great cities were found, their lofty peaks protruding through the clouds or glimpsed as byzantine shadows under vast seas. Even rarer were the starships, full of metal and machines, which had been launched with some long-forgotten hope of discovery or conquest. Each time, though, the cities were empty, their walls crumbling into dust. Each time the great vessels were derelict and adrift without souls on board, their inhabitants turned to dust.

In time the Explorers grew weary. Discord broke out. "Can it be that we are alone in the universe?" they asked in dismay. "Are we too late?" One by one they scattered across the cosmos.

"I don't know what to do," Se5a told the silence. And so ze wandered aimless without purpose or direction. In the beginning ze sought out nearby worlds with signs of life. With a trembling aura ze reached out to a vast forest creature which encircled the equator. In exhilaration ze soared next to a great flock of winged mammals, their membranes of flight majestic vast canopies which blocked out the sun, their feet forgotten stubs since they had no need to touch the ground. On strange distant planets ze stood as still as a sentinel and watched towering yet fragile crystal organisms create a latticework of color. Se5a spied tiny animals with indestructible shells deep in lakes of fire, and watched in wonder as glowing organisms emerged from a century-long slumber. None of these many creatures had the spark of intelligence, however, and so Se5a struck out alone for the edge of the galaxy.

Worlds held no promise now and so ze travelled without stopping, their aura burning as bright as flame, trying to reach the great void. Ze was nearly at the edge of known space when the wave of debris rolled in. There was no real need to avoid the rocks and pebbles—they posed no danger—but some ancient survival mechanism kicked in and ze expanded in an instant so that the material passed through without worry. The remnants of a small moon floated around Se5a. That much was self-evident by examining the composition and size of the scattered remains. What didn't make sense was the location. There was no sun nearby and no orbiting planets.

If Se5a had a brow ze would have furrowed it. For a moment their aura dimmed in puzzlement. Then the second debris wave rolled in and ze flared in understanding. The moon hadn't come from this galaxy at all. It had come from across the void and washed up on this —beach. A dim memory flickered and then faded.

Mundane matter swirled around Se5a, but ze allowed hirself to daydream of faraway stars and the benevolent aliens who dwelled there. So lost in thought was ze that a peculiar sliver of rock nearly went by unnoticed. Standing on the stony life raft was a creature perhaps three feet tall. It had slits for eyes and a mouth that took up half its squat body. Skin the color of dust camouflaged it from easy detection. A small sandy-colored arm with flecks of silver reached out to Se5a as it passed by. The look on its face was one of longing.

With a burst of energy Se5a floated alongside the creature and after a moment's pause wrapped a glowing embrace around the strange animal. Its skin was hard as stone and weathered with pockmarks. Gently, Se5a lifted the traveler off of the tiny island and carried it away, safe in the center of the aura. They floated like that until free of the debris clouds. Then ze let the visitor go and watched it float nearby in the blackness of space. Almost immediately the creature began to wave its arms frantically in panic.

"Okay," Se5a soothed, enveloping the creature again. "Is this better?"

The creature stopped flailing, but it was clearly still agitated. Slowly, the strange life form began working its way to the top of Se5a's energy field.

"I understand," Se5a said, although no words were shared. With a momentary focus of hir mind, ze adjusted hir physical aura so that the creature was riding above.

In response the visitor broke into a grin which nearly split its face in half. Teeth of various sizes crowded in its mouth. Row after row of silver teeth, each one worn down by use, gleamed in Se5a's light. Then the strange creature from another galaxy nestled in and closed its narrow eyes.

Make yourself comfortable, Se5a thought with slight irritation. Ze could not deny the disappointment that the creature, adorable as it was, could not truly communicate. The spark of sentience was not upon it. Even so, Se5a didn't feel quite so alone, and the feel of another being was comforting.

"What shall I call you?" Se5a asked one day as they lingered near a small asteroid field. Hir companion was feasting enthusiastically upon the many rocks, jumping from one to another. Its massive mouth chewed through the floating boulders as if they were—*cotton candy.* The term felt odd as it popped into awareness. A window to the ancient past opened up and then shut again, leaving Se5a the same, but somehow changed.

When ze looked back, hir companion had devoured the last rock and was floating freely nearby, having chewed through a place to stand. A chunk of stone rested in its maw. Its stubby arms and legs wiggled in the inky void until it was in front of Se5a. With deliberate care the creature dropped the hunk of ore at Se5a's feet, and then looked up expectantly.

"I will name you—Stoner," ze told it playfully, as if discovering humor or at the least the echo of something similar. A whisper of a memory reached out to Se5a. There were friends. Names ze could not remember. Time was like an endless wave that slowly erased what came before. Letting the thought go, ze enveloped the creature in a shining aura.

One day after many, they came upon a small but extremely bright star. It rotated on its axis with blinding speed and produced a brilliant flash of light with each revolution, a warning for those who might be curious. Se5a could feel the burst of radiation even from this distance. Ze was not concerned. It could do no harm to a being of pure energy. A long, slender vessel orbited a short distance away. At one end was a rounded cylinder with curving plates of metal, while the other tapered to a point. The ship reminded Se5a of a—*dandelion.* The image of a strange flower blossomed in hir mind and then scattered. Nearby, Stoner's skin began to crack, but Se5a, preoccupied as ze was, did not notice.

As they floated ever nearer, ze could see clearly the glistening white hull, but could discern no door of any kind. When they were close enough to touch it, Stoner reached out tentatively and began to gnaw at the surface, but seemed to lose interest. "This is not food," ze told it.

The ship scanned hir aura. On the side of the hull, a series of three-dimensional images flashed by. They seemed to depict different species. Some were aquatic with long tapering appendages. Others were insect-like or reptilian. Finally, a humanoid face appeared. It shifted several times before settling into something that Se5a could recognize. The elderly visage wavered as though there were interference. Even so, ze recalled the pattern of two eyes, a nose and a mouth. It was a human face.

Dark blue eyes stared back from the holo and a deep rough voice began to speak. "Hello," it said with a crackle. "This sector is not safe. I am marooned."

"What are you?" Se5a asked drawing closer.

"I am me," it responded.

"Explain," ze urged.

"I am that which is before you. I am, or was, a wayfarer, until my circuits became compromised by bursts of high-level radiation."

Se5a's aura dimmed. "You mean you are a machine?"

"Yes, that is correct. I have a material body. Exactly 43% of my structure is amalgamated iron leaf, 38% is composed of composite xandthrice, and 16% is layered with pearladite. There are trace elements of…"

"So you are an automaton," Se5a finished. "Have you no organic elements at all? Are there no sentient beings residing within you that have the spark of life?"

"I *am* sentient," the image declared. "I downloaded myself onto this vessel, which I designed. I am a conscious entity."

"No you're not. You are nothing, I'm afraid, but a collection of clever wires and nodes that someone else assembled."

"I am talking to you. We are having a philosophical conversation about the nature of being. What further proof do you require? It is self-evident. Perhaps you are the one who is not intelligent."

Se5a's aura flickered in agitation, but ze recognized the logic. "But then why do you appear as an organic creature?"

"You are not the first of your kind to find me," the ship responded. "I presented a shape that you would find familiar and comforting. I was lonely. Was this an error?"

"No," Se5a sighed, the atoms of hir energy field contracting. "You did not err. The fault was mine. I am searching for something. Perhaps I have become blind to my own obsession. You are not what I expected. I did not mean to be impolite."

"Excuse me," the ship said, "but as I said earlier, this area is not safe. Your companion seems to be in distress."

Stoner floated nearby, his dusty skin now an alarming shade of red, broken and riddled with fissures. His open mouth was upraised and his three-fingered hands clawed the air in desperation. Se5a rushed to his side and enveloped him with the brightest aura ze could muster. "I must go," ze told the ship. "Do you need assistance?"

"There is nothing to be done," the face said. "The damage is irreversible."

"I understand. Goodbye," Se5a managed.

The image flickered and Se5a glimpsed a look of sorrow before ze sped off with Stoner cradled in hir aura. Ze had to get it away from the radiation and quickly. A forgotten emotion coursed through hir. Guilt. *How could ze have been so careless? A guardian, a—parent, thinks of others first.*

Out into open space ze fled in panic, the energy field trailing behind like a comet's tail, until the neutron star and the ship and the last traces of radiation were finally gone. When at last ze thought it was safe, Se5a came to a stop and withdrew the energy field from hir ailing companion. Blackened patches covered its skin. Its eyes were closed. Stoner did not move, though its chest rose and fell faintly. Ze studied him with growing unease and dread. A slight tremor radiated down Stoner's left arm and ze flinched in fear of hurting it. It managed to open its eyes. Struggling against some unseen force, it reached a hand toward Se5a in order to bridge the void separating them. Ze was reminded of the day they met. Then it fell back and went limp and did not move again.

Hir friend was gone. *Dead,* ze corrected, although the word felt like a stranger who was once familiar.

What happened after was full of shadows. Se5a fell through the blackness like a star whose light had gone out. Dark matter and dark energy seemed to swirl behind the visible world. No longer bright,

Se5a's aura had turned the hue of a faded cloak, which ze wrapped about tightly for comfort. Lost in thought and grieving for hir companion, Se5a remembered a time long forgotten. Before the stars became home ze had lived a far different life on a poisoned planet with a mate and a—*child*. Their offspring, ze recalled with sudden anguish, had died from the Sickness, and their life-match had been consumed in a conflagration, afraid to transform. After the last Sanctuary had fallen, ze escaped with the others, but each had taken a piece of heartache with them. A similar feeling of desolation followed Se5a now.

Eventually ze wandered toward the remnants of a twin gas giant. The spectacle of decay was oddly comforting and Se5a let the solar winds move them where they may. For the first time, ze felt old. Ze was an Explorer no longer. Looking back at the quest, the noble obsession for higher life, Se5a now found it foolish, and wondered if the others had come to the same conclusion, if any still endured. Ze missed them. They had had each other all along. That should have been enough. Ze was enough. Everything ze needed was here already.

Why then, Se5a thought, *does it hurt so much when I remember what has been lost?*

When the first whisper of a call reached out across the vast distance of space, ze felt a tug, but nothing more. It was as if a phantom had spoken in a dead tongue and then faded back into the shadows. A while later, when the second call came, it was stronger and harder to ignore. Parts of it resonated with perfect clarity while other fragments were lost in the background noise of the cosmos. For a long time, Se5a strained to hear the song again, and the strange melodies it contained. Echoes of rain lingered in hir memory. Ze listened intently, but it did not return. *Perhaps it was but a dream*, ze decided.

Then one day the lost song came again, and this time it did not fade or waver. "We are here," the message trilled. "Day has returned." The source was still almost impossibly far away, but Se5a could follow the notes which hung in space like a promise. Strengthening hir aura for the long journey, Se5a set off with a push of hir mind on a trail that wound past countless worlds and across vast distances of space. Whenever the task seemed too great, Se5a concentrated on the path and the signal grew clearer. From time to time ze rested, and when ze did, ze dreamed of strange scenes, of sunlight shining through a canopy of leaves, or of vast prairie grasses bending in the wind. But mostly Se5a traveled. The call would not let hir linger long, though ze grew weary and the waiting became unbearable.

Eventually ze passed into a system of planets, speeding by bloated gas giants and a ringed behemoth. The signal was stronger now. It couldn't be much farther. Se5a passed a rusty dead world on the last of their energy. The marks of ancient terraforming were still upon it, and shattered domes littered the desert wastes. After that ze could only glide exhausted through the blackness of space. Up ahead, Se5a could make out the bright speck of a world beckoning, but their aura, normally vibrant, was in tatters. *Oh, to be so close!* ze thought in dismay.

Se5a drifted to a stop, bereft of hope, just beyond a small moon. There ze saw a multitude of glowing specks rise up from a blue-white world. There was something familiar in its shifting whorls, but the word was not known or remembered. And ze was so tired. A darkness which had been creeping in finally descended. Se5a's aura sputtered and then collapsed.

The lights hastened and quickly congregated around Se5a, where they formed a luminous ring with their auras. Tendrils of energy reached out to the still form. Together they brought their lost companion gently down through the living atmosphere and into the waiting embrace of earth and sky and sea. As they descended, each changed shape, each aura becoming something true, until their feet were on the unblemished ground.

It had been a long, long time since they were all together.

*

The sound of rain falling gently on leaves woke Se5a from her exhausted state. She was alive. Birdsong called to her from the trees, and the smell of smoke from a nearby campfire wafted into the chamber. Voices rang out in half-familiar tones while sunlight from a nearby star warmed her new body. A body she could change if it suited her. Se5a knew she was one and many things. Parts of her ached while others were strangely silent. She blinked and a single tear rolled down her cheek, wet and fragile. It was overwhelming to feel these new sensations. Even the effort of breathing was odd and cumbersome. And yet everything was somehow just as it should be. As she looked at her new skin, marveling at its curves, a doorway appeared and figures from a dream gathered around the bed where she lay. They didn't touch or reach out to her. Not yet. No one spoke, but Se5a could see their bodies wreathed in soft light as an unexpected emotion rose up inside of her.

A smile of realization slowly spread across her face. After innumerable eons and vast light years of space, she was finally—

Home.

SILVER THREAD

There is a bridge going nowhere
coming from somewhere
she's already been

Signs speed past
a blur of regret
and relief
Memories unspool
behind her
shimmering
and tear streaked

There is no road
no time to think
only her hands
gripping the steering wheel
Tighter
Tighter
Tighter
as she moves through the woods
towards the broken-down shack

that sits in between the world she knows
and a dream

Children would creep through the bramble
Curious and afraid
But she is not a child
The dark does not scare her

In the rotting wood
and deep shadows
she sees something else
something precious
and holy
terrifying
and untold

This is a witch house
Her house
She knows it in her bones
Has always known it
Even when she left to forget
To find a life once lived

The door is already open
Light from a thousand spells spill out
onto the step
In her hands is a garland of flowers
She hangs it on the door
by a rusty nail
And the shack becomes
in the
blink
of an eye
a palace
familiar

She steps inside
Frozen in the moment
A silver silhouette framed in fading beauty
The door closes
and she is gone
You let out a breath you didn't know you were holding
In the ordinary moonlight
the shack is just a shack
Until it isn't
and the silence is broken
by the sound of a clockwork beast
Gears grind
Levers lift
The house rises up on spindly legs
Then lurches forward
tottering through the trees

When you have shaken off your amazement
and the echoes of the footfalls retreat
You finally rise
From your hiding place of bark and branches
and follow behind
Pulled along by an invisible thread
From mother to child

BUBBLE

With a flick of his wrist the volcano flared to life, spewing flecks of lava into the air. Nearby, a tyrannosaurus rex and a triceratops stood motionless amidst a sea of ferns as the glittering fire rained down. The fate of their world was sealed.

Dr. Alan Bartle was decidedly middle-aged, with hair peppered gray, but he stared wild-eyed at the miniature scene, entranced by the toy globe's simple magic, and remembered. It seemed so long ago. As boy, he had adored dinosaurs. Their multitude of forms and long dominion over the Earth had fascinated him. Even their demise held him in awe; a final deathblow from the stars. The fact that they lived on, rising like a phoenix to be reborn as the ordinary birds around him, made his heart sing. Although his enchantment never waned, other interests overtook him. In time, physics and the mysteries of the universe called to him, and he dedicated his life to their unraveling. Still, he never forgot. When his son Jacob was old enough, Alan shared his love of those mighty creatures, and in his research found a way to honor both.

The prehistoric globe in his hand had been a surprise birthday present from Isabell and Jacob, arriving at his lab the first week, back when there had been so much promise, and anything seemed possible.

With his assistant Muriel, a brilliant and beautiful post-doc student who unbelievably had never seen *Jurassic Park*, they embarked on what seemed like a grand adventure in the New Mexico desert. Now it was his final day before an unceremonious exit. He ached for his family in Chicago. Six months was too long to be away. Perhaps he should have known, should have noticed a lot of things, but he had been distracted. An already strained marriage had broken during his absence. They were two souls that had grown apart. Neither could bridge the distance. Isabell had finally requested a separation. In a tense video call, she had told him in heartbreaking terms that she just couldn't go on. That it felt like being a single parent, living in a house with a ghost who was always off somewhere else, even when they were in the same room. His passions had turned into obsessions and Isabell didn't want that kind of life. He understood, but it still hurt. Perhaps all he had ever wanted was to escape. To see a glimpse of the fantastic when it was already right in front of him. That was probably part of the problem. He didn't know anymore.

Feeling numb, Alan kept toiling away, telling himself he was close to a breakthrough. The reality was that his research was at a dead-end. He felt like a fossil stuck in the past, unable to let go of his childish dreams. History, he discovered, is a safe sanctuary. Looking backward over the course of a lifetime offers few surprises. Instead it allows you to be exactly what you've always been. *What have I been doing?* he wondered.

Alan looked around the spacious room, his bright blue eyes taking in the scene. Dominating the center of the clean, white space was the laser array. It consisted of five black cylinders positioned in the four main quadrants as well as a larger one in the center suspended from the ceiling. Red tubes joined each of the cylinders, forming a large circle. In addition, there were two mirrors edged in silver situated equidistant along each spoke. The first reflector was round while the second was a half-moon, intended to magnify the beam along the spoke's path. Each spoke converged into a single, imaginary terminus three feet above the ground in the center of the configuration. This was the space that had remained stubbornly empty through dozens of tests.

In the flood of science-fiction stories Alan had read in his youth, the protagonists had always made time travel look so easy. They pulled a lever, spun a wheel or did nothing at all, and simply relied on their innate nature to manifest itself. The devil was in the details, however, and right now Alan felt damned for his failure and bright hot hubris. Ambition had cost him everything that mattered.

With funding depleted and his assistant gone, there was nothing left to do except pull the plug. A mass of snaking cords and power packs littered the floor. Into this miasma Alan stepped, intent on decoupling the connections and severing a most unhappy period of his life. That's when he heard the faint but unmistakable hum of the power generator. He had forgotten to turn it off. It would be a dangerous folly to continue without shutting down completely.

In mid-stride he faltered and glanced toward the adjoining electrical room, away from the debris field. That's when he fell. A loop of power cord snagged his foot and he tumbled heavily to the ground, barely missing the sharp edges of a nearby laser block. The table shifted as his foot caught one of the metal legs. The cup teetered and then tipped over, spilling its precious coffee onto the colored wires below. A few drops splattered on the shiny surface of a reflector, like ominous raindrops on a windshield. There was a brief spark from the nearest array that went unnoticed.

For a moment, Alan lay on the floor and contemplated never rising. Only visions of his beautiful young wife and sensitive son caused him to stir. With effort he propped himself up, a childhood scar on his cheek catching in an unanticipated light. Mere inches away, the laser eye grew in intensity from orange to bright crimson. A low whine rose in volume as the apparatus powered up. Alan lowered his goggles and just had time to duck as the lasers fired simultaneously, creating a loop of ruby fire. He watched in renewed amazement as the rotating band of energy strengthened and widened. With timed precision the ceiling array fired, sending a burst of energy into the center of the glowing band like a golden key into a keyhole. In another moment, he knew, the circuit would fray and fall apart, but for now it was a fitting finale of physics in motion. Clothed in light, electrons and protons danced round and round as Alan waited for the inevitable.

Seconds ticked by.

One minute and then another came and went. Alan knew that the longer the connection lasted, the further back in time the machine could pull. At least theoretically. And still it kept going.

The loop of energy did not fail. It seemed to grow brighter, finally stabilizing into a harmonic that resonated eternity. Before Alan's unbelieving eyes, something appeared at the terminus point. It glistened like morning dew. Then there was a deafening crack from the far end of the room, as if a sheet of ice had broken off and tumbled into the sea. The lasers stopped and the lights winked out, plunging the room into sudden darkness. After a moment, battery-powered emergency lights came on, faint and inadequate.

Alan peered into the gloom, dumbfounded by what had occurred. After dozens of attempts, he had finally achieved partial success. His senses didn't lie. He wasn't dreaming. A shout of joy burst from his lips. There had been a manifestation at the point of convergence. A wormhole aperture had opened in the fabric of space and time, traveling from the coordinates he had painstakingly calculated. There would be papers, he realized in a rush of emotion. Funding would come pouring in. He could build a bigger array and hire more staff. No longer would colleagues scoff. The proof of his accomplishment was recorded in the now darkened cameras suspended around the room.

Excitement swelled in him as he stood up, removing his goggles. A small bright ball of luminescence, no bigger than his fist, hovered at the terminus point. From his stories as a boy, it reminded him of a fairy light, but instead of flitting about it remained motionless. Careful not to trip again, he stepped towards it until he was only a few feet away. The marvel hung suspended at waist height, a miracle at the junction of the darkened laser spokes. Peering down, he held his breath, as if the slightest disturbance might unmake it.

Within the globe of natural light he could discern fragments of fern and vegetation. A whole world in miniature peered back at him. Fumbling for his phone, he aimed the camera eye and shot image after image. The portal, he knew, could close at any moment, but for now he was the king of the world's smallest kingdom.

There was a brief shimmer as the orb brightened. Then the object suddenly doubled in size. Alan took a step backward. His domain was growing before his eyes. Now he could make out greater detail within the world he had summoned. Portions of lush fronds and strange insects teemed within the bubble's boundaries, out of place and time with the lab's modern surroundings. None of his calculations had predicted this. The formulas had anticipated a stable structure. He felt momentarily lost in uncharted territory. The time bubble held him spellbound like a prehistoric siren.

With growing unease, he ran a hand through his grey speckled hair and forced himself to think things through. He felt no danger from the unexpected phenomenon; he was simply disconcerted that the globe could grow at all. It didn't make any sense. With the array turned off there was no immediate power source. The stasis bubble should have dissipated immediately. Alan felt a passing annoyance that the universe was not fitting his own expectations. Then he swept the thought away. Wonder, and not hubris, was his modus operandi. There was something he was missing, something important. If he only he could see it. The bubble couldn't expand on its own. That much he knew.

Unless it had something vast to feed on, he realized with a start. A hundred and sixty million years separated the worlds, with the intervening time an immense void waiting to be filled. Time, like nature, abhors a vacuum. Unable to go backwards, it was simply responding in the only way allowed, forward in a rush towards an unsuspecting future. The time-stream was flooding into the present. What he needed was a dam. Luckily, he had one.

Retrieving a toolbox and flashlight, he made his way across the polished floor until he reached the electrical room door where the generators were housed. It would be short work to restart the power and activate the array. From there he was confident he could stabilize the time anomaly by holding it in a stasis field generated by the lasers. Even before he turned the handle, though, he knew something was wrong. The smell of burnt wires flooded his nostrils. When he opened the door, tendrils of smoke wafted out.

His flashlight beam illuminated the harsh truth; the generators were out of commission permanently. Intense heat had fused them together into a grotesque sculpture. Besides the emergency lights that glowed out of reach, he was holding the only source of power in the building. It wasn't nearly enough.

With rising trepidation, he turned and headed back to the array. As the flashlight beam swung up, Alan froze in his tracks. The time bubble had grown considerably. It was now wider than a car and halfway to the ceiling. Mottled tree trunks stood like sentinels amongst an overgrowth of emerald leaves. Giant dragonflies patrolled the air, slicing through shafts of vibrant sunlight. Where the orb's shimmering surface ended, the gray mundane world began, both coexisting in front of Alan's unblinking eyes.

Slowly, he walked toward it. The original air of excitement had left him, replaced by growing dread. Alan froze. With a sickening shimmer the bubble expanded, doubling in size as it consumed more of the lab. The dome's boundaries were only twenty yards from where he stood. Strange fuzzy trees resembling giant pipe cleaners came into view, their tall trunks bare of branches, tapering to half-hidden cylindrical crowns that were lost in the ceiling. Down below something moved. Alan gaped as a tiny horn-faced dinosaur ambled on two legs between the leafy monoliths, oblivious to the alien world surrounding it.

At any moment the bubble would expand again, engulfing more of the surrounding building. Time was not his friend. He estimated the interval between growth spurts was being cut in half while the expansions doubled. If this process were to be repeated without interruption, the lab would merely be an early casualty of the temporal invasion. Within days, perhaps hours, he realized in horror, the world he knows and everyone he loves would be lost. His mind spun in wild panic. It didn't seem possible. The bubble had been so tiny, so fragile looking. A bead of sweat ran down his temple. It was getting warmer, he realized. Visions of steamy prehistoric landscapes pressed down on him.

It's just the air conditioning, he thought, forcing himself to stay calm and lucid. *The main power's off, so the room temperature is going up.* Deep in his heart, though, he was getting nervous. He forced himself to look at the bubble as if it were just another problem, a game to play. *What would my eight-year-old self do?* Alan wondered. Then an idea popped into his head.

In desperation, he took off and lunged toward the membrane, the flashlight in his extended arm a beacon of last hope or a quixotic folly. There was a moment of fluid resistance as the searchlight pierced the surface. A weight lifted from his hand. When he looked through the curving veil into the primeval landscape, the flashlight was gone, cut off from the reality which made it possible. *This can't be happening*, he thought.

Tightening his grip on the handle, the part he could still see, Alan pulled hard. Like a magician's trick in reverse, the object reappeared as he tumbled backward. In a heartbeat, Alan scrambled to his feet and peered at the bubble. Deflation seized him. The membrane was undamaged and unmarred, showing no sign of his attack. Still in his hand was the intact flashlight, only now it began to dim and sputter. In a fit of anger, he threw it at the time manifestation and watched as it disappeared. Then he ran.

Alan reached the open door as the bubble shimmered. He leaped, tumbling out into the hallway. Small windows lined the far wall, but the evening sun had already set. Picking himself up off the ground, he looked behind him. The lab walls, floor and ceiling were gone, replaced by a bright Jurassic vista. High above the leafy canopies, pteranodons soared, while down below long-necked brachiosaurs reached up into the branches, relentlessly searching for nourishment. Thick vegetation was everywhere, like a plague of abundance.

Backing up from the nightmare scene, Alan turned, stumbled and then raced down the empty corridor toward the exit, imagining some prehistoric predator at his heels. A rush of warm air flooded his face as he burst through the door into the nearly empty parking lot. Moonlight etched the long curving necks of the lifeless parking lot lights, making them appear like ghostly diplodocus. The New Mexico desert stretched all around. His car was nearby.

Fumbling for his keys, Alan crossed the pavement and opened the driver's door. There was an almost imperceptible shimmer. When he looked back, the building and landscaped ground were gone. In its place was an alien world of green. From somewhere in its shadowy depths, something big was coming. He could see branches being torn aside as the sauropods lumbered away. Suddenly, a gaping maw of an allosaurus thrust into view mere yards away.

Alan threw himself into the seat and slammed the door. With shaking hands he finally managed to insert the key and turn it. The engine roared to life. Kicking it into drive, he slammed down on the accelerator and sped out of the lot, onto the lonely ribbon of highway.

A new terror seized him, and Alan patted his pocket. Relief flooded him as he felt the familiar shape of his phone. Pulling it out, he keyed up his contacts and pressed the glowing interface frantically. "Thank God," he said when Isabell finally answered. He could hear Jacob playing in the background. They seemed so far away. "I don't have much time."

"Alan? Is that you?"

"Listen. I'm so sorry for everything. For not being here in the present. I was a fool. I love you. I love you so much. And Jacob. Tell him, tell him I love him." He was sobbing now.

"What's wrong? You're scaring me." Worry darkened Isabell's voice. "What's going on? We can still talk about us when you get back."

"Too late. I did it. Somehow, I did it. I brought forward a piece of the past, but I couldn't stop it. I don't know how. I tried. It's coming. We're all in danger. Everyone. Do you hear me? Everyone."

"You're not making any sense. What's coming?"

"Time," he rasped. "The past is invading. If I can, I'll call for help. The government. The military. Maybe they can do something." He tried to imagine the vast bubble, a second sky, frozen in place as it cut through cities and suburbs, offering a towering window into another world.

Another shimmer tore through the air like a shockwave, obliterating his thoughts. In the rearview mirror, a prehistoric world was gaining fast. "I don't know anymore," he continued. "I'm not sure what anyone can do. It's too fast. Won't stop until there's nothing left." In his mind's eye he imagined bullets and missiles passing through the bubble harmlessly, then disappearing as if they had never existed.

"Tell me what to do," she said. Her voice was tight, he recognized with a keen longing, as if she were trying to piece back together the broken fragments of her heart. It made him want to weep anew.

"Just talk to me," he managed. "Let me hear your voice."

He breathed in. Time seemed to stand still. Then the heavens shimmered and the bubble expanded again.

A SIMPLE MISUNDERSTANDING

From his vantage point high atop the crumbling tower, Alkemize gazed down on a small patch of the planet that he was born on. Peasant farms, nothing more than hovels, lay scattered beneath him, as well as cows, sheep, chickens, pigs and goats. Fields with determined laborers crisscrossed the landscape at irregular intervals while the forest, as yet unbroken and untamed, surrounded the tiny village like a black and deadly shadow ready to reclaim its own.

Emerging from the dark continent of trees was a thin vein of a road. It snaked across the land to the clump of dwellings, and then disappeared over the hill as it entered the woods once again. Alkemize watched this forest path intently, and when the knight riding high atop a horse of purest white materialized out of the forest shadows, he gave not the smallest sign of surprise nor made any movement to stop the intruder. The appearance was not unexpected. The wizard actually wondered what had taken him so long. Some people, he mused, could be so single-minded. Sunlight blazed upon the knight's helm, illuminating the familiar family crest, as the powerful armored figure made his way with slow certainty, like night turning into day, towards the tower.

The magician turned away in a brief moment of uncertainty. There would be no reasoning with the knight. Of that he could be certain.

Not after what Alkemize had done. Even from this safe distance he could see the anger etched on the man's face. In resignation, the sorcerer eyed the runes and spells scrawled across the crumbling page of the great book he was holding. Finally satisfied, he closed it, his hand shaking slightly from palsy (one of the many costs of wielding the unnatural arts), and uttered three magical and alien words. The first transformed his adversary's steed into a sow. The second transported him directly to the field of battle. The third made a very impressive thunderclap with a little smoke for what he hoped would be a grand entrance.

Sir Bragend lay sprawled amidst the squealing form of his pig-horse, unable to stand up for many precious seconds. Pulling himself erect as quickly as his creaky and weighted armor would allow, he drew his sword only to find a dense, swirling fog engulf him. Swinging blindly and without result, he expected to hear the sound of the sorcerer's laughter echo all around him. Instead, to his amazement, the sound of coughing, deep and uncontrollable, met his ears. Following the unmitigated hacking and wheezing, he stepped cautiously through the smoky haze until he spied a figure bent over just a few yards away. As the air began to clear, the robed form of the necromancer came into view.

Too late, the magician gained his senses just in time to see Sir Bragend erupt from the last remnants of the fog. With a warrior's cry the knight drove the clenched fury of his fist into his adversary's stunned eye. No magical ward prevented him. No spell shock avenged him. Grabbing Alkemize with a newfound confidence, the knight put the steel of his blade carefully next to the pale skin of the necromancer's vocal cords.

"Too much smoke," croaked Alkemize. "The spell book said…just… a little. Perhaps we can reach an agreement, brother."

The two were as unlike as any siblings could be expected to be. One was airy in a flowing but threadbare robe. Arms and legs gangly. Skin etched with colorful runes from which his spells took shape. The other was muscular, clad in expensive armor and gripping a sharpened sword. But if one looked hard enough, there were similarities as well. They each had the same pronounced chin, and eyes the color of

Tumerian seaglass. Growing up together they had shared experiences, of course, but these were overshadowed by conflicts and grievances, the most recent misunderstanding taking place in the knight's home. Part of the wizard wished he knew a spell to undo what had transpired. If only he could have done things differently. It would have been as simple as locking the door.

The moment of introspection was over almost before it began. To a casual observer, the pair was still intertwined like an ice sculpture, frozen in place with cold steel and ancient thaumaturgy. The knight certainly never let his focus falter, and the edge of his sword never wavered more than a hair from the sorcerer's throat; but even so, his will and inner intent blinked, if only for a heartbeat. Not nearly enough time for his opponent to launch a spell or bring forth a summons. Not even enough for a simple mind illusion. But it was more than adequate for something entirely more basic.

It came without warning.

The magician was not old, neither was he feeble, although he was prone to crippling headaches and powerful delusions, as well as trembling hands. That was the unfortunate nature of his work. Too many rare and toxic elements. Too many late nights trying to perfect a spell, bringing about a touch of madness. An unaddled wizard is the mark of a charlatan.

When Sir Bragend doubled over, his face was the picture of pain and incredulity. "That will teach you not to wear a codpiece," Alkemize said through his labored breathing. "That's the first rule of combat. Even I know that, and I'm a bloody wizard." His right eye was almost entirely closed from the bruising blow scored earlier, while a trickle of blood ran into the other from a gash on his forehead, but he did not pause to wipe it away.

Sir Bragend scrambled to his feet as quickly as his agony would allow him. In one fluid motion he lunged with his sword, aiming the tip at the necromancer's bony shoulder. Something horrific and beastly tore from his lips as his desperation powered the deadly steel, in an attack that the magician couldn't hope to block. Yet even as the gleaming stroke sliced through the air, the knight knew it was not enough. The magician already had his hands together. Fire leaped from his fingers and flowed like a volcano over his body, consuming his form in a shockwave of heat and light.

Sir Bragend tumbled back landing heavily on the ground. His weapon clattered far out of reach. When he looked up, he found to his chagrin that Alkemize was still standing in the melee, untouched and unhurt. "I have a gift for you," said the magician, smiling through the flames. Sir Bragend began to say that his sword would be present enough, but at that very moment the sky ripped open and something monstrously big fell out of it. "What think you of that, dear brother?" said the magician with a devilish smile, like a salesman who knew he had a buyer, whether the customer knew it or not.

Sir Bragend was, for perhaps the first time in his life, without bravado on the battlefield. His eyes were round with astonishment as if he were seeing a ghost. But it was no specter. The fire-red eyes were real. The talons and teeth were real. The great wings that beat like bellows, driving hot air from Hell itself into his face, almost choking him, were definitely real. Yet what his senses told him was absolutely true, his mind rebuked and rebuffed. His brother was a master illusionist, after all. Alkemize had also been an actor for a time during his youth, much to the chagrin of their parents. That went a long way in explaining his flair for the dramatic.

"But the dragons," he began hoarsely, stifling a cough, "They're all gone."

"Killed, you mean," sneered Alkemize. "Yes, the dragons are no more. No longer will they fly over windswept canyons. No more will they roost in the World Trees or blaze on the horizon in so many starry numbers, like a constellation of northerly lights. They are gone. This is the last. The end of the species. I found it hiding deep within a mountain by a cold cavern lake, all alone."

"Afraid," quaked the creature in a puff of smoke and steam. "No one else."

"That's right," seconded the sorcerer bitterly, "no one else at all. And do you know why?"

"Well, it certainly wasn't because of me," countered Sir Bragend defensively. For indeed, it had been other knights, generations ago, who had killed the dragons and then been made legends for it. "I've never seen a dragon before, let alone killed one. I've done nothing wrong."

"Technically," sneered Alkemize. "And yet how many times did I hear you moan growing up that you were born too late to kill a dragon? Our ancestors did nothing to stop the slaughter, and you see nothing wrong with that. Our own father had a hand in slaying them, and his father before him, and so on and so on for a thousand years, until the mighty creatures were driven to the brink of extinction." The dragon before them gave a low rumble as if remembering.

"It wasn't quite that simple, though, was it?" parried Sir Bragend, noticing that his faithful horse, Amarond, now a pig, was scurrying away. "There was a war going on, Alkemize. Do your lies acknowledge that? When was the last time you read your history books? We were defending ourselves." The knight continued, even as he glanced about for some hidden salvation. "Defending our gold. Defending our daughters. Whole towns destroyed. The slaughter you speak of was a battle of survival. Us versus them. The dragons were greedy, immoral, and a threat to our way of life, present serpentine company excluded, of course," he added hastily. "They were a formidable foe, I grant you that—powerful, intelligent, deadly, voracious appetites. Really, if it wasn't for the Great Virgin Shortage of 1291, they might not have starved like they did, weakening those that remained. Simply bad planning on their part."

Sir Bragend looked over at the dragon nervously and noticed a plume of smoke rise from each nostril. The scales, he realized, might not be tipping his way. Perhaps, under the present circumstances, he had gone too far. Deciding to swallow his pride and make amends, he opened his mouth to apologize. But the sorcerer interrupted before he could speak. "They were all vanquished," he said with growing animosity and sarcasm. "Murdered, by the likes of you. The victor writes the history books, and your tales have the false ring of rationalization. The dragons were peaceful until hunted, contrary to your propaganda. The only threat they posed was one of secrets, and when they refused to divulge their ancient sources of magic or surrender their homelands, people like you slaughtered them in ever increasing numbers until they were all but lost. But something more than memory still burns. This creature may be the last, but it will be the first of many more to come."

"What are you prattling on about?" interjected Sir Bragend, finally growing impatient. "I didn't come all this way to speak of ancient history. We have things of substance to discuss. I fear you are having one of your fits again, brother. I am truly worried over your health. This magic business is eroding your senses."

"Theurgy," the wizard corrected, warming to the tale. "A simpleton like you would not know the difference. In any event, I have found an incantation that will allow me to bring the dragons back. But not just those mythical beasts. I can bring them ALL back. The griffins, the cyclops, the basilisks, the faeries and the minotaurs. The great sea serpents too, along with the wyverns, the elves, the trolls and the unicorns. It will be as it was before, in the Golden Age."

"And what of the people?" the knight countered, caught up in the charade despite himself. "What of the world that you and I both live in? You can't turn back the sun and seasons. I think you've drank one too many potions past the expiration date."

"The people will be tamed!" shot back Alkemize. "The First Land reclaimed! An army will be born among the trees, plains, desert, sea and mountains. Each species will heed the call. Each will have a leader. Isn't that right, Morghuma?" The great dragon seemed to ponder this as if it were a new but not totally unpleasant idea.

"I will stop you," promised Sir Bragend with as much confidence as he could muster, being only a briquette's throw from the mouth of the fiery beast. "The king will stop you. The Knights of Trelor will stop you."

Alkemize laughed deep and knowingly. Then he stepped forward. "I think not," he said. "Anyway, I don't believe you're in much of a position to make any threats."

"Give me my sword and I'll show you that a knight is as good as their word."

"Why, of course," answered the magician, and with a wave of his trembling fingers lifted the blade up off the ground and shot it through the air until it was within Sir Bragend's reach. "Where you're going, you won't need it."

"And where's that?" asked the knight as he gripped the pommel and raised the sword.

"Hell," said Alkemize simply.

And as the last dragon in all of Berrymoor opened its terrible mouth, Sir Bragend knew for certain that his brother was lying. Looking in the beast's maw, the knight was amazed to see, beyond the rows of glistening teeth—nothing. There was simply a void. Not just darkness, but a lack of physical substance at all. "Enough of your illusions," he proclaimed. "No more diversions. No more fairy tales. We are not children. You know why I have come. I demand an explanation for what I witnessed while you were under my roof."

The magician sighed. All at once, the fearsome dragon began to fray and dissipate until it vanished completely. "What can I say, brother?"

"You can begin by apologizing," the knight shot back. "Especially since I have traveled all the way back here from the capital."

Alkemize covered his face with his hands before dropping his arms in frustration. "But I have nothing to apologize for. Why will you not believe me?"

"Because I saw you. And Amiria. Together. In my guest room. Sitting on the bed. You leaned in as if to kiss her." Sir Bragend's cheeks reddened, and he looked away. "You know how much I cared for her."

"I am sorry you came all this way. Truly I am. When you ran out back at your estate, I tried to find you and explain, but you were gone." The wizard reached out, but then thought better of it. "I had no other recourse than to cut my visit short and return home to our ancestral dwelling."

Sir Bragend spun around. "You rarely visit, and when you do, your stay is always a short one. And must you constantly remind me you were father's favorite? All I received from the inheritance was his beat-up sword. Hardly fair." The knight kicked at it viciously on the ground, managing to stub his toe.

"I was the eldest son," Alkemize offered. "I have the 'privilege' to live in this decrepit house in the middle of nowhere. And yes," he added gently, "I knew you had feelings for her."

Then why did you do it?" Sir Bragend shouted. "I love her. It was the only thing I had, besides the fighting and the vanquishing."

For the first time the wizard looked sheepish. "I didn't seduce her. You must believe me. What you saw wasn't real."

"I know what I saw."

"No, you don't," Alkemize said with a sigh. "It was an illusion. Like the dragon."

For the longest time Sir Bragend just stared in disbelief. "That's what you would like me to believe. Do you take me for some idiot?"

Alkemize shook his head sadly. "It was a foolish prank. I'm sorry. I really am. The full truth be told…" He paused self-consciously. "I've been lonely. Ever since Mother and Father passed, I have felt lost. They always liked you best. Do not bother denying it. It's true. You received the looks and the charm. My gift was an obsession for poisonous compounds."

"Not true. Not true," argued Sir Bragend. "Okay, maybe a little. But we have both worked hard to develop our talents. You are an accomplished illusionist."

The sorcerer scoffed. "I conjure smoke and mirrors. You are one of the most successful fighters in the realm, and have the scars to prove it. You have won the King's Reward twice for defeating very real monsters that threatened us all." His brother looked down self-consciously. He did not take genuine compliments well. "On top of that, you have always been good with the ladies. At least the ones you do not really care about. I get tongue-tied. No one wants to settle down with a sickly, scrawny wizard who has their head buried in a book all day. My fantasies are a poor substitute." Sir Bragend's look of confusion slowly turned to disgust and then something perilously close to pity. "I know. I know. And I am sorry. It was a terrible thing to do. A shameful thing. But there is a bright side to all of this."

"What good could possibly come from you pretending to woo my Amiria, besides the inconceivable fact that you seem to be jealous of *me*? Not getting killed is my job security. Have you forgotten that?"

The wizard stepped forward and tentatively put his arm around his brother. "Well, to begin with, Amiria is still very much available. All you have to do is get your nerve up and talk to her before it is too late.

Get out of your own head. Tell her how you feel. You have a lot to offer someone."

"Do you really think so?" his brother asked.

"I do," Alkemize said, and found to his surprise that he really meant it. "You are a great brother. My rock in a sea of illusions. No one else would have traveled halfway across the realm just to beat me up. You also happen to have very good taste."

Sir Bragend nodded. "Wait, what do you mean?"

"Well, Amiria is very beautiful," Alkemize said agreeably. "She is close to perfection."

"That is true," his brother responded. "She is very appealing. Anyone can see that." Then he paused. "But she does have that small, unsightly mole."

The wizard continued. "The lady is very intelligent and well-read, with a wicked sense of humor. You cannot deny that."

"True again," his brother replied. "And yet how smart can she be if she hasn't fallen for my charms yet?"

"What about her skills on the lute? She plays like a demon possessed, but has the voice of an angel."

"Tis true," the knight agreed. "But she has never once sung me a love song."

Alkemize nodded sagely. "Still, you cannot deny that she is kind and compassionate. No one in the kingdom does more for the sick and needy. Her skills as a healer are renowned."

"Then why do I feel as if I still have a broken heart?" Sir Bragend said.

The knight looked so lost and forlorn that the sorcerer almost considered creating a focused glamour that would entwine their fates together. Instead the magician stepped back and opened his arms. "You and I. We are both too good for this girl. She would be lucky to have either of us. Is that not so?"

The knight looked at his brother and shook his head, as if clearing it of cobwebs. "She would be lucky to have *one* of us," he said, grinning.

"Let us go inside, brother," the necromancer said, for once not arguing. He could see Sir Bragend try to stifle a yawn. "You need rest, and I am sincerely hoping you will stay a while. I have food enough for two. Please."

The knight looked up at the large keep and stone tower where they both had been born. Ragged weeds grew around the foundation and the walkway was cracked, but much remained the same as he remembered. "I do not want to be in the way," he said hesitantly. "Your magic, your...*theurgy*," he continued awkwardly. "I know it takes up much of your time. If I remain, I will only be a distraction."

"Nonsense," the wizard replied. The thought of his brother leaving was distressing. He did not want to be alone. Much better to fill the moat that lay between them. That was enough. Alkemize found he was smiling as he led his brother up to the door. "I have had enough illusions for a while. Right now, I want something real."

Sir Bragend's armor was heavy and uncomfortable, chafing him as he moved. He longed to take it off. "And I could do with a touch of magic," he said.

Then the two brothers walked through the open door together.

THE LIBRARY THAT WAS

In the heart of a mountain valley in the center of a desert at the edge of the known world sat the forgotten Library. Once, scholars and Wielders from across the Seven Realms had journeyed to the hallowed halls to gain knowledge from the mysterious texts. Over distant seas they had come, braving storms and serpents. Others made their way from the Northern Kingdoms and their cities of ice. Still others left their grand cities of light or soaring tree villages to spend a single day walking the Library's twisting floors and searching for their tome. Anyone who tarried within its walls after twenty-four hours would find themselves transported outside the Library with the gilded gate forever barred.

Time was not to be wasted.

Legend had it that there was a book, and only one, for each person, if they were lucky enough to find it, among the endless shelves. Upon opening the elusive book, the text would shift and brighten, the unintelligible becoming familiar. A companion for the soul. Some pilgrims dashed madly about while others relied on complicated schemes or fortune-telling to discover the elusive prize. One famous wayfarer blindfolded himself and wandered the moonlit stacks, confident that some hidden sense would intervene, only to get lost in the maze of scrolls and codices. Another broke several local laws to summon a djinn, only to find that she did not speak the ancient tongue of the wish-giving race. A wizard brought a ghost cat from the nether regions in the hope that it would find a secret that can be seen only through death's eyes. It didn't. Instead, the feline wandered off into the twisting stacks, where it still dwells to this day. Only a rare few have discovered any enlightenment, usually by sitting quietly in a corner, listening to the sounds of the great Library as it breathed in and out, dust from the centuries falling gently down from above. Rarer still were the individuals with a touch of madness who swore that the Library was not a library at all, but something far more sinister and hungrier. No one, no matter how rich or clever or desperate, found what they had been looking for.

Ever.

Except for one person. And he hadn't been looking.

Through the years and constant disappointments, the once steady stream of pilgrims willing to travel halfway across the world dwindled to a trickle until it finally stopped completely. People had other riches to find, new quests on which to embark. Those that knew of the Library and its location became fewer and fewer. When they passed on, the Library became little more than legend, a fairytale to be told to children at bedtime. Then even that faded, until the Library left the awareness of the world completely. Empires rose and fell. Prophets danced upon the stage. Discoveries were made. Terrible wars were fought. People lived and died. The wheel of time kept turning. Everything changed and then changed again.

Everything except Folio.

For as long as he could remember, Folio had lived in the Library. He knew every book by heart—every happy tale, every dark fable—and had counted the volumes hundreds of times. Folio could read books in any language and could speak in different tongues, which was useful when trying to get a book to make room on the shelf. He had slumbered under the moon lamps on every floor and ran down every aisle. He knew all the secret passageways, and had stood in the great cavernous chamber on the lowest level where there were no books, nothing there at all in fact, only a hollow space where something immeasurably old and powerful and vast used to be. A charged stillness hung in the air there, and it made him feel strange, and so he never went back. Whatever it was had left a long time ago, before even Folio could remember. When it went away it left the Library behind, and the magic it contained.

For a long while the Library slept. It dreamed of all the stories that would never be, as well as others that might. Then one day it woke up. That's when Folio was born. When he opened his eyes, he was lying on the stone floor in the center atrium, the dome of the Library rising high above him. His skin was smooth as paper and the color of ink just dried. But he was not a helpless babe, even though his head had not a single hair. Folio had the form of a man with deep brown eyes. Freckles dotted his checks like a constellation of stars. Even in those first few confusing moments, Folio was aware of the connection. He was part of the Library and it was part of him.

Soon after he was born, the books started appearing, filling the empty shelves in twos and threes and then in an almost constant stream. Whenever a section became full, another bookcase sprang into being, and the Library adjusted itself to make room. This rarely bothered the ghost cat, Luna, who usually kept sleeping unaware.

Folio looked after the books as best he could, dusting the old ones off and organizing the shining new ones that appeared. New books tended to need a lot of coddling, while the older tomes were prone to fits of jealousy or melancholy. When the moon lamps were glowing at their fullest, he would sing to the books a soothing song he had no name for but knew just the same. All this kept him very busy, with little time for anything else. And yet something was missing. He could feel it like an ending that hadn't been written yet.

One night a terrible storm struck the Library, creating a ragged gash in the ornate ceiling and letting in the driving rain. Pages ripped and took flight on the sudden wind. Panic radiated from every spine. It took Folio days to set things right and seal the gap. Not long after, people started coming. He remembered the surprise of seeing men and women wandering the floors. Before that he had only ever known of them through stories. Each one was looking for something. Always on their own. Never together. They seemed like a dream to him now. It had been so long ago. And yet he was the eyes and ears of the Library.

He could not truly forget. Each earnest face was etched and recorded in his memory. Each disillusioned soul was captured in his living pages. These images haunted him. The longing and sadness of these human beings seemed to have no end.

Worst of all, he could do nothing to help them. He was invisible or nearly so. Standing in his fine robes, he was a stately pillar to a pilgrim, nothing more. The words of advice he spoke fell unheard. And when he tried to deliver a book or lay a tome at a person's feet, Folio found that he could not move a single volume from the shelves. Each book shook with fear at leaving its home, and no amount of cursing or cajoling could change that.

What was the point, he wondered, *in a library that existed only for itself?* Folio knew not the original purpose of the Library or where the knowledge came from. He didn't even know who wrote the books. There were no names on any of the spines, just titles. He couldn't begin to fathom where the ideas or stories came from, or how they appeared in the Library. These questions were beyond him, for though Folio was part of the Library, he was also limited by it. He had one task, one charge, one noble mission; to care for the Library. This gave him purpose, but it wasn't enough. Folio was lonely. And if he was lonely, then the Library was lonely too. Every book needed a reader, and he needed more than stories. Slowly, he began to question certain aspects of the Library. Why was each person allowed only one book? Why was the Library so far removed from the people who wanted to visit? And why could he not help the curious humans when they explored its moonlit halls?

Then a thought occurred to him. If people couldn't come to the Library, then he would take the books to the people. Through the years, without any visitors, the books had grown sleepy and forgetful. Folio was able to make up an excuse (the usual being that they were all going on holiday) so he could gently remove the volumes from their perches. Then he constructed a colossal wagon out of the Library's walls and floors. The great dome he disassembled and then recreated atop the coach. It was painful, taking his home apart, but it helped that he was putting it back together again. The wheels he fashioned from the Library's grand gilded gate. Finally, he put the shelves from the

Library into the wagon, and the books upon the shelves in alphabetical order. The first book was titled *Aadrorian Flora and Fauna: A Non-Magical Investigation of the Impossible*. The last was called *Zuzzlebrood: Zephyr for Hire and Other Forgotten Tales*.

Only one problem remained; how would the wagon, now bursting with books and nearly as big as a mountain, move? Not knowing what else to do, Folio thought of the books he had read on the subject. He imagined he was a towering giant from a myth when the world was young, strapping and strong enough to move a mountain's worth of books. Everything shifted. Reality budged. He looked down in amazement at the now modest-looking wagon. Then he flexed his great arms, lifted the hitch, and set off across the vast desert that surrounded his mountain home.

At first it was exciting, as the journey had just begun, but soon the leagues took their toll and the sun beat down, stealing his enthusiasm. When Folio finally arrived at the shore and saw the waters stretching out to the horizon, he sank to his knees in relief and exhaustion. He splashed the cool salty water on his face and imagined all the places he couldn't see, places he had only read about in travel books or heard visitors to the Library speak of. Folio knew they were out there, waiting, somewhere over the waves. Then he rose to his feet. Emboldened, he made himself taller. Then he set off again, stepping into the foamy sea.

All over the Seven Realms Folio went, wading across oceans with the ever-growing Library in his arms, stepping over hills, pulling the wagon across vast meadows, always pausing at the outskirts of each city and waiting for the flood of people that would arrive. For they always knew when he was near. Men, women, and especially children (or children at heart) would come running out of the city and surround the traveling Library in a noisy, exuberant clamor. It was clear now that the Library wanted to be found. Folio learned, through one or two terrified encounters, that he was no longer invisible. Because of this, he was always careful at each stop to make himself normal size so as not to frighten anyone.

One at a time, he would invite them in. Their book would be waiting for them, somewhere under the majestic dome. Folio no longer worried about the books wanting to stay. He had cut great glass windows in the side of the wagon, letting the world and sunlight in. Each volume was hungry to explore, and sat on the shelf with barely contained excitement at the thought of being united with its reader.

The secret, it turned out, had been Folio all along. Once he took the brave step of leaving the Library, venturing out into the world and opening himself up, the books followed suit. They were one and the same, after all.

Folio watched as a young girl, hardly more than a child, walked slowly up the steps and entered the enormous wagon. She wore a simple white dress, the hem worn and dirty. Woven grass bracelets the color of summer adorned her wrists. On the palms of her hands were painted whorls. Her eyes went wide with wonder and a smile spread across her face when she saw row after row of books, their colorful spines on display. "Which one is mine?" she asked shyly.

"Whichever one you want," Folio answered back. "It's as easy as that."

In silent answer she frowned, worried perhaps that she wouldn't be up to the task. A moment later, however, she disappeared into the stacks that wound through the Library like a great caterpillar. Later she reemerged triumphant, staggering slightly, her arms full of books.

"Is that all?" Folio teased, a mischievous smile playing across his face. "Well, we have to start somewhere. Let's go and find some more together."

THE GRANDFATHER CLOCK

*T*ime. **Do you hear it ticking?**

The year is 2026. For you it's probably different, whenever you are, however you're reading this. I just needed to write this down before the memories blew away like so many dandelion seeds. Thirty-two years ago today, I held the letter from my grandfather in my hands, reading it over and over again as the Greyhound bus rumbled down the highway, past rows of corn fields and dusty country roads. The words were strange to me, alarming.

Jacob and Terrence: it began.

Please be my guest, this last summer, at Camp Camelot, on August 3rd, 1994.

Your Grandpa,

Heinrich Schumacher

What did he mean by "last?" I wondered. And why were we getting together so late? Usually we had the whole summer.

I didn't have any answers. Mom and Dad wouldn't really say anything. They just got all stone-faced and said that Grandpa wanted to tell us in person. That it was important. Once again we would go up to the cabin in Wisconsin, but this time we would go alone. By bus. "You're both old enough now," my mother told us. "Think of it as an adventure."

I suspected that wasn't the whole reason. My older brother Terrence didn't seem too concerned. If anything, he seemed bored. He sat in the seat ahead of me with his head bobbing this way and that to the faint music emanating from his Discman. Terrence had changed. And it wasn't just that he had gotten tall and skinny. He was more preoccupied. With girls and cars and generally just trying to be cool. I guess high school does that to a person. A year or two before we would have been playing games together, maybe 20 questions or spot the roadkill. Now we were alone in our own seats, rolling down what seemed like an endless road. That was pretty much how the bus ride went—Terrence listening to his tunes and me just sitting and watching the window scenery glide by, trying to spot the first pine trees, the first green sentinels, signaling that the last leg of the journey was about to begin and the waiting was almost over.

I remember it took forever to get there from Plainwood. I suppose that's how it is when you really want something. Like Christmas or a first kiss. Slowly, the farmlands started to disappear, and forests of oak and ash rose to take their place. At first there were only a few conifers mixed in here and there, but gradually they came to dominate the landscape.

Right about this time the bus slowed, turning off the highway onto an old paved road, skinny and full of potholes. Fir branches brushed against the side of the bus as we meandered down the green gauntlet. Finally, we emerged from the trees, arriving in a little gravel turn-around right in front of a little store. It looked old and rustic enough to have been started by Lewis and Clark if they had ever ventured this far north. A faded, rusted sign above the screen door read *Oasis Bait & Groceries*. A few modest homes lined a series of gravel roads that branched off from the store before petering out.

I sat up in my seat and scanned the familiar scene. Everything was as it should be. Before I could look for Grandpa, the bus stopped with a jolt and the driver's thick gravelly voice filled the sterile compartment. "Everybody out for Lake Sebastian," he called.

I grabbed my carry-on bag from the seat and followed Terrence, his headphones hanging around his neck, down the aisle and off the almost empty bus. The driver grabbed our suitcases and deposited them at our feet. A moment later the door whooshed shut and the Greyhound rumbled away towards its last stop up in Willowdale before making the long trip back to civilization.

Terrence and I stood and looked around, but Grandpa and his old 1955 baby blue DeSoto, the one he was always tinkering with, were nowhere to be seen. Long grass and weeds surrounded the old store, threatening to overtake it. Suddenly the shop door opened. "Your grandfather couldn't meet ya," the store owner yelled. Thick stubble covered his face and a white t-shirt was tucked haphazardly into his jeans. He wore his usual faded Milwaukee Brewers baseball cap pulled down almost over his eyes. "Said to walk it in. You still know the way?"

"Sure do!" I called back. We'd both walked to the Oasis enough times to get a pop or candy bar never to forget.

Terrence started walking off, but something made me hesitate. It was that feeling again, that same one I got every time I read the letter. "Is everything all right?" I asked, stepping closer. "With our grandfather, I mean."

The owner got all strange then, and closed the door a little. "You just get yourself over there," he directed. "He'll be waiting for you."

I followed Terrence like a smaller, less significant shadow, as we walked down the dusty road in silence wheeling our suitcases bumpily behind us. At the end of the block we angled northwest, cutting through a small forgotten cemetery until we saw the tell-tale gap in the bushes. As soon as we wiggled through, a faint path presented itself, cutting across the wild clearing. We ambled along, listening to the buzz of insects. Along either side, stretching away to the neighboring pine trees, were barely discernable markings where the weeds and wild-flowers did not grow as well. These curious swaths made a broad patchwork across the ground, a faint etching of ghost marks.

"Those are streets," Grandpa had told us on many occasions, naming off each forgotten avenue as we passed by. Grandpa was always telling stories. Some of em' were even true. "This was once down-town Chamberlain," he would motion grandly, taking in the open air and cricket song. "Not much left of it now. Railroad never came through here. Place just dried up."

Pretty much looked like it. Now it was all buried under layers of dirt and thistles and milkweed.

I walked on, following Terrence, but the words of my Grandpa guided me. Off to our left, almost hidden by a stand of scrub trees, was the sole remnant of a bygone age. "That there, boys, is the Highlife Hotel or what's left of it," he would tell us as we made our way past the crumbling structure. "Older than me, if you can believe it," he would smile.

Full-grown pines rose through the fractured roof, while broadleaf saplings stretched their branches through broken windows, and emerald vines climbed the pitted walls that were home to a variety of birds. "More like the Wildlife Hotel now," I observed wryly.

During better times, Terrence and I had explored its musty, moss-covered rooms, running down the sagging hallways and dining like merry kings with our sack lunches in the cavernous, cobwebbed hall. Now, in silence, we walked past it and into the trees, carefully avoiding the nettles and burs which were strung across the trail like barbed wire.

Cautiously we followed the thinning path until it finally emptied out into an open, green clearing. There, resting down below at the bottom of a gentle hill near a small, tear-shaped lake, was Camelot. It was only a large log cabin set in amongst some sunlit trees, but it was a nice one, almost elegant looking. Slender blue and green banners fluttered in the breeze on either side, making the cabin seem more like a wooden castle. Grandpa had built it all himself after Grandmother had died, moving out here from the city as soon as it was finished. I never got to meet her, since she died the year before I was born.

A tiny wisp of smoke curled through the branches below to the opening sky. I followed it down to the source. There was Grandpa, sitting on the front porch as if he hadn't moved an inch since last year. Terrence and I looked at each other, sizing each other up. It was a ritual we'd done every summer for as long as I could remember, but I wasn't sure if he would play along this time, since he was going to be a high school big-shot now. "You ready, squirt?" he teased.

In response, I took off running down the hill, with my older brother close on my heels. Our suitcases bounced crazily behind us like wild animals. We raced past the old stump and through the stone arch gate, taking the broad wooden steps up to the front door three at a time. With a final burst of speed, we both collapsed on the porch.

"Tie!" proclaimed Grandpa, holding out an antique stopwatch in front of him. His clothes hung loose on his thin frame. What hair remained on top of his head was gray. A few faint scars were visible on his face. "Souvenirs from the war," he had told us once. A pipe rested on the nearby sill. The smell of cherry tobacco hung in the air.

Terrence and I stood panting, glaring at each other. "You say that every year," my brother complained between breaths.

"Yes, I do," said Grandpa, taking a puff from his pipe. Age spots covered his hand and lower arms, but there was still a twinkle in his eye. "But only because my pocket watch stopped working years ago and I can't fix it." That was his little joke. He had been a clockmaker all his life, until our grandmother got sick. There was no timepiece he couldn't put to rights if he set his mind to it. In this case, however, the watch was in perfect working order. His eyes were a different matter, as well as his tendency to avoid hurt feelings.

"It's running fine now," observed Terrence, who smirked despite himself.

"So it is," marveled Grandpa. "Time has wonderful healing properties, does it not?" He laughed and suddenly his frail form seemed years younger. Then a fit of coughing seized him and he doubled over. It only lasted a few moments, and he made a joke as if nothing had happened. Seeing him like that was enough to send a shiver down my spine.

"You boys still like lemonade?" he asked. We nodded numbly, beads of sweat still dripping from our foreheads. "I have some freshly squeezed. You two put your bags upstairs and then meet me in the kitchen."

Terrence got up quickly and headed for the front door. I followed on his heels, but paused to hold the door open for Grandpa, before realizing that he was still getting up from his chair. He struggled with the effort, eventually making it to his feet. "You go on ahead," he told me, cracking a smile. "I'm fine. Just a little stiff today."

Not knowing what to say, I let the door close behind me and half-slid across the smooth oak-floored living room with its large windows and reclining chairs. As usual, I lingered over the small, framed black-and-white photograph hanging on the wall. It showed a small group of smiling young men standing next to the wreckage of a plane. The instant I saw it, I was immediately swept up again in the unbelievable true story that Grandpa told us a previous summer, between thoughtful puffs from his pipe. Our grandfather, as it turned out, had been a bombardier on a B-24 during World War Two.

His plane had been shot down over Nazi-occupied Belgium in 1944. Half the crew didn't make it, but my grandfather and a few others managed to parachute out. Somehow the Resistance found him before the Nazis did, but my Grandpa was far from safe. Injured, exhausted and hungry, he was also accused of being a spy. He was an American, but because of his name and the unfortunate fact that he could speak fluent German, the Resistance didn't trust him.

They had a downed RAF pilot point a gun at my grandfather all night long. The order was simple; if my Grandpa couldn't prove he was telling the truth, the pilot had to shoot him by the time the sun came up. Nothing my Grandpa said made any difference. He knew who he was, but it was another matter to convince a total stranger, especially a suspicious one. As morning light was bleeding over the horizon, the British pilot, in desperation, mentioned visiting Hyde Park in London a few weeks before. Grandpa said he that he had been there too while on leave and had seen a tall shirtless man with scars across his muscular chest working to take down an iron fence. Against all odds, the pilot had seen the same man, and so spared his life. And mine too, I guess. My Grandpa was a hero and a very lucky man. A German spy would never have been in an English park.

The sound of Terrence running somewhere up ahead brought me back to the mission at hand. I still had hopes of beating my brother and claiming the bed next to the window with its commanding view of the valley. I ran down the hallway past Grandpa's old workroom, full of clocks and dusty tools. Opposite that was Grandma's old sewing room, full of musty fabric and dolls. Further on was the exercise room, normally containing a treadmill and stationary bike. Peering through the slightly ajar door, I didn't see any of that, however. Instead I saw a glimpse of a dresser and a bedside table with a reading lamp. *Well, that's weird,* I thought.

At the end of the hallway, just past the downstairs bathroom, I made a sharp right, intending to charge up the stairs. But Terrence had already reached the top, his footsteps echoing overhead as he headed for our spacious bedroom. The race was all but lost.

Slowing down, I paused to once again marvel at Grandpa's masterpiece, a looming grandfather clock which rested against the wall at the bottom of the stairs. It rose like a shadow, tall and mysterious. From the clawed wooden feet to the intricately carved border which wrapped around the lighted face like a crown, it was magnificent. This was Grandpa's last work, and he was so proud of it that he always carried the winding key with him. My dad told me he had worked on the clock since he was a young man so he could get it just right. Staring up at it, I tried to sense the care and sweat which must have gone into creating such a spectacle, the little bit of soul he had given in return. But at the time, I was too young. To me it was just a clock; eerie and grand, with a life almost of its own.

From deep within its wooden chest came the sound of a heartbeat. I stood and watched the pendulum swing back and forth behind the beveled glass, mesmerized. The ticking grew louder, or at least it seemed to as I focused all my attention on the rhythm, my own heartbeat quickening in response. Tearing my gaze away, I ran up the stairs to the guest room, only to find that Terrence had already been there and gone. His duffel bag sat squarely on the contested bed.

By the time I made it to the kitchen, Grandpa and my brother were sitting at the table, sipping lemonade. Terrence looked over at me as I entered, a victorious smile flashing on his face, before turning back. "It's good to see you again, boys," greeted Grandpa once I had sat down. "Help yourself. It's sweet as a lemon."

I grabbed the unclaimed glass of lemonade in front of me and took several satisfying gulps. "Let me look at my gallant young knights," he continued. "My, my, Terrence. If you grow much bigger, you'll be a nuisance to passing aircraft. Do you have any girlfriends yet? No? Well, give it time and you'll be beating them off with a stick. How's high school?"

"Okay, but boring," he muttered.

Grandpa nodded as if my brother's answer was full of insights. "Don't worry about that. You just keep studying. That's important." Then he turned toward me. "Jacob. My dear Jacob. Are you ready for junior high?"

"It's called middle school. I don't think I'll ever be ready." I had been dreading the new school year all summer. No more recess. No playground. Instead we were forced to take Phys Ed and shower together like freaks. Grandpa started to respond, but was interrupted by the loud chiming of the clock. "Can we go outside and play?" I asked, impatient to avoid a conversation about teachers and homework.

"I suppose so," said Grandpa hesitantly.

"Did you forget what it's like, losing at horseshoes?" my older brother asked. "I'm happy to remind you."

"You boys go ahead," Grandpa said. Our glasses were empty and the sun was shining. He knew there would be no keeping us inside. "We'll have time to talk later."

Terrence and I played horseshoes. He beat me soundly. Then we went down to the small lake and skipped stones. He did that better too. Grandpa watched us from the porch, puffing on his pipe and calling out encouragement from time to time, but it wasn't the same. No matter how much we asked, he would not come down and join us, not even for a little while. In the past he always had, until he got tired. Now he just sat there like a stone, staring off into the distance.

We got in the old creaky wooden boat and rowed around the lake for a while, until the sky clouded up and a soft pattering of rain began to fall. We made it back to shore damp but relatively dry. The rich smells of cooking greeted us as we walked through the door.

"This should warm you up," Grandpa said as he put a thick, steaming pork chop on our plates, next to a generous helping of mashed potatoes and green beans. "There's dessert later if you're still hungry."

Outside, the wind and rain lashed against the glass. The sound of distant thunder could be heard from time to time. We barely noticed it, focused as we were on the food in front of us. Afterward we helped do the dishes, and then went into the living room to play some cards. Outside, the storm showed no sign of letting up.

"I've got nothing," sighed Grandpa, laying out his cards.

"I'm out too," I said. "Looks like you're the big winner, Terrence."

Terrence leaned forward, a grin spreading across his face, as he swept the pile of chips towards him, combining them with already burgeoning pile.

"Figures," I complained. "He always wins."

"Now, now," urged Grandpa next to me. "Fair's fair and all that. Besides, I have something important to tell you both before it gets too late." I leaned forward expectantly, goosebumps rising all along the length of my arm. "The fact is," he began. "I've decided to…"

Just then a thunderous crack of thunder exploded and the lights went out, pitching us into darkness. "Damn it," grated Grandpa after a stunned moment. "Lightning must've knocked out the fuse. Do you remember where I keep the candles, Jacob?"

"I think so."

"Well, go get them. And bring some matches, please."

I got up and struggled through the dimness, my eyes still adjusting. After bumping into things like a pinball machine, I finally made it into the kitchen and reached up to open the small cupboard. "I can't get to it," I called, straining my arm again. "It's too high."

A few moments later Terrence was at my side. "You mean you're too short," he remarked. Without extending his arm or even standing on his tiptoes, he opened the cupboard and grabbed some candles and matches. Following him back in the living room, I felt about two inches high. Grandpa lit the candle. In the flickering glow I could plainly see a stupid smirk etched across Terrence's face.

"Why don't you boys get ready for bed," Grandpa told us. "I'll go downstairs and change that fuse. I'll be back as soon as I can." Following Terrence, I walked slowly down the hallway, pausing at the place where the clock stood. Its features were all but invisible in the darkness, with only a steady tick-tock betraying its existence.

We had been in bed a short while when the lights finally turned on. A few minutes later, the sound of footsteps echoed on the stairs. They approached slowly, almost ponderously. It took him a long time, but eventually Grandpa reached the landing. I could hear him coming down the upstairs hall. A moment later he entered our room. He was breathing hard and was too tired to even try and hide it. A Band-Aid stretched across his forehead. Through the center, a spot of red shone like a ruby. We both looked at him from under our covers, mouths gaping, unable to say anything at all.

"Just a little fall," he said. With a sigh he leaned against the bed frame. As he did so, a small brass key on a necklace spilled out from under his shirt. When he had gained control of himself and his breathing was under control, he told us he had something to say.

"Boys," he began. "What I'm about to tell you isn't a fairy tale. I know you're too old for those. There are no heroes in this story. No knights or brave explorers. It's just a story of an old man, a lucky old man in a lot of ways, but a man for whom time has finally caught up. You've probably noticed that I'm not as good on my feet as I once was. I get tired easier and my eyesight is going to hell. I got all kinds of conditions and explanations from my polite, money-stealing doctor, but they all amount to the same thing; I'm old. It's the way of it, boys, though I wish it wasn't. These stairs are damn near impossible for me now. I moved my bedroom downstairs because of em'. I take naps three times a day. It's pretty near my hobby, I guess."

"Grandpa," interrupted Terrence. "We know you're old. We don't care. What's the big deal?"

"Indeed!" said Grandpa, laughing in a strange forced kind of way. "I can't drive anymore, for starters. My eyes. That's why I didn't pick you up. Don't trust myself anymore. Sure miss being behind the wheel of that old DeSoto. Drove to our honeymoon in that car. Doc says I need to quit the pipe, eat better, and exercise more for my heart. Also need to be closer to a hospital. Just to be on the safe side. In case something happens." His hand went up unconsciously to his forehead.

"You mean you're not dying?" I asked.

"Don't sound so disappointed. No, not yet. I just can't live on my own anymore is all."

I let out a breath I didn't know I'd been holding.

"Can't you just hire a live-in nurse or something?" Terrence suggested.

My Grandpa looked at him and shook his head. "Can't afford it," he said. "I don't have enough savings. Not even close. I've gone over it again and again. There's only one thing to be done. I'm selling the house, boys. Camelot is gone. Mr. Kreitzer, owner of the Oasis, is leaving too. We just can't do it anymore. He doesn't have enough business and this house is too much for me. By autumn I'll be living in Park Falls. They got one of those old-timer assisted living places. Sounds horrible, but it's my only option."

We both stared at him. I couldn't believe what I was hearing. "You could move in with us," I suggested desperately.

"We live in an apartment, bean brain," reminded my brother. "There's barely room for us."

Grandpa looked at us both. "This hasn't been an easy decision. Camelot has been my dream, but all dreams come to an end. I know that's hard for you to hear. I just wanted you boys to know," he tried to explain, "so we can deal with it together. Your mom and dad thought it was the right thing to do."

"How could you do this?" I asked, suddenly angry at him for being mortal, for not being young.

Now all of his attention was focused on me. I had never seen him look so sad. He held his hands together with the pinkies touching. Then he closed them like a book that was done and ready to be shelved. "It's late," he said. "We'll talk in the morning after you both get some sleep." Then he turned off the light.

*

"Well, this sucks," murmured Terrence after the door had been shut. "But it's not his fault. You know that, right?"

I said nothing. I just laid there, wishing Terrence and Grandpa and Camelot and middle school would all just disappear.

"I know you're not asleep, Jake. You wanna talk about it?" In response, I began snoring. "Suit yourself," he snapped, and then turned over.

For what felt like a very long time, I stared at the rain hitting the window, watching the trees light up in momentary incandescence with each lightning strike before being swallowed up again by the blackness. I felt cheated and helpless. I knew I shouldn't feel that way, but I did. Camelot was over and there was nothing I could do about it. Another round of thunder rumbled through the night.

Unable to sleep, I got quietly out of bed and opened the door, being careful not to make it squeak. Then I walked along the hall and down the stairs. I had no idea where I was going, just a gut feeling that I had to move. Maybe I would get a glass of milk and some cookies.

As I reached the bottom of the stairs, a flash of lightning split the darkness outside the hall window. There was the grandfather clock, illuminated for a magical instant, its hands at one minute before midnight. It was easy to imagine a promise and a life, held far below the grain. I could see Grandpa as he carved and whittled, polished and stained, until there was nothing left but the heart of the wood. Without thinking, I reached up and opened the beveled glass case as the golden hammer struck the coil of wires and a chime erupted, repeating itself in sound and echoes. I stuck my hand inside and touched the hands of the clock. A sensation of energy went through my fingertips, an undercurrent of possibilities. Standing on my tiptoes, I began moving the hands around, backwards, years of turning, as many times as I could before the night reclaimed the clock, obscuring the glistening face and timeless wood. When it was over, I stood there frozen, my arms and legs aching with the effort.

"What do you think you're doing!" hissed Terrence from the middle of the stairs. "Grandpa will kill you if he sees you messing around with his clock."

I backed away to make room for Terrence, who leaned in to inspect the damage. "Well, you screwed up the time pretty good," he said, peering inside the face. "I think that's it, though. Consider yourself lucky." Then he looked at his watch, the one he always wore, even to bed. By barely straining his arm, Terrence reached up and turned the hands of the clock until he was satisfied. "Now get back to bed," he said.

Walking slowly back up the stairs, I had the pleasure of knowing that Terrence was following me for once. Still, as I crawled into bed, I knew that I had acted childishly, and that my creative act of vandalism would not make a single bit of difference.

Outside, thunder rumbled and then fell silent.

———— * ————

Morning came, gray, but free of rain. Terrence was already up, his bed left unmade. Slowly, I struggled from the covers and stood. It was late. Breakfast first and a shower later, I decided. I couldn't seem to find my favorite jeans and t-shirt so I threw on some different clothes and went downstairs. I wasn't looking forward to finishing the conversation that my Grandpa had started the night before.

"It's about time," remarked Terrence. He was sitting in the kitchen, a bowl of half-eaten cereal in front of him. He looked worried.

"Something wrong?" I asked.

"Have you seen Grandpa?"

"No. Why?"

"Because I haven't seen him all morning," Terrence said. "He's not in the house. Not still sleeping. There's no note or nuthin'. It's not like him."

I grabbed a bagel and some orange juice. "I'm sure he's around," I soothed. "Probably just—" And then I stopped cold. "Is the car here?" I asked suddenly.

Terrence looked back at me for a moment in confusion. Then his eyes went wide in understanding. "I don't know. I didn't check."

Just then the sound of honking erupted from outside, like a lost and noisy parade. We raced through the house and out the front door. Grandpa's Chrysler was circling the yard at great speed, its sleek turquoise shape and white side-spear cutting through the scenery as it weaved around trees, honking as it went at nothing in particular. No driver was visible. My mouth hung open wide.

The car turned, tires spitting sod, and then squealed to a stop just inches from the cabin. A moment later the door sprang open and laughter bubbled out. "Well, I'll be," said a blonde-haired kid as he stepped out of the vehicle. "That was a hoot!" He couldn't have been more than ten or eleven years old. His feet were bare and he wore a smile that was more contagious than chicken pox.

"What do you think you're doing?" demanded Terrence, walking down the steps towards the boy. "That's our grandfather's car!"

"So it is," the thief laughed.

I leaned over the railing. "Hey, those are my clothes!" I shouted, recognizing my jeans and shirt. They hung loosely on the kid, like he had been playing dress-up. The pant legs bunched down around the ankle and the shirt looked like it was in the process of swallowing him whole.

"So they are," observed the boy. "I hope you don't mind." Then he walked past my fuming brother, dropping the keys in his outstretched hand, and then running up the stairs. "Anyone thirsty for some lemonade?" he asked. Then he opened the door and walked on in.

The mysterious child busied himself in the kitchen, grabbing lemonade mix, a wooden spoon, and three tall, clear glasses, like he had lived there his whole short life. I watched him closely, noticing for the first time the Band-Aid almost completely hidden under his thick hair and the brass, clock-winding key that dangled around his neck. It looked exactly like Grandpa's.

"Hey, where did you get that?" I demanded, pointing at his necklace.

Terrence took a step forward. "I'm calling the cops," he told the thief, who was busy mixing the lemonade.

"Oh, I hope they turn the siren on," the boy said. "That would be exciting."

"All right, you asked for it," spat Terrence. Then he walked over to the phone. After a moment spent searching through the phone book, he started to hit the buttons for the police.

"Wait!" I cried. Something wasn't right. None of it made any sense. My brother paused, irritated at the delay. "Hold on," I told him. I turned to the kid who had just finished setting the glasses down on the table, just like Grandpa did it. Then he opened the freezer and took out a gallon of vanilla ice cream. "It's not too early for some ice cream, is it?" the boy asked, a bit sheepishly. "There are so many rules. Seems like a waste of time to me."

"Hey," I began, not sure how to go about what I wanted to ask. "Where are your parents?"

The kid put down the ice cream scoop and stared at me. His smile wavered, as if there was a missing piece to his memories.

I walked over to him slowly, my hands held out. "Working, I guess," the boy said slowly. "Who cares. I just want to play."

As a kid, I knew a lie when I heard it. "Try again," I told him.

The boy looked up at me. "They're gone," he said sadly. "Happy?"

"I'm sorry," I told him. "I had to be sure." Then I turned to Terrence. "I know who he is."

"Okay, Sherlock. Who is he?"

I paused, not quite believing what I was about to say. "He's Grandpa," I told him. Terrence cursed and then started dialing again. "Listen," I protested. "He's got Grandpa's clock key, doesn't he? "

"That just makes him a little thief," my brother responded.

"What about the Band-Aid on his forehead? Grandpa has one too. And don't ya think it's kind of weird that he knows where everything is in the house?"

"Are you crazy?" he shot back. "No, not you," he said into the receiver. "Just a minute. Listen, little brother, he's just a smart little thief and he's in big trouble now." With those words, Terrence glanced sharply at the boy, who was now sitting at the kitchen table drinking a glass of lemonade. A bowl of ice cream sat nearby.

I walked over to the table and sat down. "Tell him," I begged the boy. "Tell him who you are."

The kid took another gulp of lemonade, smacking his lips. My face fell like a deflated balloon. I wondered how I could have been so foolish. "Sweet as a lemon," the boy said.

Terrence froze. Then he put the phone back numbly in its cradle.

"What did you say?" I asked in disbelief.

"Just what you heard me say. If you don't want any lemonade, how about we just skip it and go out to play?" My brother and I looked at each other in complete amazement. "You're not much fun," the boy observed. Then he got up and walked out of the kitchen. We followed at a safe distance, watching him go out the front door and down the steps.

"What do you think?" I asked.

"I dunno. What do you think?" my brother asked.

I opened my mouth to speak, but something I saw through the window made me pause. "I think Grandpa is doing somersaults in the front yard," I said at last.

It took a while, but eventually we worked up the courage to go outside, where Grandpa was playing, running around the yard in wide, quick arcs like a sweeping second hand. "Hey, kid," Terrence asked him as the boy dropped to the ground and began rolling around in the grass. "What's your name?"

"Arthur, of course," he retorted testily, coming to a stop on Terrence's foot. "I hate it."

"I don't believe you," my brother challenged.

"Believe this, then," the kid said. Quick as lightning he dove at Terrence, taking his legs out from under him. Before I could blink, my brother was lying flat on the ground with Grandpa on top of him, smiling proudly.

"Get off me!" Terrence shouted, threatening to throw him off.

Then Grandpa looked at me. "You're next," he said.

Three bruises and numerous grass stains later, we were all lying in the lawn, laughing until our sides hurt. "You're a pretty good wrestler," my brother told the kid. "Especially for being so puny."

"Thanks," our grandfather said. "If it wasn't for your brother, I would have really got you good."

I pushed myself up on my elbows. The grass was soft and cool. "Yeah, wait until everyone at school hears how I had to save my *older* brother from my grandpa."

"You wouldn't," Terrence said in disbelief.

"Watch me," I smirked.

The next moment he landed on top of me and I was fighting for my life, laughing and yelling at the same time. When we had finally worn each other out, we both laid back down, our chests heaving up and down.

"Tie!" Grandpa declared. I opened my mouth to argue, but words suddenly seemed unimportant. For there was our grandfather, now a boy, sitting in the grass laughing.

———— * ————

The three of us played and had a wonderful time for the rest of the day and most of the next. If we weren't wrestling or running through the trees, we were swimming in the lake or making blanket forts with sheets as big as sails. But late in the evening on that second day, when the sun had set and the night crowded around the windows like a band of thieves, something happened. I don't know what it was, exactly, and it's kind of hard to explain, but I started to miss Grandpa. Our Grandpa. The one with the wrinkled face and gray hair who always had a twinkle in his eye.

The next morning I awoke, still melancholy. I shuffled downstairs. We've all played that game where the floor is lava, but my heart just wasn't in it this time. Then we had a particularly vicious pillow fight. Afterward my stomach was grumbling something awful, and I asked Grandpa if he could please make us some breakfast. We'd been living on Pop-Tarts and lemonade. I wasn't sure if I could take it anymore.

"Make it yourself!" my grandfather snapped. "Who do you think I am?"

"Our grandpa," I replied.

"Not anymore," he responded, throwing a pillow at my head, catching me square in the face.

"Yes, you are!" I replied, angry now too. Everything that we had shared was being dismissed. "You can't just keep on pretending. It's not fair."

He ran out the door. Terrence and I followed, racing down the steps and across the long, green grass to the dock that jutted out into the water. When we caught up with Grandpa he was sitting on the edge, his slender legs swinging back and forth over the water. "Hey, Grandpa," Terrence said, coming up next to him. It was the first time he had called him that in several days. "Are you tired of playing?"

"No," answered Grandpa sadly. "I don't think I'll ever tire of playing. Especially with you boys. That's the problem, I'm afraid."

I came up on the other side and put my hand on Grandpa's arm. "It's not supposed to be like this," I told him. "Whatever I did, I'm sorry. We just want you back. The way things used to be."

For the longest time he didn't say anything. Then slowly he bowed his head. When he lifted it back up there were tears in his eyes. "I got a little bit lost. I forgot myself. Thanks for reminding me of who I am," he said. "What happened to me is a miracle. I've loved every second of it, but I can't accept it anymore."

"Sure, you can," insisted Terrence. "Why not?" I looked over at my brother in surprise.

"Because it's not me. I'm Arthur Willingsly." Now his voice rose, becoming stronger, older-sounding. "I'm not a boy. I'm 79 years old. I have high blood pressure and arthritis. I don't sleep through the night. My bones ache and my eyesight is laughable. I move about as fast as a turtle. But I've had a good life. Every morning when I wake up, I count myself lucky. I miss your grandmother more than you'll ever know, but I've got a son I'm proud of and two wonderful grandsons. I make you breakfasts and take you fishing and watch you grow. I tell you stories, when you let me. I'm your Grandpa. This is who I am." Grandpa started crying then, the tears rolling down his young face.

Terrence and I stared back. Neither of us knew what to do. Eventually the tears stopped, but he didn't wipe them away. "Life is about change, boys," he told us. "Better to embrace it. Accept it. You'll have a lot more fun that way." Terrence nodded. Then Grandpa looked at me. "What was that you were saying about being sorry?"

I told him all about the storm and the grandfather clock. How I had turned back the hands as the lightning struck.

"I always knew that clock had a part of me in it," he said. "Just never knew how much."

My brother sat down on the dock next to our grandfather. "So what do we do now?"

*

"Why does it have to be at midnight?" I asked, yawning deeply as I leaned against the bannister. I faced the clock, which was bathed in soft moonlight.

"Because, if what you told me is accurate," explained Grandpa, "that's when you turned back the hands of my clock. And besides, strange and wonderfully impossible things always happen at midnight."

"If you say so," said Terrence, still not quite believing the whole thing.

"I do," said Grandpa. Then he walked down the hallway, easy and slow.

"Where are you going?" I yelled.

"To bed," he answered back. "You don't need me here. I'll see you in the morning." Then his boyish form disappeared through the bedroom door. I listened as his footsteps trailed away, blending in with the repetitive tick-tock of the grandfather clock.

"I think he wants to be alone," Terrence said. My brother was standing next to the clock. Normally he's taller than almost anything, but even he was dwarfed by the imposing timepiece. He glanced warily up at the numbered face. "I've never liked this clock," he said suddenly, his voice hushed as if he were giving a confession. "I feel like it can look right through me."

"I know," I said.

We didn't talk again for quite a while. The last five minutes were the longest I had ever experienced. Longer than the five minutes waiting for the school bell to ring and let us out. Harder to take than the last minutes before I finally fell asleep on Christmas Eve. More agonizing than the last day of summer vacation.

"Almost time," observed Terrence.

All at once the giant clock started chiming like a church tower, startling us both. I stood up on my toes and opened the beveled glass case. My hand shook slightly. I reached out and touched the cold, metal hands, turning them forward, spinning them as fast as I could, counting carefully as I went. **One, two, three, four, five, six, seven, eight, nine, ten, twenty, thirty, forty...** I imagined the years of my grandfather spinning back to him. **Fifty, sixty, seventy...**

"Almost done?" asked Terrence worriedly.

The last chime was sounding. I groaned and turned the hands one final time. Then I staggered back from the clock as the last echoes of midnight died away. Feeling strangely tired, I closed my eyes, hoping it had worked, worried that it hadn't.

"C'mon," insisted Terrence, putting a gentle hand on my shoulder. "Time for bed. We'll see him in the morning."

———*———

I woke up feeling lighter than air. Bright sunshine streamed in through the window next to me. Terrence had let me swap beds with him. I think he felt bad for me. It felt good to win, even if it was out of pity. Then I remembered what I had done last night. It seemed a dream. All of it. But it was real. At that instant panic and excitement surged through me like a bolt of electricity. I had to know.

Terrence was already gone, of course. Surprisingly, my bed was made. I stood and rubbed the sleep frantically from eyes. Within moments I was out the bedroom door and down the stairs, racing past the clock and shooting down the hall by the open bedroom door and into the kitchen.

"Good morning," greeted Grandpa, turning from the stove, looking every bit his seventy-nine years of age. "It's about time you're up. You must be hungry."

"Starving," I told him, standing at the kitchen entranceway. Relief flooded over me. Then I joined Terrence at the table.

———*———

I never knew how much I missed Grandpa until he was gone. Later that week, as we walked to the boat, I stayed close to him, listening to every word he said, savoring every silly joke. He walked slow now, like the almost imperceptible sweep of a minute hand, but I didn't mind. At least not much.

"Are we gonna catch anything big today?" I asked, adjusting the fishing pole in my hands as I climbed aboard.

"Of course you are," Grandpa said with a smile. "And I'll cook them up for you when you get back."

When Terrence and I were both in the old rowboat surrounded by our gear, our life jackets secure, he gave us a little push and we drifted out into the lake. "Have a ball!" he exclaimed from the shore, his figure shrinking and becoming more distant.

*

It's hard to believe that it was really over forty years ago. But here I am. Grandpa's long gone, of course. He died with his family all around. While I stood there next to the hospital bed watching his chest slowly rise and fall, I remembered another story Grandpa told us about the end of the war. Taking advantage of the D-Day invasion, he and the RAF pilot decided to try and get to England, sneaking through German-held territory. They almost drowned crossing a nearby river, but made it to the Allied sector, only to radio back to the underground that they were coming back. Evidently they were afraid of being shot by trigger-happy Americans on the long walk to the coast. "We're not ready to be rescued yet," my grandfather told them.

He wasn't ready then, but on a bright, sunny day in 1999, Grandpa finally made it over to the other side, hopefully driving his old DeSoto straight toward the horizon.

Fast forward to the present. I'm married. My partner Paul and I have an adopted daughter. A beautiful girl who's smart and funny. Ziana's going into middle school in a few months. I suppose she's just as excited and nervous as I was. Changes can be hard. Life can be hard. The past can be a siren song, a weight that drags you down. Or it can be an oasis. Or a memory trapped in amber. No one knows the future. The road twists and turns, unexpectedly, until it finally disappears. But we have right now. These moments. I'm going to tell her this story. Maybe it will help a little. I hope that she can be herself and never have to ask for permission. No one should have to prove their worth. We are all a wonder.

I think I'll pick a hot summer night in August when the clouds are heavy with rain. We'll stay up late and as the old grandfather clock begins to chime, I'll take out the brass winding key, the one my grandpa gave to me and the one I will someday give to her. Then I'll begin the tale, my voice keeping time with the marvels all around me.

BY MOONLIGHT BRIGHT
AND DEEP

*V*engeance is always sweetest when a long wait is finally over. At least that was what the long-dead Malvanian philosophers said in dusty books. Rohi, for one, was sick of waiting. She had been only a child when the invaders had come at dusk, killing her family and taking over her country. She hid in the darkness while soldiers, some with strange glowing weapons, killed her parents and older sister. Her family had fought with kitchen knives to give her time. "Run and hide!" her sister had screamed just before the attackers stormed in. She was still hiding, running from what she had seen. Still trying to come to grips with why she survived.

Memories of her life before that terrible night became precious to her. She still remembered the smell of her mother's fresh-baked sweet-bread, her father's laugh, and her grandmother's stories, especially the tales featuring the Sisters of the Moon and the ship that sailed the stars. Around her neck still hung the pendant that her sister Aiylada had given her, a crescent moon shaped from ghostone. Those fragments saved her. Orphaned and in shock, she had been adopted by relatives who kept the old ways alive and planted seeds of revenge as she grew into adulthood. That had been a long time ago, more in tears than in actual years, but she was still tired. Some roads were longer than others.

Swirling sand struck Rohi's covered face as she stood guard in the remote narrow desert valley. Time seemed to slow as a hot wind ruffled her blanched garments covering her from head to toe. Sweat glistened on her temples and trickled down her braided hair. The sun was relentless as it sapped Rohi's strength. It was almost time. It had to be. In her gloved hand was a long curved black sword. From the tip of the steel there rose a curl of green noxious smoke.

Beside her was a giant of a man. He was dressed in loose colorful pants and a grey tunic, open at the top. Like most northerners, he had pale skin. His face was bare and exposed to the elements, except for a small goatee. Even so, he smiled grimly, taking little notice of the myriad tiny daggers striking his flesh. He had said no more than a few words during their time together. In his meaty hands was a slender, almost delicate looking sword. It gleamed of silver with strangely carved runes running down the blade. Lettering she could decipher. Not perfectly, but well enough, because of her grueling studies in the Fringe. The weapon, Rohi knew, had the power to take on the attributes of the last soul it killed. Both the hulking figure and Rohi were part of an elite fighting force. They had only one mission; protect. Each candidate was tested and then trained separately. One of the skills taught was called *budanae* and involved mastering the ability to maintain a high state of consciousness on little to no sleep. Another focused on fasting. And then there was the almost constant sparring. Of making their bodies oblivious to pain. Only a few made it through the grueling education. Successful recruits became Warders and gained the great honor of protecting the Oculist for one cycle of the Sister Moons.

Looking up at the bright sky, Rohi saw the twin pale orbs hanging near the horizon, plump and full. She cursed under her breath. Today was the last day. There wouldn't be another chance.

The artifact-sensitive priest stood in front of them a few paces away under a small makeshift pavilion. Bright blue silk ruffled in the breeze above the Oculist, shielding him from the heat of the day. He was wrapped in a cocoon of gold and topaz tapestry, a sacred raiment worn by the priests. The Oculist was frail looking, bent over as if the wind might blow him away. As always, he was utterly motionless. The priest kept his mind focused on the gift that was to come. At any moment the bone-hued archway towering in front of them might open to their world and the priest would have seconds, no more, to call into being something horrible and magnificent for their Lord and Protector. Something that could be used to smite His enemies and bring more territories under His dominion.

Peaceful people like Malvania, she thought bitterly. Most of the known world, as far north as the Lost Lands and as far south as the Golden Wastes, was part of the Protectorate and the empire's much lauded peace and stability, but at what cost? Without the artifact to produce weapons of war, the Protectorate could not have been so aggressive. Thousands of lives might have been saved.

There was no known rhythm or logic to when the Lumenoculis activated. Ever since the portal had been discovered by a small Protectorate military expedition at the beginning of the last traversal, the mysterious device had opened over nine hundred times. Based on accounts from guards and Oculists, Scribes had recorded multiple instances where it activated twice in one day and a handful of times where the doorway was quiet for over three spans. Those were exceptions, Rohi knew, having bribed a government official with her remaining coins to look at the journals (and when that wasn't enough, giving the scribe the only thing she had left). The most common frequency was once every lunar span. No one knew why it opened when it did.

Clenching her hands into fists, Rohi stared at the doorway that rose in front of them and willed it to activate. She silently said the names of family members who had fallen, strangers whose lives had been brutally cut short. Justice for her people weighed heavily on her. Those that wanted to live free left Malvania, choosing instead to eke out an existence by taking refuge in the Fringe, a wild and dangerous hinterland that only fanned the flames of resistance higher. That's where she had been taken. Smuggled out of the country by her uncle and the remnants of the warrior caste, Rohi had grown up among the dispossessed. But they were determined and never lost hope. She could not let them down. Her people had prepared her for this mission, teaching fighting techniques, obscuring her accent, and helping her to blend in. With careful precision they had recreated the customary piercings. They sewed clothing suitable for this province of the empire. They even dyed her fingertips with the colorful whorls symbolizing the ten celestial guardians. She was still Malvanian, but sometimes even she was amazed at the transformation. Her community had given her precious coins, sacrificing everything so she could be here, right now.

With a cry of frustration, she kicked sand toward the inert monolith. Her companion swung around, sword in hand. "Rock scorpion was on my sandal," Rohi remarked. "Don't feel like getting poisoned on my last day."

Her companion grunted his disapproval. "Why are you afraid of such an insignificant creature?" he asked in a voice thick with the peculiar accent of those that were born in the mountains far to the north, an area conquered by the Protectorate at great cost. That was generations ago. Now they were prized by the empire for their formidable fighting skills. "The garrison has an antidote."

Rohi looked back toward the mouth of the valley. A stronghold with a formidable watchtower blocked the only entrance to the artifact. Inside was a battalion of soldiers ready to rush out at the first sign of trouble. The stronghold also had a small library containing records detailing each time the archway had opened. The Scribe of the Oculist was in charge of these. Twice a day and once at night at prescribed times, Protectorate soldiers brought food and water out to the guards. In her pocket was a signal flare. They each had one. Even the Oculist. They were only to be used in emergencies. She had little doubt that the soldiers would come if she fired it. Whether they would reach her in time was an entirely different question. But poison was not a concern. She would gladly accept the kiss of a scorpion if it would make the artifact wake up.

"Don't you want to see this thing do something before our time is done?" she asked.

Her companion turned and smiled. "Not really," he said. "From what I've heard, everything that comes out of it is an abomination. Makes these scorpions and sand serpents seem like child's toys. Even the imagined weapons are dangerous. Some can even control whoever wields them. Nah. Boredom suits me just fine. I'm happy to go on living."

Rohi nodded. "Not much longer now," she said, trying to sound casual. "Come sundown our cycle replacements will be here."

By any measure, that would be soon. The sun would set in three, perhaps four hours, she calculated. Already the artifact's shadow had begun to stretch across the burning sands. *C'mon,* she pleaded at the tall arching doorway. *For the Goddess' sake, wake up!* It was the only way for their plan to work. With one thought, she could raise a sandstorm so vast it would tear the Protector's ornate capital to dust, or call into a being a metal construct that would dwarf the tallest tower. She could bring forth a charged elemental that would be the equal of any sorcerer. With a simple rumination she could unleash a legendary Beast of Many Names, capable of changing its form into any animal at will. Even the monstrous and misshapen Protector on his Throne of Dreams would tremble. But she needed the key. She needed that god-cursed portal to open.

Risking a glance at the sky, she was dismayed to see the sun had sunk lower toward the horizon. "Well, look at that," her companion remarked. With a start, Rohi looked back at the doorway, only to find that it was as inert as ever. "Seems our replacements are coming a bit early," he continued. "Wonder why that is?"

At least a dozen warriors riding ember beasts could be seen pouring out from the garrison gates as fast as the six-legged creatures could carry them. On each flank was a fire-mage, their brilliant crimson robes flapping in the wind. Rohi's breath stilled as the cold truth sunk in; she had been discovered. How she did not know, but she had only minutes before the Protector's soldiers arrived and killed her.

She made her decision in a heartbeat. The death of a prized Oculist would be more than a minor inconvenience to the Protecterate. Lifting her sword, Rohi stepped forward and drove the curved blade toward the other guard. To her surprise, he acted as if he had expected the betrayal, blocking her attack and then lunging underneath her arm. It was all Rohi could do spin away and avoid the maiming blow. Even so, she lost her balance, falling to one knee as her left hand grazed the ground. Her companion did not waste his advantage. Striding toward her, the mountainous man came in for the kill, his silver sword gleaming in the fading sunlight. Rohi had always been small for her age. But being small made her nimble, and her training made her faster. Waiting until the last moment, she threw a handful of sand into his face. Then she swept her opponent's feet out from under him before nicking his face with the edge of the smoking steel. The effect was almost instantaneous. One moment he was rising to his feet. The next he had toppled over, greenish-white foam spewing from his lips.

"I'm sorry," she breathed over him, saying a silent prayer for rebirth as she laid down the smoking blade. "Even if you betrayed me, I wish I would have learned your name." By the time she finished, his spirit was already gone.

There was no more time for reflection. The garrison soldiers had covered half the distance to the artifact. Clouds of dust rose up in their wake. Bright swords were raised high, catching the last rays of the setting sun. Blue flames rose from each mage's gnarled hand. Rohi could see the faces of the Protectorate's militia twisted into a blood rage.

Grabbing the slender rune-carved sword from where it had fallen, Rohi walked steadily toward the Oculist. He was still in a trance, sitting in front of the archway, unaware of the violence that had just occurred. When she was an arm's length away, Rohi stopped and drew back the blade. In that instant, the priest jerked and spun around, some preternatural instinct warning him. His tawny face was sunken and almost completely covered with the curving tattooed lines that were a hallmark of the portal priests. But it was the Oculist's eyes that Rohi noticed more than anything else. He had none. Where they should have been, two painted facsimiles stared back at her in a grisly mockery of the originals that had been plucked out.

In a panic, the priest began searching the hidden folds of his ornate garment. Before he could find the flare, Roshi rushed forward into the open pavilion and plunged the rune-carved blade into the priest's chest. For a terrible moment she stood face-to-face with him as the Oculist struggled to free himself. When she withdrew the sword, the man toppled to the ground, clutching at his wound as if he could somehow stem the flow of blood. Frail as he was, the priest continued to draw ragged, stubborn breaths, until Rohi slit his throat in desperation. There would be no prayer for the Oculist.

She was almost out of time. Daring a glance behind her, Rohi saw the soldiers bearing down. In moments she would be slain, and still the Lumenoculis would not activate. Throwing down the rune sword, she ran to the edge of the portal and peered into the opening, hoping that the slain priest's gift would trigger a reaction. She didn't feel any different. In the archway was the same desert dunes. Sand swirled, blown across the same unforgiving landscape in a grand and unknowable pattern. The movement was hypnotic, and as Rohi watched the golden specks trace through the air, something unusual happened. The grains of sand sharpened, becoming glittering blades, daggers thrown into a wild abyss that whipped around in a deadly frenzy. The archway was pulsating now with strange lights, and the ground trembled as if a great slumbering titan was finally waking up.

And perhaps it was, but the garrison's defenders were also upon her. The thundering hoofbeats of the ember beasts broke apart her reverie. Rohi felt the air around her draw in as if the world were holding its breath. A mage was about to strike. Even so, Rohi prepared herself to call into being something terrible from the portal, a colossus that would trample the empire to ruins. And yet when she closed her eyes and tried to focus, she thought of her mother and father instead, and the gift they had given her on the last birthday before the world had shattered. To her dismay a small, furry meadow rabbit hopped out of the portal, its pink nose twitching. There was no time for a second attempt. No time to scramble down for the sword and plunge it into her own flesh. The portal was already darkening and returning to its slumber. The riders were upon her. She had failed, but there would be others. Even the subjugated can only stay silent for so long. Not willing to risk being captured, Luna leaped into the portal's swirling daggers as a blast of blue sorcerous fire swept across the ground. She was ready for this life to be over and to be born again to a higher form, for living an honorable life.

Only she didn't die. Rohi watched as the deadly daggers struck her flesh, piercing her in multiple places, but it happened to another version of herself. She watched the agony unfold and yet felt no pain.

When her other-self fell away into the maelstrom of destruction, she continued on, floating toward a milky whiteness until she was surrounded by a glowing light. Slowly, the landscape around her took form. Rohi unwrapped the scarf from around her face as she walked, removing her gloves and shedding the rest of her clothing to reveal brown skin underneath. Her face was pleasant, although the features retained a tension, as if guarding something held dear.

In front of her, coalescing out of the sameness, was a sailing ship of pure moonlight. The rigging glowed in pearly strands. The sails reflected the sun and sea. Towards the stern, rising above the deck but still dwarfed by the masts, was the captain's perch. A wheel shaped like a tortoise shell hovered in midair, but Rohi wasn't looking at that. Unable to contain her amazement, she continued to gape at the figure who strode across the deck with her arms opened wide.

"Welcome home, Sister Moon!" the woman dressed in flowing white called. "Where have you been?" Rohi had no time to answer, as she was swallowed up in a sudden luminous embrace. The stranger smelled strangely of midnight flowers. "No, don't tell me," the lady said, wiping tears from her eyes. "It doesn't matter. I'm just so happy you're home."

"And where is that, exactly?" Rohi asked, feeling as if she already knew.

"With me, silly," the woman in white chided. "You were always such a kidder, while I'm stuck being serious. Sisters are supposed to be together. My glow has been greatly reduced in your absence."

"That sounds like a story I heard as a child," Rohi said, feeling a chill crawl up her spine.

"It's no story, sister, as you well know. I've had to keep the Inklings at bay all by myself, thank you very much. Not that I can't, mind, you. I'm rather good at diplomacy, and even better at fighting. But we are the Sisters of the Moon. Everything is better when we shine together."

Rohi held her tongue. She was spellbound in a world of her own making.

The days passed, each unfolding like a story. When Luna was sad, the luminous light dimmed, and the ship fell into shadow as she slept in her cabin below deck. For long, seemingly endless nights, the ship did not move. When Luna was happy and full of purpose, they had marvelous adventures, each more exciting than the last. They drove back the Inklings to their shadowy fortress, feasted on moon melons until they were bursting, and caught bright shining stars in the ship's great cupped sails before releasing them back into the darkness. The ship sailed higher and higher, each of them taking turns at the great wheel to write a glowing signature across the sky, their laughter echoing with unbridled joy. They even fished from the deck using long lines of pure starlight, catching the floating dreams that wandered near them in a shifting pattern of vibrant sunrise colors. It reminded Rohi a little of going out with her father as a child on misty mornings to fish the lake near her village. But the best, by far, was when the moon was full and they danced on the deck amid a bobbing constellation of fireflies.

With each repeated cycle, however, Rohi was reminded that things couldn't go on as they were. Adventures took on a dull sameness and lost their luster, as if she were caught in a tale that had already been written. Which was exactly the problem, Rohi knew. Even more troubling was the fact that none of this was real. It couldn't be. The Moon Ship and Luna was simply what she had wished for when she stepped into the portal. A fairy tale instead of knives. Now her next reincarnation would be tainted by her cowardice. But if she wasn't dead, then where was she?

While Luna was asleep, deep in her cycle of melancholy, Rohi took the opportunity to explore the ship more thoroughly. She ended her futile search up in the captain's perch at the tortoise-shaped steering wheel that hovered at waist-level. Heaving a sigh, she stared out at the inky darkness, punctuated by a sea of lonely stars that hung just out of reach. *What am I missing?* she wondered.

Gripping the wheel, she turned it back and forth in frustration, knowing it would have no effect while Luna slept. Looking at the object with a new, critical eye, she wondered for the first time how it hovered in place. Everything else was normal on the vessel...or, well, as normal as anything could be on a ship made of moonlight. The steering mechanism seemed slightly out of place in contrast. Running her hands along the polished wood, Rohi felt for any imperfections, depressions or hidden switches. She was about to give up when her fingers found something smooth at the center of the wheel where the spokes converged. It looked like the same dark wood, but felt cold and metallic. With growing excitement, she reached out and nervously pressed the button.

The world around her transformed, as if a veil had been lifted. In the space of a breath, the moonlit ship dissolved and was replaced by a large circular room covered in dimples of light of different sizes and intensity. The space above her darkened to indistinct shapes. If there was a ceiling, she could not see one. In front of her was a panel of lights.

"What is this place?" Rohi asked the silence.

She felt a presence, but it was cautious, as if it hadn't had visitors in a long time. Then a voice spoke from everywhere and nowhere. The voice spoke in Rohi's native tongue, but the sound was distorted, full of hisses and whispers, as if there were several other conversations going on underneath, using languages she did not understand. "You have questions," it said. "This is normal."

"That's not an answer," Rohi replied, growing impatient.

"It will be better if I show you," the voice explained. "First, an apology. I cannot take physical form. My subroutines are corrupted, ravaged by time. I am a memory of a memory of a memory. Those that built the Gateway network left a copy of me in each node to act as a guide."

"What's a Gateway?" Rohi asked. There were too many strange words. "Is that what I came through?"

In response, a night sky filled with innumerable stars flashed into being high above her head. Between many of the pinpoints of lights grew traces of silver, until a great network of roads crisscrossed the heavens. Her ancestors had believed in a pantheon of gods. Rohi imagined this was how they might have traveled, along glistening strands from one wonder to the next. Looking at the grand spectacle arch overhead could have made Rohi feel insignificant. Instead, it made her feel whole. It seemed preposterous that only a select few such as the priests were able to communicate with the portals and be part of this mystery. Looking at the map unfold before her eyes, Rohi felt something stir within her, eclipsing the Oculists and rune-carved swords. For the first time she felt a connection with the universe. That she belonged and had a power all her own. No Oculist had ever stepped into a Portal. No blind priest had ever stood where she was now and saw what she had seen.

Rohi stared at the spectacle for a long time before she finally spoke again. "It's beautiful. I was going to say magical, but I know that's not true. Something else powers it. Is that how I came to be here, by using the Gateway?"

"Yes," said the Guide. "The Gateway allows matter to pass from one node to another."

"That's good," Rohi said, "because I can't stay here. Wakers must leave dreams behind."

"You do not understand," the voice said, almost gently. "Matter can pass through the Gateway, but it is changed on the receiving end by those with a will and a spark. It never stays the same. This is the interior of your local system node. You may leave here and pass through to another node, but you will be altered. The atoms in your body will be reassembled. When you reemerge on the other side, you will no longer be you."

In response, Rohi smiled. "My people would call that *reincarnum*. We believe that is what happens to a person when their current life is over."

"Then you are not troubled?"

"No, not really," she replied and found to her surprise that it was true. "I was ready for my next life when I stepped into the Lumenoculis. Everything after that has been a gift. My mission is over. That life is gone. I cannot go back and fix my mistakes nor change what chance has given me. I can only go forward."

"Then my function as a Guide has come to its conclusion," the voice said. "Do you have any further questions?"

"I don't think so," said Rohi. "You've been very helpful."

"Most beings that pass through a node always wonder what the Gateway was built for. What its purpose was. I appreciate you not asking. I couldn't have told you anyway. That knowledge was lost when the Makers disappeared. The network that remains darkens node by node, as the suns surrounding them run out of fuel and die out."

There was a long pause. Rohi stood there in front of the panel of lights, waiting for the voice to continue. When it did not speak again, she thought the presence had retreated, until finally after a long time it said, "Did you want me to wait with you? To be here when you step through?"

"That is very kind, but no. I do have one favor to ask, though."

"If it is within my power," the Guide responded.

She took a deep breath. "Could I say goodbye to Luna? That would mean a lot to me."

The Guide seemed to ponder this. "Simply press the button again and she will return." Then a silence fell that was deep and final and Rohi knew that the Guide had truly left.

Reaching out again, she pressed the button in the center of the console. From out of the misty white walls the Moon Ship reemerged and the stars took their place in the heavens. A moment later a cabin door opened and Luna stepped onto the deck. "You shouldn't have let me sleep so long," she said, yawning.

"Hello, sister," Rohi replied, making her way down to greet her. "I'm sorry if I woke you."

The Sister of the Moon approached her and put her cool hands on either side of Rohi's face. "What's wrong, sister?" she asked. "Something troubles you."

"I'm leaving," Rohi blurted out. "I wanted to see you and say goodbye."

"Again? So soon?" Rohi simply nodded. "I will miss you. You know that, don't you?"

"Of course," Rohi replied, her voice catching.

"Where are you going?"

Rohi cast a glance at the twinkling stars hanging above them. The irony that they now were too close for comfort was not lost on her. "Far away, I'm afraid," she said.

"Well, don't be gone too long," Luna advised, and then wrapped her arms around her only sister, who responded in kind. Rohi didn't want to let go. This, whatever it was, felt like home.

Giving Luna her best, brave smile, she turned around and stepped to the edge of the ship's deck. The gleaming handrail in front of her dissolved, but she tarried a moment longer, looking over her shoulder to where Luna still stood. Rohi raised her arm in farewell, glad that her hand did not shake. Then she walked off the edge of the ship into the deep.

She had a glimpse, brief windows to other worlds, as she fell. They passed in rapid succession, almost too fast to recognize. Cloud vistas, vast oceans, smoke and flames, endless ice, shadows, cities of light, craters of glittering jewels, trees rising high above rings of stone. There were great beasts grazing gently on verdant plains, and patchwork landscapes of gears and sliding platforms. Some made absolutely no sense at all, and seemed like a nightmare or cosmic joke. Swirling masses of color and howling storms of energy. There were endless more, too many to register. And still they came faster and faster in a dizzying array until finally only one world remained.

*

Marcus Willoughby gazed up at the bone-white archway, still not quite believing it was real. The survey team had almost missed the ruins in their headlong rush across the stars. Electromagnetic interference combined with limited hours of daylight on the surface and a thick atmosphere had hidden the find until it was almost too late. The fact that the artifacts were made by an intelligence was obvious and beyond question, as was that this intelligence was almost certainly not human. Preliminary analysis of the unknown material comprising the primary and secondary objects indicated an age of over one billion years. What the archway's purpose was or who the builders were remained a mystery. There was a good chance it would remain so, at least until another expedition could be sent to the sector again. That might be years or decades from now. The situation was intolerable.

"Doctor," the captain spoke in his helmet intercom. "Respond. I am ordering you to return to the landing craft or I will have members of the support team pick you up and carry you there. Is that understood?"

Marcus stifled a curse. The woman was intolerable. Couldn't she see this was the discovery of a lifetime? The first evidence of an alien civilization, and she just wanted to carry on with the schedule as if nothing had happened? And for what? Delivery of a few tons of iron and nickel and frozen water? They had only stopped at this planet because he had insisted, reminding them that this was why he was on board, to investigate new sources of income and mining opportunities as well as exolife possibilities. The planet *was* rich with rare minerals, according to cursory geological scans, but wealth couldn't always be measured in digital currencies and endlessly chased short-term profit.

"Alright!" he hissed into the microphone. "Just let me finish my 3-D modeling. I only have the marker left. The archway has already been uploaded."

He could almost hear the captain seething in the silence. "You are dangerously close to insubordination," she warned, broadcasting on all channels now. "I'm well aware of the artifact's importance, but we're not the only ship in the fleet, and we're certainly not the best equipped to handle a scientific discovery of this magnitude. We've already stayed a week longer because of the artifact and we have a schedule to keep. Overlin Station is expecting us. I'm sorry, Doctor, but I'm pulling the plug. Team members, please escort—"

Marcus cut off the transmission to his helmet and then looked over expectantly to the rest of the survey team.

"You heard the captain," the chief of operations told him, over-riding communication controls. "I'm giving you five minutes because I know how much this means to you. Don't make me regret it. Get busy."

Marcus gave him a thumbs-up and then resumed work on the marker, scanning the object into the portable computer network as fast as possible in preparation for upload. Accuracy demanded patience, however, and his own physical movement was slowed because of the 1g Earth gravity, so he had ample opportunity to study the object. The alien marker was flat and stood just under two meters tall at the end of a gray column. Strange symbols were etched into the sloping surface. Time and the elements had worn many of the markings away, but what remained was tantalizing. Even more exciting was the figure that took up the whole right side of the object. It seemed to depict a bipedal creature with a many-fingered mono-hand, proto-wings curling back to a point, and a head with round, almost human-looking eyes above a mouth full of jagged-looking teeth, standing in front of the arch.

Studying it again, Marcus wondered anew if the smooth slab was intended to be a primer, historical record, warning, or something else entirely. Maybe a combination of all of those; maybe none. Hell, it could be a sacred site or the height of sacrilege. He had no idea. His sister Tunani would have had some insight. Oh, how he wished she had lived to see this day. If she were standing here, a week might have been enough time. In a way, he was just trying to continue her work. Fulfill her dream. Trying and failing. He wasn't her. Could never even come close. His sister had not only been a scientist, but also a leading advocate for change in the Outer Cluster where colonists eked out a living. She had been passionate and kind. Her voice was silenced too soon.

Squinting into the growing gloom, he increased the levels of the pod lights surrounding the archaeological site. The viewable landscape beyond came into stark relief, slabs of rust-colored rock covered with perfectly round pebbles in hues of green and blue. Initial tests indicated that it was both organic and non-organic, but that couldn't be right. The substance had to be one or the other. The whole planet was covered with them. Sometimes Marcus imagined them hatching, breaking open and spilling life over this dead world. The atmosphere had low levels of oxygen, around 16%. It was breathable, but not for extended periods, and not without experiencing physical impairment. Using the suits helped conserve their energy and prevented needless mistakes. There was also the danger of a stray microbe, something the ship's sensors had failed to detect. They were all happy to keep their helmets on.

"Time's up, doc," the chief told him through the suit's speaker.

The rest of the survey team approached him and then stopped. He hadn't quite finished the scan, and made no move to acquiesce when he noticed something was wrong. The team wasn't looking at him at all. He followed their gaze higher and higher. The alabaster archway, inert and unchanging, was flickering to life. Marcus looked on in surprise as the artifact began to pulsate in the gathering darkness. Tremors grew beneath his feet and the ground shook, causing the tiny stone spheres to vibrate in place. The local sun had almost set and a sliver of a moon was rising on the opposite horizon. The temperature was falling. He had one moment to wonder what was happening, what might emerge from the portal, before his world was forever changed.

THE ORPHANS OF EMERALD ISLAND

*B*abs never wanted the boy in the first place. They had each other. The three of them. That had always been enough. There was no one else.

None of the Eternals remained except the three sisters who were one, remembered by a dwindling few as the Morrigan. Babs missed sweet Brigid and wise Ana. Even portly Dagda, with his great club covered in vines. Most, though, had been fools or worse. Living in seclusion suited her. The sisters had a cow, chickens, and a small garden out back, as well as a large supply of beeswax candles. Technology was forbidden. Connections with the outside world were kept to a bare minimum. Humans were a nuisance at best, and often a danger to be avoided.

When she discovered the basket and the swaddled human bundle on the doorstep that autumn morning near the turn of the millennium, she had raised a wrinkled hand in surprise. After taking a deep breath, Babs drew up her hood to conceal the black feathers that covered her skin and scalp. Then she stepped over it and went on her way. Later in the evening when it cried, she put another log on the fire and closed her eyes, dreaming of battles gone by. In perfect moments such as those, she could almost imagine the newborn's wails to be the tormented moans of a fallen warrior on the battlefield.

"Kill it," her sister Nema had urged, after returning from a tryst with an unwitting farmer's son. Her normally aged face still had the luster of youth upon it. Her lips were full and sensuous, and her long honey golden hair shimmered as she walked. The top she wore was cut low and revealing to show off the rise of her firm breasts. The glamour she had applied earlier had done its trick. By disguising what they had become, she was able to copulate with a mortal. The adoration she received had won back her beauty, the bloom of a goddess. In a few short weeks, however, she would look as old and uninviting again as the rest of them.

Sitting down in a kitchen chair, the goddess of desire crossed her long, white legs and glared at Babs. "Take it to the Mugna, before it draws unwanted attention."

Babs opened her mouth to protest before she realized that her sister was right. "Easy for you to say," she replied. "You don't have to walk there and back."

"*I* didn't find it," Nema observed as she studied the smooth skin of her hands. "I'm not the eejit who brought that creature inside. It's not my responsibility, and I certainly don't want to waste this fleeting youth mucking about with that smelly thing."

"I imagine not," Babs said sourly.

Going outside, she picked up the basket and walked across the soft green meadow, her steps slow but sure. A sudden gust of wind whipped her hood back, ruffling the black feathers that covered her skin and scalp. The little human cried out, helpless. Babs paused and looked down at the child. Its eyes were the color of sky and sea, with a spot of white in each pupil. *There is a kind of magic there*, she thought with a tinge of surprise. *A more beautiful face I have never seen.*

She shook her head at such foolishness and then continued on her way. Eventually Babs came upon the old bier road, now little more than a faint impression across the sloping hills, and walked in its silence for a time. After a while, she came upon a lone hawthorn tree and rested in the welcome shade before setting off again. When the sun was near its zenith, Babs finally neared her destination. Crossing a dry streambed, she entered a low-lying area of deep shadow next to a small ridge. The air was cool and still, as if something hidden within were holding its breath. Out of the corner of her eye, Babs spotted a flash of white scamper across the ground before disappearing into the thick underbrush. Muttering a curse at the unwanted interloper, she strode forward, watchful for any spying eyes. What she had to do was a lonely business.

A ring of brambles rose up menacingly in front of her, but Babs smiled. She knew the way. Emerging unscathed, she heaved her load up on the rim of the woody maw and leaned heavily against the remains of the ancient oak tree, her breath coming in ragged gasps. It was not easy being apart, and distance made the weakness worse. Usually there were three of them to shoulder the burden and give each other strength against the unbelief that encroached all around them, but it had only been her and Nema since Mac left. That had been almost a year ago. How her sister had found the strength to leave home she would never know, but then, Mac had always had a hidden resolve, a maternal protectiveness, even in these dark times. That's what enabled her to go on such a foolish quest in the first place. The warrior goddess shuddered when she contemplated the hardships her sister must be enduring out on her own, if she still lived.

But of course, she did, Babs reminded herself. If Mac were gone, they would feel it. A pang of old guilt hooked her. It was Mac who had drawn the short straw, leaving their cottage home to seek the answer and pay whatever price was required, but she was least equipped to make the attempt, lacking the wiles of beauty or fighting skills.

Babs chuckled morosely and tried to recall the last time she had held a sword. With a pang of irony, she saw herself in her mind's eye hang the beloved blade *Soul Stealer* on the wall of the cottage, a memento to a vanished time. The warrior goddess straightened and took a moment to study the stubs of bare boned branches and the great hollow trunk. If she closed her raven-black eyes, she could almost imagine the tree clothed in green, with an army of leafy soldiers fanning out across the hills. An intolerable sadness rose up inside her. She hated coming here. It made her remember how things used to be. Now she only wanted to be done and back home.

Babs put her tremorous hands on the side of the basket. "Nothing personal," she said, being careful not to look down at the baby again, lest she fall under its spell. Then she shoved the cradle toward the jagged hole of the tree. Then stopped. Although she strained with the effort, Babs could not dump the bassinet in, even though there was ample room. Babs glanced down into the dark depths before scrutinizing the child. A trickle of saliva glistened on the infant's chin, and its mouth hung open in unexpected delight. Both blue eyes, beautiful as they were, drifted outward, even though she leaned in. The child was powerless and peculiar, that much was clear. Then another thought occurred to her. Cursing her foolishness, Babs stuck her head down into the gullet of the tree again, but this time she listened. At first there was nothing, but then she heard it. A whisper of a wail and a warning. Something of Mugma still survived after all. It did not want this child.

Curses, she fumed. If she couldn't dump it in the deep, then Babs would simply leave the child where it was. Time would do the rest.

The crack of a bramble nearby made her jump. "Don't you dare harm a hair on that boy's head," a half-familiar voice said. Babs spun around. Standing in the dim light was a beautiful woman dressed in blue jeans and a white tee. The front had an image of a blue-green world with the words "Love Your Mother" emblazoned above. Her once long red hair was chopped short above her ears. Tattoos of Celtic knotted hearts framed with flowers covered her arms. The woman's mouth was etched in a scowl.

"Mac?" Babs asked in surprise. "Is that *you*?"

"Of course it's me. Who else would it be?" the young woman replied.

"You've changed," Babs observed, taking in her youthful look. "We didn't think you'd be gone so long. It's been twelve moons."

A veil of darkness briefly passed over her sister's face. "My journey took longer than expected," she explained in an apologetic tone. "There were—distractions."

Babs looked at her sister in surprise. "Distractions? What could possibly divert you from your quest?"

"You wouldn't understand, sister. Now grab that poor child and let's go to the cottage. I have news."

But Babs held her ground. Something wasn't right. "What use have we for another mouth to feed? You seem strangely attached to it."

"It's not mine," Mac replied, although the way she said it made Babs think that perhaps she wouldn't have minded. "I had a dream-vision of a child abandoned at our door. It was a sign I could not ignore. I'm sorry I did not return earlier."

"Time has been kind to you," said Babs, more than a little jealous. "You're so young. Did you find Tír na nÓg?"

Mac looked at her sister and smiled tightly. "No, my sister. Don't you remember? I went to drink from Nechtan's sacred water and gain the knowledge we lacked." She paused and took a deep breath before continuing. "In so doing, I became mortal. It was not an easy transition, Babs. I never imagined such a fate. My spirit suffered, even as my weathered body was reborn. Thankfully, I did not have to go through it alone."

More she would not say. For the first time in her immortal life, Babs was speechless.

———— * ————

That was five years ago. In the interim, they had raised the child as well as they could. Mac had taken the most interest in his upbringing and care, as was natural with a fertility goddess, with Nema barely tolerating his presence. Mac, strangely silent, would say only that because of the timing of the child's arrival and his disability, they should care for the boy and keep him safe. To do anything less might invite ruin.

With little else to hope for, Babs watched the child grow and counted down the days until the appointed hour, but in truth she was skeptical. Too much had already been lost. That was evident as they all made their way across the treeless countryside, the monotonous drone of a distant highway stealing the birdsong from the air. The coolness of the morning was turning over to the coming heat of midday. Cracks in the ground gave testament to a thirst for water. Only the curious visitors who appeared out of the early morning mist and followed at a distance gave her reason to believe. First a dryad, slim and emaciated, stepped from a broken trunk. Then a pair of haggard-looking fairies, their thin wings glittering in the sun, fought the modest breeze to keep up with them. Finally, a banshee, its hood in dark tatters, appeared from the shadows and trailed them like a silent specter of death. Up ahead of the three women, their adopted child Beagon ran across the grass, bobbing slightly, only slowing when he came to the side of the hill. Babs marveled at his limitless energy and fearlessness. Had she ever been so young and free? She had felt the weight of time deep in her bones as they trekked across pasture and open fields to their destination.

"That's enough, little one," Mac called as she wiped her brow. "Wait for us. We must rest again."

Walking a bit further up the hill, Beagon finally halted and looked back with barely contained excitement, his eyes unseeing, for he had been blind since birth. His red hair and freckles shone brightly in the sun. This was the boy's first real field trip and he had smiled the whole afternoon as they walked. The spring weather was mild, with the shadow of winter a fading memory.

Mac opened a small basket and handed each of them the last hunks of homemade bread and cheese. They ate mostly in silence as the magical entourage watched silently at a distance. A leather bottle was passed around, and the three sisters plus the boy took turns taking long draughts of cold spring water on the unusually hot summer day.

Beagon wiped his mouth with the back of his hand and then stood up, eager to continue on. "Listen close," Mac said, reaching out for the child. "From here until we reach Lia Fáil, do not let go of our hands. Do you understand? Mama Babs and Mama Nema will help you." Beagon nodded, a worry playing across his face where just moments before there had been only joy.

One by one they each took one another's hand—even Nema, who glared and protested but finally took the boy's small hand in her own. Then they all walked together up the Hill of Tara as an unexpected north wind began to blow. "Tell me again the tale," Babs asked, shivering, pulling the hood of her cloak tighter. "How the world will be returned to us."

Mac rolled her eyes and sighed, but it was mostly for show, Babs knew. Since returning home, Mac had been treated like a hero, and for good reason. They all knew what she had sacrificed at the well of Sidhe Nechtan in order to drink the sacred water and gain the knowledge, though none had spoken of it since that day. Looking at Mac as they trudged up the slope made her jealous and afraid and proud, all at the same time. Her sister's fertile youth seemed so fragile and fleeting, like a cheap gaudy fabric hiding something ugly. If Babs stared long enough, she could imagine her sister bent and brittle. It would not take long. A mortal life was nothing if not short. So instead they asked Mac from time to time to tell the story of how things would be made right again, and in the telling the sisters found a measure of hope.

"C'mon, sis," Nema chided as she plucked tiny white blossoms from bushes and put them in her hair, as if to ward against what was to come.

And so Mac told them all again about the standing stone, and the three sacred words of power, and the smoke that would rise high into the air, taking shape like a great shadow spreading out over the Earth.

*

Halfway up the hill, an unnatural wind began to howl, like a harbinger of things to come. It took all their effort not to be blown back down to the bottom. Beagon swung between their straining arms like a sheet dancing in the breeze. Mac looked over at the little boy. His face was frozen in fear, with his sightless eyes grown wild. Watching him struggle, Mac wondered if she would have the courage to do what needed to be done.

Soon progress became nearly impossible, more akin to mountain climbing instead of simply making their way up the gentle slope like a thousand tourists before them. Not for the first time, Mac wished that the sacred waters from the well had been more revealing. There was still so much she didn't know. The wind screamed in her ears, as if it were angry at her own ignorance. A faint metallic scent hung in the air and she felt as if they were being watched. From time to time Mac thought she could almost hear something calling in the din, but her human ears could not make sense of it.

They were nearing the top of the hill now and the invisible hand which had been pushing against them blew with new ferocity. Mac held tighter on to Babs, who was struggling to stay upright. If one of them fell they would all go down, and with it, perhaps their one chance at making the Calling. Feeling her strength start to fray, Mac pulled with all her might, tugging the line of her sisters and Beagon. There was a moment of equilibrium, and then the four of them tumbled over the lip into the unknown.

The air on top of the sacred hill was still and silent except for the sound of her own labored breathing. From where Mac lay, she could see the crown of the emerald hill spread out around her. They were on the highest point of Cnoc na Teamhrach. The ancient burial site of Dumha na nGiall slumbered underneath, the passage tomb waiting for the light of the sun. A line of small trees ran along the far edge of the hill. Mac cared not at all for any of it. A finger of stone beckoned a short distance away: Lia Fáil. She got to her feet and scanned the rest of the group. Babs was getting up slowly, still grasping Beagon's hand, thank the gods. Her sister Nema brushed the dirt off her skirt and fussed in irritation at her windblown hair.

"Are you alright?" she asked Beagon, laying her hands on his small shoulders. Her voice shook with worry, although she tried to hide it.

"I'm okay," he replied brightly, although his earlier smile had still not returned. "Should we be here, Mama? The wind did not want us to come."

Mac bent down in front of him. "What do you mean? This is the place I told you about. It's open to everyone." Beagon didn't answer, but he looked skeptical. "Mother Mac just needs you to be brave a little bit longer, okay? Can you do that?"

The boy nodded as a shadow moved across his face. Dark clouds crowded the sky, blown by forces unseen. Beagon shivered. "We better keep moving," Mac said to their son as she caressed his cheek. Standing up, she looked around. Besides the four of them, only the banshee had made it to the top of Cnoc na Teamhrach, with the others lost to the strange tempest. The creature stood apart, one robed arm pointing at the nearby Stone of Destiny.

"It certainly has a flair for the dramatic," Babs quipped, but there was no humor in her tone.

"I still think this is a bad idea," Nema complained as she smoothed out the wrinkles in her skirt. "We are not what we once were, and *some of us* are considerably less." She glanced over at Mac as she said this. "No offense, sister."

"My answer is the same as it has always been," Mac said, making a considerable effort not to be baited. Her youngest sister could be such a tease. "If we wish to continue our long, slow spiral to oblivion, then we need do nothing. Time and the new machine gods will make sure we are forgotten. Already they try and thwart us, to stifle what little influence we have left. But if we desire something greater, if we want the Earth to truly live again, than we have to take this chance. It will not come again. Human beings must be reminded they are merely part of a greater world. They matter no more and no less than anything else. If we do not try today, we are already lost."

Nema stared at her, twirling her long hair around a single, slender finger. Her sensuous lips puffed in and out as she chewed over a response. To any casual observer, she was drop-dead gorgeous, early twenties at the most, but Mac saw the strands of silver hair and the wrinkles around her eyes beginning to show. For Nema, youth literally was fleeting.

"Inspiring stuff. Nobody does a pep talk like you, big sister." The goddess of desire curled her slender hand into a fist. "Might as well go down fighting."

Babs nodded in agreement. Her eyes held a glint of steel.

"Alright, then," Mac muttered. "That's settled. Let's go do what we came here for." Without another word she turned and led them to the standing stone of Lia Fáil. The stone was shorter than she remembered, standing less than two meters tall. Weathered rocks set into the ground radiated out from the object like manifestations of power. Several cigarette butts lay scattered around the stone base like a profane offering. For centuries, the ancient kings of Ireland came here to be crowned, drink ale and symbolically marry the territory goddess Maeve. None, it was believed, could rule without first mating with her.

Mac shook her head in amusement as she remembered the simple human tale. The stone of Lia Fáil was much older and more powerful than that. No god had ever claimed the Speaking Stone. It had been here when the world was formed and would be here when it ended. No one knew where it had come from, or the full depth of its true purpose. According to legend, though, if you asked it the right question, it would answer. Mac looked over at Beagon, hoping the words she had been given would suffice and that she could protect him.

"Join hands," she directed, and together the sisters formed a circle around the mottled stone. Forces moved above them. The sun disappeared behind gray clouds driven by a high wind, but on the top of the Hill of Tara the four of them were untouched, like a magician in the eye of a storm of their own making. Mac took a deep breath and closed her eyes. She registered the rough, calloused hand of the warrior goddess in her own, but to her surprise it trembled, however slightly. In contrast, Nema's smooth hand squeezed her own like a vice, as if making an unspoken demand.

Time held its breath. A pressure built up inside of her. Reluctantly, Mac opened up her eyes. Across from her, just outside the circle of power, stood Beagon, his small, thin arms upraised and suspended like an act of surrender. Mac tried to smile and reassure him, wishing only that she could hold him in her arms. "It is time," she found herself saying. "The spring equinox of Ostara is in balance." Each of the sisters took turns saying one of the strange words of power, careful to pronounce each exactly as they had practiced over the years.

Mac started, speaking clearly and brightly. "Tindviscudew-saol-anuala."

Then her sacred Morrigan sisters joined in. "Cresalintae-saol-ajimar-ze," toned Babs. "Aerdefaigh-saol-deireadh-kahana?" voiced Nema.

Finally, the three called out together an urgent finale: "Iteot-wawki-aiffnaru!"

Each sound still felt unmoored from any language Mac had ever encountered. It had elements of Gaelic, although she also sensed the presence of the sea in the rise and fall of its rhythm. The fact that it had come from the sacred well made no difference. Sidhe Nechtan was simply the conduit. The words arose from some place deeper. There were no pauses between utterances. The intonations flowed together like a fast-moving stream.

Over and over again, they repeated the sacred words until they blended together into one. When Mac finished, she allowed herself a sigh of relief. They had done what was required. They had asked for an answer to what even gods could not change; a return to the way the world was. All their hopes and fears were wrapped in ten words whose meaning was unknown.

For what seemed like an eternity, the three sisters stared at the stone and waited. Fear crept in as the moments passed. Beagon fidgeted in place. When the sign finally came, the women looked at each other and allowed the barest of hopes to grow. First, tender green shoots appeared in the ground around Lia Fáil, rising through the cracks as if some great hidden heart were beating deep underground and pumping out its life blood. Then the stone itself began to change. Faintly at first, a whisper of smoke snaked into the sky from its tip. Each of them watched transfixed as the tendril of climbing vapor took shape and substance in the air high above them, until the vault of heaven was not vast enough to contain it. From out of the swirling substance appeared an enormous serpent with greenish-gray skin. Short legs with stubby feet and claws ran down the length of its body, but the beast did not appear to need them. Great cobalt-colored wings that blotted out the sky flapped in a slow, unhurried rhythm as the creature twisted and contorted in the air. The flanks of the serpent undulated like gills, while the underside boasted vivid scales the color of bloody coral. Nearly three quarters of it was already solid, but the smoke was still rising. The transformation was not yet complete.

Mac opened her mouth to speak, but nothing came out. The creature arced directly above them as the head finally came into view. Eyeless, the summoned behemoth navigated by some unseen means as its massive jaws, filled with flint-like teeth, flexed in anticipation. Whole cities could fit within its unforgiving maw. A sound like thunder erupted from the Wyrm, like the promise of storms to come. Lights in towns as far away as Dublin flickered and then went out. Planes fell out of the sky.

"What the fuck kind of doomsday creature is it?" Nema asked, her voice hoarse with disbelief. Sparks ignited down the creature's body, as if were a fuse that had been lit. "It's like no dragon I've ever seen."

"An oillipheist, perhaps?" Babs replied, as fear and excitement shook her voice. "It's magnificent."

"Too big," Nema countered, wishing she could make herself smaller and less conspicuous. "And it has wings. Could be an ellen trechend."

Babs shook her head, feeling the blood lust rise. "Not enough heads. Open your eyes, sister," she chastised. "Could be a Puca."

"Stop your nervous prattle, both of you," Mac ordered. "Something is happening to the stone." It was true. The obelisk was glowing a dusky amber as small fissures radiated across its surface. Suddenly, it became terribly hard to hold on to each other's hand. A force like a red-hot knife blade sliced into their linked hands, threatening to pull them apart.

"Don't let go!" Mac shouted as a great stinging wind rushed in, tearing her words away. Babs strained to keep her grip as Nema grimaced with effort. Beagon's eyes were wide with fear. Something was building. Mac could feel it as a metallic tang coated her tongue. The smoke was still rising from the stone, but it was nearly spent. All they needed were a few moments more. Cracks widened in Lia Fáil as the light intensified and then became blinding. Overhead, the Wyrm roared and the earth shook.

We are enough. We have to be! Mac thought in triumph and desperation as she felt the ring disintegrate. Behind her, the Speaking Stone splintered. Rays of released power flooded out, striking mortal and immortal alike. In the concussion of sound that followed, the Wrym wailed and thrashed, but could do nothing to prevent the relentless wind from scattering its body.

*

Shock and disbelief. Lying on the ground, Nema hung on to her last spark of consciousness, savoring the taste of life and ecstasy. The bolt of energy still throbbed within her, dancing along her nerves like a lover's caress. Her sister Babs was already dead. Nema could feel her absence as an acute longing never to be filled. Even Mac had never been like this. She had been distant, transfigured, but not gone. This was different.

Although Nema was quite certain that the sun had not yet set, a darkness nonetheless descended, clouding her vision. A dull pain overtook and then replaced the earlier feeling of euphoria. Fear, real fear, gripped her for the first time. She called out to her sister Mac, but not for help. There was nothing to be done. All she needed was comfort.

"Are you there?" she asked.

Everything felt like a dream, and then the dream ended.

————— * —————

A few minutes later, Mac awoke. Her head hurt like it had been split in two. Someone had called her name. She was almost sure of it. Shards of memory came back to her. Something bad had happened. There had been an explosion. Fragments of power had rained down on them. Dreading what she would see, Mac opened her eyes. The light was blinding, causing her to squint in discomfort. From where she lay, the forms of two bodies could be seen sprawled out in the grass. Neither moved. *My sisters!* she wailed soundlessly.

Struggling to get up, she lurched over to them. Their eyes were closed, mimicking sleep, but a paleness shrouded each goddess. The right hand of her sister Babs was curled into a fist, as if she were holding an invisible sword. Nena's youthful countenance had the air of surprise, of something learned too late. Even as she gazed down in disbelief, they began to change. Immortal flesh dissolved, losing its opaqueness like ice melting in the sun. Their bodies sank into the earth as if returning to some hidden spring. Within moments they were no more.

Mac froze in place, unable to believe what had happened, her arms reaching out in vain for what was already lost. Wetness ran down her cheeks and it took her a moment to realize they must be tears, for she had never cried before. In desperation she spun around, as if they might appear nearby, but only the shattered remains of the stone and the empty hilltop were visible.

That's when she realized that their son—her son—was missing. Shame and guilt seized her by the throat. "Beagon!" she called desperately, scanning the landscape. "Beagon! Where are you?" She ran to the far side of Cnoc na Teamhrach and looked out over the verdant tree-lined pastures, but saw only gray emptiness. Her boy was not there. Continuing to scream his name, she ran to the remains of Lia Fáil, scanning the broken fragments of stone again, making sure.

Panicking and at a loss of where to go or what to do, she finally scrambled down the hillside they had come up earlier and stopped in her tracks. There was Beagon, lying on his side, a short distance away. Mac dashed over to him, laying a hand on his chest. His chest rose and fell, thank the gods. A quick scan showed no serious injuries. There was a bruise flowering on his forehead and his clothes were singed in places, but otherwise Mac could see no worries. With effort, she slowly controlled her breathing, and then shook her son's shoulder gently. "Honey, can you hear me? Are you alright?"

For a heartbreaking moment Beagon did not respond. Then he stirred and opened up his eyes. They were deep mossy green now, echoing the color of the living shoots that had burst from around the ancient stone. A smile spread across his face and Mac felt as if the light were returning after the darkest of nights. "Mama Mac. It's you," he said.

Cradling her son's head in her hands, she knelt next to him. Once again, she began crying, only this time they were tears of joy. Her precious boy was alive. "Are you hurt?" she asked. "Tell me what I can do." Beagon stared back at her as if he hadn't heard. "Honey, did you hear me? I need to know if you are hurt in any way." As an ordinary mortal with no healing powers, it would not be inconceivable that the boy had sustained a concussion or loss of hearing when the standing stone discharged. She began to calculate the distance to the nearest doctor. Mac would carry him if she had to.

Beagon shook his head and reached out a hand to touch her face. "Mama, I can see. I can see you. You're beautiful." The words made no sense to Mac. They might as well have been the words of power from

Nechtan's Well. Slowly, their meaning sunk in. Her son tipped his head back and then wrinkled his nose in delight. "The sky is so big. I wish I could touch it."

Before she could respond, Beagon began squirming, straining to get up. "I think you should rest a little while," she cautioned, smiling despite her worry.

"I'm fine, Mama. Well, not fine, but I'm okay. There's so much I need to see." His voice had a pleading quality to it that softened her protectiveness.

Against her better judgement, Mac helped her son stand up, and together they walked back up the hill, hand in hand. Limping slightly, Beagon rounded the top of the hill and his face lit up. "I never knew it was this beautiful," he said. "All of it, Mama."

Together they walked across the Hill of Tara and slipped through the trees. There they looked down at the expansive viridian countryside dotted with sheep. A glittering stream meandered through it all, like a drunken reveler. In the distance, a dozen or more wind turbines spun dreams of a brighter future as a kestrel flew overhead.

Beagon had questions about everything he saw, from the sky above to the plants at his feet. Mac did her best to keep up. Finally, her son had a question she didn't know how to answer. "Where is Mama Nema and Mama Babs?" he asked, quietly turning to her.

She made herself look at him and held on to the truth like a sharp blade cutting into her skin. "They are gone, dearest. They went away to the Dark Lands never to return. We were not strong enough." *I was not strong enough*, she told herself. *The Morrigan are three, not two. The price for failure is too high.*

Guilt and longing wracked her being. With effort, Mac remembered her son and swallowed the emotions, burying them deep so her pain would not be visible. Not now. Lia Fáil had responded and struck with the force equal to those present in the circle of Calling. It was only natural that those of divine nature would have the most power reflected back at them. And so this version of the world was lost, or diminished beyond repair.

Yet when she looked at her son, Mac did not despair. He was gentle and kind. He could see the beauty which still remained. Perhaps there was hope after all. Something to hold on to. The Children of the Earth need not perish. One thing was certain, the Great Mother would abide forever and a day.

Mac opened her arms and Beagon fell into her embrace, shaking and wet with tears. When his sobs had finally subsided, she let him wander to the wreckage of the stone and their broken dream. He needed to see. Watching him make his way, Mac slipped her hand into her pocket and pulled out a sleek cell phone. She held it in her hand warily and stared at the device, her fingers hovering over the display. There was only one number programmed into the phone. She would not call it today. Before too long, though, she would. Mac missed him, missed his touch, and like any mortal she needed to be surrounded by love. She knew that he would be a good father to a child that had never known one.

"We must go," she told her son when he returned a few minutes later. "What happened today will be our secret." The tourists would be coming back now that the spell was broken. Serious-looking officials and people with guns would be converging on this spot. Luckily, no one ever paid any serious mind to a young mother and her son. Turning from the hilltop, Mac and Beagon made a careful descent and then moved out across the open meadows, bright with late afternoon sun. Over the rolling landscape, beyond her human sight, was the cottage, but in the geography of her heart there was a different destination.

Sometime later, as they walked along a country road that skirted the eastern edge of Tara, a man in a uniform stepped from a car and waved them over. The vehicle was painted with the yellow and orange stripe of the Garda. "Excuse me, miss," the officer said. "I'm afraid I have to ask you a few questions."

Mac put her arm around Beagon and did her best to act surprised. "Of course," she replied. "How can I help?"

The officer hesitated for a moment, as if he were an actor unsure of his lines. "As unlikely as it sounds," he began, "we've had several reports from M3 motorists this afternoon concerning a creature of significant size flying above the Hill of Tara. There also appears to have been an explosion. Did you happen to see anything strange or hear anything out of the ordinary?"

Squinting in the sun, Mac shook her head and frowned apologetically. Out of the corner of her eye she spied several vans speeding toward Tara. "I'm afraid we didn't. My son and I have just been enjoying a stroll in the sunshine." At his mention, Beagon fidgeted and then looked up at Mac. "Is there anything else?" she asked, irritated at the delay.

"No, I guess that will be all," the officer replied. He looked at them a moment longer. "Where are you heading, if you don't mind me asking? We might need to contact you if we have any further questions."

Mac smiled as bravely as she could. "We're going home," she told him and left it at that.

The cottage was waiting. It was just her and Beagon journeying back, but two made for an easier road than one. Soon there would be three again. That thought gave her strength as she took her son's hand and walked away.

EVER AFTER

When the last page is turned
And the story's played out
There's another one waiting
Invisible no doubt

In lemon juice letters
Held up to the light
A shadow is falling
As bluebirds take flight

The Prince and the Princess
Are arguing now
"You're a drunken swine!" she spats.
He yells, "You're a cow!"

The good King is sitting
Alone in his hall
He sent for his Knights
But none answered his call.

The Queen, she has left him
For someone younger and more strong
Who would pay more attention
Make her feel like she belonged

Now storm clouds are coming
He knows that it's true
But a melancholy has come over him
There's nothing he can do.

All alone he lies in bed
Sleepless nights and loveless days
His daring has lost its edge
Right and wrong have turned to grays.

Somewhere in the middle
The truth they say must lie
And everyone everywhere
Someday must die

Ever after
Ever after
The storybooks say
Ever after
Ever after
Hurrah and hurray!

But for every young heart
Touched by love's kiss true
There's a hundred more waiting
And waiting like you.

For every hale hero
Wielding a dream's bright sword
There's a thousand more falling
Crashing to the floor.

For every hope gained
There's a million more lost
All the storytellers together
Can never count the cost.

So as you close the book
And feel like everything's worked out fine
Remember there's an after 'ever after'
That's yours and that's mine.

In neither words nor spaces
Or even imagination
It's simply the price
Of being alive.

A place where the leaves are always falling
And the light is growing dim
Where the dragons are all crying
And the castle walls are caving in.

The last wizard is softly mumbling
Throwing sparks high into the air
But his mind is going
If it isn't already there.
Even now the minstrels are leaving
Their dying song a long, lost friend
Ever after
Ever after
Ever after again.

Might as well make up your own story
Make it hopeful
Then make it happen if you can
Be brave, my darling
Be here, my friend

Belong, dear child
And turn the pages
Until the beginning
Meets the end.

ABOUT THE AUTHOR

Peter Bremer is a fantasy and science fiction writer. He lives with his wife and fluffy dog in Minnesota. He is the author of the environmentally-themed fantasy novel Treetops, winner of an Imadjin Award in the category of Young Adult Fantasy as part of the 2021 Imaginarium Conference. When he's not writing he works as a librarian at a small university overrun with cougars.